AN ILL WIND

by

WERoberts

3 MARCH 2016

FOR TIM,
THE NEXT ADVENTURE
FOR ARNIE. HOPE
IT GRASS YOU!
ALL BEST,

Bill

For Carolanne Lyme, without whose enthusiastic support, patience and help this book could never have been completed.

Acknowledgements

Over the past months many people have contributed in one way or another to the completion of this novel, so many that I might inadvertently have overlooked one or two in my listing. If I have done so I offer heartfelt apologies.

There is only one person I hold responsible for the initial idea for the book and that is my old and dear friend Joan Forsht of Smith River, CA, whose experiences both as a Del Norte County Deputy Sheriff and as a Correctional Officer at Pelican Bay State Prison – relayed to me in many wine-lubricated chats over the years – contributed enormously to the idea of setting a novel in Del Norte County and, eventually, to my conception of the character of Deputy Geri Mitchell. From that point on all I needed was the incident that set the story rolling, and once that had suggested itself to my imagination the rest, bit by bit, fell nicely into place. Thanks, Joni, for those many fascinating conversations about your life! Thanks also for your subsequent guidance regarding Sheriff's office and Pelican Bay procedures and practices.

My sincere thanks, too, to Jane Conway Gordon for reading the overlong and over-written first draft of the book, and for making so many useful suggestions for cuts and improvements.

Though I undertook a great deal of research in order to get the main facts right in this book it is entirely possible that I have made errors in my depiction of the drug scene in northern California, and elsewhere – as well as in other things – and if so I apologize for my ignorance/negligence. I have tried to make the story plausible as an event involving real people in a real community, and to create scenes that might happen to anyone anywhere in America, and apart from seeking to place these characters in situations that are superficially recognizable and truthful I have taken many liberties of omission and invention with the details of actual places, institutions and procedures. Insofar as my treatment of illegal drug selling and manufacturing, cartels and gangs is concerned, hopefully most of my facts are genuine. Again, for all those who see the holes and the mistakes, I apologize.

Though I am American, raised and educated in Oregon and northern California, my residence in the United Kingdom for 48 years has meant that many 'Englishisms' have crept into my syntax and vocabulary. Clearly I needed more than just the computer's facility for translating English spellings to American to insure the book's 'American-ness', and I have relied heavily on West Coast friends to read my manuscript and offer suggestions for the non-American words and expressions I too often unwittingly used. Among those to whom I owe enormous gratitude for their painstaking efforts and suggestions are Christa Agee, Jan Rothrock, Brian Keith, Lark Weston, Doris Whalen, and Jessica Cejnar. For his help with the description of the Pelican Bay interview facility and prisoner's garb I am greatly indebted to Danny Blackburn. For their help with suggestions and corrections regarding the Los Angeles scenes I am also hugely beholden to Herman and Judith Poppe. For her warm encouragement, and help with all things Mexican, including correcting and improving my creaky Mexican Spanish and the names used in the story, I am immensely grateful to Cristina Aragón.

Finally, my eternal thanks and love to my long-suffering partner Carolanne for being my first reader, primary editor and proofer. Her herculean efforts and support can never be adequately recompensed or acknowledged.

WERoberts
London, October 2015

'An yll wynde that blowth no man to good...'
[1546 J. Heywood Dialogue of Proverbs ii. ix. L1]

Prologue

The buzz of his second cell phone hummed from the suit jacket hanging on the coat rack and the man stepped across the room to remove it from the inside pocket.

'Yes?' he said as he clicked the receive button, simultaneously closing the door that connected his office with that of his secretary.

'Bad news, I'm afraid, sir.'

The voice at the other end was breathy and deep, with a Latino accent.

'What kind of bad news?'

'He's dead. They had to take him down.'

The man in the office jerked upright, his face contorted with shock.

'They what!'

'He was raising hell. They had to shoot him.'

The man paced before his large desk, running a hand through his grey hair.

'Goddammit!' he rasped, trying to keep his voice low. 'I told you I wanted him roughed up, that's all! Given a lesson that would drive him off. I didn't say to terminate him.'

'I know that, sir, but there was no choice. It was either him or us.'

'Look, I know killing is common where you people come from, but we don't do that kind of thing up here. How the hell can we keep it from coming out, huh? What am I going to do about it when it does?

Any ideas?'

'It shouldn't come out, sir. The body will never be found.'

'I certainly hope not. What have they done with it?'

'Removed all means of identification. Put it in a place where nobody can ever find it.'

'Good. Where's that?'

There was a pause at the other end.

'The river.'

'What!'

'Do not worry, jefe. *They dropped him in the South Fork, well upstream. There is a deep pool at the bottom of a narrow ravine between rocky cliffs. The body should stay there till it rots.'*

The man stopped his pacing at the window, looking out at the street and the city buildings beyond.

'That was foolish. Hunters walk through that country. And hikers. Someone might see it there. Why did they dump the body in the river? Why didn't they bury it somewhere out in the woods?'

There was another pause.

'I'm sorry, patrón. *We thought it best to get rid of it as soon as possible. Also, there was no shovel.'*

'There's one at the cabin.'

'We weren't at the cabin, and we couldn't carry the body around. Clearly we had to dispose of it quickly.'

'What a mess,' the grey-haired man said, turning away from the window and shuddering. 'How could such a thing happen? I thought they were professionals.'

'They didn't expect to have to kill him. And they're not professionals, patrón. *They're just gangbangers from the plantation down south on loan to you. They're used to rough stuff, but not to killing. The shooter only acted out of self-defense.'*

'Well, it sounds a complete fiasco to me. This could bring my whole operation down like a house of cards.'

'Do not worry, sir. Even if someone did go there it is hard to see the

water from the cliffs. I checked it myself. Trust me, the body will not be found. It will stay there until the floods of next winter carry what's left of it out to sea.'

The man in the office took a deep breath.

'You'd better hope it does. What about the other problem? Have they handled that yet?'

'That should be dealt with in the next couple of days, sir. Certainly by the weekend. Then they go back south.'

'Good. I want them out of here before they screw something else up. Do not contact me again unless something else goes wrong. And nothing better go wrong. Understood?'

'Nothing will go wrong, patrón. *I promise you. Do not worry.'*

'All right. Tell the men to give my regards to the top man when they speak to him. Tell them to tell him I'll be in touch soon.'

And he hung up.

Chapter One

Saturday, May 10

Helen Babich thought her head was about to explode. The migraine had come down suddenly as they always did, just as she was supervising the exodus of the children from the school bus. Standing outside the door, ticking off the names on her clipboard as they filed past, she felt like crumpling to the ground, dropping everything to cradle her head in her hands. If she'd been at home she might have done so, but here she just set her jaw, squinted her eyes and fought against it, forcing herself to focus on the stream of teenagers as it moved past her into the picnic area and off towards the rippling river beyond. It was not the first time she'd had to cope when the excruciating pain had hit her like a thunderbolt at the most unexpected and inconvenient moment – in the midst of a class, or during a faculty meeting, or while grocery shopping in the local Fred Meyer. This was just the effects of her menopausal progression, she knew. But would it never end?

'You all right, Mrs. Babich?'

Linda Baron, a wisp of a girl with acne spots and reddish hair, had halted at the foot of the bus's steps and was staring at her, frowning.

'You don't look so good.'

Helen forced a smile. 'I'm fine, Linda. Thanks for asking. Just one of my headaches. It'll pass in a while. Go along now and find your friends.'

Smiling back, but with a trace of concern still in her eyes, the girl moved on and the exodus resumed.

The annual Redwood Elementary School eighth grade picnic in Jedediah Smith Redwoods State Park always took place on the second Saturday in May, when the warmth of spring was an almost dead certainty. This year proved the rule, with bright sunshine glinting through the canopy of trees and off the emerald waters of the broad Smith River, promising another hot summer to come. They had been lucky. The previous week had seen an unusual sequence of heavy rainstorms coming through one after another that had drenched the coastal mountains and raised the rivers high above their normal springtime level. As Helen fought against the waves of throbbing pain she thought that at least the weather had been kind to her today. Trying to supervise a picnic in the rain would've been a nightmare worse even than her headache.

As the last of the kids stepped down and away she ticked off their names and reached for her bag, rummaging inside for her super-strength Tylenol and the small bottle of water she carried for just such emergencies. Popping two of the painkillers into her mouth, she washed them down and glanced ahead.

In the open space under the trees between the parking area and the river bar Joe Meeks, the other eighth grade teacher at Redwood, was organizing things – unpacking the boxes and bags filled with containers of food and drink, paper plates and utensils, showing student helpers where to put them on the trestle tables beside the barbecue grill. This was Joe's first year at the school and Helen was pleased to see he had taken charge so efficiently. That made it easier for her. Looking after forty-five pubescent youngsters let loose beside a river in a redwood forest was a difficult enough assignment. She was glad she didn't have to supervise the picnic as well. There were a few mothers, too, who had turned up to help, and now they bustled around the tables, opening bags and boxes and laying things out, chatting happily together. Apart from her throbbing head, Helen thought things looked promising for a pleasant and very successful outing.

Putting the water and pills back into her purse, she made her way forward to give the others a hand.

Forty minutes later Helen was standing before the smoldering barbecue, nursing a Diet Coke and rotating hamburgers and hotdogs on the grill with a pair of tongs, when a girl's distant scream cut across the picnic area like the wail of a banshee. She turned towards the river.

'What the hell was that?' Joe Meeks asked beside her, frowning. 'Was that in fun? Or something else?'

'Don't know, Joe. But I'd better find out.'

Laying down the Coke and the tongs Helen lit out towards the riverbank where groups of kids were standing, staring upriver. Helen hastened in that direction.

She found the path leading from the rocky bar up onto the sand bank flanking the river and forced herself to run, the now muted headache pushed to the back of her mind. A hundred yards along she came to an elbow in the river beyond which the trail dropped again beside a clump of thick brush and alder trees that cut off her view of the water. Standing just beyond in the middle of the path, clutching her elbows and obviously shaken, was Linda Baron, the girl who had spoken to her at the bus.

'What is it, honey?' Helen asked, breathless, as she reached her. 'What's the matter?'

The red-haired student could only shake her head, raising an arm to point towards the secluded stretch of water shaded by the fringe of trees.

Helen turned.

At first she couldn't make out what it was in the shadows there, the white blob floating in the dark water, circling slowly in the river's eddy. When she stepped closer, however, she could clearly make out the form of a body, the white blob resolving into the back of a light-colored sweatshirt bobbing on the river's surface, a head of longish blond hair spreading out beyond it.

Thinking it must be one of her charges Helen waded briskly into the thigh-deep water. Grasping the sweatshirt at the shoulder she pulled the body around so it was face-up.

And screamed herself.

Because there was no face.

No eyes, just gaping holes where eyes had once been.

No mouth, just a wide gash above the chin with broken-toothed, smashed gums grinning out from the mangled opening. It looked like the whole face had been beaten with a hammer or some other blunt instrument. In revulsion Helen let go of the cloth and stepped back.

Left alone the body gently turned downward again, closing off the horror of the non-face. And opening a new one. For as the body resumed its former position, bobbing gently in the current, the arms slowly splayed out to the sides. And at the end of each arm, where hands should have been trailing through the water, there were no hands – just ragged, fleshy stumps where the hands had been hacked off.

Helen felt her stomach rising and turned to lose her breakfast in the green water.

When she finished and had recovered some degree of composure she waded back to the shore, reached for her cell phone and punched in 911.

* * *

Deputy Sheriff Geraldine Mitchell settled back in her seat and reached a hand up to adjust her sunglasses as she guided her unit south along ruler-straight Highway 101 toward Crescent City.

There was nothing unusual about Deputy Mitchell's ride – it was the same trim, white SUV with the same green and yellow markings and Sheriff's Office shield emblazoned on the front doors that all the other deputies drove around Del Norte County. And it was equipped the same, with the flat band of flashers across the top, the whooper and siren, short wave radio, the usual trunkful of accessories (plastic sheeting, fingerprinting kit, flares and other emergency gear), and the same lethal scatter gun clamped ready just to the right of the steering wheel. The only unusual thing about Geri Mitchell's ride that day was that I was sitting beside her on the front seat.

My name's Arnold Rednapp and normally you'll find me down in San Francisco where I work as the senior investigative reporter for the *South Bay Bulletin*, a small but highly respected weekly newspaper based in a university town in Silicon Valley. Had I been riding around in a sheriff's department rig anywhere in that area it wouldn't have been in the least extraordinary, such a trip being probably related to some current investigation of mine. But what was I doing in one at the top end of the state, in remote Del Norte County on the coast just below the Oregon border?

Well, it's like this.

Some months earlier, during an investigation into a mysterious death in another coastal town a couple hundred miles north of San Francisco, I happened to meet a waitress with whom I shared several nights of great sex and unusually relaxed companionship. In spite of my resolve to avoid long term involvements, after the investigation was concluded and I had returned to the bay area I found myself missing this lady a lot, and wanting to spend more and more time with her and her quirky but delightful teenage daughter. As a result I'd travelled up to see them as often as I could, and over the months we've become an item. The waitress's name is Lorraine, and the kid's name is Mandy. Both of them are good people, and Lorraine is one of the cleverest and most perceptive individuals I've ever known. She's also a stunner in the looks department. Suffice it to say that I have still not tired of spending time with these ladies, and for a re-confirmed bachelor like myself (with a divorce behind me and a daughter of my own living with her mother back east) that is a somewhat alarming, though admittedly very pleasant, state of affairs.

On this occasion Lorraine and I happened to be in the latter stages of a week-long spring vacation, having driven together up into Oregon and Washington to visit the cities and natural wonders that I, as a relatively recent arrival from Des Moines, had heard of but had not yet seen. Lorraine managed to persuade a work colleague with a similar aged daughter to let Mandy stay with them while we were away, and over the preceding days the two of us had enjoyed exploring Portland and Seattle together, had savored the views of majestic Mount Hood and the famous Crater Lake National Park, and were now on our way home – having stopped for a couple nights in Del Norte County so that Lorraine could visit her friend and college roommate Geri Mitchell, who'd become a law enforcement officer.

The previous evening the three of us had enjoyed a delicious home-cooked meal at Geri's renovated farmhouse just outside the little town of Smith River, and talked late into the night — mostly about Geri's work as a deputy. After describing the ennui of her patrol duties she told us she felt she was doing particularly good work for the young people of the area, trying to befriend them while at the same time keeping an eye out for any potential threats, from within their ranks or from outside. As a result she admitted shyly she was getting something of a reputation locally as a law enforcement officer that could be trusted. That, coupled with the fact that in her five years of doing police work she had loved every minute of it, was the up-side of her working life. The downside was that from the beginning even of her training she had encountered no small degree of chauvinism from certain of her teachers, colleagues and superiors, varying in severity from throw-away sexist jokes and muttered comments to blatant demonstrations of outright disrespect. Geri had made an effort to ignore these taunts, but she admitted that at times it'd been hard, and that there'd been occasional tears along the way – never, however, in front of her tormentors.

Moreover her work had recently become more challenging owing to an increase in serious drug trafficking in the county. Apparently cocaine and methamphetamines were being transported up from L.A. by the Mexican cartels to be distributed by local dealers – mostly Chicano fieldworkers employed by the lily bulb farms and dairies that flourish in the rich bottom lands beside the mouth of the Smith River. In fact, however, these Latino dealers are almost all cartel plants, many of them illegals who – seeking a better life – had been spirited into the country from Mexico and beyond by cartel affiliates, transported up-state to take agricultural jobs, then forced by their masters to moonlight as drug dealers – or see their families back home murdered by cartel thugs. Geri told us drug-related crime was by far the most common in the county these days – amounting to nearly seventy percent of the total – and that just as soon as one dealer was busted another would arrive to take his (or her) place. Keeping on top of this situation was an endless and frustrating task for the local law enforcement officers.

Sniffing a potential story I had asked Geri if I might spend some time with her out on patrol – to get a feel of the county and its problems first hand – and she was more than willing to comply.

As it happened Lorraine wanted to do some shopping that morning in Crescent City, so that left me free to avail myself of Geri's invitation to accompany her for half of her shift.

All of which explains why I was sitting beside her in her unit that Saturday morning.

As we headed towards town for the morning Sheriff's briefing Geri was describing another problem Del Norte County law enforcement officers were facing – an apparently all too lenient policy of drug dealer prosecutions by the Del Norte County District Attorney's Office, the incumbent D.A. being one Lamont Gregory, Republican pillar of the local community, friend of the state's Governor and Attorney General, and holder of the office for the last two terms. According to Geri Mr. Gregory's method of dealing with apprehended drug dealers, especially those with clear cartel affiliations, was far too soft – charging them only with low level felony offenses and negotiating plea bargains, all of which kept the court roster relatively uncongested, but which also resulted in minimal sentences that obviously failed to deter the seemingly endless stream of dealer replacements. An election for District Attorney was scheduled for the following July and Geri was about to describe the policy changes proposed by the opposition Democrat candidate when our conversation was interrupted by a call on her shortwave radio.

'Radio, 416.'

Geri reached for her microphone.

'Go ahead, Radio.'

'What's your 20, 416?'

'Current 10-20 southbound on 101 near King's Valley Road. What you got?'

'Gonna need to you break off at 199 and head east, 416. Got a situation developing in Jed Smith State Park with suspicious circumstances. 1144. Possible 187. Vic discovered by a party of kids at the park for a school outing. Contact is a teacher, a Mrs. Helen Babich. Got that?'

Geri was making notes on a notepad she kept on the island between the seats.

'Copied. Anything else?'

'Not at this time. I've already dispatched Ambulance and Fire. They'll be staging at the park entrance.'

'10-4, Radio. 416 en route. Turning onto 199 now.'

Dropping her notebook and pen, Geri pulled the car abruptly onto the access road leading to Highway 199 and reached down to hit her lights and siren.

Ten minutes later we crossed the Hiouchi Bridge over the Smith River and soon after Geri killed the flashers and siren and turned into the approach road for the Jedediah Smith Redwoods State Park campground. At the check-in gate a park ranger stepped out of his hut to meet us. Geri rolled down her window.

'Morning.'

'Morning, Deputy.' The smiling ranger removed his flat-brimmed Smokey hat and leaned down to peer across her at me. 'My boss Ranger Barker's waiting for you guys down at the riverbank.' He turned and pointed ahead. 'Follow that road around to the right and you'll come out at the picnic area. It's a short walk from there to where the body is.' He nodded to a brown state park pickup. 'Want me to lead you down there?'

Geri smiled. 'No, thanks. I've been here before. I can find my way.'

The young ranger stepped back, tipping his hat as he resettled it on his head, then murmured into his shoulder radio mic as we rolled away.

We got to the picnic area a couple minutes later and Geri tucked her unit in beside the back end of a yellow school bus that was taking up several of the diagonal parking slots. She got out and I followed her around to the back of her vehicle, where she opened the trunk and removed a roll of yellow and black incident tape. Then she closed the trunk and looked up at me.

'I don't know if you understood what that call was about, Arnie, but this business involves a death of some sort and a body. You can come along if you want, but if I tell you to stop and hang back you'll have to stop and hang back. If it's a crime scene I can't have you accidentally contaminating it.' She smiled. 'Even if you are a hot shot reporter.'

'I wouldn't want to,' I told her. 'And thanks for letting me tag along.'

Geri nodded and turned away, striding off towards the picnic area where a crowd of school kids and parent helpers was milling around picnic tables and scattered in groups out on the river bar beyond, all working on paper plates of food and talking in low voices. On one of the tables a boom box was belting out heavy metal music. Sitting across from one another at the other end were two grim-faced grownups holding Styrofoam cups of coffee – a man in his early thirties and a middle-aged woman. When they noticed us coming they got to their feet.

'Mrs. Babich?' Geri asked.

The woman put a hand to her forehead momentarily and smiled, weakly.

'That's right. I'm one of the teachers looking after these kids.' She turned towards the man. 'This is Joe Meeks. He's the other one. We're from Redwood Elementary in Fort Dick.'

Geri nodded. 'I saw the name on the bus. You're here for a school outing, is that right?'

'Yes. Our annual spring picnic for eighth graders.'

Geri glanced past her towards the river.

'Can you take me to the body, please?'

'Sure can.' Mrs. Babich glanced at her colleague. 'Joe, can you hold the fort till I get back?'

'No problem, Helen,' he said.

The woman turned towards the river and the three of us set off over the rocky bar, angling upstream to a sandy rise and along a trail beside the river.

We had walked a hundred yards or so when, turning a corner, we encountered a park ranger waiting by the water with his arms crossed. Removing his hat to expose a head of greying hair, he stepped forward.

''Morning, Deputy. I'm Chief Ranger Tom Barker.'

'Ranger Barker. Geri Mitchell.' Geri shook his hand, then nodded to me. 'This's a friend of mine, Arnold Rednapp.'

'Mr. Rednapp.'

'What have you got to show me, Ranger Barker?' Geri asked.

He led us a few steps along the path past some low trees and brush to the water's edge. Stopping, he raised his arm to point out along the shadowy shoreline.

'There he is. Or what's left of him.'

He stepped back, folding his arms again.

Geri swung around to view the white blob floating a dozen yards away. Then she turned back to the teacher.

'Was it you that found the body, Mrs. Babich?'

'No. One of my students found it. Linda Baron. She screamed and I came running.' She glanced out at the river, then quickly away again. 'I waded out to take a look at it – I thought it could've been one of the kids. But when I turned it over...'

She shuddered.

Geri reached out to touch the teacher's arm.

'Mrs. Babich, I won't see the body till the ambulance people bring it in,' she said gently, 'so could you please describe to me what you saw?'

Babich took a deep breath, then told her story. When she'd finished there was silence as everyone digested the details of her grim description. Then Geri spoke, now all business.

'Right. Ranger Barker, I'll need you to call in a couple of your staff to block off this trail a hundred feet along in both directions, then stand by to keep out all gawkers.' She handed him the roll of incident tape. 'If you wouldn't mind, you could also mark out the crime scene for me. It'll want to go into the trees at least fifty feet from the water's edge all along the way – like a rectangle. Then I want you to stand here and keep an eye on that body till the fire and ambulance people arrive. Can you do that for me?'

Barker reached for the tape.

'Only too glad to help.'

He set off upriver, talking into his radio's shoulder microphone.

Geri turned to the teacher.

'Mrs. Babich, thanks for your help. I'm going to call for back-up and for the department detectives. From what you've described we're obviously not dealing with just a drowning here. When they arrive you'll be free to go, but make sure someone takes statements from you and the girl who found the body before you do.'

'I understand.'

Now Geri turned to me.

'Arnie, I'm afraid you're stuck with me awhile. I hope that's all right?'

'Don't think about it. I might even learn something.'

She nodded, glanced at her watch.

'It's almost lunchtime. I'll do what I have to do and drop you back home soon as I can.'

'Fine.'

Geri turned and walked off towards the picnic area. Allowing Mrs. Babich to fall into step behind her I followed the two of them downriver.

Chapter Two

When we got to the picnic area Mrs. Babich rejoined her school party and Geri walked out to sit in her car. Picking up the radio mic, she first summoned the ambulance and fire people who were waiting at the park entrance. Then she contacted Dispatch in Crescent City and told him to send out the Sheriff's Department detectives as well as another deputy as backup. When she'd finished Geri just sat there with her door open staring out at the river, her brow drawn in a troubled frown. I knew all this because I had come out to the car with her and was standing beside it with my hands in my pockets, watching her.

'You okay?' I asked her finally.

She glanced up at me with a weak smile.

'Yeah, I'm fine. Just don't get this kind of call very often. Still gives me the willies – though I've seen worse things, believe me.'

I nodded. 'I'm sure you have. So what happens now?'

She sighed. 'Well, first we wait for the detectives. Then the paramedics and firemen will bring the body in and we'll check it out. Then it'll be transported into town to Wier's Mortuary where it'll be kept till the investigation's over and it can be released to the family – if we find them.'

'You don't have a county morgue in Del Norte?' I asked.

'No. We don't get enough mysterious deaths to justify one. We always use Wier's. Autopsies are also done there.'

I nodded. 'So what happens when the detectives arrive?'

'I'll have to hang around to help secure the site until the detectives release me.' She glanced up at me. 'If there's ID on the body and it turns out he's some local guy I might have to visit the family.' She sighed. 'Sorry, Arnie. You could be stuck with me a couple hours more before I can get you back home.'

I shrugged. 'No problem. It's interesting to see how these things work. Anyway, if I get bored I can always call Lorraine and ask her to come pick me up. Speaking of which I'd better give her a call now, let her know I might be delayed.' I reached for my phone. 'Okay to tell her why we're out here?'

She smiled. 'Sure, but I wouldn't give her the gory details.'

'I won't.'

The two Sheriff's Department detectives arrived half an hour later, hard men with the look of seasoned professionals about them. One of them was in a deputy's uniform, the other in casual civilian attire. I hung back and kept out of the way, trotting along behind to watch them and the ambulance and fire people doing their business – wading out to pull the body in and transferring it to a stretcher and a body bag. Geri had allowed me to observe while this was going on, but the minute the detectives noticed me I was challenged, then told to beat it back to the picnic area, which I did. I was out there long enough, however, to watch the body brought in and saw for myself the horrors described by Mrs. Babich. I was also present when they searched the pockets of the corpse's worn jeans and found nothing in them – no coins or keys, no wallet or comb. Nothing. Certainly no ID. Clearly, the terrible things that'd been done to him had been done to eliminate all means of identification. The only facts that were definite were that the victim was male, Caucasian, and aged somewhere between late twenties and early forties. A small bullet hole in the back of the head seemed the obvious cause of death, but that would be confirmed at the autopsy. It appeared that the body had been in the water something over two days, and that it hadn't been dumped in its present location. The detectives reckoned it entered the river somewhere upstream and had drifted down with the swollen current from the recent rains – until it was caught up in the eddy at the river's elbow, just above the shallows.

Before I was given my marching orders I overheard one other interesting comment. The two detectives were standing beside the stretcher, examining the body.

'Certainly a thorough job,' one of them said. 'Haven't seen anything like this since I was a rookie down in Inglewood. This looks like gang work, this mutilation.'

Gang work. Meaning it was done by gangbanger thugs used to carving people up for their masters and turning them into unidentifiable mincemeat. But Del Norte County's a long way from L.A. What were they doing up here? Just who was this poor guy? I wondered. And what had he done to deserve such a death?

I had to wait some time at the car before the professionals came back and the bagged corpse was loaded into the ambulance and taken away. Then Geri was cut loose. Mrs. Babich and her colleague and all of the eighth graders had long since re-boarded their bus and gone home – after the second Sheriff's deputy had taken statements.

On the way back to Geri's place we spoke of the morning's events.

'You got a bit more than you bargained for I think, Arnie,' she said. 'Hope it won't keep you awake.'

'Not for the reason you're thinking,' I replied.

'Meaning what?'

'The whole thing's very mysterious. Why attempt to hide the guy's identity then just dump the body in the river rather than burying it somewhere? And how could there be a possible gang connection this far north?'

She glanced across at me.

'Gang connection? Where'd you hear that?'

I told her about the overheard conversation between the two detectives.

'Hm,' she said when I'd finished. 'That'd be Nelson. Heavy-set guy in the jacket and chinos?'

'Uh-huh.'

'That's him. Detective Sergeant Craig Nelson. A real chauvinist hardass. Doesn't like me, but he has to tolerate me and that rankles.'

'Why doesn't he like you?'

'Because I'm a woman. He doesn't think women should be out looking for bad guys. He thinks the only jobs they're suited for in law enforcement are secretarial and making the coffee. Also we had an issue over a drug bust once.'

'Ah.'

'But he's a good detective. And he did spend twenty years in L.A., so he ought to know what he's talking about.' She paused. 'Gangs, huh? Well, we won't know what that connection might be until we discover the vic's identity.'

I asked her if there'd been any missing person reports locally in the last few days. She responded by radioing Dispatch and putting that question to him.

'Far as I know, 416, there's been no such reports.'

'10-4, Radio.'

Geri replaced the mic and we drove on in silence for a bit. I was about to ask her about the drug bust with Nelson when a sequence of white blobs along the roadside ahead caught my attention. I watched as they grew in size into publicity posters for the upcoming county elections. There were several offices being contested, including County Sheriff and District Attorney. From one of the bigger posters the chiseled face of one of the District Attorney candidates smiled out at me, an older man with a thick head of grey hair. Below the picture were the words 'Vote Lamont Gregory for Del Norte County D.A.! Vote for Experience and a Proven Record!' That pulled my thoughts in another direction.

'What else can you tell me about Lamont Gregory, Geri? Apart from the fact that his prosecution policy has been too lenient.'

She made a face and ran a hand through her short brunette hair.

'What can I say? He grew up here, son of a prominent family of devout Catholics who made their money from logging and lumber milling.' She smiled across at me. 'That was back in the old days, when it was still legal to clear-cut old growth redwood without any limitations. That isn't allowed anymore, not since LBJ turned most of the redwood forests into national parks. When that happened the Gregorys shifted to farming lily bulbs. When his parents died Lamont inherited one of the largest farms in the area. We passed it a minute ago. It's just off 101, between the Dr. Fine bridge and my house.'

I remembered it. A white two-storied farmhouse surrounded by a cluster of outbuildings, the whole lot set back from the highway against the foothills of the coast range and flanked by vast fields of lily bulbs.

'I noticed it,' I said, nodding. 'Impressive spread.'

'He also has a place in town overlooking the ocean. He spends most of his time there, since it's closer to his office and the Court House.'

'How old a man is he?'

'He's now about sixty,' Geri replied, 'and manages somehow to run both of his houses, the farm and the court house without conflict.' She shook her head. 'I don't know how he does it, really.'

'He must have help.'

'He does. His manager on the farm is an old beau of mine named Ryan Garrett. Ryan inherited and managed a lily farm of his own – until Lamont bought him out. When he did he hired Ryan to look after his entire outfit. Apart from Ryan there's a Latino who's been with him for years that maintains his house and yard. The guy's wife works as his cook and housekeeper. Those are the only full time employees. Of course, they hire casual field labor when they need it. Mostly Mexicans.'

I nodded. 'And he's always been a lawyer?'

'Oh, yes. He's a bright boy. Got his law degree at the Gould law school at USC, then passed the bar exam and worked in L.A. for some years as a criminal defense lawyer. Made quite a reputation for himself. Then he was taken into the L.A. County District Attorney's Office as a junior prosecutor and slowly worked his way up to Assistant D.A.' She smiled. 'He knows a lot about Chicanos and gangbangers. He's put lots of 'em away.'

'But you say his prosecution record in Del Norte County has been too lenient?'

Geri scrunched her mouth in a moue.

'Well, let's just say he seems to be getting a bit soft in his old age.'

'And the candidate running against him wants to change all that?'

'Yes. He's a Democrat, obviously. And a friend of mine. A Native American named Thad Wilkins who's been practicing law in the county for the last half-dozen years. Gregory's come out very aggressively against him. In his press statements he accuses Wilkins of proposing as an alternative a naive and ultimately undeliverable plan for drug dealer prosecutions.'

'What's Wilkins want to do that's so different?'

'Thad has watched the rising numbers of drug addicts on the county's rolls – not least in the local Native American community – and has been sickened by that increase. He wants to come down hard on the dealers, using the full weight of the law to secure long prison sentences. Gregory argues that would result in longer court trials and fewer convictions. His more measured approach, he claims, results in more and quicker convictions, costing the county a lot less in court expenses – thereby saving taxpayers' money.'

'Seems a fair argument. People hate paying taxes.'

'Maybe. Gregory's also attacked Wilkins for publically confessing that as a student he occasionally used marijuana himself and therefore feels better qualified than Gregory to understand the drug culture temptations faced by today's youth. Gregory, of course, interprets this confession as evidence of character weakness, a trait clearly undesirable in a District Attorney.'

'Hm,' I mused. 'When did he move back north from L.A.? Gregory, I mean.'

'Ten years ago. He came back when his parents died and he inherited the farm. But growing lilies wasn't for him. Within a year he'd bought the house in town and entered the race for District Attorney. He got himself elected with no trouble. He's been re-elected once since and will probably get elected again next month.' She shook her head, resigned. 'No matter what I think of him he's certainly popular and he runs a tight ship. It's hard to fault him. Either that or he's just very careful. And he never busts the budget, which makes the local taxpayers very happy.'

'What's his family like?'

'Apart from an older sister who lives in Portland Lamont's the last of the line.'

'He has no children?'

'Nope. Never married. Claims he's never had the time. But there's been a lot of speculation as to why he's not tied the knot.'

I shrugged. 'Maybe he's gay.'

Geri laughed. 'Lamont Gregory gay? Arnie, I doubt it. He's one tough son of a bitch, believe me. I wouldn't have thought it was possible, but then I'm no expert in those things.'

When we got to the house Lorraine was there with lunch waiting for us. Geri stayed long enough to grab a sandwich and a cup of coffee, then she hit the road again, back on patrol.

That night we took her out for dinner at a seafood restaurant overlooking the ocean in Brookings, just over the Oregon border. It was a good dinner and a very pleasant evening. When we got home we talked into the wee hours about all kinds of things. But no mention was made of the mutilated body.

The following morning, we said our goodbyes and headed south.

Chapter Three

The grey-haired man sat in his home office, staring out at the Pacific through the sliding glass doors that gave onto the redwood deck. On the mahogany desk before him was a short tumbler of malt whiskey. In his hand was his second cell phone. He held the phone to his ear. The number he had dialed rang for some moments, then was picked up.

'*¿Bueno?*'

'It's me.'

'Ah, yes. So, how's it going? Business is good?'

'Business is fine. But there's been another complication. What I was afraid might happen *has* happened.'

'What do you mean?'

'The package your people disposed of has reappeared. It turned up at the weekend in a very public place. The authorities are now all over it.'

'Really? That's most unfortunate.'

The man at the desk ground his teeth. 'You could say that, yes.'

'Do they know who it is?'

'Not yet, no. But it's only a matter of time till they do. What I want to know is what're we going to do about it?'

For a moment there was silence from the other end.

'I am sorry for your predicament,' the voice said finally, 'but you know, *amigo*, this is really your problem, not ours.'

The man fought to keep his temper. He was not used to being spoken to like this, but he couldn't afford to compromise their relationship.

'I know that, Marcos. But it wouldn't have happened if your amateur heavies hadn't panicked and overstepped their instructions. That was down to them, not me.'

The Latino at the end of the line sighed, wearily.

'I told you. They had no choice.'

'So you said.' The man sat back in his chair, watching the sea undulate beneath the late afternoon sun. 'All I know is their over-reaction has created a situation up here that might be difficult to contain. Frankly I'm quite worried about it.'

'It sounds to me like you need to make your problems disappear. Want me to send another team up? True professionals this time?'

'Good God, no! It was that kind of thing that created this mess in the first place. I'm not going to compound it by resorting to the same tactics again. This is not Los Angeles, remember? You can't do up here what you do down there and get away with it.'

'Whatever. Anyway, the offer stands if you need it.'

'I'll remember that. Hopefully it won't be necessary.'

'You're a man of influence and connections. Can't you just call in some favors?'

'I'm thinking about that. Rest assured I'll consider all options.' The man glanced at his watch. 'I've got to go. I've got guests coming.'

'Ah, the good life. Always nice talking to you, *compadre*. Let me know if I can help with anything. I know you'll take care of things, one way or another.'

'I shall do my best.'

And he cut the line.

Chapter Four

Friday, May 16

I got back to my apartment around mid-day on Monday and for the next week I was tied up chasing a story and far too busy to think about the body found in the Smith.

My story concerned a couple dozen local veterans of the Iraq and Afghanistan wars, documenting how many of them were finding it difficult if not impossible to adjust to normal life after the horrors they had witnessed. It was a story I cared a lot about since I'd had grave doubts from the beginning about the efficacy (not to mention ethics) of American military involvement out there.

So I had been out and about, visiting military hospitals, rehabilitation centers, and the usual haunts of the homeless and dispossessed, working my way down a list of veterans I hoped to find and interview, veterans whose dedicated service to their country had left them refugees in their own society, unable because of their emotional, mental and physical scarring to take any active part in it, and whose plight for the most part was being ignored by everyone except the members of their immediate families, the few poorly-funded governmental agencies established to rehabilitate them, and the charity organizations that kept them from starving to death.

Friday night I was in the process of collating the material and writing my article when I received a telephone call at my apartment that, for the moment at least, changed the focus of my thinking.

'Hello?' I said, irritated by the interruption.

'Arnie, this is Geri, from Smith River?'

Suddenly the whole corpse-in-the-river episode flashed clear in my memory.

'Geri! How are you? I'm so sorry. I've been meaning to call you all week but an assignment came up that's completely taken me over. What's happened about the body in the river? Has it been identified?'

'No, it hasn't. But something else happened that I think you ought to know about, since you were in on the case from the beginning. I'd like your advice on what to do about it.'

'Fire away,' I told her.

For the next twenty minutes she filled me in on the moves that had been made by the Del Norte authorities to discover the identity of the mysterious corpse. The first thing the detectives had done was to check all Missing Person reports within a five hundred mile radius. They'd come up with nothing. No blond-haired man of that approximate size, weight and age had been reported missing in the last three months. So that avenue was closed. Having had his hands severed and his teeth smashed to jagged stumps there was no way to check the identity through fingerprint databases or dental records either. There was DNA profiling, of course, but without knowledge of where the man came from or where his family might be it was useless going down that road as well. Their last effort was to create a photofit image of the man's artificially reconstructed face which they had run on the front page of the *Triplicate*, the local paper, two days before. Although no one came through with a positive identification, a few people in the county did report they remembered seeing a man over the previous days with long blond hair that looked vaguely like the photofit image. He'd always been on his own, and on one or two occasions was seen driving a motorcycle. Every account described the man as quiet and reserved. No one had seen him before and it was almost certain he was not from the area. So who was he?

Then Geri'd had a call on her landline from a man who gave his name as Josh Bridger. She said his voice was distinctive – low and breathy – the kind of voice you wouldn't forget. In essence what the man said was that he'd been told she was someone he could trust, that he'd called her because he was pretty sure he knew who the mysterious corpse was and would reveal its identity to her – if she would come to his cabin up near the Oregon border. She asked how she could find the cabin and he gave her a rendezvous point at a roadside rest stop on Highway 199 just below the state line. If she came there at 10 in the morning the following Sunday he would meet her and escort her the rest of the way.

'Don't bring any other cops,' he'd told her. 'I don't trust anybody but you.'

Geri told him she wouldn't meet him on her own. After all, he could be a complete loony and she wasn't prepared to take the risk. He had offered her a compromise: she could bring a companion, but not another cop. Someone who was just a friend.

'So,' I said when she'd finished. 'Are you going? And who're you taking with you? It'd better be someone you can depend on for help if the guy is a psycho.'

'I've thought of that, but there's something about this business that makes me unwilling to trust just anybody. The only person I thought I might take with me – is you.'

'Me?' I squeaked.

'Why not? You were in on this from the beginning. I trust you and you're a no-nonsense guy.'

'But I'm no green beret, Geri. I couldn't protect you. If this guy is a psycho he could walk all over me and then go after you.'

'Something tells me he won't do that.'

I chuckled. 'Well, I sure hope you're right.'

There was a pause.

'So,' she said finally. 'Could you come back up here for Sunday and meet this guy with me?'

I blew out air.

'God, Geri. I'm working on an article that's due Monday. I'm nearly done with it, but...'

'Can't you finish it tonight, or tomorrow morning? If you drive up tomorrow you could spend the night. Then you'd be rested when we see this guy on Sunday.'

'Geri...' I started, then stopped when she hit me with another closer.

'If you do come up, Arnie,' she cooed, 'you could stop off in Shelter Cove on the way back to see Lorraine and Mandy. Does that make the idea any more attractive?'

That was unfair. After spending a week with Lorraine on our vacation, the previous five nights without her had been lonely as hell. I missed her, and the chance to curl up close to her again, if only for one night, was too tempting to refuse. In any case, before I could respond Geri added:

'I phoned Lorraine. She's delighted they might see you again so soon.'

I sighed. 'All right. You win. I'll break my butt and wrap this thing up tonight. Once my editor has it in his hands he won't mind if I skive off for a night or two.'

'So you'll come?' she asked.

'Yeah, I'll come. I'll phone when I set off tomorrow to give my ETA, leave a message on your voice mail if you're out. I'll try to get there in time to take you out to dinner.'

'Great! Thanks, Arnie.'

'Oh, Geri?'

'Yes?'

'You didn't mention the autopsy report. What did that reveal?'

There was a pause as she shifted gears.

'Well, you know what his injuries were. The only thing the coroner confirmed was that the mutilation took place after he was dead.'

'Thank God for that. And he was shot, wasn't he? That's how he died?'

'Yeah. From the size of the entry wound it looks like it was a 9mm pistol. The bullet exited through the left eye. There was no sign of a powder burn, which means the muzzle was not held against his head when it was fired. So it doesn't look like an execution. He died instantly, but it's possible he was beaten beforehand. There were bruises on his body and in the tissue under the mutilation of his face. Of course we don't have his hands so we don't know what they could've done to them.'

'Nothing else was discovered that could identify him? No tattoos or birthmarks?'

'Nothing but a scar on his back, up near his right shoulder. The Coroner said it looked like a war wound of some kind so he must have been a veteran. We're checking that out, but there've been so many vets with wounds over the last few years it'll probably take some time to narrow it down.'

'A vet, huh? More interesting still. Anything else?'

'Not really. His stomach contents indicated he'd ingested some fast food for his last meal. Whatever that tells us.'

'Hm. That everything?'

'Pretty much.'

'All right, then. I'll set off as soon as I can tomorrow. Probably around noon.'

'That's wonderful, Arnie. Thanks a bunch.'

'Oh, one more thing. Any indication yet who's going to win the coming elections?'

Geri laughed. 'It's almost a foregone conclusion. The incumbent Sheriff and District Attorney will almost certainly be re-elected, unless the sky falls in. No surprises there. Drive safe, Arnie. See you tomorrow!'

She hung up.

I put the phone down and returned to my desk, focusing my mind again on my elegy for former warriors with broken minds and wasted bodies.

I finished the article shortly after midnight. Then I had a shower and hit the sack, exhausted.

The next morning, Saturday, I re-read my article, made a couple of minor changes and emailed it to my editor, Abe Rawlings. He wouldn't get it for a few hours as he spent every Saturday playing golf with his cronies at the Palo Alto Hills Golf and Country Club, and I thought I'd better talk to him before I set off for the north again so I called him on his cell. Luckily I caught him while he was waiting for one of his partners to take a shot. If he'd been lining up one himself I would either have been ignored or shouted at for breaking his concentration.

'Yeah?' he breathed down the line. I could hear distant chatter and birdsong.

'Abe, it's Arnie.'

'Hey, fella. What can I do you for?'

I wondered how I could best put this to him.

'Remember the story I told you last week, about the body in the Smith River?'

'Sure, I do. Very intriguing.'

'Well, my deputy sheriff friend called last night and asked if I could spare a day or two to come up and help her out with something related to the investigation.'

'"Something related to the investigation,"' he echoed. 'What the hell does that mean?'

I sighed. Then spent five minutes filling him in on the information Geri had relayed to me in her call – finishing with her request to accompany her on the visit to the cabin of the mysterious Josh Bridger. When I finished there was a long silence at the other end. So long that I thought I'd lost the connection.

'Abe? You still there?'

'Yeah, I'm here. Just thinking.' There was another pause. 'You finish the article on the veterans?'

'I just emailed it to you.'

'You're pleased with it?'

'As pleased as I am with any of my writing. It says what I wanted it to say.'

'Then it'll be good.' He sighed. 'Okay. You can go north again. But let me know how long you'll be soon as you can, all right?'

'I will, soon as I know myself.'

'I suppose you'll stop for a night to see Lorraine and Mandy on the way back?'

'I had thought of it.'

He laughed, then the phone went quiet again for a few seconds.

'Do you think this's going to develop into a story that might interest us, Arnie?' he said at last.

'Can't say for sure, Abe, but my instincts tell me there's something going on up there that isn't just a local issue. I'd like a few days to check it out, if you can spare me.'

'I can do that.'

'Thanks, boss. I appreciate it. I'll keep in touch.'

'Gotta go now. My turn to tee off.'

'Enjoy the game.'

'I always do. Ciao, kid.'

The phone clicked off.

Chapter Five

Being used to driving every other week up to Lorraine's place on California's Lost Coast, my trip to Del Norte County was a dawdle, with most of the time spent listening to an audiobook of a Robert Crais detective novel and enjoying the scenery. Passing the turnoff to Shelter Cove two and a half hours after leaving San Francisco was a bit of a wrench, but I calmed myself with the thought that I'd be seeing Lorraine and Mandy on the way back. Mandy was beginning to accept me as family now, though I still officially slept in the guest room. Both of them had met my daughter Lisa a month before when she'd come out to spend a week with me and we had passed two nights together in Shelter Cove. Lisa took to Lorraine immediately, and Lorraine to her, and though there was an age gap between our daughters they got on well. Frankly it was a little frightening to see how much we were becoming like a family together. Lorraine and I had both been burnt by painfully dysfunctional marriages and we weren't about to abandon our independence easily, no matter how great we felt together. The only thing I knew at present was that I missed her and wanted to be with her again as soon as possible.

It was 3:30 when I drove through Crescent City. Minutes later I passed the turnoff to Highway 199 that Geri and I had taken the week before on our way to Jed Smith State Park. A couple miles after that I glimpsed off to my left, through a thin veil of second growth redwoods, the grim walls and towers of Pelican Bay maximum security state prison – the principle source of income for the county after tourism and fishing. I'd noticed it before, and it always gave me goose bumps to realize that beyond those concrete walls were sequestered some of the most evil people the State of California had ever incarcerated.

I passed Smith River around 4 PM and turned up Geri's drive a couple minutes later. She lived off the highway on a winding road just north of the town in an old farmhouse with a covered porch at the front. Behind the house up the hill was a small barn and an old chicken house, now used for storage. The barn was her garage. The double doors were standing open and her red Toyota GT86 sports car was gone when I drove in, so I assumed she'd slipped off to do a bit of shopping. I parked beside the front porch, climbed out of the battered blue Chevy Cobalt I've been driving for the past five years and sat on Geri's front steps, enjoying the warmth of the spring sun. Overhead large cumulous clouds floated across the sky like lazy white whales surfing the air currents. It was a lovely afternoon.

Five minutes later I heard a car approaching along the road and glanced up to see the distinctive black and white markings of a California Highway Patrol SUV that slowed and then turned up the drive, pulling to a stop behind my car. I could see the patrolman inside eyeing me suspiciously before he climbed out of his rig and sauntered up the drive towards me, surveying my dusty Cobalt on the way. He was a tall man somewhere in his late thirties with a slim athletic build, and as he neared me he pulled off his Ray-Bans to reveal penetrating blue eyes.

'Afternoon,' he said, running a hand through his sandy-colored hair. 'Geri around?'

'Nope,' I replied. 'Must've gone to get a quart of milk or something.'

He nodded. 'She expecting you?'

'Yep. I'm a friend of hers from San Francisco.' I stood up, dusted off my pants and extended a hand towards him. 'Arnold Rednapp. I'm a reporter for a bay area paper.'

He shook my hand.

'A reporter, huh? Up here on business, or just for a visit?'

'Well,' I hesitated, 'a little of both, really. But I don't expect to be here more than a day or two. You a friend of Geri's, too?'

'Yeah. I stop in sometimes for a coffee when I'm out this way. Thought I might find her home this afternoon.' He turned to look along the empty roadway. 'Well,' he said finally, smoothing his hair back with one hand, 'tell her Sam stopped by, will you? I'll give her a call sometime in the next day or two.'

'I'll tell her.'

He smiled. 'Enjoy your stay.'

'I will. Nice meeting you, Sam.'

'Likewise, Arnold.'

'Arnie. Please.'

'Ok, Arnie.' He cocked his head to one side. 'You a close friend of Geri's?'

I smiled. 'My partner is. They were roommates at Sac State.'

'Ah.' He nodded, his face relaxing. 'All right. Take it easy.'

'I'll do that.'

Slipping on his sun glasses he turned and walked back to his ride, nodding back at me before settling himself inside. Then he started up and drove off, leaving me in silence once more.

Geri drove in twenty minutes later and parked behind my car. When she got out she was carrying a paper sack full of groceries. I'd been right. She'd gone out for some last minute shopping – a bottle of wine and some nibbles. For the rest of the afternoon we watched the sun go down together from her back deck while chatting about miscellaneous subjects. I told her about Sam's visit and she smiled. When I gently pressed her for more info on him she shrugged.

'His name's Sam Buchanan,' she told me. 'We met not long ago at a restaurant in town where we'd both stopped for coffee. The uniforms drew us together and we started talking. Sam's only been here a few months. He's a transfer from the bay area. He's just been through a difficult divorce and wanted some distance from the memories. He thought a posting up here would open new possibilities for him.'

'You one of those new possibilities?'

She laughed. 'We'll see about that. I like his company, but we're taking things slowly. Ask me again in six months and I'll be able to give you a more definite answer.'

I raised my wine glass in a toast to the pair of them. Then we spoke of the reason I'd driven up there.

'Have you learned anything more about the mysterious Josh Bridger?' I said, topping up her glass with the last of the wine.

She shook her head.

'I've asked around, but no one seems to know anything about him.' She lifted her glass and sipped. 'I was in Gasquet yesterday – up near the state line – and stopped in at the store there. The owner – an old guy who's been running the place for years – was behind the counter and I told him about the call and asked if he knew such a fellow. When I described his voice and mentioned that he apparently had a cabin somewhere up that way the owner said he thought he knew who I was talking about. Said he'd come in now and then to buy a backpack full of staples and then just disappear. Always paid cash. Said he was tall, with long dark hair and a beard. Rode a motorcycle, he thought. He didn't have a name for him and didn't recognize the name Bridger. But the old man assured me he isn't a loony. Seemed too calm and collected for that, he said. Just a quiet guy who kept to himself.'

'That's reassuring. Still no news about the unidentified body?'

'Nope. That's still a complete mystery.'

'Well,' I said, finishing my wine, 'here's hoping tomorrow night we'll know more about him.'

'Amen to that,' she said, emptying her glass.

'And now,' I said, standing, 'how about that dinner I promised you?'

We went back to the Brookings restaurant we'd gone to during my visit with Lorraine, and again the food was great. The place was busy during the early part of the evening but by the time we'd gotten to coffees it had thinned out. A glass or two of wine had relaxed us even more and I suddenly found myself describing for her my pre-Lorraine love life – the gradual dissolution of my ten-year marriage, the months of fruitless counseling, the eventual sad decision that divorce was our only option. Having bared my soul to Geri I asked her how it was she was still single, or if she too had been married before. She nodded grimly.

'I was married for almost five years to my college boyfriend. Wayne was a jock, played offensive end for the football team and scored lots of touchdowns. A hunk. We went together for the last two years I was at Sacramento State – during the time I was rooming with Lorraine. I was very much in love with him. When we graduated we got married. He wanted to be a lawyer and I agreed to work to support us so he could get his law degree and pass the bar. I figured once he was qualified he'd give me a good life with lots of creature comforts to make up for my years of sacrifice. Unfortunately it didn't work out that way.'

She took a sip of coffee.

'What happened?'

She sighed. 'Four years later he got his degree, passed the bar exam and set up a practice down in Salinas where he'd grown up. We bought a house there and settled down and I thought everything was going great until...'

She stopped and looked down at her lap.

'Until what?' I prompted.

'Until he told me one night that he was in love with his secretary and wanted a divorce.'

'Just like that?'

'Just like that. His secretary turned out to be a girl he'd dated in high school – a bit of information he'd neglected to mention before. Apparently their close proximity brought all the old feelings back, or so he told me.'

'What a sweetheart.'

'Yeah.'

She sighed again, took another sip of coffee. So did I.

'Lucky you didn't have any kids,' I offered.

'He didn't want them,' she said. 'Said it would complicate our lives too much, that until his practice was going well we couldn't afford them. He was right about that.'

'But you still do? Want kids?'

'Sure. One day. If I can find the right guy to father them.'

I smiled at her. 'You will. What's more, Ger, you're going to make one hell of a mom.'

Chapter Six

Sunday, May 18

I woke up at 7:30 next morning in Geri's guest room to the sounds of movement in the kitchen and the scent of freshly ground coffee. That did the trick.

Ten minutes later I was dressed and leaning against the kitchen door frame, sipping a mug of strong black Columbian and watching Geri put together two plates of scrambled eggs, bacon and toast. It smelled good.

'You slept well, then?' she asked, smiling towards me as she carried the plates to the kitchen table.

'Like the proverbial log.' I slid onto the nearest chair. 'But I miss my bed warmer all the same.'

She laughed. 'I'll bet you do.' She sat down opposite me and reached for her coffee cup. 'Never mind. You'll be with her again soon.'

'I can't wait.'

We ate in silence for a few minutes. The breakfast was as good as it smelled.

'So,' I said finally, wiping my mouth with a paper napkin, 'how do you want to play this meeting?'

She took a sip of coffee and sat back, looking at me and thinking.

'By ear, I guess,' she said at last. 'It takes about an hour to get to the Collier Tunnel Rest Stop where we're to meet him. We'll leave so we get there early, just to check things out. I don't know what this guy looks like, of course, and he probably won't know me either, so I don't know how we'll recognize one another.'

I smiled. 'From what he's told you I reckon he's seen you before. It wouldn't surprise me if he's been shadowing you over the last week, checking you out. He sounds a very careful man.'

Geri nodded. 'I think you're right.'

'That early in the day there probably won't be many people at the rest stop anyway. He'll know who we are.' I sipped more coffee. 'You taking your weapon?'

She glanced up sharply. On our earlier stay Geri had shown Lorraine and me the little snub-nosed .38 police special she often carries in her purse.

'No,' she said. 'I thought it better not to.'

'Fair enough. From what you've told me I don't think we'll need it.'

We left the house at 8:30, taking Geri's red Toyota. The day was grey and cool, with the usual coastal overcast that might or might not burn off as the morning progressed. But the skies would be clear thirty miles inland – at least, the forecast gave that prediction. It was supposed to be warm and sunny in the mountains.

We took the highway south towards Crescent City, then turned left to take the North Bank Road along the Smith River to join Highway 199 at the Hiouchi Bridge. Moments later we passed Jed Smith State Park and the events of our recent shared time there flashed through my memory.

From that point on all cloud dissipated and the skies remained cornflower blue from mountain crest to mountain crest. Watching the Smith swirling through the gorge below the roadway I marveled once more at the natural beauty of the area.

We passed through the tiny village of Gasquet with its gas station, fast food joint and long, one-storied Market stretched out beside the highway. Then we wound onwards through the redwoods and beside and over various branches of the multi-forked Smith until at length we approached the southern opening of Collier Tunnel a few miles short of the Oregon border and Geri signaled to turn left into the adjacent rest stop.

As the car eased into the parking area with the restrooms at its center Geri slumped forward over the steering wheel, scanning the lot and the surrounding trees. As expected, there was hardly anyone there. Only one vehicle was parked beside the restrooms. Beside it a young couple were shepherding a small boy and girl back inside its open doors. There was nobody else around. We pulled to a stop three car widths away and sat watching the young family preparing to hit the highway again. Finally the car started and backed out – revealing a motorcycle parked beyond it. But there was no one around that seemed to belong to it, and when the family drove off we were left with nothing but silence.

An intense silence.

Minutes ticked by as we waited. There was no movement – only the mountains and the trees and the blue sky and the rest stop facilities. No people. No animals. No sound at all save for the occasional cry of a distant soaring hawk or the squawk of a bluejay disturbed somewhere in its foraging.

Nothing.

Until suddenly there was.

The man called Josh Bridger appeared from nowhere. One moment there was nothing, the next moment there he stood in front of the car, a tall figure somewhere in his late thirties with his hands in his pockets. He wore jeans and a grey sweatshirt, its sleeves cut off below the shoulders revealing muscular arms. On his feet were heavy boots, and on his head, over shoulder-length dark hair, he wore a black woolen navy cap. His eyes above his beard were hidden behind sun glasses.

The man had appeared so suddenly that both Geri and I gave involuntary 'Oh!'s and sat bolt upright. While he stood watching us, we shook ourselves into some degree of composure and climbed out of the car to join him.

'Josh Bridger?' Geri asked, shielding her eyes from the sun with her hand to peer up into his face.

'That's right.' He pulled off the glasses. 'Pleased to meet you, Deputy Mitchell.'

'Call me Geri.'

'Okay ... Geri,' he said. Then he turned to me, his steel grey eyes seeming to dive deep into my soul. 'Who's this?'

'A friend of mine from the bay area. He's visiting and I thought I'd ask him to come along. Hope you don't mind?'

'No, I don't mind. Long's he's not a cop.'

'He's no cop. He's a reporter.'

Bridger's eyebrows lifted. 'Reporter?'

'That's right,' I told him. 'Arnie Rednapp. I work for the *South Bay Bulletin*. Heard of it?'

'I have, actually. I spent a couple years at San Jose State. Your paper has a solid reputation. I'm glad to meet you, Arnie.'

'Likewise.'

He nodded, then looked me up and down more closely.

'You a vet?'

'Nope. I've always thought it best to leave fighting wars to the professionals.'

'Wise move.' He turned to look off at the mountains to the north. 'Well, shall we go? It's not far, only five minutes away. The cabin's just across from the bug station.'

'Okay.' Geri nodded at the parked motorcycle. 'That yours?'

'It is.'

'Nice bike.'

'Thanks.'

Bridger turned away, donned his sun glasses again and produced a pair of leather gloves from his back pocket. Slipping them on, he stepped astride the bike and swung up the kickstand while Geri and I climbed back into her Toyota and strapped ourselves in. Bridger fired up his ride and swung it around and we followed him back onto 199, heading north.

The bug station he'd referred to was the California Department of Agriculture border checkpoint whose purpose was to prevent contaminated fruit and vegetables being brought into the state that could devastate California's extensive fruit crops. For the last several years, however, owing to the state's continued budget shortfall after the crash of 2007, the building had remained mostly closed.

Exactly five minutes later, just as the dark two-storied bug station loomed up ahead, Bridger signaled a right hand turn and jockeyed the motorcycle onto a narrow road that led off through the trees. Slowing, Geri followed him.

A few hundred feet along the trees on the left thinned out and the road followed the bank of a pond opposite a large, ranch style home. Just beyond that the asphalt paving ended and the road that carried on was graveled. This we followed another quarter of a mile, skirting the pond for a time until we crossed a cattleguard and the road broke off to the right through some trees and climbed a low hill. At its top, set back against a forest of scrub oak and pine, was an ancient-looking log cabin with a stovepipe poking through its shingled roof and an open garage beside it. At least a third of the garage's space was taken up by rows of split and stacked firewood. At the side of the cabin's screened front door were a picnic table and two benches, together with a small barbecue on a tripod stand.

Josh Bridger pulled his motorcycle into the garage and shut it down, balancing it on its kickstand and climbing off. Meanwhile Geri eased her Toyota to a stop and the two of us got out.

Peeling off his gloves, Josh stepped up to the cabin's screened front door.

'Welcome to my humble abode. We can sit inside if you like, or we can do our talking out here.'

'Outside's fine,' Geri said, looking around.

'Mind if I have a look inside?' I asked. 'I'm curious.'

'Help yourself.'

I stepped through into the interior, Geri at my heels.

There wasn't much to see. The main room was a long rectangle, with a kitchen at the left end and a living room area with a sofa and armchair at the other. There was clearly no electricity, and positioned here and there around the room were candles in metal holders and hanging gas lamps. In the back wall an open doorway led into the shadowy bedroom beyond.

The armchair set in the corner to the right was obviously Bridger's favored perch, given the stack of books and the kerosene lamp on the end table beside it. On the back wall a gun rack held a double barreled shotgun and a lever-action Winchester 30-30, with boxes of ammunition on the shelf below. I leaned down to look more closely at the books by the armchair – and was surprised to find amongst them a few of what I would call serious titles, things like Thoreau's *On Walden Pond*, and Tom Paine's *The Age of Reason*. For a bearded roughneck Josh Bridger obviously had refined intellectual interests.

'What do you think?'

Bridger's quiet voice from outside broke the spell and we pushed our way out the screen door to join him. He had removed his sun glasses again.

'It's amazing,' I said. 'You live out here all year long?'

'Pretty much. I head off now and then to take jobs to earn some money. Then I come back.'

'What kind of jobs? And where do you find the work?' Geri asked. 'Around here? In the lily fields?'

Bridger shook his head.

'No. I go into Oregon to pick grapes for the wineries along the Rogue River and the Applegate. Or I travel on up to the Willamette Valley. Look for whatever short-term agricultural work I can find.'

Geri looked toward the garage.

'You use your motorcycle to get around? You don't have a car?'

Bridger nodded. 'That old bike's an antique. It belonged to my father. It's a '48 Indian Chief. Bit of a collector's item now.'

'Lovely machine,' I said. 'Must take some work to keep it running. You do all that yourself?'

'No. Guy down in Gasquet looks after it for me. I let him ride it sometimes and he gives me a good rate for maintaining it.'

'Why don't you find a room in Gasquet?' I asked him. 'What makes you stay up here on your own?'

Bridger looked at me. Then he reached up to pull the woolen cap from his head and shook out his long dark hair.

'Like I told Geri when I called her, I'm a private person and I like to keep to myself, away from people. That's why I asked her to meet me up here. Let me make you guys some coffee and I'll try to explain why. Then I'll tell you about that body in the river.'

Chapter Seven

Bridger produced a small gas camping stove from within his cabin, placed it on the picnic table, then lit it with his lighter. He disappeared inside for a moment and reappeared with a metal tray. On it were two cups and a spoon, a plastic water bottle, a small pot and a bottle of instant coffee. He filled the pot with water from the bottle and sat it on the stove to boil. Then he put coffee into the cups and set them ready – one for Geri, one for me. The pot and cups were aluminum and had seen a lot of use.

'Aren't you having any?' Geri asked him.

'Nope. I have my coffee when I first wake up.' He chuckled. 'Anyway, I've only got the two cups.'

Geri looked around. 'You got plumbing here? Or an outhouse?'

'Toilet's inside off the bedroom,' he said, smiling. 'Ain't got electricity, but I do have running water and a flush toilet. There's a spring above the cabin that runs all year long. Help yourself.'

Geri excused herself and went inside. While Bridger was working over the coffee things I noticed for the first time that the backs of his hands had tattoos on them. Between the knuckles at the tops of the fingers of each hand three black stars were spread across in an arc. Centered below that was a black triangle with a thick red arrow within it pointing forwards into the triangle's apex. Beneath the triangle two words were etched into his skin. I couldn't read them and asked him if I could take a look.

'Sure,' he said, holding up his right hand, back upwards.

Now the words were clear: '*Nulli Secundus*'. My high school Latin back in Iowa finally paid off.

'"Second to None",' I said aloud.

He grinned. 'That's right.'

'Is it the same phrase on the other hand?'

'Yep,' he said, switching hands so I could see. 'That's from my Army days. Everyone in my unit had the same tattoos, except the number of stars varied according to rank. I was a sergeant so I had three stars. The lieutenant had four. The other three guys had one or two each, depending on whether they were a private or a corporal.'

'You were a soldier then. In Iraq?'

'Yeah. I'll tell you all about that in a minute.'

Geri rejoined us and Bridger reached for the now boiling pot.

'Have a seat,' he said.

Geri and I sat on the side of the bench facing the cabin while Bridger poured water and stirred the coffees. Then he killed the gas and passed us our cups, seating himself opposite and crossing his arms before him on the tabletop. The day was warming up but it was still cool enough under the trees for the hot coffee to taste good, even if it was instant.

'So,' I said, 'tell us why you choose to live way out here by yourself.'

Bridger smiled. 'That's an easy one. I grew up on a ranch in Montana. My Ma died when I was only six, and apart from a Cree Indian woman who cooked and cleaned for us I was brought up by my old man and my older brother. We raised cattle and horses and I was always at home in the outdoors, enjoyed hunting and fishing and so on. But I hated cattle, hated ranch work. I tried college for a couple years but couldn't settle to anything. After Sadam Hussein invaded Kuwait and the Desert Storm campaign was fought I decided I'd join the Army, maybe see a bit of the world myself. I spent eight years in the service; saw a fair amount of action in Iraq and elsewhere. After my discharge from the Army a few years ago I felt nervous about settling back into civilian life. I would've gone back to the ranch but my dad had passed on by then and the ranch was being run by my brother. He and I don't get along so well so that was that. My father gave him the ranch in his will. All I got was the old man's Indian and his shotgun. I guess he thought I'd turned my back on ranch life so he cut me out.'

'How did you end up here, in Del Norte County?' Geri asked.

'I'd been through here once as a boy when Dad drove us down to collect an Arabian stud horse he'd bought from a ranch down near Santa Rosa. I liked the redwoods, loved the Smith River canyon. I've always remembered it, and when I couldn't think of anywhere else to go this seemed a good choice. I asked around and found this cabin. It'd been empty a lot of years and the owner's pleased to have someone living in it and looking after it again. I've been here four years now.'

'Will you ever move back closer to civilization?' Geri asked.

He shrugged. 'Maybe. One day. But I'm still happy the way things are so it ain't going to happen for a while.'

'Don't you miss people?' I asked him. 'You must have friends, other family besides your brother?'

He nodded. 'Sure, I have friends. Pals from high school, old hunting buddies, a cousin or two I visit sometimes. A couple of people from college. I don't see them much but I do try to keep in touch.'

'What about Army friends? You must've had soldier buddies?'

He stared at me a time before answering. Then he nodded again.

'My best friends are Army friends. Those who are still alive I see whenever I can. One of my closest friends was the man whose corpse I reckon you pulled out of the Smith a week ago.'

Geri put her cup on the table. 'He was a friend of yours? Who was he, and where did he come from?'

Bridger scratched an elbow.

'His name was David Colson. Everyone called him 'Davey'. He turned up here two and a half weeks ago. I'd gone down to the Post Office in Gasquet on the Wednesday to get my mail – I have everyone write to me there care of General Delivery. Davey knew I'd come there sooner or later and he was waiting for me. He'd hitched down from visiting a cousin up in Tacoma, Washington. He spent a few nights with me here.' Bridger rose to his feet. 'Before he left he gave me this.'

Pulling his wallet from a back pocket he extracted a photograph from it and handed it across to Geri. I leaned over to have a look. It was a black and white photo of a boy of about thirteen or fourteen with an older man standing beside him. They were posing before a barn door. The boy's face was impassive, almost resigned. Certainly not happy. The older man was wearing a smart dark suit and had his arm around the boy. He was smiling.

It was a face and a smile I had seen before, on a roadside election poster. It was definitely the same man, though much younger and without the grey hair.

Geri glanced at me. 'Do you know who this is? The man?'

'Yes I do. I saw his face on a poster a week ago. It's Lamont Gregory. We talked about him.'

She nodded. 'That's right, we did.' She looked up at Bridger. 'The boy is Davey Colson?'

'Yes.'

'Do you know who the man is beside him?'

'I do. The current District Attorney for Del Norte County.'

Geri frowned, glanced down at the picture, then up at him again.

'Do you know why they're together in this picture?'

Bridger nodded, then sat again.

'I'd better tell you the whole story from the beginning. And, uh, you might want to take notes.'

Geri pulled out a pad and a pen from her jacket, settled herself, and Josh Bridger commenced his tale. It was a long story, and it took almost an hour to tell.

David Colson had grown up in the L.A. area, living in various scruffy apartments and duplexes around Inglewood and Lennox. His father was a drunk and ne'er-do-well who had abandoned his wife and son when the boy was only a couple years old. Davey's mother had tried to raise him on her own, hiring baby sitters and taking on badly paid sales work, but it wasn't easy and in his teens Davey had fallen in with a bad crowd. He started experimenting with drugs, and at thirteen was arrested for dealing pot to his schoolmates. Lamont Gregory was then an Assistant District Attorney for Los Angeles Country. He prosecuted Davey's case and succeeded in convicting him, the sentence being eighteen months' detention in an appropriate youth facility. The ideal institution had just been created a year or so before. Gregory pulled strings and got the boy sent to this special place. It seemed a generous, positive thing to do, but his underlying motive was much darker.

Apart from prosecuting drug dealers and gangbangers, Lamont Gregory had gained a reputation in those years for being public-spirited. He had founded – partly with public money, partly with his own, and with donations from various philanthropists of his acquaintance – a ranch for delinquent boys out at the edge of the county. The ranch was known as Camp Belleview, and it was run by a clutch of former soldiers, prison officers and cops whose brief was, ostensibly, to inspire their charges to lead responsible lives by exposing them to a regime of strong discipline and hard work. The boys planted vegetable gardens, learned to ride and care for horses, bred cattle and chickens, and generally undertook to turn the ranch into a profit-making enterprise through the sale of their produce: vegetables, eggs, hay and beef. It was a good idea. For a time Davey had done well there and, according to Bridger, had come to regard Gregory – who visited the ranch regularly – as a kind of proxy father. Then one night during one of Gregory's visits the boy was called to see him at the big house (the boys slept in bunkhouse-like dormitories nearby). Over the next two hours Davey was subjected to a heavy sexual assault, culminating in him being sodomized by the older man. When he had done his business Gregory threatened to have the boy killed if he ever spoke a word to anyone about what'd happened. Terrified, Davey had kept silent. Over the following months this abuse continued – until Davey's sentence was concluded and he was released. Long before then, however, he had learned that he wasn't the only boy being treated in this way, and that some of the guards were also involved in the sexual abuse. The experience left him, understandably, with deep psychological scars. All the same, after his release Davey somehow managed to keep himself out of trouble. He graduated – eventually – from high school, then immediately joined the Army.

Which was where Josh Bridger had met him.

After boot camp Colson was posted to the 75th Ranger Regiment at Fort Bragg, North Carolina. Bridger was already there, a Corporal in the company Colson was attached to. Colson, both at boot camp and in training exercises at Fort Bragg, had distinguished himself as a daring, dependable and fast-thinking soldier, and had caught the attention of his superiors. After 9/11 and the destruction of the Twin Towers both men were sent with their regiment to Afghanistan to fight in the Enduring Freedom campaign, the objective being to root out and capture the Al Qaeda leader Osama bin Laden. The 75th was involved in several heavy engagements with Al Qaeda forces in the Bora Bora Hills, and both Colson and Corporal Bridger had been cited for courageous service above and beyond the call of duty. Bridger was promoted to Sergeant, Colson to Corporal, as well as being awarded a Distinguished Service Medal. Back at Fort Bragg at the end of their tour, the long days of waiting and inactivity began to chafe. Then news came through that changed their lives. The two soldiers, who at that time only knew each other vaguely as company colleagues, were invited to take part in a selection process – along with two dozen others from the 75th – to join the 1st Special Forces Operational Detachment-Delta, otherwise known as 'Delta Force'. After weeks of rigorous training the two dozen candidates had been reduced to a hard core of five men. Among these five men were Corporal Davey Colson and Sgt. Josh Bridger. When they were all declared members of Delta Force in the autumn of 2002 Bridger said it was the proudest day any of them had known in their lives.

These five men – led by a hard young Lieutenant from Arizona named Dawson – were to work together as a unit for the next six years, being deployed in both Afghanistan and Iraq to infiltrate insurgent hot spots, eliminate their leaders, or to free kidnapped NGO workers, American and European civilians and United Nations personnel. In all their operations the team worked together with exceptional bravery, efficiency, and speed. Their professional lives seemed charmed.

Until their last operation changed everything.

In April of 2008 the squad was ordered to undertake what seemed a routine operation on the edge of Helmand Province in Afghanistan. At their briefing the men were given clear instructions and shown aerial photographs and detailed plans of the town they were to penetrate. Their target was a mid-ranking Taliban leader who had been creating severe problems for the Coalition forces – organizing ambushes that had resulted in dozens of deaths (mostly among Afghan forces), and planting IEDs along Coalition supply routes that had destroyed two armored personnel carriers, killing eight American soldiers. It was time to close his operation down, and Bridger and Colson's unit had been selected to do just that.

The drop was made by helicopter at night in the desert a mile or so from the town in which the Taliban leader was based. With blackened faces, wearing dark battle dress and helmets, Kevlar vests, mini headsets and night vision goggles – and carrying automatic assault rifles – the five men had moved forward through the stony fields into the houses at the edge of the town, clearing each hundred yard section carefully before advancing further. Whispering terse comments to one another over their radio mics, the five men had slowly worked their way through the dark streets.

Everything had gone like clockwork – until the last moment, when the Taliban leader's headquarters had been located and the first steps were being taken to gain entry into his compound.

Then things went horribly wrong.

Chapter Eight

The compound faced a broad square, at one corner of which a stubby fountain trickled water into a shallow stone basin. At this time of night the square was deeply shadowed, with only a couple of feeble street lights at opposite corners offering any illumination. There was no sound as the five men dropped one by one behind the cover of the stone basin, and there was no sign of anyone about. Bridger, Colson and the others had listened as the lieutenant whispered last minute orders. Then they had separated to take up their positions.

The plan was to enter the compound from several points at once – after creating a diversionary explosion at a doorway in one corner of the square. Colson's closest buddy in the unit, Dylan Porter, a young African-American from South Chicago, had been detailed to plant the explosives. From behind the fountain Colson and Bridger had watched Lt. Dawson and the fifth member of the group – a first-generation Irish-American named 'Paddy' Carmichael – creep around the walls to take up positions on the compound's far side. Then they watched Dylan slip forward toward the doorway where the charge was to be placed. Near the doorway a stretch of earth had been cultivated with a few sparse bushes. As Dylan stepped through these his foot must've snared an alarm trip-wire because suddenly the entire area was bathed in bright light and there were shouts and bursts of gunfire. Crouching behind the fountain, Colson and Bridger found themselves lit up like actors on a stage while a wave of gunfire poured down on them from the wall above.

Spraying bullets from their own weapons towards the lights, Colson and Bridger managed to keep clear of the rain of lead, huddling behind the stone basin. Meanwhile Dylan Porter had dropped his explosives and was sprinting for cover at the far side of the square, moving towards a dark alleyway that seemed to lead off in the direction from which they had come. Colson and Bridger watched as Dylan took a hit and dropped, a few feet short of the alleyway. Without thinking, Colson screamed his friend's name and lit out towards him across the open square. Shouting at him to turn back, Bridger had given him cover fire, spraying the walls of the compound with a full magazine. But Colson had not turned back. He had run on and was now dragging his wounded comrade around the alley corner to safety. Meanwhile on the far side of the compound all hell was breaking loose. Lt. Dawson and Paddy Carmichael were now under heavy attack. Bridger could hear their excited exchanges over the radio mic and knew they were being hammered with all kinds of ordinance. Then two loud crumps came from the back of the compound – the unmistakable sound of RPG explosions. Bridger knew that meant the probable end for both men. Whispering desperately into his radio mic he had tried to raise them – once, twice, three times – but without success. Both of them were almost certainly dead.

Inserting a fresh magazine into his weapon, Bridger had fired a quick burst first towards the Taliban positions, then at Porter's gelignite-filled backpack, which erupted in an explosion and a cloud of smoke. Then he set off running across the square to join Colson and Porter. Once he made the alleyway and the compound was no longer in sight, the three men together had retreated as quickly as possible towards the post-op rendezvous point at the town's edge – the wounded Porter hobbling between his two colleagues, who were half-dragging, half-carrying him, their weapons held ready in their free hands. Breathlessly, Sgt. Bridger had radioed for the return of the extraction helicopter and was assured it was on its way.

The noise of gunfire and explosions had awakened the little town. Now there were dogs barking everywhere, people at doorways and faces poking out of windows. Aiming their weapons at them as they passed, the men pushed on. They were left alone until – at the edge of the town and opposite the field where the chopper was to evacuate them – they suddenly came under fire again, from two sides. Porter's body jumped as heavy caliber bullets slammed into his back, one of them smashing into his head and splattering blood and brain matter over Bridger. Colson was also hit, high in the right shoulder. All three went down. Then Bridger and Colson had scrambled for cover, leaving their colleague's lifeless body and crawling along a ditch toward a stone wall that surrounded the field.

The next ten minutes had seemed an eternity, with Taliban warriors maneuvering ever closer and bullets flying over their heads. Bridger had radioed their situation and position and finally the two men could hear the chop of rotor blades approaching from the east. There were two helicopters, the first an Apache attack chopper that swept into the area like a dark nemesis, pouring rockets and torrents of heavy machinegun fire into the Taliban positions. Behind it came the second one, a UH-60 Blackhawk, which hovered at the back edge of the field, waiting for their extraction targets to reveal themselves. Bridger had grabbed Colson and dragged him onto the field, waving a hand to draw the chopper's attention. The Blackhawk moved forward and settled. With the help of the crewman on board, Bridger was able to push his wounded friend up into the opening in the chopper's side. Then he'd scrambled in himself, the Blackhawk had lifted off and both choppers had angled away back into the eastern darkness, leaving in their wake sporadic weapons fire, the cries of the wounded and dying and a swirling cloud of dust.

When Bridger had finished his story Geri and I sat for several seconds, stunned to silence. It was Geri who spoke first.

'Jesus,' she said, almost in a whisper. 'What a story.'

'Amazing,' I concurred. 'What happened after that? How bad was Davey's wound?'

Bridger leaned forward over the table.

'Fortunately it wasn't too bad. It wasn't the machinegun that'd hit him but a bullet from some kind of small arms fire. It passed through his shoulder without doing any serious damage, other than tearing a few ligaments and splintering a bone or two. When we got back to base we were both taken to the field hospital. I was covered with Dylan's blood and they wanted to make sure none of it was mine, that I hadn't been hit somewhere without realizing it.'

'And you hadn't been?' Geri asked.

'No. I was clean. Or at least I was after I'd had Dylan's remains sponged off me.'

Geri shuddered. 'Yech!'

'What happened then?' I pressed him.

He shrugged. 'I was debriefed by the unit commander. I was pretty shaken up, as you can imagine. Losing almost all our squad at one go was hard to take. Those guys had been family to me. Like brothers. We'd been through a lot together. You don't get over something like that quickly.'

'No,' I said. 'I'm sure you don't.'

'They sent us back to Fort Bragg. Davey spent a month in the hospital there while his wound healed. I attended counseling sessions with the base shrink. I was still having nightmares weeks after we got back. Finally I submitted my resignation to the company commander. I'd had enough. Davey, too. We both felt the same way. After going through something like that, losing so many of our buddies, it was natural to want to quit and get the hell out of it.'

I nodded. 'And they let you out, just like that?'

He smiled. 'They kind of had to. We'd given them eight good years, with a string of successful ops to our credit. We'd earned it.'

'I'll say you had,' Geri said.

'What happened to Davey after he left the Army?' I asked. 'Where did he go?'

Bridger had produced a tobacco pouch from his hip pocket. Now he pulled a cigarette paper from within it and commenced to load it with tobacco. When he'd finished he dropped the pouch onto the table and rolled the cigarette expertly into a tight cylinder, licking it sealed.

'He went home,' he said, sticking the cigarette into the corner of his mouth and digging in a pocket for his lighter. 'His mother still lives in L.A., down in Long Beach. Davey went to stay with her.'

'What did he do? How did he get along?'

'Badly.' Bridger lit the cigarette, took a long puff and exhaled. 'Davey always had difficulty holding down a job. He had a hairline temper and didn't like being bossed by anybody. Wanted to be his own man. He was also drinking a lot. He'd find something and stick with it for a few weeks, then he'd have a run-in with the foreman or the boss and that would be that. Either he'd deck the guy and be fired or he'd just walk off the job.'

'How did he survive when he wasn't working?' Geri asked. 'Did his mother support him?'

Bridger shook his head. 'She couldn't. May lives on welfare herself. She has bad asthma and can't get around much without her meds and oxygen pump and inhalers. No, when Davey wasn't working it was real hard for both of them.'

'But you kept in touch during all this time?' I asked.

'Yes. We'd write postcards to one another. Once or twice we met in San Francisco, after he'd been working and had a bit of money saved. Sometimes I'd call him at his mother's. We were usually in touch one way or another every two or three months.'

'Why did he make the trip to Washington?'

Bridger took another puff.

'He went up to see a cousin of his, to try to persuade her to take his mother in. It wasn't any use. The cousin was as poor as they were. When he came through here he was pretty much at the end of his rope.

Didn't know which way to turn. Then he saw something along the road that changed things.'

'What was that?' Geri asked.

'An election poster. For the District Attorney race. Davey saw that smiling face and recognized the man who had abused him all those years ago – the man he had sworn he'd get even with if ever their paths crossed again.'

I leaned forward. 'What did Davey intend to do?'

Bridger smiled. 'Initially his plan was to waylay him, beat the living shit out of him. Leave him scarred up so bad the world would see his ugliness and be repelled by it. But then he got a better idea. One that'd not only satisfy his desire for revenge but would also take care of all of his financial problems.'

Geri frowned. 'What was his idea?'

Bridger smiled again, wider this time, showing a row of even white teeth.

'He decided to blackmail the son of a bitch.'

Geri's mouth dropped open.

'*Blackmail* Lamont Gregory? How did he plan to do that?'

Bridger scratched the side of his beard. 'He sent him a photocopy of that picture with a note on it telling him he'd better pay or Davey was going to the press with his story and ruin his career. He wrote the note up here on the Sunday, then he rode into town on the Indian to drop it and the picture off at the Court House so Gregory would find it first thing Monday morning.'

'Was Davey trying to set up some kind of a meeting with Gregory?' I asked. 'And how was he going to get Gregory's reply?'

'Apparently he told him to send his answer via General Delivery at Gasquet Post Office – using my example.'

'Did he get an answer?' Geri asked.

'Don't know. He waited around here Monday and Tuesday, then Wednesday morning he walked down and was going to hitch into Gasquet to check if anything had come in. The mail arrives at the Post

Office from Crescent City at about 11:30.'

'Had it arrived?' I asked.

Bridger shrugged his shoulders.

'I don't know. Davey never came back. I went down myself Thursday in the pouring rain to see if anyone at the Post Office had seen him, but the regular postmistress was off for the day and the guy taking her place didn't know anything about it. So I don't know if he got a reply or not. In any case, that Wednesday morning was the last I ever saw of him.'

'What did you think about that?' I asked him. 'When he didn't turn up that night?'

Bridger shrugged. 'I wasn't worried. Davey was one wild sumbuck. He did things his own way, often changing his plans without giving any notice. I figured he'd come back when he had something to tell me.'

'What did you think he was doing?' Geri said.

'Didn't know. Maybe he'd got to the Post Office and there was a letter waiting for him. Maybe a meeting had been set up. Maybe he'd collected his payoff and was off somewhere counting it. I only started worrying when I hadn't heard from him by the weekend. Then the following Wednesday I saw in the *Triplicate* that a body had been found. I figured from the description and the photofit picture it was probably his.'

'Why didn't you go to the police?' I asked. 'He was your friend, your buddy. If it was Davey's body surely you'd want to find the people who did that to him?'

'Sure I did. I still do. But I figured after what he told me it'd be best to keep out of it – at least, for the moment.'

'I don't understand,' I said. 'What did he tell you?'

Bridger looked across at me.

'Davey gave me that picture the night before he left. He said if anything happened to him I was to find someone I could trust to give it to. Somebody in the law. I asked him what he was afraid of and he said he'd been doing some poking around up in Smith River. I'd loaned him my Indian a couple times and he'd gone off to find and talk to people who worked for Gregory on his lily farm. He wanted to see if there were any rumors around, anything that might suggest he was still at it, abusing young boys. Davey said he'd been lucky, turned up some information that was even more damaging for Gregory than the sexual abuse story if it ever came out.'

Geri frowned. 'What kind of information?'

'Davey spoke a bit of Spanish, had a lot of Chicano pals as a kid down in L.A. I gather he went drinking in a bar in Smith River with a few of the Latinos who work on Gregory's place, and that after a few beers they opened up to him – or one of 'em did, a kid.' Bridger took a last draw on the cigarette and, bending down, ground it to bits in the dirt. 'It seems that lily bulbs aren't the only things sold off that farm.'

'What do you mean?' I asked.

'Davey said the kid told him Gregory's workers were the main dealers of cartel drugs in the county. Methamphetamines, heroin and crack cocaine, not to mention weed. He also hinted that Gregory knew about it, that in fact he ran the operation – saying he had connections with L.A. gangs and the cartels dating back to his days as Assistant D.A. in Los Angeles. Davey said the boy warned him to be careful who he talked to because the word on the street was that the people Gregory fronts for are tough sons o' bitches, real gangland hardass types.'

I glanced at Geri. She was frowning at Bridger.

'You're saying that Lamont Gregory, Del Norte County's District Attorney, is also the kingpin behind the county's drug racket?'

'I'm saying that's what Davey told me. What he suspected was the case from what he'd been told. He didn't have time to find out for sure.'

'Do you think that was why he was killed?' I asked. 'Because he'd been asking around about Gregory and the word got back to him?'

'Could be. He might've been worried about Davey nosing around and decided to have him snuffed before he stumbled onto something big.'

'Hm. Maybe,' Geri said.

'One thing is sure,' Bridger said.

'What's that?' I asked.

'If he did send a squad to do for Davey they would've taken some grief before they got him subdued – unless they killed him right away. He would definitely have put up a fight. Were there signs of a struggle? Bruises, cuts?'

'There were bruises, yes,' Geri said. 'On the body and the face.'

Bridger shrugged. 'There you are. I'd venture to say one or two of the bad guys had a bad time of it, too.'

'I guess we'll find that out when we know who did it.' Geri glanced off toward the cabin door. 'Did Colson leave anything with you that night? A bag or anything?'

The bearded man shook his head.

'Davey travelled light. He had a backpack that he always took with him. He never knew from one moment to the next where he was going to end up so he was always prepared. He took it with him the morning he went to the Post Office.' He scratched his elbow. 'How did Davey actually die? Was he shot?'

Geri nodded. 'A bullet to the back of the head.' She frowned. 'Was Davey a user?'

Bridger shook his head. 'Not since he was a kid. Booze was his weakness. He fell into heavy drinking for a couple months after his discharge – ended up sleeping rough on the streets some nights. But after his mother took a bad turn one time he decided to clean up his act. She needed him, and he wasn't any good to her drunk. From that time on he never drank heavily again.'

Geri crossed her arms. 'Why couldn't you come to my home with this information, Josh? Why'd you make us come all the way up here?'

He glanced around, then back at her.

'I told you,' he said. 'I don't like people knowing my business. If I'd met you in town somewhere or at your house someone would've seen me talking to you. It was better this way. Anyway,' he grinned, 'apart from Davey you're the only ones that've ever seen this place. You should feel honored.'

While Bridger gathered up the coffee gear Geri outlined her intentions. She was going straight to her boss, the Sheriff, to pass on the information about the river corpse's identity. She wouldn't mention Bridger's name, just say that an 'informant' had passed the name to her. She'd asked to keep the photograph of Davey and Gregory, and Bridger had agreed. She told him to stay around, not to take off on one of his trips into Oregon for a while, that she might need to talk to him again. If that was the case she'd leave a note for him in the General Delivery drawer in Gasquet. She told him to check there every other day. She also told him to keep his head down, and to call her again at home if he noticed anything suspicious.

We helped him carry the stuff into the house, then he walked us out to the car.

'I can't thank you enough for getting in touch with me, Josh,' Geri told him. 'I promise I'll do my best to find the men who did this to your friend.'

He smiled. 'I'm sure you will. Just keep me in the loop, okay?'

Geri said she would and we climbed into her red Toyota. Bridger stood outside the cabin's front door watching us as she backed the car around and headed off downhill to catch 199 back to Crescent City.

Chapter Nine

We didn't talk much on the way back down the gorge, until I suddenly remembered something.

'Geri,' I said, 'Did you notice the tattoos on the backs of Bridger's hands?'

'Yes I did. I figured they were Army tats.'

'They were. Bridger told me about them while you were off using the toilet. He said that all five of the men in his Delta Force unit had those same tattoos, the only difference between them being the number of stars on the knuckles, depending upon rank.'

She nodded. 'Interesting. So?'

'That's surely why Davey's hands were hacked off. It wasn't just for the fingerprints. It was also to get rid of the tattoos that might've helped identify him.'

Geri stared at the road ahead as she negotiated its twists and turns.

'That's got to be it.' She frowned. 'But why didn't they bury the body if they wanted it to disappear? Why just throw it in the river where it was almost certainly going to be found?'

'That was my question last week.'

She smiled across at me. 'I remember.'

'Maybe they were just stupid,' I said. 'Or maybe they panicked and tossed it in a place where they thought no one would ever find it and then the unseasonal rains that raised the river levels brought it downstream? Maybe they thought by the time anyone found it there'd be nothing left but bones.'

She looked across at me. And nodded.

'You could be right.' She smiled. 'You know, you're a useful man to have around. You might not make it back to San Francisco for a while.'

I was beginning to think the same myself. In fact I'd be phoning Abe Rawlings that night, to tell him that things were beginning to look very promising for an important story of state-wide interest and I was going to urge him to let me spend enough time up here to get that story written.

'What're you going to tell the Sheriff?' I asked Geri after a while. 'You going to show him that picture?'

'No, I'm not. Not yet, anyway. I'm going to sit on it. I'm not saying anything to him about Lamont Gregory yet. Gregory's almost his boss. I want to have watertight evidence before I lay all that before him.'

'How're you going to get that?'

'Don't know yet. Maybe talk to some of Gregory's fieldworkers on the lily farm, check the bar in Smith River where Davey met the others and see if the bartender remembers anything useful.'

'How will you know which bar it was?'

Geri grinned. 'There's only two in Smith River. It won't take long to find out.' She was silent for a moment, staring at the road. 'I'd like to know more about that boys' ranch, too. Camp Belleview. I wish I knew someone down there – someone who'd be willing to dig around and find out what was going on in that place.'

I chewed on that for a while. I had a friend in L.A. who owed me a favor – a journalist who'd once been a cop. He still had a lot of contacts.

'I might be able to help you out there, Geri,' I said at last. 'I'll see what I can do.'

Del Norte County Sheriff Harvey Cantrell was a big man with a booming voice, but underneath the voice and the swagger you could detect a pretty decent guy. I liked him immediately, even if he wasn't too happy about Geri's reluctance to divulge the name of her informant about the body.

'Goddammit, Geri! You can't just clam up about something as important as that!' he shouted at her from behind his desk. 'If somebody knows who the body is, they probably also know who he was associating with and how he came to end up in that river.'

'I can assure you he doesn't,' Geri told him, which was almost true.

'Ha!' he said, smiling. 'At least I know it was a "he". That's a start.'

'Harv, if and when I think it'll help the investigation to bring my informant in I'll do it. But please, leave that to my discretion. For the moment, at least.'

He levelled a steely glare at her from across the desk.

'All right. I'll do that. For now. But if I find out later you've been withholding information that could advance this investigation I'll bust your ass. Understood?'

'Understood.'

Cantrell nodded and sat back.

'Well, I'd better tell Nelson and Ross we've got a name for the John Doe now, get them gathering information about him. I'll contact the Army at Fort Bragg; see if they can give us any medical info that can confirm the identity of the body as David Colson. When that's done, I'll phone the Los Angeles Sheriff's Office and ask them to take the sad news to his mother. You don't have an address for her, do you?'

Geri shook her head. 'No, but the Army should have it. It's somewhere in Long Beach, I understand.'

'Hm,' Harv grunted. 'I sure hope you're not leading me down the garden path with this thing, Geri. The minute you get anything useful you let me know about it, y'hear?'

'I hear.'

'What're your intentions now? Got any leads to follow up?'

Geri grinned. 'One or two. I'll let you know if I find anything.'

'Do that. And be careful. Whoever did those things to that guy might still be around. Don't take chances and get yourself in trouble.' He paused, staring across at her. Then he stood up. 'All right. I've got things to do.' He looked over at me, where I sat in an armchair against one wall. 'It was great meeting you, Arnold. You going to be around awhile or are you heading back to San Francisco?'

'Thought I'd hang on here a day or two,' I told him. 'Got one or two things I'd like to do.'

He looked at me sternly.

'Well, I hope those things are beach walking and sightseeing because I don't want you aiding and abetting this young lady in her sleuthing. That wouldn't be proper. Worrying about one of you getting into trouble's bad enough.'

'Nothing to worry about, Sheriff,' I told him. 'And rest assured. As far as I'm able I'll prevent Geri taking any unnecessary risks.'

'Good man,' he said.

Five minutes later we were back in Geri's Toyota heading north to Smith River.

Geri dropped me at her house, then backed out and headed into town to do a bit of shopping for our dinner. I used her spare key to let myself in, dropped my jacket on the couch, took out my cell phone and sat down, scrolling through the directory till I found the number of my L.A. contact, Martin Taylor.

I'd met Martin two years before, just after I'd arrived on the West Coast, when we'd both attended a convention of newspaper publishers, editors and journalists in Anaheim. Martin had spent twenty years as a cop with the L.A.P.D., worked his way up to lieutenant, then decided he wanted to fight not only street crime but also the corruption and injustice within the system he had spent so many years working for. Through his many VIP friends he'd managed to wrangle a reporter's job with the *Los Angeles Times*, and in the last six or eight years had been ruthless in his pursuit of bent cops and fraudulent civil servants, with a handful of sensational exposés to his credit. Six months ago Martin had called me at my desk at the *South Bay Bulletin* and asked if I could help him by doing some legwork for him, tying up a few loose ends in the bay area on an investigation he was involved with regarding a state-wide car theft syndicate. I'd been able to uncover a couple of things for him that enhanced his story, resulting in a dozen successful local prosecutions. He had told me he longed to return the favor just as soon as there was something he could do for me. Well, I thought, something had just come along.

Martin lives in northwest Los Angeles, in Westwood, with his wife Connie, who I'd met at the convention. I didn't know if I'd catch him at home or at his desk at the paper so I tried his home first. I was lucky.

'Hello?'

Martin's voice was gravelly and deep.

'Hey, Martin. It's Arnie Rednapp, from the *South Bay Bulletin.*'

'Arnie! How you doing, buddy? Haven't heard from you in ages.'

'I'm good, Mart. Keeping busy. How's Connie?'

'She's fine. She's out front pruning the jacaranda.'

'Good. Good. Give her my best. I'm glad I caught you. Are you busy at present? In the midst of something?'

'Actually, no. I've just finished a piece on kids accessing internet pornography and am taking a well-earned rest. So to what do I owe this call, Arnie? Just keeping in touch or is there something I can do for you?'

'As it happens there is something, Mart. Have you got a few minutes?'

'Sure. For you, Arnie, always. Fire away.'

I filled him in on the developments in the Colson case thus far – a tale of gangland murder, drugs, sexual abuse and corruption allegedly involving the county's highest legal authority. Martin was more than interested. The story appealed both to his hunting instincts as a cop and to his thirst for another good journalistic windmill to tilt at.

'Tell me how I can help, Arnie,' he said. 'I'll give it my best shot.'

'That's great, Mart. There're two things in particular I'd like you to look into for me.'

'I'm all ears,' he said.

I asked him to find out anything he could locally about David Colson, and about the Camp Belleview boys' home where Colson had passed his two year sentence. In particular I asked if he might be able to track down any of the staff members or inmates from Davey's period of incarceration. What we desperately needed, of course, was corroboration from other witnesses – or victims – of the sexual abuse Davey had suffered that would nail Lamont Gregory and the guilty members of the Belleview staff. I also asked Martin to check into the years Gregory had practiced law in Los Angeles – both as defense lawyer and as county prosecutor – and to pick out anything from his record of court appearances and associations that might prove a link between him and the cartels. Martin said he would use his contacts and see what he could find.

'Great, Mart. I'll be up here in the north for a day or two more, then I'm heading back south. But you can always get me on my cell. For safety's sake you'd better not mention to anyone why you're making these inquiries. We don't want to spook the baddies into going into hiding.'

'I'll be as discreet as a nun,' he said. 'Give me a day or two. I'll get back to you soon as I have anything.'

'Thanks, old friend.'

We said our goodbyes and hung up.

Chapter Ten

Twenty minutes later I'd just emerged in fresh clothes after taking a quick shower when I heard Geri pull into the drive. I met her at the door and took one of her grocery bags.

'Wow,' I said. 'Looks like you bought the store.'

She moved past me into the kitchen, placed her bag on the counter and started to unpack it. I followed her, putting my bag beside hers.

'Actually I thought it was time for a little celebration,' she said, 'given the breakthrough I've just had.'

Geri reached into the bag and produced a bottle of chilled champagne, depositing it on the counter with a flourish.

'Double wow,' I said. 'So what is it we're celebrating? What's the breakthrough?'

She returned to emptying the bags while I stood in the doorway watching her.

'I stopped by La Cantina, the local watering hole in Smith River, on the way in,' she said. 'It's the bar most of the field workers use – especially the Latinos. The owner's an old high school friend of mine, Tracy Abromovitch. She was there and I described Davey Colson and asked if she remembered him coming in in the last couple weeks with any of the lily farm workers. She did. She said four of them – Colson and three Latinos – came in around five-thirty one afternoon a couple weeks ago. She thinks it was a Sunday. After an hour or so two of them left, leaving Colson with the other. I asked her if she knew who the men with Colson were and she said she didn't, though she recognized them as regulars. Then she called her cook from out the back. La Cantina does a brisk trade in short order Mexican food. The cook's the wife of a Mexican laborer at one of the local dairies. Her name is Conchita Guillén, and she gets to know the Mexican regulars pretty well. As it happens, Davey and the boys had ordered some tacos to go with their pitcher of beer and Conchita had delivered them to the table. She said she knew all three of the Latinos and spoke with them briefly. She also said she chatted with Davey in Spanish and that his Spanish wasn't half bad.'

'Did she identify them? The three Latinos?'

'She did.'

Geri reached into her jacket pocket and produced a scrap of paper which she held out to me. On it were three names: Manuel Fernandez, Alejandro Moreno and Pablo Ortega.

'Conchita told me it was Moreno who stayed with Davey when the others went. She knew this because they ordered some cheese nachos to have with their second pitcher and she delivered it to them. Apparently Alejandro's a lot younger than the other two Mexicans, a fairly recent arrival. Tracy said the two of them stayed another half hour or so, then left.'

'Great sleuthing, kiddo,' I told her, returning the paper to her. 'So what now?'

'I called my friend Ryan Garrett on my cell from the bar. He's the foreman on Lamont Gregory's lily farm, remember? I asked him if he'd like to drop by later for a glass of wine and to meet a friend.' She turned from the counter, where she had placed two champagne flutes side by side, and looked up at me. 'Ryan knows those men. He works with them every day. He can tell us things about them – and perhaps about Gregory and the rest of his staff – that might be useful.'

I smiled. 'Well done, Deputy. I can see why the Sheriff trusted you to pursue your own leads. This could open a lot of doors.'

'That's my thinking,' she said, smiling back. 'And now, how about opening that champagne?'

Ryan Garrett arrived at about 9 PM, just as we had finished eating. We'd worked our way through the champagne, had half-killed a remarkable bottle of South Australian red during dinner, and were just finishing our coffees when her doorbell rang. We'd been on the deck watching the light slowly disappear over the Pacific but when Ryan arrived we moved back indoors, taking the bottle with us. While Geri went to the front door I went to the kitchen to grab a third wine glass. Then I joined the two of them in the front room.

Geri made the introductions. Ryan was older than I expected – a tallish, slightly balding man in his early fifties, thick-set and rugged-looking, with the demeanor of a man who spent most every day outdoors.

He agreed to a glass of wine and I poured him one. Then I refilled Geri's and my glasses and sat down at the other end of the sofa from him. Geri sat in her usual recliner in the corner.

'So,' Ryan said. 'Geri tells me you're a reporter, Arnold?'

'Arnie, please. Yeah. I write for a paper in a town south of San Francisco.'

'Would I know the paper?'

I shrugged. 'You might. The *South Bay Bulletin*?'

He nodded, appraising me now in a slightly different light. 'Oh, yes. I've heard of it. It's done some useful exposés over the last few years – of corruption and indulgence in high places, if I remember correctly.'

'That's us.'

'Arnie had a hand in several of those,' Geri contributed. 'In fact, for the last year or so he's been their number one investigative reporter.'

'That a fact?' Ryan reached for his wineglass and raised it in my direction. 'Well, here's to all the good work.'

'Thanks.'

We all sipped wine in silence for a few moments. Then Geri cleared her throat and made a start.

'Ryan, you remember the body that was found in the Smith a few days ago?'

'Yeah. I read about it in the *Triplicate*. Sounded like some kind of drug-related execution. Strange, that kind of thing happening up here, so far north.'

Geri nodded. 'Yes, it is unusual.' She sat forward in her chair. 'Ryan, I'm going to be frank with you, tell you most of what we know about this case so far. Some of it I haven't even told the Sheriff so I'd appreciate it if you didn't breathe a word of this to anybody. I know you, and I know I can trust you to do that if you give me your word.'

Ryan nodded. 'You've got it. So what's the story?'

Geri told him the main points of the murder investigation thus far – including the highlights of Bridger's story. When she finished, there was silence for a few seconds. Then Garrett sat forward, his face a mask of sobriety.

'You're saying Lamont Gregory's the county's drug godfather?'

'I'm saying he might be, based on the story the informant gave us.'

'But he's the District Attorney.'

'So? It wouldn't be the first time a senior public official has used his position to hide criminal operations. In any case, I've decided to keep the suspicions about Gregory off the record for the moment, and not pass that information on to the Sheriff. We want to do some poking around ourselves first with the local Latino field workers – see if we can get them to corroborate the story. Or to discount it. We thought you'd be the ideal person to help us out.' She produced the scrap of paper from her jeans pocket. 'Are these men on Gregory's payroll?'

She read out the names for him: Manuel Fernandez, Alejandro Moreno and Pablo Ortega.

'Yes,' Ryan said, frowning. 'All three work at the lily farm. Why?'

Geri explained that Colson had been seen drinking with them a few days before he disappeared. Ryan's frown got deeper.

'Hell, Ger, I know all those men well. They've been working for us for months now. I'm sure none of them could've had anything to do with that fella's death.'

She sat back in her chair. 'Probably not. All the same, tell us about Alejandro Moreno.'

'Of the three he's been here the shortest time – he arrived about six months ago. Alex's just a kid, only turned twenty-one a month ago. Comes from down near Guaymas, and he's a damned hard worker. Why do you want to know about him especially?'

'Because he spent the longest time with Colson, talking for some time with him alone after the other two had left.' She looked at me, then back at Ryan. 'We'd like to know what they talked about.'

Ryan Garrett looked from her to me, then back again. 'I don't understand. Is Arnie working with you on this?'

'I was with Geri when she answered the radio call that day about the body,' I told him. 'She didn't have time to drop me off so I went with her to the discovery scene. So I've been in on this from the beginning. Geri asked me if I'd mind helping her out with it over the next few days. I had nothing on so I agreed.'

'I see.' Ryan sat back again. 'And you want to talk to Alex, is that right? Want me to introduce him to you?'

'If you wouldn't mind,' Geri said.

Ryan scratched his head. 'Well, I don't mind, but I haven't seen Alex for a few days. He phoned in sick last week. Far as I know he's been home in bed all that time.'

Geri and I looked at one another.

'Can we see him anyway?' she asked.

'What, now? All of us?'

'Sure. If that's all right.'

Ryan's eyebrows raised and he exhaled a chestful of air. 'I guess we can. His shack's just down the road.'

Geri stood up. 'Then let's do it.'

The clapboard house Alejandro Moreno lived in was situated behind a derelict garage at the edge of Smith River. The house was tiny and sat amongst a half-dozen rusted out hulks of abandoned vehicles covered with blackberry vines. There were no nearby neighbors. We had taken Ryan's Chevrolet Captiva SUV, and when he parked it outside Moreno's front door we climbed out and stepped up in the darkness onto the small porch, Ryan in the lead. There was a pale light seeping out from the edges of the drawn curtains on the front window. Pulling open the screen, Ryan tapped on the door. When there was no response he knocked again, louder.

'Alex! It's Ryan Garrett. You in there?'

After a few moments sounds of movement could be heard inside. Shuffling noises and a feeble cough. But the door stayed closed. Garrett tried again.

'Hey, *amigo*! I hear you in there. It's Ryan. Open the door, will ya?'

'Go away, *Señor* Ryan,' said a muffled voice from inside. 'I am not well. Please, leave me alone.'

Ryan looked at us and lifted his eyebrows. Then he turned back to the door.

'You don't sound too good, Alex. Open up and let me get a look at you. You might need a doctor, ol' buddy. I can get one for you if you do.'

'I don' need no doctor, *Señor* Ryan. I just need res'. I'll be back to work on Monday, I promise.'

'Come on, Alex. You're not in any trouble but I'm not going without I get a look at you. I don't want to have to kick the door in so you'd better open up.'

There was a long silence, then the sound of bolts being drawn and keys being turned. Finally the door opened a couple inches and a face appeared in the crack – a mightily bruised face with two very black eyes.

'You see, *patrón*? I am all right. I just need to be left alone.'

Ryan pushed open the door, forcing the boy back into the room and stepping in after him. The light came from the kitchen at the back, angling in through the door. As Alex retreated from his foreman's gentle push, Geri and I moved into the open doorway. Reaching out, Ryan switched on the overhead light.

Alex tried to cover his face with his hands but he couldn't hide all of his wounds. There were bruises and cuts all over his cheeks and head, and it was clear it hurt him to move. Someone had really worked him over.

'Jesus!' Ryan said. 'What the hell happened to you, boy?'

'Nothing,' Alex murmured. 'I fell off my motorbike, that's all. I'll be okay.'

'It'd take more'n a fall from a motorbike to do that to you,' Ryan said. 'Now why don't you sit down on that couch over there and tell us what really happened.'

But Alex wouldn't. He kept insisting he'd gotten his injuries falling from his bike, asking us to go so he could get to sleep and get better. He wouldn't change his story so finally we had to leave him to it. Ryan told him to call if he needed anything. Then we all stepped outside, climbed into Ryan's rig, and pulled out.

As we did I could see the curtain at the shack's window parted as Alex watched us go.

Chapter Eleven

We hadn't travelled a quarter mile down the road when Geri broke the stony silence.

'Pull over, Ryan. We need to talk.'

At the next wide spot Garrett eased the Captiva onto the shoulder and cut the engine.

'Okay. What next?' he asked.

'That's a good question,' Geri said. 'Obviously your Alex didn't get those injuries from falling off his motorcycle. He should heal all right, but since he can't or won't tell us what really happened to him we've got to find that out some other way.' She turned to Ryan from where she sat on the front passenger seat. 'Do you think one of the others might know?'

'Pablo or Manuel?' He shrugged. 'Who knows? Maybe.'

'Careful,' I said from the back seat. 'One of them could also be the informer who tipped off the bad guys about Davey's poking around. We don't want to rush into this or we might be inviting the same treatment for ourselves.'

Geri turned to look at me.

'Good point.'

I grinned at her in the darkness.

'Just trying to stay alive.'

She smiled, then looked at Ryan again. 'Do you know those men well enough to trust them?'

Ryan met her eyes, then turned forward again.

'I've known both of them two or three years. But the one I'd feel safer going to is Pablo. He's my age and we've a lot in common. We drink beer together sometimes and watch the sun go down. I don't think he'd deliberately expose me, or anyone with me, to that kind of danger.'

'Then let's go see him,' Geri said, firmly.

'Now?'

'Now.'

And we did.

Garrett restarted his vehicle, pulled back onto the road and drove another mile or so along it till he turned off to the right and we rumbled for a couple hundred yards over a badly holed dirt track between fences. At the end of it the road widened into a graveled driveway before a double-wide trailer. There was a porch deck stuck onto its front with a short flight of stairs up to it. A white Nissan pickup that'd seen years of hard use was parked at one side. Ryan pulled up next to it and we all climbed down.

The outside light beside the front door came on before we reached the steps and the trailer's front door opened. Pushing the screen back, a Latino man in his fifties with salt and pepper hair and a lined face stepped out onto the deck in his shirtsleeves.

'Ryan?' he called out, shielding his eyes from the bright light. There were moths circling the light fixture already.

'Yep, it's me,' Garrett responded, grabbing the railing beside the stairs and hauling himself up. 'Brought some friends with me. You okay to talk a few minutes?'

Pablo Ortega was about five foot six, and beside the figure of Ryan Garrett he looked a bit like a child. But his eyes showed kindness and intelligence, and his welcoming smile to Geri and me was genuine.

'Sure, we can talk. Want a beer?'

'No thanks, *amigo*.' Ryan turned to us. 'This here's Geri Mitchell, the resident Sheriff's Deputy here in Smith River?'

Pablo nodded. 'I recognized her. *Bienvenida, señora*. It's an honor to meet you.'

Geri smiled. 'Thanks, Mr. Ortega.'

'Please, call me Pablo. Everyone does.'

'This fella is Arnie Rednapp, Pablo,' Ryan went on. 'He's a friend of Geri's who's helping her out.'

'*Señor* Rednapp. I am happy to meet you, too.'

'Likewise.'

The Mexican gestured back toward the door.

'You want come in? My wife, Juanita, she's watching the television.'

'No thanks, Pablo,' Geri said. 'What we have to say won't take long.'

Pablo nodded. '*Muy bien*. What can I do for you?'

She stepped closer to him, keeping her voice low.

'You know about the body that was found in the Smith just over a week ago?'

He nodded, his face suddenly grim.

'Yes. Everyone was talking about it.'

'Well, we know who the man was now, and a bit about why he was here in Del Norte County. He was doing some investigating on his own, it seems, and I have it on good authority that sometime around that time you met him and spoke with him for an hour or more.'

Pablo frowned. 'Me? Who do you...?'

'You were with two other Gregory field hands, Manuel Fernandez and Alejandro Moreno.'

'Ah. You mean the *gringo* with the blond hair?'

'That's the one.'

Pablo frowned. 'That was the man found in the water?'

'Yes, it was.'

'*Santa Madre*,' Pablo muttered, crossing himself. '*¡Pobre gringo!*'

'How did you meet him, Pablo?'

The Mexican frowned, thinking back.

'He came to "La Joya" one Saturday when we were watching a soccer game.'

I glanced at Geri with raised eyebrows.

'"La Joya" is an informal hangout for the local Latino population,' she told me. 'It's a Mexican market on 101 near Smith River with a field beside it where the men and boys play soccer. It's very popular at the weekends.' She turned back to Pablo. 'And this man Colson came there?'

'*Sí*. Yes. He was there a couple hours, watching the game and talking with the people. He told us his name was Davey. He spoke Spanish not badly and seemed a good guy. *Un buen hombre. Muy simpatico.* There was another game the following afternoon and he came to that one, too. Afterwards Manuel and Alex asked him if he wanted to go for a beer at La Cantina. They asked me if I wanted to come, too, and I said "*¿Porque no?*"' We went there and the four of us had beer and tacos and talked for maybe an hour. Then Manuel and I went home.'

'Leaving Colson and Alex together at the table?'

'*Sí.*'

'Can you remember what you talked about?'

Pablo shrugged. 'About many things. About work. About him growing up in Los Angeles. About the time he spent as a soldier in Iraq and Afghanistan.'

'That was all? He didn't ask you ... about your boss? He didn't ask any questions about Lamont Gregory?'

Suddenly Pablo looked distinctly uncomfortable. It took some time before he could bring himself to speak, and that after a long look exchanged with Ryan Garrett.

'*Sí* ... yes. He did ask about *Señor* Gregory. He wanted to know if we knew much about him, what went on in the big house, if he ever had any visitors – especially young visitors, boys and young men.'

'What did you tell him?'

'We told him no, we didn't know what went on in the big house. That it was none of our business. And that we'd never seen any young people visiting – except when *Señor* Gregory was having one of his barbecues or dinner parties with lots of invited guests. He does that sometimes. Especially in summer.'

Geri nodded. 'I see.' There was a pause while she considered her next line of enquiry. 'Pablo, I'm going to ask you a very important question and I want you to answer it honestly. By being honest with me you will run no risk of getting into trouble. I promise you that. Do you understand?'

'*Sí*. I understand.'

'Good. Now then. Can you tell me – honestly – if you're aware of any kind of drug dealing being done on that farm – either by the people in the big house or by any of your fellow workers? Remember, you won't get into any trouble if you tell me the truth.'

Pablo cast a glance back toward the open door of his trailer, from whence the low murmur of the television could be heard with occasional bursts of canned studio laughter. He clearly wished he was back inside there and not out on the porch with us, facing a grilling by an officer of the law – even if she was treating him with kid gloves. Finally he seemed to steel himself, took a deep breath and turned to face Geri again.

'*Señora* Mitchell, please forgive me. With great respect, there is nothing I can tell you. You have to remember that I am Mexican. At this moment my country is being torn apart by the cartels and their battle with the government. Many people are dying. It's hard to stay alive in such a place. It's much better for us here. Now it seems the cartels are reaching deep into your country, bringing their poisons to towns and cities in the north. Maybe they are even here. And with them come the *sicarios*, the thugs who murder and hurt people. *Lo siento, señora*. Even if I did know something I could not speak.' He shook his head, then nodded toward the open door. 'Do you want to see my Juanita made a widow? Do you want to see the two of us murdered, perhaps? Like that poor man in the river? Please, *señora*. Do not force me to answer your question. It is too much.'

Geri stared at him. Then she nodded.

'I understand. Thanks for your explanation.'

Stuffing her hands into her jacket pockets, she stepped toward the stairs down to the driveway. At the top she stopped and turned back.

'*Señor* Ortega, we've just come from the house of your friend, Alex Moreno. He's been badly beaten. Did you know about that?'

Pablo's lips became a tight line.

'I had heard something of it.'

'Is there anything you can tell us about that? Why it happened? Who did it?'

He looked at her, his brows knitted fiercely, and shook his head once more. Then he lifted his two arms high into the air and dropped them in a gesture of resigned impotence and shame.

There was nothing more to say.

Garrett and I followed Geri down the stairs and we all climbed into his Captiva and drove away.

'So,' said Garrett, twenty minutes later. 'You're not any wiser now about what was said in that bar than you were before.'

I had opened a new bottle of red and now Geri sipped her fresh glass of wine and stared at him over its rim.

'I wouldn't say that. It's now been confirmed Colson was in La Cantina talking to those three men. We obviously can't know for sure what he and Alex talked about after the others left, but I think it's fair to assume the question of drugs and drug dealers came up and that Alex felt relaxed enough to tell Colson what he knew or had observed. Or at least what he suspected.'

'And somehow that got back to the drug boss,' I added, 'who decided to nip Davey's investigation in the bud before he stumbled upon something really incriminating.'

'And to teach Alex a lesson about what happens to people with loose tongues,' Geri concluded.

'Precisely.'

I sipped some wine.

We were seated once more in Geri's front room – Geri back in her recliner with her legs drawn up under her, Ryan sprawled on the sofa, and me this time on another armchair across the room.

'What about you, Ryan?' I said, resting my wineglass on a nearby coffee table.

'Me? What do you mean?'

'You're on that farm every day. You virtually live there. Have you noticed anything suspicious, either among your field workers or in the movements at the big house?'

He frowned across at me.

'Do you think I'd condone drug dealing on that farm, Rednapp? Or that I wouldn't speak out if I suspected there were perverted sexual shenanigans going on? What kind of man do you take me for?'

I held up a hand.

'Calm down, Ryan. I'm not making accusations. But after what Pablo told us tonight I thought it was worth asking you because it might've jogged something from the back of your mind, some memory of something you'd seen that seemed slightly odd at the time but which you dismissed as unimportant. That's all I was asking. I know you're a man of integrity, otherwise Geri wouldn't have you as a friend.'

Garrett relaxed slightly but he was still unhappy.

'No. In answer to your question, Pablo's remarks didn't make me think of anything from the past that seemed suspicious or out of line.' He sat forward, toying with his wineglass on the table in front of him. 'You've got to remember, I'm just the farm manager. My job is to organize the field work, order and get the lily bulbs in, keep them nurtured and healthy, then harvest them for shipment when they're ready. My laborers are good men, men I can trust. Otherwise

I wouldn't have them working for me. During the day they do what's required of them. I have no idea what they do after hours. That's their business, not mine. But, to be honest, if I had to pinpoint anyone among them that I thought might be a dope dealer on the side I'd be hard pressed to do it. They're all hard-working men and women, and from what I can see all they want from life is a good job and fair pay.'

I nodded.

'What about the big house?' Geri asked. 'Do you spend much time there? How much contact do you have with Gregory?'

'I see him once a week, on average. He usually comes out to spend the night on Saturdays and he likes me to drop by in the afternoon to give him a run-down on things. He trusts me absolutely running the farm so it's really only a question of keeping him informed.'

'Why does he trust you so much?' I asked. 'Have you known him a long time?'

Garrett nodded. 'His family and mine were close for years. My dad and his used to hunt together in the mountains. The Gregorys had a cabin up there back then. The two of them would go off for a week or ten days, then come home with a big buck each. They were good friends.'

'You never went on these hunting trips?' Geri asked.

'No. Well, once when I was very young.' Garrett took a sip of wine and put his glass down again, putting his hands on his knees, palms down. 'Staying at the cabin was great, but I've never been much for hunting – much to my father's disgust. I guess Lamont and I were alike in that. It was his older brother who was the hunter.'

'I didn't know he had a brother,' Geri said.

'Oh, yeah. He died in Viet Nam. Almost five years older than Lamont. His name was Clark. I remember him as big, quiet-spoken and strong. I was always in awe of him. Maybe he was a kind of idol for me. It was sad when he was killed. I was only a boy, but I remember how it devastated his family.'

'You and Lamont weren't close, were you?' I asked. 'I mean, he's a few years older than you, isn't he?'

'Nearly ten years older. And no, we weren't close. Lamont's always been a loner. Kept to himself. Never had many close friends.'

'So you don't have any social contact with him?'

'No. I'm just his manager. He knows I know bulbs and he trusts me for that. That's as far as it goes. Then there are lots of weeks when he isn't there at all.'

'Why is that?' I asked. 'Does he do a lot of travelling?'

'He does. Whenever he can get a break from the Court House.' Garrett sat back, more at ease now that he was off the hook. 'He has friends in Sacramento. He's a pal of the Attorney General, knows the Governor. And he has a house down in Mexico where he spends as much time as he can.'

Geri and I exchanged a glance.

'Where in Mexico?' she asked.

'I'm not sure. But I've heard him mention flying into Puerto Vallarta so it must be somewhere near there.'

Puerto Vallarta. On the western Mexican coast. The playground for rich gringos. It figured he would have a place there.

'So he's a friend of Anthony Baldini?' I asked.

Ryan shrugged. 'So I'm told.'

'Has Baldini ever visited him here?'

'At the farm? Not so far as I know. I've never seen him. Baldini regularly sends his Citation jet to pick Lamont up at the airport, but he never stays at the farm. If he spends the night he must stay in Lamont's house in town. Or they meet in Sacramento. Or down in Mexico. I gather Baldini also has a house there, not too far from Lamont's.'

Geri and I exchanged another glance, interesting possibilities of criminal collusion in high places rumbling around in our heads.

'What about the man that looks after the house ... what's his name?' she asked.

'Félix. Félix Calderón. He's been with us five years.'

'Do you work with him closely?' I asked.

'Not really. His duties don't overlap with mine. Félix has a double-wide trailer on the farm, beyond the big house and the barn. His wife Teresa is Gregory's housekeeper and sometimes cook.'

'Any other staff at the big house?'

'Nope. Only Félix and his Mrs.'

'What about you? Do you live on the farm?'

'Not on that farm. I live on my old place, in the old family home. It's part of Gregory's spread now but he lets me stay there.'

'I see. And Félix? You trust him absolutely?'

Garrett shrugged. 'I've never found reason not to.'

'Well,' Geri said, swinging her feet down from the recliner and sitting forward. 'I guess all we can do is ask you to keep your eyes open, Ryan. I know if you see anything suspicious you'll tell me about it.'

'You know I will,' Garrett said, standing and glancing at his watch. 'And now I'd better say goodnight to you both and get my beauty sleep. I've got a busy day tomorrow.'

Chapter Twelve

Geri went off to bed after Ryan left and I called Lorraine on my cell, even though it was late. I caught her just as she'd stepped out of the bath. The very thought made my skin tingle. Lorraine took the call on the phone at her bedside. I could imagine her lounging back on the pillows in her fluffy white terrycloth bathrobe, and I well remembered the smell of her shampoo and the lotion she used when she'd come from the bath. I was missing her a lot.

'So, how're things going with the investigation?' she asked after the preliminaries. 'Will there be a story for you there?'

'It begins to look like it.'

I filled her in on our meeting with Josh Bridger, the news derived from Geri's bartender friend at La Cantina and the evening conversations with Ryan Garrett and his workmen. When I finished there was a pause before she responded.

'Arnie, are you sure you aren't getting into something out of your depth?'

'How do you mean?'

'Well ... the cartels for a start. They kill people for fun, honey. If this man Gregory is involved with them then it's likely he'll use them to eliminate any potential threats – like you trying to expose his seamy past and his control of the drug dealing in that area. I'm just worried for you, that's all.'

'Lorraine, you've got to trust me. I'm no hero. I'm not going to knowingly put myself in danger from these people. But if there is a story that links Gregory and the state Attorney General with the Mexican cartels I can hardly back away from it. You can understand that, can't you?'

'Of course I can. I just worry for you.'

'Well, don't. Anyway I'm thinking I'll be coming south in a couple days. I'm dying to see you and Mandy and I want to do some digging around in other corners of the state.'

'But you'll go back to Del Norte County?'

'Almost certainly, yes. I want to keep close to the situation up here until we know exactly what happened to poor Davey Colson and why.'

She sighed. 'Well, we'll talk more about it when I see you. We miss you here, honey. I miss you.'

We didn't use the 'L' word when we signed off. I think both of us – as victims of bitter divorces – were reluctant to show that depth of affection yet. We were far too wary of being hurt again. But the feelings were clearly there all the same.

The next morning Geri set off early to check in at the Sheriff's office, leaving me to get on with my own business. I called Abe Rawlings at the paper, described the events of the previous day and told him I wanted to spend some time on this story, unless he had objections. He didn't. Like me, his feeling was that if a county district attorney, and perhaps even the state Attorney General himself, was in bed with the Mexican drug cartels, then that affiliation had to be exposed and prosecuted. That was what the *South Bay Bulletin* was all about.

Then I did some research, checking out as many online repositories of information about the Mexican cartels, their current status and practices, as I could find. I also looked into Los Angeles gangs and their associations with the cartels, and the more I read the more depressed I became. There was increasing evidence all across the continental

United States of cartel – and gang – involvement in government at all levels, with law enforcement officers being corrupted and the legal process manipulated at the highest levels in exchange for lavish bribes.

Sometimes it feels like a losing battle, fighting against such a wave of unconscionable selfishness – as if there's only a small percentage of the population left that really cares and who can resist the temptation to get rich quick by turning criminal or by compromising ethical and societal standards for personal gain. It's like a pestilent wind that has swept across the nation – and the world – eroding old values, numbing the corrective effects of conscience, reversing the evolution of society toward a more compassionate, tolerant civilization into a backward slide to that primitive earlier world of basic tribal loyalties and indulgent self-gratification at the expense of all other considerations. Less survival of the fittest than survival of the most cunning, most brutal and least empathetic. But we still have to fight on – have to try to stem the tide of egocentricism that is dividing us so dangerously into two opposing camps: the callous and indifferent rich, and the struggling and embittered poor. Or there won't be a free society left to fight for.

Geri was back just before noon in her Sheriff's Office SUV, and she brought with her a pizza for lunch and a sheaf of printout information on Davey Colson, including his criminal record and service history. While she laid out the plates and made a quick salad I looked through the pages.

There were photographs as well: two mug shots from Colson's booking for drug dealing at age fourteen, and an official photograph taken by the Army of Colson as a new soldier fresh out of boot camp. In the latter picture he looked happy and self-confident in his uniform, as if he'd at long last found his place in society and was content. The Army had obviously been good for him. At least for a time.

Colson's criminal record was sketchy, just the bare facts of his arrest, the booking and final conviction – plus a document covering his months spent at Camp Belleview, which indicated that he had served his time there without incident.

The military record was a bit more revealing, reporting his movements from North Carolina to Iraq and his activity within that country during his period of duty there – including his receipt of the Distinguished Service Medal – and his return to Fort Bragg at its conclusion. A brief entry indicated that he had, shortly after his return, been selected for inclusion in the 'Delta Force' program, and that he had successfully completed the training. There were, of course, no mentions of his excursions to Iraq and Afghanistan while involved with that select force, nor of the missions he'd taken part in. There was also no mention of his unit colleagues. Finally, a terse entry recorded his having been 'wounded in action', and subsequently noted his request to resign from the service, which was granted. The date of his 'Honorable Discharge' was given as 12 June, 2008 – tallying completely with Josh Bridger's account.

'Nothing new here,' I called out to Geri from the living room. 'Just confirms what Bridger already told us, more or less.'

She poked her head around the kitchen door.

'That's what I thought. While I was at the office Craig Nelson cornered me and asked if I had learned anything new. You remember, the Sheriff's detective?'

'Sure. What'd you tell him?'

'I told him I hadn't had time yet to do much. That I was going to make some inquiries today and would get back to him if I found anything interesting.'

I nodded. 'I gather you don't trust him enough to tell him everything we've discovered thus far?'

'Well, it's partly that, but...' She broke off and sighed. 'I just don't want him to take over the investigation entirely and tell me to butt out – which he's often done in the past. He might do that if he thought I was actually on to something.'

'I see.'

'I'll tell him what we know if and when I feel we have enough new information to make a difference with his investigation.'

'Has he learned anything new?' I asked her.

'Only that the body was definitely Davey Colson. The Army had his DNA recorded. They emailed the details to the lab in Sacramento that's doing the forensic work and they verified the identity.'

'Well, that's something,' I said.

'I guess so. Craig also volunteered his opinion that Colson's death was probably nothing to do with Del Norte County, that it was more than likely just a cartel hit on a troublemaker they'd trailed all the way up here. I don't think he'd give much credence to a connection between the murder and local drug dealers.' She rubbed her hands together. 'Anyway, lunch is ready. I've laid it out on the table on the back deck. Shall we eat?'

Geri's plan after lunch was to return to Gasquet to ask the local postmistress if she remembered receiving the 'General Delivery' letter addressed to Davey Colson two weeks before, and if she might have seen him pick it up. We set off together in her deputy's rig as soon as we'd finished eating.

'Geri,' I said, some minutes into our drive, 'have you thought about the possibility that there might be more cartel corruption among local officials? Involving people other than just the district attorney?'

She looked across at me.

'You mean, like, in the Crescent City police force and in the Sheriff's office?'

'Yes. For instance.'

She stared back at the roadway, taking a deep breath and raising her eyebrows, then breathing out again.

'It did cross my mind. But I rejected the idea. I don't want to believe any of my colleagues could do such a thing – work with criminal thugs.'

'It has been known.'

'I know that. But I don't think it could happen here. We're all too close for one thing – too tight a group to be able to hide such things easily. Even the people I don't get on with too well – like Craig Nelson – I still find it hard to believe they would stoop to such an alliance. They're too dedicated to bringing down the bad guys to be tempted to play ball with them, even for big money.'

'All the same,' I said, 'I think you're right to sit on the information about Gregory's alleged involvement with drug dealing and the cartels.' I paused a moment. 'Of course, we could talk to the FBI; express our concern about possible corruption within the local law enforcement community. See what they say to do.'

She sniggered. 'How can we do that? There's nothing yet about the murder that would make it fall under the FBI's jurisdiction. Why should they be interested?'

I shifted in my seat.

'Well, based on Josh Bridger's story there's a potential tie-in between Colson's death, the L.A. gangs, international drug-running, the Mexican cartels and high level governmental corruption. I would think that's enough to whet their interest, wouldn't you?'

'Maybe. But how do we contact them? And how much do we tell them?'

'I think we tell them everything. As to how we contact them, there's always the telephone.' I paused, thinking. 'But there's one other way. I've been thinking about heading south again soon – stopping over a day or so with Lorraine, then spending a couple days checking out some things in the bay area. I could drop in to the San Francisco field office when I'm down there.'

'What would you tell them?'

'I'd have to say that I'm speaking on your behalf and that you, as a Del Norte Sheriff's Deputy, have concerns – based upon information received from a reliable source – that the District Attorney's office, and perhaps even your own department, might've been infiltrated by gang and/or cartel influence, and that you're therefore reluctant to share your findings with your colleagues for fear of it getting back to the bad guys and compromising the investigation.'

'What could the FBI do about that?'

I shrugged. 'They might want to hear about your findings first so they can check them out before you share the information with the department.'

'That could work.' She looked across at me again. 'Do you really think we should do that? Lay it out for the FBI? Everything we've learned so far?'

'Yes, I do. I'd feel better knowing your back is being covered. These are nasty people, Geri. And the FBI has a lot more expertise in these things than either you or your department. They could be a big help in many ways. I also think they should see that photograph linking Gregory with Colson. They're certainly in a better position to discover what really happened at Camp Belleview than you are.'

Geri didn't say anything for a long time, just concentrated on negotiating the twisting road beside the Smith River gorge while she kicked around the ramifications of my suggestion. Then, finally, she smacked the steering wheel with her right hand and turned to me.

'All right. Do it. It might cost me my job when Harvey finds out about it, but what the hell? If these people are corrupt I want to see them taken down – even if some of them are my friends. And I have to confess I'd feel safer knowing the FBI had my back.'

'Done deal,' I said. 'I'll see them when I'm back in San Francisco. Can you get me a couple copies of that photograph Bridger gave you?'

'Yeah. I can do that.'

'Good. I'll show them that picture. It'll prove there's a connection.'

We didn't talk much the rest of the way up the gorge. I did mention Lorraine's concern that I was getting in over my head with this story and Geri laughed. But she agreed we had to be careful. She said she'd text Lorraine, promising she wouldn't expose me to any real danger, and for that I was glad. I didn't want Lorraine worrying about me.

There were few people evident on the hundred-yard stretch of highway frontage that was 'Gasquet' when we got there. A girl in shorts with a ponytail was filling the tank of her Polo at the gas station and two cars were parked in front of the fast food place beside it. There was only one car outside the Market further along. The lot in front of the Post Office was empty and there was no one inside when we entered.

There was a bell on the counter. Geri punched down on it, sending a resounding 'ding' echoing into the back room. A few seconds later a lady appeared in the open doorway behind the counter, chewing some of her lunch and wiping her hands on a paper towel. She was grey-haired and wore jeans and a large unbuttoned long-sleeved flannel shirt over a 'Bud Light' t-shirt.

'Can I help you?' she asked.

Geri did the talking.

'Yes, Ma'am. Ten days or so ago a body was discovered in the river down at Jed Smith State Park.'

The woman nodded. 'I remember. A John Doe the paper said.'

'That's right. It hadn't been identified then. We know who it was now. A man from out of town.'

'Is that right?'

'Yes. We also know he spent some days before then staying with a friend who lives up this way close to the border, and that he was expecting a letter to be delivered for him here via 'General Delivery'. That would've been about two weeks ago. The man's name was David or Davey Colson. Do you remember such a letter being delivered?'

The woman dropped the crumpled paper towel into a nearby waste basket and placed both her hands on the counter, palms down.

'Seems like I do remember that name. I noticed it because it wasn't one I'd seen before. It wasn't local.'

Geri looked at me, then back at the woman.

'Can you recall if the man collected the letter?'

'Yes, he did.'

Geri produced the army photo of Davey and handed it across to her. The woman scanned it and nodded. Then she handed it back.

'That was him. But he certainly wasn't in uniform.' She frowned. 'That was the man who was found murdered?'

Geri nodded. 'That's right. Can you describe what happened when he collected it?'

The woman chewed her lip, remembering.

'He came in one morning, round about eleven-thirty as I recall. Anyway a little before lunchtime. Long straggly blond hair and stubble. There was no one else here and he was in and out in about five minutes.'

'How was he dressed?'

'Just ordinary – jeans, pale sweatshirt, a dark blue anorak. Oh, and a baseball hat – L.A. Dodgers, I think. And he was wearing a backpack.'

'Did he open the envelope here?'

'Yes he did. There was a letter with what looked to be a check folded inside it. I remember he smiled while he was reading the letter. He walked out holding it and I didn't see him again.'

'Can you remember anything else about the letter?' I asked her. 'Was there anything about it that attracted your attention? Other than the enclosed check?'

The woman made a kind of noncommittal facial shrug.

'It looked like some kind of business letter. Typed, not hand-written. Whatever it said made him pretty happy.'

'Hm.' Geri placed her folded arms on the counter and leaned on them. 'Anything else you can tell us? Either about the letter or the man?'

'Nope. That was it. As I said he was in and out in five minutes max.' She shuddered. 'And to think ... only a few days later he was murdered. Imagine that.'

'Yeah,' Geri said. She turned to the door. 'Thanks for your help.'
And we left.

Chapter Thirteen

We had climbed back into Geri's car and she was about to start it when a California Highway Patrol black and white pulled into the lot beside us on the driver's side. Geri's friend Sam was driving it.

He smiled across at her, rolling down his passenger side window. Geri rolled hers down, too.

'Thought that was your rig,' he said. 'It's break time, isn't it? How about we grab a coffee over at She She's?'

She She's Drive In was the name of the fast food place up the road.

Geri smiled. 'Sure. Why not? We'll meet you there, okay?'

Sam nodded, rolled up his window, backed out and drove off. Seconds later we followed, moving the couple hundred yards up the road to park in the small lot before the diner. There was only one other car there now and we slipped into the empty space between it and Sam's rig.

'Arnie, you met Sam before, didn't you?' Geri asked, after we'd climbed out and joined the tall patrolman at the front door.

'Yeah. While I was waiting for you the other day. How're you doing, Sam?'

'Doing good, Arnie. So. How come you're riding shotgun today? You helping Geri keep the county in order?'

'Nope. Just tagging along to watch. I'm a reporter.'

'I remember. You working on something?'

'Doing some research.'

'On what?'

Geri answered before I could, which was fine with me.

'He's looking into David Colson's murder – the guy whose body was found in the river ten days ago. As he's a friend I'm letting him ride with me while I check out some leads.'

'Found anything useful so far?'

'Yes we have. Let's grab our coffees and sit out here and I'll fill you in on what we know.'

Ten minutes later we were seated at a picnic table at the side of She She's nursing coffees while Geri told Sam everything we had discovered up to that point – including Josh Bridger's revelations about Davey Colson and Lamont Gregory, the sexual abuse, and Gregory's alleged involvement with drug dealing and the cartels. I was surprised she chose to reveal so much, but it was a sign, I guessed, of her trust in him. It was also natural for her to want to share these things with someone local she could rely on, someone who would be there for her if push came to shove. Sam looked just the man to do that. His eyes never left her face throughout her story.

When Geri had finished Sam sat for several seconds without saying anything. Then he shook his head and sat back.

'Holy shit,' he said finally. And then repeated himself, more slowly this time. 'Holy shit.' He blew out a breath. 'That's heavy stuff, Geri.'

'Couldn't get much heavier.'

'So what're you doing up here this morning? Checking out something in relation to all this?'

'Yep.'

Geri explained about Colson's blackmail letter to Gregory, and about him leaving Josh Bridger's mountain retreat to collect the reply early on the Wednesday morning before his sudden disappearance. She told Sam we'd come here to question the postmistress.

'Did she remember him?'

'Yes, she did. And she recognized his picture.'

Geri gave him the army photograph to study while she related to him the woman's description of Colson, and the way he reacted when reading the letter.

Sam handed the photograph back to Geri and looked beyond her to the highway, then toward the few other buildings that stood along it on either side.

'I wonder if anyone else saw him that morning?' He looked at Geri. 'Have you asked?'

'Not yet, no. That was my next intention.'

'Well,' he said, lifting his Styrofoam cup to his lips and emptying it, 'why don't you guys sit here and finish your coffee? I'll make a start by asking at the garage.'

Sam got up from the table, tossed his empty cup into the waste bin at the side of the building, and strode off along the edge of the highway toward the Gasquet service station a hundred yards south of us. We watched as he stepped across the empty forecourt past the pumps and entered the open door of the garage. He was in there three or four minutes. When he reappeared he stepped to the edge of the forecourt and waved to us.

'Come on over,' he called. 'There's something you should hear.'

Geri and I dumped our empty cups and walked along the road to join him. Beside us the traffic on 199 was sporadic.

'What you got?' Geri asked when we reached him.

'Come and see.'

Turning away, Sam led us toward the open garage door where a man in a dirty blue overall stood watching us, wiping his greasy hands on a rag. Centered in the garage behind him was a battered pickup truck with its right rear axle resting on blocks. The wheel had been removed and the man was obviously working on the brakes.

'Geri, this here's Art Michaels,' Sam said. 'He owns this station and is here six days a week from nine in the morning till five at night.'

'How d'you do, Mr. Michaels?' Geri said, extending a hand which he shook. She gestured toward me. 'This is a friend of mine, Arnold Rednapp.'

'Deputy. Mr. Rednapp.'

Michaels shook my hand and then stood back, clutching the rag in one hand with his arms crossed.

'Tell the deputy what you told me, Art,' said Sam.

'Sam asked me if I remembered seeing a stranger on foot a couple weeks ago who came into town from the north sometime before lunchtime. A long-haired blond guy, he said. He told me that was the guy whose body was found in the Smith down at the park a few days later.'

'That's right,' Geri confirmed. She gave him the photograph and he peered down at it. 'His name was David Colson. That was taken while he was a soldier some years back. Did you notice him?'

'I did,' Art said, nodding. 'Fact is I'd seen him before.' Michaels handed back the picture, then looked around him as if he was concerned about being overheard. 'I look after a motorcycle for a guy who lives up near the border,' he said, dropping his voice. 'A big fella named Josh who likes to be left alone. I give him a good deal, and in exchange he lets me ride it sometimes.'

Geri and I exchanged a glance. More confirmation of Bridger's story.

'I love working on old bikes so it's a pleasure for me to do it,' Art went on. 'Anyway Josh drove in about two weeks ago with this guy Colson to get gas. He told me he was a friend of his and that he was letting him use the bike, that I was to help him out if he needed anything. Well, the guy did use it. I saw him driving by two or three times and he bought gas at least once more. So I knew who it was when I saw him that Wednesday morning.'

'What was he doing?'

'He must've been hitching 'cause a car with an Oregon plate stopped in front of She She's and he climbed out of it. Then the car drove off and he walked up and stood waiting at She She's front door. They open at ten and it was just before then. He waited about ten minutes.'

'And when the place opened he went in?'

'Yeah. He bought some breakfast – looked like a sandwich and coffee – and sat at the table outside, where you guys were sitting. It'd rained all the previous night and that morning and had only just stopped. I was surprised he'd choose to sit outside, but he did. Just wiped the seat and table off with paper napkins and sat down, all by hisself. He had his food and his coffee, then walked back north toward the Market.'

'And that was the last you saw of him?'

'Yes it was.'

'That's not all Art noticed that morning, Geri,' Sam said. 'Tell her about the Jeep Wrangler, Art.'

Art Michaels wheeled and spat, then turned back to Geri.

'Well, it was funny. All that morning, from the time I arrived to open up the station at 8:45 or so, there was this old black Jeep Wrangler that kept cruising up and down the highway, back and forth through town. I thought whoever was driving it was looking for something because he did that off and on for about half an hour. Then he must've found it because I didn't see the Wrangler again. Not till I noticed it heading south again around noon. That was the last I saw of it.'

'Could you see who was inside the Wrangler?' Geri asked.

Art shook his head. 'Nope. Windows were tinted. You couldn't see nothing through them.'

Geri turned and looked along the highway toward the market and the Post Office.

'And it came from that direction, from the north, that last time?'

'Yep.'

She nodded, turned to him again and smiled. 'Thanks for that, Art. You've been a big help.'

He grinned, showing a gap in his upper front teeth. 'No problem, Deputy. Always glad to help a pretty lady.' He turned to Buchanan.

'Be seeing you, Sam.'

He disappeared into the garage and Sam, Geri and I ambled back to She She's.

'What now, Geri?' Sam asked as we walked.

'Going to ask at the Market. See if anyone there noticed either Colson or the black Jeep that morning.'

'Good idea. It'd be good to know who was in that Wrangler.' Sam checked his watch. 'I'll have to leave you to it, though. Time for me to hit the road again.'

When we reached the cars Sam gave Geri a quick hug, shook my hand, and settled himself into his driver's seat.

'Keep me informed, Geri. And look after yourself. If you need me for anything you know how to find me.'

'Thanks for that, Sam.'

Seconds later he was gone, patrolling north along Highway 199 toward the border. We climbed back into Geri's rig and drove to the north end of town, pulling this time into the lot before the Gasquet Market, which was now empty of cars.

Chris Aikins, the old man who owned the Market, was grey-haired and amiable. Geri passed him the Army photograph of Davey Colson and asked if he remembered the man coming into the market one morning about two weeks before – a few days before the body was discovered in the Smith. Aikins frowned and looked down at the picture while he marshalled his memories.

'Well, I've certainly seen that fella before, no question,' he said at last. 'He's been in a couple times, I know. But I'm not sure he came in that week.' He handed the photograph back to Geri, who pocketed it. 'I remember something else, though, that happened that week.'

'What was that?' Geri asked.

'Well, it must've been the Wednesday...' He stared into space, remembering. 'Yes, that was it. Wednesday morning. I remember 'cause we had a truck come in late that morning with a delivery. I'd just opened up and in came these two tough looking guys. Mexicans

I reckoned. One of 'em had a huge scar down the left side of his face and a black tattoo on his neck under his chin. The scar looked to me like it came from a knife fight. Bright red it was. They bought several cans of soda and a half dozen sandwiches and then left. I was curious so I watched where they went from the front window. They were driving a dirty black Jeep Wrangler 4 by 4 – one of those that has the windows tinted so you can't see inside? It was a five-door and it looked three or four years old. Well, they got in and drove off. But they didn't go far. I watched them turn off onto that little dirt road just kitty-cornered across the highway there, a couple dozen yards or so north. They turned the Wrangler around and backed up under them trees over there next to a beat-up dark-colored pickup, both of them nosed toward the highway. I couldn't see much of the pickup, but I could see there were two people inside it. I thought that was odd; it was like the two vehicles were kind of hiding together or something. And waiting. One of the guys got out of the Wrangler with some of the soda cans and sandwiches and went over to the pickup. The pickup's passenger door opened and the food and drink was handed inside. Then the guy climbed back into the Wrangler and both vehicles just sat there. Nobody got out again so far as I saw.'

'What time would that've been, Mr. Aikins?' Geri asked.

Aikins pursed his mouth.

'Oh, they came in early, like I said. Just after I opened up. Must've been around nine-fifteen. I kept checking on the vehicles for the next hour or two and they were both always there parked under the trees, though I never saw any of the guys again. Then the truck came with the delivery and I forgot all about them. The next time I looked the Wrangler and the old pickup were both gone.'

'The Post Office is across the highway from there,' I said. 'Do you think they'd be able to see who came and went at the Post Office from where they were parked?'

Aikins thought about it. 'Yeah. There's some trees and brush at the edge of the road, but I reckon they could've.' He looked at me. 'D'you think they were waiting for someone to turn up there? Is that what they were doing? Watching and waiting?'

Geri nodded. 'Yes. That's what we think they were doing.'

'Who were they waiting for?' Aikins asked.

'The man in the photograph.'

'Hm,' said the old man, frowning. 'I thought there was something funny about 'em. Even thought of taking down the Wrangler's license number.'

Geri had been making notes in her notebook. When he said that she looked up sharply. 'Did you? Take down the number?'

'No. I went off to get a pencil and a pad, but then a customer came in and I completely forgot about it.' He thought a moment. 'I can remember the first four letters, I think. Let me see ... it was something like 6JMV. Can't remember what came after that. Sorry. And even those might not be right.'

Geri noted the partial plate number. Then she put away her pad and pen.

'That's fine, Mr. Aikins. That'll be useful to us just as it is. You couldn't see what kind of pickup it was that was parked next to the Wrangler, could you? Or see its license plate?'

'Nope. Too far away. I just noticed it was dark colored.'

'Well, you've been a great help. Thanks.'

Geri turned as if to go, then seemed suddenly to think of something and turned to scan the ceiling around us. She smiled when she saw what she was looking for – a closed circuit TV security camera fixed to a rafter beam a few feet away. It was trained down on the counter area near the till. She turned back to Mr. Aikins.

'You've got a security camera.'

'You bet,' Aikins said. 'I've been robbed twice so I had that put in some years back. Haven't been robbed since.'

'Good,' Geri said. 'Real good. But if you've got the security camera then surely you've got those men captured on film somewhere. Isn't that so?'

Aikins looked up at the camera, then shook his head and turned back to Geri, looking a bit sheepish.

'Fact is the damned thing's been down for the last two weeks. I've been calling the company down in Eureka to come fix it but they haven't turned up yet.' He shook his head and shrugged. 'Sorry.'

Five minutes later we were back in Geri's car and on the road to Crescent City.

Chapter Fourteen

There were five of us seated around the table in the Sheriff's office that afternoon: Geri and me, Sheriff Harv Cantrell, and the two detectives, Craig Nelson and Nick Ross. Cantrell sat at the end of the table, Geri and I on one side and Nelson and Ross on the other. It felt like Cantrell was refereeing some kind of sporting contest between us, because the aggressive vibes that rolled across the table toward Geri and me from the two detectives were almost palpable.

Sheriff Cantrell had been surprised and not too pleased to see that I was still with Geri, but when she explained that I was a journalist from San Francisco and that I'd decided to do a feature on Sheriff Department procedures and techniques in Del Norte County, using the investigation into Colson's death as the focus of the story, Cantrell mellowed – especially when she mentioned I'd already been impressed by what I'd seen. I guess the idea of some positive bay area publicity for him and his remote department was too attractive for him to object to. Anyway, I was allowed to stay in the meeting – though from the looks on the faces of the two detectives it was clear they thought it a very bad idea.

Once everyone had settled Geri outlined the advances that had been made that morning – reporting the conversations with the postmistress, Art Michaels and Mr. Aikins at the Gasquet Market. Notes were taken by the detectives of the names and the gist of their evidence, and of the Jeep's partial license plate number.

'And you're not going to tell us who the informant was that gave you Colson's name?' Craig Nelson asked her.

Geri sighed. 'I explained all that to Harvey. If there's a real need to have this person brought in then I'll do it. Until then they remain anonymous.'

'Real need?' Ross said, his face creasing angrily. 'Of course there's real need. How the hell do you know what that person knows or doesn't know?'

The Sheriff held up a hand.

'That's enough, Nick. I told Geri she could keep the informant's name secret and that's the way it stands. For now, anyway. All right?'

Nelson and Ross exchanged a look, then checked their notes again.

'The guys in the Wrangler were definitely Mexican?' Nelson asked Geri eventually, glowering across at her.

'Mr. Aikins thought they were. At least Latino. And the neck tat and the facial scar suggest gang membership, probably in L.A.'

'What about the ones in the old pickup? Did you get any description of them?'

'No,' Geri said. 'Mr. Aikins said they never got out, and it was too far away to see anything through the windshield other than that there were two people inside.'

'That'd make four men altogether,' the Sheriff put in. 'That we know of. Lot of fellas to go after only one man.'

Nelson sat back. 'Like I said, this was probably just a gang hit on a guy who'd pissed them off or run off with their money.'

'Or an informer,' added Ross. 'Someone who ratted to the cops about their business.' He smirked. 'They don't like that.'

'Colson had form as a drug dealer,' Nelson continued. 'And you said he was having trouble holding down jobs after he left the Army. Maybe he went back to dealing, then decided to cut and run with some of the gang money?'

'Whatever it was,' Cantrell growled, 'we've got to find those

Latinos and see whether or not they were involved – either in Colson's abduction, or his murder, or both.' He glanced around. 'Any ideas?'

Nelson sat forward again, looking at his notes.

'We can try to find the black Wrangler.' He looked up. 'Could've been stolen, of course, probably down south, in Humboldt County or below. It wouldn't be a hire car because it was too old and beat-up. We need to check out those partial license plate numbers. I'll check with the DMV. 'Course, if it was stolen it probably had switched plates on it, but I'll try anyway. The fact that it was old, dirty and beat-up might help identify it.'

'Why do you think they might have picked up the vehicle down south?' Geri asked. 'Couldn't they have driven it up from L.A.?'

Nelson shook his head. 'I doubt it. Too far to come. Unless they'd followed him from there. And if they did why'd they wait all that time to get him? They could have snatched him anywhere along the way.'

'But according to Geri's informant,' said Sheriff Cantrell, 'Colson didn't come from the south at all. He'd hitched down from up north, from Washington, where he was visiting a relative.'

'If he wasn't followed,' said Ross, 'then how did the gangbangers find out he was up here?'

Geri leaned forward. 'Somebody must've seen him and told them where he was.'

Cantrell looked at her. 'Who would do that?'

Geri shrugged. 'Somebody who didn't want him here. Somebody who wanted him dead. Or knew that the gang wanted him dead.'

Cantrell frowned and sat back, crossing his arms. 'If that was the case, and somebody did recognize him and told the gang leaders he was here, then they could have flown the hit men up by plane and they could've all gone after him together.'

Nelson leaned forward over the table. 'They've certainly got money enough for airfare. If that's what happened, the question is where did they fly into?'

Ross shifted in his seat. 'Well, it wouldn't be into Crescent City.

That'd be too obvious. The next closest commercial airport is Arcata.' He looked at Cantrell. 'I'll contact the Humboldt County Sheriff's office, see if they can get copies of the passenger manifests from United Express and the other airlines for the week Colson disappeared. I'll also ask for them for the week after, in case they dumped the Jeep and headed back again using the same IDs.'

'Might as well ask if they've had any beat-up black Jeep Wranglers stolen in Humboldt recently while you're at it,' the Sheriff added.

'I'll do that.' Ross made a note, then looked up. ''Course they could still be here. Hiding out somewhere.'

Cantrell frowned deeply. 'I sure as hell hope not. I don't want those evil sons-a-bitches hanging around in my county.' He scratched an elbow. 'You better ask them to check any private plane movements into Eureka from the south, too. They could have been dropped in that way.'

'Possibly,' Nelson said, 'but my money would be on them coming in on a commercial flight. Who knows? We might get lucky.' Nelson sat back, smiling. 'We might even get some pictures.'

'How?' I asked, daring to speak for the first time.

Nelson looked across at me. 'Since 9/11 all commercial airports have security cameras filming all arriving and departing passengers. They keep those films for a while. If we get some names off the manifests, even if they're false names, we can pull those films and try to pin the names to actual faces.'

'How would you know which were their names?' I asked.

Nelson shook his head, smirking.

'If the guys are Mexican they'd use Mex names, right? They're sure as hell not going to be down as 'Murphy' and 'Moriarty'. So we find the Latino names, marry those names to faces. Then we can use our resources to find out who they really are.'

'Good thinking, Craig,' Cantrell said. 'Anything else we can do?'

'If they are gangbangers,' Geri said, 'they might've made contact with the drug dealers here in Del Norte County. Or within the local

Latino community. They had to stay somewhere during the time they were here. I'll do some poking around, see if anyone in my area saw either the black Jeep or the scarred and tattooed guy.'

Cantrell nodded. 'All right, but be careful.' He sat back, thinking. 'What about that letter Colson received? Any idea what that was all about? Who it might've been from?'

Nelson shrugged. 'The woman said it looked like a business letter. That it was typed, not hand-written.'

'And that there was a check enclosed in it,' Ross added. 'That could be significant.'

Cantrell nodded. Then he looked at Geri. 'Any idea where that letter was from? Did you ask the woman about the postmark?'

Geri looked embarrassed. 'No, Harv. I didn't.'

He frowned. 'Okay. Well, maybe you can give her a call, see if she remembers?'

'I'll do that. Sorry.'

'No harm done.' Cantrell looked around again. 'What else? Anything we've overlooked? Anything else we can be getting on with?'

Geri was making a list.

'I'll also check with the people at She She's diner,' she said. 'See if they remember Colson or the tattooed guy or anyone else that might've come in there with him.' She looked up at Cantrell. 'Sorry, boss. I should've done that, too, while I was there.'

He smiled. 'That's all right. You're learning. I'll make a department wide memo to all deputies to ask around the county to see if anyone else remembers seeing a beat-up black Jeep Wrangler or the scarred and tattooed Latino. Maybe we can get some pictures of a dark Wrangler to jog their memories. Could even put a picture in the *Triplicate*, with an appeal for information about recent sightings. Del Norte's not that big and there aren't that many people. Somebody must've seen 'em.'

'Good idea, Harv,' Ross said. 'I'll handle that.'

Sheriff Cantrell put his hands flat on the table in front of him.

'Well. I think that about covers it.' He looked at Geri. 'I'll expect to have your report on my desk by tomorrow noon, kid – including any new information you get from the postmistress about that letter or from the people in She She's. Okay?'

Geri nodded. 'You'll have it.'

'Good. Now let's go catch some bad guys.'

And the meeting was over.

I was feeling a little hungry when we left the Sheriff's office so Geri offered to treat me to an afternoon snack at La Cantina in Smith River before she dropped me off. We drove straight there when we left town.

It was 4:30 PM when we pulled into the bar/restaurant parking lot and there were only three cars there besides our own. Geri locked up and we went inside.

It was pretty much what I expected. A long rectangular room with a bar along the back and an empty platform stage against the left wall. Beside the stage a few tables and chairs were arranged around a postage-stamp of a dance floor. Across the front of the room on both sides of the entrance door were booths. A couple sat in one of the booths near the door working on plates of food. At one end of the bar a pair of locals in baseball hats were nursing draft beers and watching a ball game on the flat screen fixed to a nearby wall. The bartender was a woman – fulsome and good-looking, with blond hair gathered in a ponytail that swung over her shoulders as she worked. I reckoned she was Geri's friend, Tracy. We sat at the bar.

'Well, hello there, Deputy,' the woman said. She finished drying a beer glass and deposited it in its rack. Then she turned to face us. 'You're starting to be a regular here, Geri – two visits in as many days? What can I get you? And who's your handsome friend?'

'I'll have a Sprite, Tracy. And my handsome friend's already taken, though not by me. Arnie Rednapp, meet my old high school rival Tracy Abromovitch. Tracy, Arnie.'

Tracy showed teeth and gave me her hand to shake.

'Pleased to meet you, Arnie. You in town for a while, or just visiting?'

'Just visiting, but you might see me again. I've got business that might bring me back a few times.'

'Well, you're always welcome here when you're in town. What can I get you? A beer?'

'Yeah, I'll have a Corona. And I've heard great things about your tacos.'

'I'll bet. Conchita cooks good Mex.'

'I'll have a couple of them, then. Beef, please.'

'Hot salsa?'

'Uh, no. Got mild?'

'I can bring you mild.'

'Then I'll have some. Thanks.'

She got our bottled drinks, opened them and filled two frosted glasses on the bar in front of us, then disappeared through swinging doors into the room behind the bar where Conchita must do her marvels. The beer tasted good.

'Do you come here often?' I asked Geri.

She smirked. 'Great line, but not very original. And the answer's no, not very. I used to. They do music at the weekends – local rock bands and occasional Latino groups from Bakersfield and beyond doing salsa music. I came here with Ryan sometimes. But no, I don't come here much now. And certainly not during the day.'

Tracy came back a minute later and busied herself giving the two game watchers another beer each from the draft tap. Then she wiped her hands and rested her crossed arms on the bar before us.

'You find those fellas I told you about? Pablo and the others?'

'Yes, I did. Thanks for that.'

Tracy shrugged. 'Glad I could help.'

'You might be able to help me again,' Geri said. 'Do you remember a couple of gangbanger types, Latinos from out of town, dropping in at any point last week or the week before?'

She described them according to the information we'd been given by Mr. Aikins – complete with the tattoo and the facial scar. Tracy thought about it. Then she nodded.

'Yeah. I remember the guy with the scar and the tattooed neck. He came in one night two weekends ago – Friday night.'

'Alone?'

'Yeah. We had some Bakersfield beaners playing Mex music and the place was full of lily workers and their ladies. Believe me, it was jumping. I noticed the guy's scar and the tattoo when I served him. He didn't talk much, and didn't crack a smile all evening. Just sat at the bar drinking tequilas with beer chasers. Then he went. I didn't see him again after that.'

Geri nodded, thinking.

'Were any of the Latinos in that night that'd been here with the blond guy?'

Tracy laughed. 'Boy, you're really pushing me today, honey. It's hard to remember who all was in here that night, there were so many. Everybody having fun, dancing and laughing. It was a good night. But were any of those three in? I'm not sure.' She stopped and frowned, trying to remember. Then she nodded. 'Yeah. Two of them were here. I remember, now. The youngest one that wears his baseball cap back to front. What's his name? Alex? Oh, and the one that wasn't Pablo.' She chuckled. 'I didn't know any of their names before then, of course. It was Conchita who knew who they were. I just knew them as regulars.'

'Was the other one Manuel?' I asked, entering the conversation for the first time.

Tracy swung her shoulders toward me, looking me in the eye.

'Yeah. You're right. I think Conchita did say his name was Manuel.'

'Were he and Alex sitting together that night?'

'No. I remember Alex coming to the bar for a pitcher of beer and taking it back to a table full of youngsters – all lily workers. Everybody was laughing. No, Manuel wasn't with them. He was sitting across the room at a table with another Latino guy.' She scrunched her mouth. 'I don't like that Manuel much. Always grim-faced, no sense of humor. Don't know why he turned up that night. He'd never come in for the music before so far as I can remember.'

'Did you notice the guy with the scar talking with anyone while he was here?' I asked. 'With Manuel or with any of the other customers?'

'No, I didn't. He wasn't very approachable, for a start. Pretty frightening guy. But he did seem to be looking for somebody. I noticed him turning around several times, scanning the crowd.'

'But he didn't find them? And no one came to join him?'

'Not so far as I know. Or saw.'

'And then he left.'

'Yep.' She looked at me for a moment in puzzlement with her head on one side. 'You're asking a lot of questions for someone who's just Geri's friend, Arnie. You a cop, too?'

I smiled. 'Nope. Journalist.'

She raised her eyebrows and looked about to ask another question, but then there was the 'ding' of a bell from the room beyond the swinging doors.

'That'll be your tacos,' Tracy said. 'I'll get 'em for you.'

A couple of young women came in after she brought my plate and Tracy spent the next quarter of an hour serving and jawing with them. That left me free to get on with my afternoon snack in peace. The tacos were good – Conchita's reputation was well-deserved. When I had finished, Geri sat back on her stool.

'Well, I'd better drop you back at the house and go do something useful.'

'What're your plans for this afternoon? Going to write up your report?'

She nodded. 'Some of it. I'll drive up to Gasquet again in the morning and see the She She ladies and the others, the postmistress and Chris Aikins. You can come if you want. I want to talk to them in person. See if any of them can tell me anything more about Davey Colson or the gangbangers in the black Jeep.'

'Sounds good.' I finished my Corona and slipped off the stool. 'I'm ready.'

Tracy saw us making to go and stepped along the bar to say goodbye.

'Good to have you in here, Geri. And it was nice meeting you, too, Arnie. You guys drop in again, y'hear?'

'We'll do that, Trace,' said Geri.

'Tell Conchita her tacos are wonderful,' I added.

'You can tell her yourself. She's on her break, having a cigarette out back. You'll probably see her outside.'

Geri raised a hand in a farewell wave and we both made for the door. Then I pulled up.

'I think I'd better make a rest stop, Geri. I'll meet you at the car.'

'Okay.'

Chapter Fifteen

Geri wasn't in the car when I got outside. She was talking to a short Latina woman I took to be Conchita at the back corner of the building. Conchita was sitting on an old kitchen chair. She wore a white apron over her sweater and jeans and was smoking a cigarette. Geri was kneeling before her and they were deep in murmured conversation when I approached. In Spanish. When she noticed me Geri stood up and smiled.

'Arnie, meet Conchita Guillén. Conchita, this is my friend Arnie.'

The woman held out her hand and I shook it. Her eyes were dark, and her smile muted. Conchita was probably in her late forties or early fifties. Her face, though friendly, was creased and worn – the face of someone who has known a lot of sadness.

'Pleased to meet you, Conchita,' I told her. 'Your tacos are to die for.'

'*Gracias, señor.*'

Geri was standing with her hands on her hips, scuffing the toe of one shoe against the asphalt. Then she looked up at me, her face serious.

'Arnie, would you mind waiting for me in the car? I won't be a minute.'

'No problem.' I smiled down at the seated woman again. 'Nice meeting you, Conchita. I'll be back to try more of your food another time.'

I left them and walked back to the car. As I reached it the lights flashed and the doors clicked unlocked as Geri hit the button on her ignition key. I waved a thank you and crawled onto the front passenger seat, closing the door behind me.

Geri spent another five minutes talking with Conchita. Again she knelt close to her, once or twice putting out a hand to touch the woman's arm. Their conversation was obviously serious for there was no smiling or laughter. Occasionally Conchita would look around nervously, seemingly making sure she was not being observed talking to this uniformed *gringa*. But there was no one on the road, and the area behind and beside the parking lot was a wilderness of scrub trees and blackberry brambles. She was safe enough.

Finally Geri stood and Conchita, too, got to her feet. The two women shook hands, then Geri turned away and walked toward the car. Behind her, Conchita dropped her cigarette to the ground and shredded it with her toe. Then, lifting the chair, she disappeared with it around the corner of the building.

'That was extremely useful,' Geri said, after we'd pulled out and set off in the direction of her house.

'What did she tell you?'

'A lot – though she couldn't be specific. She was obviously terrified of saying anything that could get her into trouble.'

'What did she say?'

Geri outlined the story Conchita had told her of why she and her husband had come to America. Conchita's husband, Raymundo, was a worker at a local dairy in Smith River. In Mexico he'd been an elementary school teacher. They had lived in a small village near Juarez, not far from the border at El Paso. All had been well for them until the cartels came to control the area in the late eighties. From that time on their lives became hell. In the battles between the various vying cartel bosses, and between the cartels and the police, many people died, including innocent civilians, and the authorities lost control of law and order. At the close of his schooling, Conchita and

116

Raymundo's only son Ernesto joined the Mexican Army. He had been in a year when his company was sent to close down a cartel transit route used to bring drugs from Columbia and Peru into the United States. Someone had informed the drug barons of the mission, however, and the Army company was ambushed. Many soldiers died in the onslaught – including Ernesto. After his death it became impossible for Raymundo to continue to teach. Things had grown so terrible that, out of fear, few people sent their children to the schools. Finally Raymundo and Conchita decided to come to America. They sold their small house and gave all of the money to a man who promised to get them across the border. It was a frightening march through the night, Conchita had said, but they had managed to cross without being seen, and had made their way first to Los Angeles, then north, to find jobs on the land in Del Norte County. Now they lived quietly, grieving for their lost son.

'An awful story,' I said when she had finished. 'And, I'm afraid, all too common.'

'Yes,' Geri replied. 'She warned me, you know? She said the cartels are definitely here, now. In Del Norte County. In Smith River.' She shook her head. 'I asked her which cartels. She answered with one word: "Sinaloa". The Sinaloa Cartel. Which is what our own intelligence has suggested from previous drug busts.'

'Did you ask her what she knew about the local dealers?'

'I did, but she wouldn't say much. She said to speak out would be too dangerous.' Geri looked across at me. 'But she did say one thing that's significant.'

'What's that?'

'I asked her if she had any idea who was controlling the drugs in the county, and she looked at me a long time before she answered.'

'She gave you a name?' I asked, hopefully.

'No. But she did whisper, "*Desde muy arriba hay mucha corrupción. Hombres muy malos y peligrosos.*"'

I looked across at her. 'What does that mean?'

'"There's corruption high up in the government. Bad men, dangerous men."'

'Confirming what Davey Colson was told.'

'Exactly.'

'And she wouldn't give you a name?'

'She didn't dare. I looked her in the eye and said "Gregory?" and she looked away and seemed to shrink within herself. But she wouldn't say yes or no. So I left it at that.'

'Holy shit,' I said in a whisper. Then Geri spoke again.

'The last thing she said to me was, "*Tenga cuidado, señora. Hay soplones en todas partes.*" "Be careful. There are informers everywhere." I took a chance and mentioned one name to her: Manuel. When I did her face darkened and she said one word through clenched teeth: "*¡Cabrón!*" Meaning bastard or traitor.'

I nodded. 'So Manuel was probably the one who tipped off the powers that be about Davey. And Scarface about Alex. Remember, he was at La Cantina that night.'

'That's just what I'm thinking. I'm also wondering if he was working at the lily farm on the Wednesday Colson disappeared, or if he phoned in sick for the day. I'll ask Ryan about that.'

'You're thinking he might have been one of the guys in the Wrangler or the beat up pickup?'

'It's possible. Manuel knew Colson. Maybe he was involved because he could point him out to Scarface and the others. Maybe he was in that second vehicle, the old pickup.'

'Does he own such a pickup?'

'Again, I'll ask Ryan. But there are hundreds of beat up old pickups around the county. Without the license number there's no way of knowing if his was the one parked with the Wrangler, even if he does own one. In any case it looks like Manuel was involved in Davey's disappearance one way or another.'

'Jesus,' I said. 'What a nest of vipers.'

'You said it.'

When we reached Geri's house she swung the SUV into the drive behind my Cobalt and stopped. Then she looked across at me, the engine rumbling at idle. I waited for her to say something.

'No,' she said at last. 'There's one more thing I want to do before I finish today.'

'What's that?'

'I want to check on Alex Moreno. Maybe he'll talk now. I'd like to know who did that to him.'

I shrugged. 'You can try.'

She backed out again and gunned the car along the road, retracing our route of the night before. When we reached the abandoned garage at the edge of town she turned off the road and eased around the corner of the building and down the short track beside it that led to Alex's shack. There was a car parked beside Alex's Kawasaki out in front of it, a grey VW Passat some years old. Geri stopped the car and switched off the ignition.

'Looks like he's got company,' she said.

'Yep. Want me to come with you?'

'Sure.'

We got out and I followed Geri to look at the bike standing beside the porch. It was an older bike and not very powerful, and it had seen some rough use. But there was no sign of any scrapes or damage that could confirm Alex's story. Geri and I exchanged a glance, then approached the tiny porch. When we got there the door opened before Geri could knock and a young woman in her late teens or early twenties looked out at us.

'Is Alex here?' Geri asked.

'He's sleeping,' she said, whispering. 'I don't think I should wake him.'

Geri nodded. Then she tilted her head slightly.

'I know you, don't I?' she said, keeping her voice low. 'You're

Verity Thomas's daughter, aren't you?'

The girl smiled. 'That's right. Hayley. And you're Geri, aren't you? I've heard Mom talk about you. All the good work you're doing with the kids around here.'

Now Geri smiled and nodded. 'That's right. Your mom and I go back a long way.' She turned to me. 'Hayley's mother works at Ray's Market in town. You might've been served by her at some point.' She looked back at the girl. 'Do you think we could talk, Hayley? Have you got a minute?'

Hayley Thomas turned to look back into the shack's shadowy interior, then nodded and stepped outside, pulling the door to gently until it clicked shut.

'Let's move away a bit so we can talk properly,' she said, and led us a few yards up the track toward Geri's vehicle. Then she stopped. 'How can I help you?'

Geri glanced at me.

'This is a friend of mine, Arnie Rednapp. He's visiting and I'm letting him tag along with me on patrol.'

'How do you do, Mr. Rednapp.'

'Hayley, we were here last night,' Geri went on. 'And we saw what happened to Alex. His injuries. Do you know how that happened? Who did it to him?'

The girl seemed reluctant to speak. Then she took a deep breath and folded her arms across her chest, shaking her head.

'He won't tell me,' she said. 'He said he fell off his motorbike, but no fall could've hurt him that badly.'

Geri nodded. 'That's what we thought.'

'But he won't change his story. And he gets angry if I press him about it.' Hayley looked at me and smiled, embarrassed. 'We're kind of together, you know? We both work at Gregory's lily farm. Since he's been off work I stop by every afternoon to look after him, make sure he has something to eat.'

Geri nodded. 'Were you with him the Friday before last at La

Cantina?' she asked. 'There was a Mex band playing there that night.'

'Yes, I was. There was a bunch of us there. Why?'

'Was that the last time you saw him without the injuries?'

Hayley thought a minute.

'Yes it was,' she said at last. 'I came back here with him that night after we left La Cantina, but I went home about 2 AM. Alex told me his fall from the bike happened the next morning.'

'Did you notice anything when you left him that night that was ... unusual?' Geri asked. 'Out of the ordinary?'

'About him?'

Geri looked around. 'No. Around here. In the lot at the garage or on the road? A strange vehicle, perhaps?'

Hayley turned to look past Geri's patrol car toward the road, then looked back at her.

'There was an old SUV parked over there, across the road. I noticed it when a car went by and lit it up. I didn't think anything about it at the time, mind – thought it was probably just somebody who'd broken down or run out of gas.'

Geri nodded. 'Can you describe the vehicle, honey?'

The girl frowned, concentrating.

'Like I said, it was some kind of an SUV. Old and dark. Maybe black. It was parked right across from Alex's driveway, pointing away from the town.'

'So anyone sitting in it could see what went on at the house?'

'Yes.' She paused. 'Do you think whoever did that to Alex was in that car?'

Geri nodded. 'We're certain of it.'

'Gosh.' Hayley frowned again. 'Why would they do that to him? What'd he done?'

Geri looked at me, then back at the girl and smiled, sympathetically.

'You'll have to ask him about that, Hayley. If he tells you I'd be grateful if you'd pass on to me what he says.' She reached into a pocket and produced a card. 'My number's on there – home phone and cell.

Call me anytime. Also call me if you notice anything else suspicious, okay?'

'Okay.'

Geri looked back toward the shack.

'You'd better get back before he wakes up and finds you gone. I'd rather he didn't see us talking to you. It might make it easier for him to tell you about what happened.'

'Right,' Hayley said. 'I'll go.'

She turned and started back down the gravel drive toward the shack.

'Hayley?' Geri called softly.

The girl stopped and turned.

'Yes?'

'Give your mom my love, will you?'

She smiled.

'Sure.'

When we got back to the house Geri opened another bottle of red and poured us each a glass. Then she excused herself and went off to her office/study to start work on her report. I went out onto the deck to watch the late afternoon sun settle toward the ocean. I'd taken my laptop out with me and spent a few minutes entering the information we had learned that day and reviewing all my previous notes. From what we had discovered so far there were certainly grounds for believing there'd be a story worthy of my efforts sooner or later.

On the way back to the house I'd told Geri my plans. I was thinking of heading down to Lorraine's at Shelter Cove the next afternoon. After a couple nights with her and Mandy I would drive on down to my apartment and check in at the paper. I could also, then, contact the FBI field office in the city and have a chat with them about Davey Colson's allegations against Lamont Gregory. Geri thought that was a good idea, and said she would keep me informed of developments.

I called Lorraine on my cell and told her of my intentions.

'Wonderful! When do you expect to arrive?' she asked when I'd finished.

'Sometime around five or five-thirty. You working tomorrow?'

Lorraine was employed as a waitress at the Cove Restaurant in the little town. With a degree is Social Sciences she was obviously over-qualified for such a job, but there hadn't been anything else available for her when she'd first arrived there a couple of years earlier. She was popular with her colleagues and her regular clientele, but I knew she wanted something a bit more challenging in her life.

'I am, but I won't be much longer,' she answered, cryptically.

'What do you mean?'

'I've given my notice. One more month and I'm a free woman. I've decided to cash in my savings and try my hand at something new – starting a business, with my friend Ardelle as a partner. You remember her, don't you? The older waitress? Married to the fisherman, Andy?'

'Sure I do. Nice lady. What kind of business are you considering?'

'Well, one of the local fast food places has closed down and the lease on it is up for grabs – at a very reasonable figure. We thought we could turn it into a classy tea and coffee shop offering home-made scones, cakes and pies, and a range of up-market sandwiches. I'll tell you all about it when I see you.'

'Sounds a great idea. I look forward to hearing about it. Mandy okay?'

'Mandy's fine. Going through a minor emotional thing over a boy at the high school who seems to be jerking her around, but other than that she's fine. Looking forward to seeing you.'

'Well, I'll be with you both soon. I can hardly wait.'

'Me, too,' she purred. 'We'll have a nice dinner on the deck under the stars, then have an early night.'

'Sounds good to me. Though I might not be that tired.'

'I hope you're not. And never mind that. I guarantee when I'm through with you you'll be ready to sleep.'

Geri came out a few minutes later and said she'd had a call on her cell phone from Sam Buchanan to see how we'd done that morning after he'd left. She'd told him, filling him in about the two Mexicans Mr. Aikins had mentioned, including Scarface's description. Sam said he'd keep that in mind and make some gentle inquiries of his own while he was out on patrol.

Geri also told me she'd given Ryan Garrett a quick call to ask about Manuel Fernandez's whereabouts on the Wednesday of Davey Colson's disappearance. As we'd suspected, Manuel had called in sick the day before and was away for two days. Garrett also confirmed that Manuel owned a battered black pickup, an old Ford.

'So his pickup could've been the one Aikins saw under the trees with the Wrangler?'

'Quite possibly,' Geri said. 'But we'd need more evidence to confirm that, and that he was inside it. Still, it does look more and more as if he's a key player in all of this. I've asked Ryan to keep an eye on him.'

'Good idea.'

It having been a long day, Geri made us a quick stir-fry dinner and we both knocked off early.

Chapter Sixteen

Tuesday, May 20

The following morning Geri knocked us up some toast and eggs and we headed off for the first half of her patrol.

My plan was to hang with her for the morning till she dropped off her report at the Sheriff's office in town – adding to it there any new information we managed to pick up during the morning. Then I'd buy her lunch somewhere before she dropped me off at her house. When she'd gone off on patrol again I'd pack my things and leave for the south.

Our first objective was to revisit the Gasquet Post Office to talk to the postmistress again about whether or not she remembered a postmark on the envelope Davey Colson had taken away. Then we'd find out if Chris Aikins at the Gasquet Market could remember anything further about either the two Latinos or their black Jeep that could help us identify them. Finally we would stop by She She's diner and ask after Davey, the scar-faced Mexican, and anyone else that might've come in with them.

The postmistress was alone again when we entered the tiny Post Office. Geri put her question and the woman frowned while she scoured her memory for any details that might help. But there were none. The letter could've come from Timbuktu for all she knew.

We had better luck with Chris Aikins. We had to wait ten minutes for him to work his way through several customers with full grocery baskets to be checked at the till, but finally the last person left and as soon as the door closed Geri and I moved to the counter.

''Morning, you two,' Aikins said. 'Any news about those Mexican fellas?'

'Not yet,' Geri said. 'Actually we're here to ask if you've remembered anything else that might help us find them – or the black Jeep they drove. Anything spring to mind?'

Aikins thought for a moment.

'Not really, no.' He paused. 'Well, there was one thing I forgot to mention. When I watched them pull out of the lot and cross the highway I remember there was a lot of mud on the tires and caked around the wheel wells of the Jeep – as if it'd been driving over muddy mountain tracks. Which wasn't surprising because it'd been raining pretty heavily the previous ten or twelve hours.'

Geri produced her notepad and started writing.

'Anything else?'

Aikins scratched his head. 'Now that I think of it, I remember when they reversed the Jeep out of its parking slot I noticed there was a pretty hefty dent in the back bumper – like they'd backed into a post or something sometime in the past.'

Geri noted that down. 'Useful. Anything else?'

Aikins shook his head. 'That's it. If I think of anything I'll be in touch.'

We thanked him and left.

We were just about to pull onto the highway when Josh Bridger swung his Indian off the road and into the nearby Post Office parking lot. While he climbed off it Geri drove us over to join him, stopping beside him and rolling down the passenger's side window. He smiled when he saw who it was.

'Arnie. Geri,' he said. 'How you guys doin'? I just came down to see if there're any messages for me.'

'There's nothing from me yet,' she said, 'but it's good to see you checking in. Thought of anything else to tell us?'

Bridger looked around the area, then knelt down beside the car outside the passenger door, his face at window level.

'No, nothing new. I did have an idea, though.'

'What's that?'

'You know you asked me if I ever worked on the lily farms in Smith River?'

'Yeah?'

'Well, it occurred to me it might be an idea for me to get a job there for a while now, if I can. It'd give me a chance to take a look at things from the inside. Maybe I'd come across something useful. How's that sound?'

Geri and I exchanged a glance, she with her eyebrows raised.

'That's a great idea. Give me a day and I'll get back to you. The manager at Gregory's farm is a friend of mine. I can talk to him, put in a good word for you.'

Bridger nodded. 'Sounds good. Don't worry about leaving a note. I'll call you tomorrow evening. Any further developments with the investigation?'

Geri filled him in on what we'd learned the previous day. When she finished, he nodded slowly.

'Sounds like Davey was set up.'

'Yes, it does.'

Bridger stood up, stared off up the highway. 'I'd like to do something to help, you know? Davey was a buddy of mine.'

'I know, Josh,' Geri said. 'Let me contact my friend at the farm. Hopefully by tomorrow night there'll be news of a job there. Okay?'

'Okay.' He slapped a hand down lightly on the car's roof. 'Well, you guys got things to do. Good seeing you. We'll talk tomorrow night.'

And turning away he walked inside to check for mail.

The girls at She She's were friendly and obliging, but couldn't offer us any new information of note. They remembered Davey – remembered serving him on two or three occasions – but he was always alone and he kept to himself, sitting outside more often than not. They didn't know anything about the Latinos or the black Jeep.

We bought two lattes to take away and set off back toward Crescent City.

Geri had just brought her unit to a stop in a parking slot outside the Sheriff's office when her cell buzzed. She switched off the engine and reached into her pocket for the phone, checking the screen.

'It's Sam,' she said, looking across at me. Then she clicked the receive button and held the cell to her ear. 'Hey, Sam.'

Their conversation was short and I could tell it brought good news. Geri broke off finally with a heartfelt 'thanks' and a promise to contact him again soon. Then she clicked off the phone and stuffed it back into her jacket pocket.

'Useful?' I asked.

'Very,' she said. 'Sam stopped this morning to buy a sandwich at Hiouchi Hamlet, a mile or two north of Jed Smith State Park on Highway 199. Remember? Just before the road turns down into the canyon?'

I nodded. The Hiouchi Hamlet market was centered on a high bluff above the river that'd years before been cleared of timber and built up with houses. Apart from the store there was also a garage, a motel and an RV Park. I remembered it well.

'Sam says he asked the woman inside if she remembered seeing a couple of Latinos come in over the last two weeks – one of them with a facial scar and a neck tattoo. As it happens she did, but said there were three of them – Scarface and two others. Said they'd been in several times – bought boxes of groceries and beer. Paid cash. Last time she remembered seeing them was the morning the body was discovered.'

I frowned. 'Wow. So there were three of them.'

'Yep. Plus the two guys in the pickup.'

'And they were obviously still around while we were at the river responding to the call that Saturday?'

'It looks that way. But here's the best bit.' Geri smiled impishly. 'Sam said the store has a couple of CCTV security cameras, one over the counter inside and another out on the parking lot covering the front entrance. He says it's almost certain we'll get some images of the men and their Jeep from the stored film.'

'That's fantastic!'

'Isn't it? Our first piece of really good luck. I'll go out there tomorrow morning and pick up the memory discs. Then we see what they have to show us.'

There were few people in the Sheriff's office when we got inside. The Sheriff was apparently in a meeting with Detectives Nelson and Ross in his office so Geri used one of the desk computers in the common office space to update her report, which she'd brought with her on a memory stick – adding the new information about the mud and the sightings of the Latinos at Hiouchi Hamlet. Meanwhile I sat at the side of the room and busied myself bringing my own notes up to date. We finished at about the same time, Geri punching a key to send the report to the printer. As she was collecting the pages the Sheriff's office door opened and the meeting participants filed out. There was one additional person we hadn't expected. Bringing up the rear, after Ross and Nelson, and talking *sotto voce* to Sheriff Harvey Cantrell was none other than the Del Norte County District Attorney himself, Mr. Lamont Gregory.

Cantrell was listening and nodding to what Gregory was saying – until he noticed Geri and me and laid a hand on Gregory's sleeve.

'Just a sec, Lamont.' He stepped toward Geri, his face clouding. 'Why the hell weren't you here this morning, Geri? I wanted you at this meeting.'

Geri looked askance.

'We went back out to Gasquet. Sorry, Harv. I didn't know you'd called a meeting. I don't remember you saying anything about it yesterday.'

'Well, I did. At least, I think I did.' For a moment the Sheriff looked sheepish. 'Maybe it was after you left and I forgot to call you about it. Anyway, Lamont wanted to know where we are on this Colson thing so we've been bringing him up to date.'

Gregory now stepped forward.

'Deputy Mitchell.' He extended a hand to her, which she shook. 'Good to see you again.' Then he turned to me. 'And this is...?'

'Arnold Rednapp, Mr. Gregory,' I told him. 'I'm a reporter from the *South Bay Bulletin*, down in Silicon Valley. I'm doing a piece on law enforcement in Del Norte County and Deputy Mitchell's been kind enough to let me ride with her out on patrol.'

'I see.' His dark eyes bored into mine for a few seconds, then he extended his hand for me to shake. 'Good to meet you, Arnold. I trust you're finding everything we do up here up to scratch?'

'Absolutely, sir. I've been very impressed so far.'

'Good.' He looked at Harv Cantrell, then back at me. 'You're following the investigation into the murder of the man found in the river?'

'I was with Geri when the call came in about it, sir. I've been on the case from the start. Fascinating, watching how things work.'

He looked at me with a half smile, still uncertain exactly how to classify me – as friend or foe, sycophant or threat. Then he nodded.

'Good. Great opportunity for you. You'll get to observe the whole thing through to the arrest, if you're lucky.' He smiled again. 'Or rather, if we are.'

'I hope so, sir. It'd make a great article.'

'I'm sure.' He stepped toward me, his eyes never leaving mine, until he was quite close, intimidatingly close. 'Why don't you drop by my office sometime and we can have a chat about things? I can put you in the picture about the whole prosecution process, if you're interested.'

I could smell his breath – peppermint. Mr. Squeaky Clean. I felt like stepping back, away from his encroaching presence, but I fought against the impulse.

'That'd be great, sir. I'm going home for a few days, but I'll be back later this week or early next. Can I make an appointment to see you then?'

He nodded. 'Court appearances permitting I'll be pleased to see you anytime. Just give my secretary, Annabelle, a ring. I'll tell her to expect your call.'

'Thank you, sir.'

'My pleasure. Nice meeting you, Arnold.'

Then, with a nod to Geri, he and Sheriff Cantrell walked out.

Det. Sgt. Craig Nelson and his sidekick Nick Ross were hovering over desks at the side of the room. They had observed the entire exchange and were clearly unhappy that I had received such a welcome from their D.A.

'I wouldn't stay away too long, Rednapp,' Nelson growled. 'We might have this whole thing wrapped up in a matter of days, the way things are going.'

'Oh?' I said. 'Why? Have you come up with new information?'

Nelson was gathering papers together into a file. Now he closed the file and stood erect, glaring at me.

'We've got good leads already, and we should be hearing from the Humboldt County Sheriff's office in the next few hours about the airport passenger manifests and the CCTV camera footage. That should be enough to put us on the right track. Things fall right the whole thing could be wrapped up by the weekend.'

'You still believe it was just an L.A. gangbanger hit squad taking down somebody who'd stolen their money?'

Nelson shrugged. 'You know these gangs, Rednapp. If they want somebody, they get 'em, wherever they are. You can run, as the saying goes, but you can't hide.'

'For someone who'd allegedly stolen gang money,' I said, 'Colson seemed pretty poor. Without wheels and apparently hitching everywhere.'

'He had access to a motorcycle, at least,' Ross said, backing his friend. 'We know that from the sightings. And he could've stashed the cash somewhere.' He crossed his arms, scowling. 'Also, he might not have stolen any money. Maybe he just ratted on somebody and they went after him for that. Who knows with these douche bags?'

I smiled.

'Whatever.'

'They really want to push that gangland hit angle, don't they?' I said to Geri five minutes later, as we pulled away from the Sheriff's office.

'Yep. For some reason they're reluctant to consider the possibility of a local tie-in with the murder. I think they'd like it all to disappear back to Los Angeles where it probably came from.'

'I'm sure they would. Nice tidy finish to it.' I grinned toward her. 'I don't think Det. Sgt. Nelson likes me very much.'

'He doesn't like anybody very much, except himself.' Geri glanced apologetically across toward me. 'Sorry you're having to suffer his arrogance.'

'No problem. I've endured worse.'

Geri directed the car north, past the gas stations, restaurants and motels that lined the road through the last quarter mile of north Crescent City. Soon we were on Highway 101 on our way to Smith River where she was dropping me before heading off on patrol again.

When we passed Pelican Bay prison a thought occurred to me.

'You mentioned before that there was a particular reason Nelson took against you,' I said to her. 'Want to tell me about it?'

She shrugged. 'He pulled some stuff I thought was unprofessional and wrong. When I called him on it he turned against me big time.'

'What kind of stuff?'

Geri sighed. 'Well, over the years I've seen him take liberties with several investigations – altering measurements at accident scenes, being selective about what he chose to include as evidence in his reports – doing things that would ultimately help the prosecutor nail the offender, or to get him off if the perp was a friend of his. But there was one big instance of evidence manipulation that really put me off him. I've never been able to fully respect him after that.'

'What was it all about?' I asked.

'It was back when I first joined the department. I was partnering him for a few weeks till I got used to the routine and could manage my own unit. He stopped a Latino kid one afternoon who he claimed had pulled out in front of us dangerously, though it didn't look that way to me. Instead of just giving the kid a warning he made him get out of the car and did the full search routine on him – spread-eagling him against the car and frisking him. The kid was rightly surprised and got a little lippy about being treated like a common criminal. His girlfriend was on the front seat and he got the hump over being humiliated that way in front of her. Nelson didn't like him talking back. When he searched the kid's car and found a small bag of weed under the driver's seat he went ballistic. The kid was hauled off to the office and booked for possession. But that wasn't enough for Nelson. He wanted to make an example of the kid, make sure he learned never to sass a cop again, so he arranged a search warrant to turn over his house. I was with him when we served it, and the boy's poor mother was completely shocked by the way Nelson handled things. The warrant gave us permission to toss his bedroom and together we did a pretty thorough search of the room – checking drawers, stripping the bed, looking through clothes in the closet and on shelves, emptying boxes. I thought I'd done a good job and told him I'd found nothing on my side of the room. Nelson hadn't found anything either, it seems, and he wasn't too happy about it. "We'll switch sides and have another look,' he said to me, and while I went through the stuff he'd already searched, he went across to search the kid's chest of drawers again. I watched as he went through the same drawers I had gone through before. When he rummaged through the bottom drawer his face suddenly brightened. "Come here," he said. When I did he showed me at the drawer's bottom a small plastic bag. It turned out to be crystal meth. I was shocked, because I'd searched that drawer carefully and the bag wasn't in there when I checked it.'

'You're sure of that?'

'Positive. There was nothing like that in the drawer when I searched it before.'

'Meaning Nelson must've palmed the bag and planted it in the drawer himself?'

'Exactly. I told him I'd checked the drawer carefully and the bag hadn't been there. He just smirked and told me I hadn't done my job well enough. What could I do? I couldn't call him a liar.'

'What happened to the kid?'

'He was tried for possession and dealing, was convicted, and sentenced to three years in a youth facility. Fortunately he was out after eighteen months for good behavior.' She glanced across at me, shaking her head. 'But it shouldn't have happened. His parents and friends all swore he never used crystal meth and never dealt drugs to anyone. He was a good kid with a clean record. He just smoked a little dope and got caught with a trifling amount in his possession. I could never respect Nelson after that.'

I nodded. 'People like that shouldn't be cops. Sadly, though, there're too many just like him out there.'

'So it seems.' She smiled across at me. 'But I'm not one of them.'

'I know that, sweetie. And your friend Sam isn't either. That was a very useful break, what he discovered at the Hiouchi store.'

'Sure was,' Geri returned. 'That's a pretty clear indication that the men in the Jeep were based somewhere out that way – around Hiouchi or Gasquet or off on one of the side roads.'

'Are there many side roads?'

'A few. Later on I'll drag out the maps, get online and check out the area on Google Earth. Maybe I'll find something worth taking a look at.'

'That'll keep you busy,' I said. 'Good luck with it.'

We had lunch again with Tracy at La Cantina – the full nine yards this time, with cheese nachos, enchiladas, tacos and tamales. We didn't see Conchita, but Geri sent our best regards to her via Tracy. Forty minutes later Geri dropped me at the house, passed me two scanned and slightly enlarged copies of the photograph of Gregory and young Davey Colson at Belleview and sped off to talk to Ryan Garrett. I gathered my stuff into my bag, locked up the house and put the key under the flowerpot. Then I climbed into my dusty blue Chevy to head south for the long awaited rendezvous with the woman in my life.

Chapter Seventeen

The pleasure I felt walking into Lorraine's arms again was greater even than I'd anticipated and I held her a long time before letting her go, relishing the scent of her freshly shampooed hair and the soft fullness of her body. Then she drew me inside to the living room where Mandy was parked in front of the television. Smiling, the teenager got up from the sofa to give me a hug before returning to watch the current Mylie Cyrus video on MTV.

It was good to be back.

That evening the three of us sat together on the back deck of Lorraine's house, enjoying a great dinner of fresh Dungeness crab that I had picked up from a fisherman at the Crescent City marina on my way through. Lorraine told me more about her plans for the tea room and I filled them both in on the major recent developments in the body-in-the-river story. At my mention of the possible cartel connection Mandy looked up with wide-eyed interest, and when at the end of the meal her mother left us to organize the desserts indoors, she felt she could reopen the subject with me.

'Cartels, huh? That's pretty heavy stuff.'

'You'd better believe it,' I said.

'Did you ever use any drugs, Arnie? When you were young?'

I smiled at her. 'I tried pot like most college kids – smoked a bit off and on for a year or so at parties when everyone else was doing it. But

I never really got into it. And I've never tried anything else, nor had any desire to.' I took a sip of my Chardonnay, held up the glass. 'This is my poison. Why do you ask?'

She frowned. 'There're some boys in school that are selling stuff. I know some of my friends smoke marijuana, and have used uppers or taken ecstasy. At dances and things.'

'Have you tried any of it?'

'No. But it's hard sometimes when your friends are doing it and you're the only one that doesn't.'

'I think you're wise, Mandy.' I took another sip of wine. 'Have you talked with your mother about it?'

'Yes. Like you she said she smoked grass when she was in college, but didn't try anything else. And like you she told me to keep away from all of it.'

I nodded.

'That's good advice, my girl. When you turn eighteen and go to college, then you'll be an adult and if you want you can try marijuana. But be careful.' I lifted my wineglass again. 'Since I'm prone to the overuse of this particular mind-bender I'm in no position to preach abstinence. But I think it'd be best not to experiment while you're still in high school. There'll be plenty of time for that later on. Who knows? The powers that be might even get smart and legalize pot in the next couple of years. Then there won't be anything to worry about in terms of breaking the law. But if that happens you'll have to treat it carefully, just like alcohol. A little goes a long way.'

Mandy nodded.

Lorraine returned with three plates of freshly-made apple pie *à la mode* and the conversation went off in another direction.

Half an hour later Mandy had left us to watch a film on the TV and Lorraine and I were enjoying our coffees in the falling darkness when the phone rang indoors. Lorraine got up to answer it, bringing the receiver back with her onto the deck. It was Geri, and for a minute or two the two old friends chatted amiably about Lorraine's new plans.

Then Lorraine handed the phone to me.

'Geri says there've been developments,' she said.

I lifted the receiver to my ear.

'Hey, Deputy. What's happening?'

'It's been a busy day,' she said. 'Harv Cantrell called the Humboldt County Sheriff's office this morning. They've not had any black Jeep Wranglers stolen in Humboldt County in months.'

'Any luck with the airport security cameras?'

'No. The Humboldt deputies went over the passenger manifests and the CCTV films for all incoming flights at the Eureka/Arcata airport for the week before the body was found and the outgoing flights for the week after.'

'And there were no Latinos matching the descriptions we had? No Scarface?'

'No. They didn't see anyone resembling our profiles in any way.'

'Shit. What about other local airports? Anybody check that out?'

'Yeah. Nelson did. There're two airports serving the Eureka/Arcata area, the main commercial one just north of Arcata, and a smaller one, Murray Field, on the northern edge of Eureka. All the others are probably too far away. Murray Field is mainly used by general aviation aircraft. It has a short runway and fewer facilities. But there is quite a lot of traffic that comes in from outside. Craig telephoned the airport and asked about any flights in or out of Murray Field in the last few weeks from the L.A. area.'

'Were there any?'

'Oh, there were several. But none that left any Latino passengers – certainly none with scarred faces and neck gang tats.'

'They're sure about that?'

'Positive. The airport administrators keep a record of all aircraft that fly in and out of there.'

'So we still don't know what happened to the Jeep or the three Latinos?'

'Not yet, no. We can only hope that something turns up in the next couple of days.'

'Right.' I sighed. 'Anything else?'

'Well, I talked to Ryan after I left you and he's holding a job for Josh at the lily farm. They're actually looking for casual laborers just now so it worked out just right. Josh can take a job and not stand out, since there'll be other newbies besides him.'

'How will he contact you?'

'On my cell. Once he's settled we'll arrange some way to meet face to face, if necessary.'

'But not at your house.'

'God, no. It'd be too easy for someone to see him here.'

'Right. That it?'

'Not hardly. On the way back from Gasquet I stopped at the store in Hiouchi Hamlet and picked up the memory discs from the security cameras. When I got back to the office Harv and I went over the relevant dates. We found the guys.'

'Great! What's the picture quality like?'

'Not wonderful, but good enough to put together some useful stills.'

That was more like it. I sat up straighter.

'That's fantastic.'

'There's more. The CCTV films are time-coded, so we know the date and time the perps appear on the screens. The two Latinos Aikins saw plus one other appeared with their Jeep first on the Monday afternoon. They bought some groceries and beer and headed off, seemingly toward the north. On the Wednesday morning, the day of Colson's abduction, a dark and very dirty pickup appeared in the parking lot outside the store at just after 8 AM and parked at the edge of the camera's range. The driver and his passenger remained in the truck until the three Latinos appeared in the Wrangler a few minutes later and parked beside it. Then they climbed out and joined the men from the Wrangler on the pavement. The pickup's passenger seemed to hang back a bit, as if he was reluctant to meet the other men. He's the one we're going to have trouble identifying because he was wearing a hooded sweatshirt that covered his face, and he always kept his head down with his hands in his pockets. The other men greeted one another and spent a couple minutes talking and smoking. Then all of them climbed back into their separate rigs and the two vehicles drove off together – toward the north.'

'How did they greet one another?' I asked. 'I mean, were they pally? Did they seem know one another?'

'I can't say for certain, but from what we saw I'd say it looked like it was the first time they'd met.'

'So the guys in the pickup could've been locals sent to help them out?'

'Very possibly.'

Now the big question.

'Was one of them Manuel?'

'I can't tell you that yet. I'll have to wait till we get some pictures made so I can show them to Ryan.'

'Well,' I said. 'That confirms five guys altogether, not four. At least that explains how Davey Colson was taken, in spite of his Delta Force training. Sheer weight of numbers.'

'True. But there's something else. When the Latinos reappeared with their Wrangler on the CCTV at the store the following Saturday morning – the day we found the body – two of them looked like they'd been in a brawl. One had his arm held in an improvised sling, the other had what looked like a broken nose. Only Scarface appeared unharmed.'

I couldn't help but crack a smile.

'Bridger was right. Davey didn't go down without a fight. Anyway, you think the TV images will give you pictures good enough for identification?'

'We can only hope so. Harv's having the best images enhanced. Then he'll send the results down to our colleagues in Humboldt and Los Angeles to see if anyone down there can put names to them.'

'What about the Jeep? Did you get a clear image of the license plate?'

'Sadly, no. The camera's fixed to a light pole at one side of the entrance so all the cars are viewed side on.' Geri paused. 'You're going to talk to the FBI in San Francisco in the next couple of days, right?' she asked suddenly.

'Yeah. And I remembered something on the way down that might help us. A year or so ago I actually met one of their senior agents at a cocktail party. I can drag his name out of my notebooks and give him a call. I think telling Bridger's story to someone I've met before might get a more sympathetic hearing.'

'Fair enough. Let me know how he reacts. When do you think you'll be up here again, Arnie?'

I exhaled through my pursed mouth.

'Well, I'll be here another day. Then I'll need to spend a few days at home. I want to have that meeting with my FBI contact. So unless there's some pressing reason for me to be up there with you again sooner I guess I'll hang down in the south for a bit, maybe make my editor happy by doing a story or two for him in the meantime.'

'That should be fine. No point in you twiddling your thumbs up here waiting for something to happen. I'll let you know if anything new turns up.'

We said our goodbyes and switched off.

The rest of that evening was taken up by Lorraine walking me around to her recently leased shop and opening it up to show it to me. It was a light and pleasant space with a kitchen at the back, a reasonably sized dining area and a walled-in garden and patio on one side with wooden tables and benches. As it had been a fast food restaurant before, there would be no difficulty in securing a license for that purpose again. She outlined her and Ardelle's plans for the place and I thought they had some great ideas. The way the tourists were flocking into Shelter Cove during the summers these days, it was almost certain they'd do good business. Like all tourist-based enterprises, however, it would be the slack winter months that would be the testing time.

'Doesn't matter,' Lorraine told me. 'We did a projection of probable income and expenses for the seven or eight months of good weather, and if we're careful we can earn enough during that time to see us through the winter. If necessary we can always close the place down between, say, late October and the 1st of April.'

'You'd be able to do that?' I asked. 'What would you do for an income?'

She shrugged. 'If there's a problem Ardelle and I can go back to waitressing or tending bar part time at the Cove. It just happens that our landlord for this place is none other than Dale Anders, the Cove's owner and my boss. He's agreed to help us out if necessary over the first couple of years, to give the place a chance to catch on. It's obviously in his interest to have a successful business here.'

Lorraine locked up and the two of us walked down for a nightcap at the Cove Lounge, beside the restaurant where she worked. Apart from the bartender and a couple of young guys playing pool in the corner we had the place to ourselves. I was beginning to feel quite attached to the quiet easy pace of the little town.

When we got back to the house Mandy was still watching television – some documentary about wildlife in Yellowstone National Park. But she turned it off when we came in and said she was going to bed. Lorraine went off to empty the dishwasher and I wandered down the hall to the guest room to fire up my laptop. I was trying to keep accurate records of all the material relating to the Colson murder, and I wanted to enter in the latest information I'd gotten from Geri. While I was peering at the screen, pecking away on the keyboard at the small table in the room, there was a knock at the open door. I glanced up. Mandy was standing in the doorframe in flannel pajamas.

'Hey, there, young miss. What can I do for you?'

'Lisa texted me tonight.'

'Oh, yeah?'

Lisa's my sixteen-year-old daughter. She and Mandy had hit it off when they'd first met some months earlier and despite the three years age difference had kept in touch ever since.

'What'd she want? Anything in particular?'

Mandy shrugged. 'No. Just asked how school was going and what was happening about Brad. When I texted her back I told her that you were here.'

Brad, I remembered, was the boy Lorraine had mentioned that Mandy had fallen for, but who apparently did not share the same feelings for her – after having flirted outrageously for a week or two. It was one of those terrible emotional crises that all young people create for themselves, all the more disturbing because auto-generated.

'What's happening about that?' I asked. 'The relationship with Brad?'

Making a face, she rocked her head from side to side.

'He's a jerk. I don't care about him anymore.'

'That's good, Mandy. To hell with him if he can't appreciate what a great girl you are.'

'Anyway, I've found someone else I like. Someone much nicer.'

'Glad to hear it. Just go easy. Don't let yourself get hurt again.'

'I won't.'

Mandy stepped into the room and moved across to stand behind me, stooping to put her arms around me and to rest her chin on my shoulder.

'What you doing?'

'Typing up notes.'

'About the body-in-the-river case?'

'Yep.'

'Mom's worried about you getting involved with cartel people. She's afraid something could happen to you.'

'Well, she needn't be.'

'You will be careful, won't you?'

'Of course. I'm always careful. Cowards have to be.'

'You're no coward.'

'Don't bank on that.'

'Lisa wants you to phone her.'

'I'll do that. Anything wrong?'

'I don't think so. I think she just misses you.' She squeezed me in her arms. 'I know the feeling.'

I gave her clasped hands an affectionate pat.

'The feeling is mutual, angel. I miss you guys, too, when I'm away. And thanks, I'll phone Lisa tomorrow night. I've been missing her, too. Now you'd better get yourself to bed. Tomorrow's another school day.'

'Don't I know it.'

She gave me a quick kiss on the cheek, then stood up and walked back to the door, stopping there to look back at me.

'You know, you don't have to keep pretending you sleep in here, Arnie. I'm not a child. I know you spend most of every night in Mom's room.'

'Does that bother you?'

She grinned. 'Of course not. I like to see Mom happy.'

I stood up, stuck my hands in my pockets, looking at her with a sheepish grin.

'You're a piece of work, girl. Thanks for that. But for the moment I think we'd better leave things as they are. Your mother might not want us to be that open about things just yet.'

'Whatever. But it doesn't bother me one way or the other. You might as well sleep together all night long if you want to.'

I nodded. 'I'll talk to your mother about it and see what she says. Deal?'

'Deal.' She smiled again and blew me a kiss. 'Sleep well.'

'You, too.'

Then she was gone, her slippered feet scuffing down the corridor toward her room.

Chapter Eighteen

The shot-caller was in his car on his way home when the second cell phone buzzed. He pulled to the side of the road and stopped, reaching into his jacket to take the call.

'Yes?'

'It's me. I gather you wanted to talk?'

'That's right. This time I've got bad news for you, I'm afraid.'

'How bad? And what is it?'

'Nothing you won't be able to handle, I'm sure. The three soldiers you sent up to help me have been made. They were filmed by a CCTV camera and the authorities now have their pictures and their vehicle. They've even got half the license number. The L.A. police will have that information, too, later today or tomorrow. I'd advise you to get those men into hiding as soon as you can.'

'Understood. They're back at the plantation but I'll arrange to send them south for a time, over the border. Are the pictures clear?'

'I've not seen them yet, but apparently they're good enough for identification. In any case, the gang tattoo is a dead giveaway.'

'I'll make arrangements tonight.'

'Good. I don't want anyone picked up that can link me in any way to that package in the river.'

The man at the other end of the line chuckled.

'How could that happen? The men don't know who you are.

Remember, they never spoke directly with you. Don't worry. Your secret will be safe. Can I tell the company you'll be bringing another payment soon?'

'I'm contacting my partner tonight. We'll arrange a trip south in the next week or two.'

'The company will be glad to hear that.'

'I'll contact you again when I get back. I've got to go now.'

'Have a nice evening, *amigo*.'

'You, too.'

The line went dead.

Chapter Nineteen

Wednesday, May 21

Lorraine and Mandy both left early the following morning – one off to work, the other to catch the bus to school in Fortuna – leaving me alone in an empty house. I made my breakfast, took it out to the deck to enjoy it, and was just finishing my coffee when my cell buzzed in my shirt pocket and I pulled it out to check. It was Martin Taylor, my L.A. journalist friend. I clicked the talk button.

'Hey, Mart. How's it going?'

'Going good, pal. I've got some info for you. Which do you want first, the Colson/Camp Belleview stuff or the dope on Gregory?'

I dug out my notepad and pen.

'Let's have the Belleview stuff.'

'Right,' he said. I could hear him flipping pages in his notebook. 'Here goes. As you probably know, the place was founded by Lamont Gregory with additional financial contributions from a couple of his rich friends in L.A. and Palm Springs, and with a matching grant from the state government. It was located out in the Sunland-Tujunga Valley, up on the foothills of the San Gabriel Mountains. It opened in 1993 and had a capacity of forty-five boys and young men, with a complement of fifteen guards, two teachers and a nurse on the regular staff. The guards were mostly former cops or soldiers, and some had obviously been known to Gregory because they'd worked in departments that had frequent dealings with the L.A. D.A.'s office. The records show the camp functioned well for the first few years, with only a few minor incidents.'

'Colson was there from '94 to '95,' I said. 'Did you get a listing of all the inmates who were resident there during that period?'

Taylor laughed, dryly. 'Funny thing. For some reason all the records for that period have gone missing. I could confirm from Colson's own record that he'd been there, but I couldn't find any listing to show who else was in the place then. I'd have to go through the individual records of all the convicted youngsters in L.A. County to find out who was sentenced there, and obviously that's too much work.'

'Why should the prisoner records go missing?' I asked him. 'Isn't that a bit suspicious?'

''Course it is. Especially since the place closed down eight years later, in 2003.'

'Closed down? Why? It was only ten years old.'

'Apparently there were rumors of some shady things going on there.'

'What kind of things?'

Martin sighed. 'I had to call in some favors from old department colleagues to get the skinny on this because since its closure there seems to have been a deliberate attempt from somebody high up to bury all information about the place. But I did find out that apparently over the years there were a number of complaints raised by lawyers and parents alleging that their boys had been violently assaulted at Belleview. There were rumors of boys being taken to the hospital with severe injuries after being worked over by the guards, and even whispers of sexual abuse. Then in 2001 and 2002 a boy went missing, presumed escaped, and two of the younger inmates committed suicide. Gossip started to spread that the place was out of control and in 2003 it was decided to shut it down rather than open the can of worms that an official investigation would've unearthed.'

'Did you find a list of the guards that worked at Belleview during the period Colson was there? Or any of the other staff?'

'Nope. All staffing info went with the inmates' records. Only the Camp Supervisor's name was listed – one Clifford Marshall. He remained there for the duration. I did a search on him and discovered he'd been running a similar facility in Arizona a few years previously, and that before that he'd been warden of a state prison in Louisiana. After Belleview closed down he seems to have retired. Don't know where he is now. I'll keep looking.'

I was noting down the salient facts, holding the cell to my ear with the other hand.

'Anything else about Belleview?'

'Nope. That's pretty much it. Except to say that in the early years Gregory made a big show of visiting the camp regularly, apparently to help the boys adjust to the routine of the place. Lots of newspaper photo ops. I can send you some of the pics, if you'd like. I copied a few of them.'

'Yeah, please. I'd like to see them.'

'I'll email 'em to you.'

'Great. Now, what about Lamont Gregory himself? What did you find out about him?'

'A whole shitload of things. Hang on to your hat.'

'Let's have it.'

'Okay. As you probably know Gregory graduated *cum laude* in law at USC in 1976, and passed the California Bar exam shortly after. Within six months he'd set up a law practice in Pasadena with one of his friends and co-students at USC, a guy named Anthony Baldini. That name ring a bell?'

'Sure does. He's the current Attorney General for the State of California.'

'Exactly.'

'Which explains why Gregory's so pally with the guy.'

'Yep. They spent six years practicing together, criminal defense mostly – a lot of dopers, gangbangers and drug dealers. Both of them were hot shit lawyers and the practice developed a reputation for getting their clients off the hook – either freed altogether, or their sentences hugely reduced through plea bargaining.'

'Interesting. Any clients of note?'

'A couple.' I could hear him shuffling through his notes. 'In 1986 he represented one of the top shot-callers in a local Chicano gang, a guy named Marcos Galvéz. That name mean anything to you?'

I thought back. 'No, can't say that it does. But remember, I'm only a recent arrival in California. I don't reckon much L.A. gang news would've made it as far east as Des Moines.'

'Of course. Well, Marcos Galvéz is now reputed to be the head of the Varrio Pasadena Rifa gang, one of the strongest and nastiest in the whole L.A. area. They're big into all mainline criminal activities – drugs, prostitution, protection rackets, even human trafficking. Rumor has it they have close relations with the Sinaloa cartel in Mexico. They're a rough bunch.'

'What was the case Gregory defended him in?'

'Murder One. He was charged with killing a rival gang member from the next neighborhood. There were witnesses who saw him pull the trigger.'

'What happened at the trial?'

'The case collapsed and Galvéz got off with only a conviction for weapon possession.'

'How could that happen if there were witnesses and he was in possession of the murder weapon?'

'First of all the gun that was found on him when he was arrested wasn't the murder weapon. That was never recovered. Secondly, during the trial the key witnesses all retracted their initial statements, swearing they'd been coerced by the police into identifying Galvéz, that in fact they hadn't had a clear view of the shooter at all, and that therefore it could easily have been someone else. Galvéz did his year inside and that was that. In no time at all he was back on the streets again, running his crowd of pimps and cutthroats.'

'Interesting. So the thinking was that someone had gotten to the witnesses and bribed or forced them to retract their statements?'

'Yep. But it couldn't be proved.'

'Hm. Any other cases like that in Gregory's past?'

'A few, but none so blatant. He was known as an attorney who could always get short sentences for his clients, even when their guilt was beyond doubt. Gregory was a master, apparently, in finding legal glitches or mistakes in law enforcement and prosecution procedures that either got his man off altogether or resulted in a lesser charge and a greatly reduced sentence. He also became a master at plea bargaining.'

'Hm,' I said. 'Sounds pretty much the way he's running the D.A.'s office in Crescent City right now – keeping the public happy with convictions, but only on relatively minor charges – not going for the felony convictions and longer sentences that the crimes and the evidence would seem to warrant.'

'That doesn't surprise me. Leopards don't lose their spots.'

'What about his time in the L.A. District Attorney's office? Were there any other cases that caught the limelight for being controversial during his tenure there?'

'Depends which side of the political spectrum you sit on. Gregory was brought into the L.A. County District Attorney's stable of counselors in 1988, and was appointed Assistant D.A. in '92. During all those years, from the uninformed, conservative point of view, he appeared to be doing a good job as a prosecutor, putting the bad guys away and keeping them off the streets. But from the vantage point of the law enforcement agencies he was far too lenient – opting too often for lesser charges and to plea bargain when he should've pressed for felony charges with long sentences. Eventually his notoriety as a 'soft' prosecutor got to be an embarrassment for the D.A.'s office. According to my sources he was finally given an ultimatum – either resign and move on or be fired. He chose to move on. That was in 2004.'

'And he returned to Del Norte County shortly afterwards,' I picked up. 'Where he was elected District Attorney less than two years later – for the first of his two terms.'

'So it would appear.'

I glanced at my notes, trying to tie this new information in to the facts I had already learned about Lamont Gregory from Geri and elsewhere.

'Do you think Gregory could've formed a clandestine association with any of the bad-asses he represented during those early years as a defense attorney?' I asked Marty eventually. 'This guy Galvéz, for instance? I mean, do you think he got anything more out of his bending of the rules on their behalf than the fees he charged?'

'You mean do I think he was being regularly paid off under the table by the gangs?'

'Yeah. I guess that's what I mean.'

Martin sighed, the sigh of a man who's become resigned to a world that is decidedly other than what he would have it be.

'I would think it very likely,' he said at last. 'But proving that is another thing altogether. People like Lamont Gregory don't get to their high positions in the establishment without being cagey.'

'And dangerous?'

'Probably. If he has friends in the L.A. gangs he's got an army of thugs at his disposal. So,' he said, after a moment's pause, 'anything else I can do for you?'

'You've done a lot, Mart, and for that I'm very grateful.'

'No problem. You did a lot for me a year ago.'

'There is one thing, though, that I'd appreciate your help with – if you have the time.'

'What's that?'

'The L.A. gangs. Do you still have friends in the LAPD that could bring you up to date with what's going on with them today – particularly with regard to their associations with the Mexican cartels? I'm just wondering if you might come across a mention of some bigwig in northern California that's handling their business for them up there?'

'Meaning Gregory?'

'Yes. Possibly.'

'I can poke around, but I wouldn't hold out much hope of learning much. These organizations work because no one in the chain knows anyone other than the links directly above and below them, and then seldom by their real names. But I'll ask around.'

'You're an ace, Mart. Also, if you can track down an address for Davey Colson's mother, May Colson – an asthmatic invalid living somewhere in Long Beach, I think – I'll be eternally grateful. That'd save me bothering the Del Norte Sheriff's office about it, which might make them suspicious about what I'm up to.'

'No prob. I'll add that to my list. So, when will we see you down here next?'

'Probably fairly soon,' I told him. 'I want to come down to check into a few things. When I do I'll let you know and we'll get together.'

'Hell, you can stay with us, *amigo*. You know Connie and I would love to have you.'

'Thanks, Mart. I might well take you up on that.'

For the next couple of hours I amused myself online, digging out all the details I could find about the current Attorney General of the State of California, Anthony Baldini. There wasn't much, but it was all interesting.

Baldini was halfway through his second term of office, and was a quintessential Republican success story. What struck me immediately was how everything he was as a man seemed the direct opposite of Lamont Gregory, his old friend and colleague. Gregory was a confirmed bachelor. Baldini was married to a former movie actress and had three beautiful teenage kids. Apart from occasional politically motivated dinner and cocktail parties and catered barbecues at his

Smith River farm Gregory was mostly reclusive, spending the bulk of his free time in the seclusion of his ocean-side property in Crescent City or in his house in Mexico. Baldini on the other hand was a social butterfly, partying frequently and publically both in Sacramento and in Los Angeles, where he and his wife had many friends among the Hollywood glitterati. Although a dedicated Republican, Gregory was relatively inactive politically apart from campaigning in his own elections. Whereas Baldini was constantly in the news, pushing the Republican line up and down the state on a variety of issues. In short, Baldini was the obvious extrovert while Gregory chose to lead his life in comparative silence and privacy. It was an interesting contrast.

I also discovered that besides owning a villa on the coast near Puerto Vallarta, Baldini was also a friend of the current President of Mexico, and was a frequent guest at the President's residence in Mexico City, where they both enjoyed golf weekends at the finest Mexican courses. One would think with all that travelling that Baldini would've had little time to see to his duties as Attorney General, but it appeared that that was not the case. He seemed to be well-liked and highly regarded by his governmental colleagues, and I could find no rumors of ill feeling or accusations of inattention to his duties anywhere on the web. Another Mr. Squeaky Clean, to all intents and purposes. I wondered about that. How could he be such a close friend of Lamont Gregory without sharing at least some of his alleged malevolence?

I had lunch at the Cove Restaurant, served by my lovely Lorraine, then took a drive up to Eureka, where I intended to have a chat with the Humboldt County Sheriff if he was available. The weather was cool and the skies overcast and Eureka is bleak enough even in good weather, in spite of its broad bay and atmospheric waterfront, and the wonderful collection of 19th century buildings lurking on the side streets. I found the tall modern building that housed both the jail and the Sheriff's office downtown on the main drag, put the car in a nearby parking lot, and went inside.

Amazingly the Sheriff was both in and able to see me, and without delay I was ushered up stairs and down corridors until a knock at a door gave me entrance into his expansive office. Sheriff Michael 'Mickey' Dunlap was a short, round man with greying hair and a powerful grip. He shook my hand, offered me a chair across the desk from his, and we both sat down.

I had met the man the year before while I was in the area investigating another mysterious death – the same event that'd brought Lorraine and me together – and judging from the warmth of his welcome I could tell that he both remembered me and respected the paper I write for.

'So, Mr. Rednapp,' he asked, 'to what do I owe this visit?'

I told him about my covering the investigation into the body-in-the-river case in Del Norte County and asked if there had been any new word regarding the missing black Jeep Wrangler or the Latinos seen riding in it.

'Well, no. We've been passed the CCTV pictures of the vehicle and the men, but we don't recognize any of them from our known offenders mugshots. Hopefully the Del Norte detectives can get the Wrangler's registration from the partial plate reading. Maybe the police down in L.A. will be able to identify the Latinos – especially the one with the scar and the tats. Of course, there's no absolute guarantee they even came into Humboldt County. It's common knowledge the cartels and the gangs use I-5 to run their drugs from L.A. up into southern Oregon. And I-5 is inland, miles from the coast. It's quite possible they arrived and went back that way.'

'Right,' I said. 'And your department is convinced they didn't dump the vehicle somewhere and just fly out of here south, either commercially from the Arcata airport or on some private plane out of Murray Field?'

'We've looked over the CCTV footage of the Arcata passengers for both of the weeks in question and there were no Latinos that remotely matched the descriptions sent to us. Certainly nobody with face scars and tattoos. So yes, we're sure they didn't fly in or out of here through Arcata Airport or Murray field.'

I sat forward in my chair, frowning, trying to think outside of the box.

'Sheriff Dunlap, I don't suppose it's possible they're still here somewhere hiding out – if indeed they came through Humboldt County? Could they have friends here, gang people already based in the area?'

'Oh, sure, it's possible. We've had gang sleepers and active members here since the '80s. Over the last few years we've had ample evidence – derived from drug busts and arrests of drug dealers throughout the county – that the illegal substance supplies on sale here in Humboldt County are coming, at least partly, from gangs in Los Angeles and elsewhere. Not so much the marijuana, but methamphetamines, coke and heroin. Most of the marijuana comes from the local growers in the Emerald Triangle – though there are plenty of gang and cartel people involved in that, too. An increasing number, as a matter of fact. Hell, in the last six months alone there've been several busts in Humboldt County of huge cartel growing operations involving tens of thousands of plants – some of the busts even resulting in fatalities, when the law enforcement officers surprised Chicano minders who were crazy enough to engage in fire fights with them. The cartels are big into weed production in the northern mountains, now. Saves them the hassle and expense of transporting it up from the south.'

The Emerald Triangle, I already knew, is the rugged mountainous area of northwestern California comprising great chunks of Mendocino, Trinity and Humboldt Counties, where for the past thirty or forty years – effectively since the end of the Viet Nam War – illegal marijuana farms have sprung up all over on Bureau of Land Management and National Forest land, hidden away under the forest canopy on mountain tops and hillsides. In recent years, however, the situation has become more critical, with some growers actually clearing away the forest, creating exposed growing plots and erecting greenhouses on

156

the tops of mountains – using harsh herbicides, pesticides and poisons and diverting natural springs and waterways, thereby upsetting the delicate ecological balance of the area. Over the last several years the alternative press – *Mother Jones*, for instance, and *The North Coast Journal* – has published numerous articles documenting the damage such operations have caused to the region. And whereas traditionally it'd been local people who created these clandestine mountain farms in relatively limited operations – former hippies and desperate timber industry workers with no more jobs to find – they have recently been superseded by a wave of cartel-sponsored crews of illegals coming up from the south and slipping quietly into the mountains to create their own vast marijuana plantations, driving the locals away with threats and intimidation. This expanding enterprise has become so widespread now that anyone using Google Earth to scan the mountains of northern California can easily spot these illegal farms right there in the open, as if their makers were daring the DEA and local drug enforcement agencies to try to stop them. It's even rumored that the U.S. Forest Service has detailed maps of the plantation sites, partly so they can avoid stumbling onto them themselves and being shot at. Owing to the severe budget cuts of the last decade, however, the law enforcement agencies are powerless to do more than make token forays into the mountains to close down the illegal nurseries, recovering and destroying only a tiny fraction of the total amount grown. The whole thing is a shocking tragedy for the environment in terms of the destruction caused by these operations and the garbage their tenders leave behind.

There were, however, some hopeful signs, as I knew from my research.

In the summer of 2013, North Coast Congressman Jared Huffman took a step forward by introducing the Protecting Lands Against Narcotics Trafficking Act (PLANT), a law establishing new and stiffer penalties for the damage caused by illegal growers on lands belonging to the state and the nation. Already some raids had been made under this new law and the results were encouraging.

'Isn't it entirely possible,' I asked Sheriff Dunlap, 'that these guys might've come from here or somewhere near Humboldt County in the first place? That they were plucked from their duties as plantation minders by their shot-callers and ordered to drive north to take care of gang business in Del Norte County? Maybe that's where their Jeep has disappeared – back into the mountains, hidden under branches on some barely accessible logging road. Sound feasible?'

''Course it's feasible. We know there are scores of illegals in the mountains working under gang and cartel orders. Hell, we've even found Bulgarians and Romanians out there! What's to stop them being used for occasional other jobs as well?'

'They'd already have weapons,' I added. 'It's common knowledge they're heavily armed.'

Sheriff Dunlap nodded slowly. 'That idea has crossed my mind. In fact, I've got deputies checking with the various Latino communities around the county now, trying to find someone that knows or has connections with cartel or gang growers, and who's prepared to talk. But it's almost certainly a lost cause. These people won't rat on their own. They're too scared.'

'Which gangs are involved up here?'

The Sheriff shook his head, resignedly. 'We've got several. The most active locally are the Norteños and the Sureños – gangs originating in Mexico and San Salvador. But there are others that come through occasionally, as well. The MS-13 out of L.A. is moving out all across the states, sending drug mules and dealers into communities that've never before had a drug problem.' He laughed. 'We've got hundreds of gangbangers working here, Arnold. Do bears shit in the woods? They sure do, and we've got lots of woods for them to shit in. Up to now we've been able to keep the pot growing situation pretty much contained. But it's getting worse, no question. And without more government help I don't know how we're ever going to hold it in check anymore, let alone stop it.'

'The simple answer, of course, is to legalize it,' I suggested. 'Pot at least.'

'Maybe so. But it'll take a sea change in government thinking to go down that road.'

Unfortunately, I believed he was right.

Chapter Twenty

I got back to Shelter Cove in time to shower and change and to walk Lorraine back from the restaurant at the end of her shift. When we got to the house Mandy was home from school. I had offered to take them out for a meal in Fortuna as a last night gesture before departing south in the morning, and while they got ready I phoned my daughter on my cell. I reckoned with the time difference she would've just finished dinner. I was right.

'Hey, Dad,' she said when she picked up. 'Thanks for calling.'

'How's it going, squirt?'

'All good at the moment.'

'School okay?'

'Fine. I talked with my counselor today about where I should go to college.'

Lisa was due to graduate in just a couple weeks.

'Oh? And what schools are you considering?'

'I'd kind of like to go to somewhere in California, if you wouldn't mind paying the out-of-state costs. I'm sick of the Midwest.'

'If your Mom's all right with that I think we could manage it together, she and Jack and I.'

My ex had remarried three years earlier, to a city accountant that made good money cooking the books for a major Midwest construction company. To say they were 'comfortable' was a drastic understatement. Unlike me.

'Anyway,' I went on, 'you might be able to use my residence in California to avoid paying the out-of-state costs. What schools do you have in mind out here?'

'Well, maybe U.C. Santa Cruz, if they'll have me. Or Santa Barbara.'

'They're both great universities, Lisa. I'd be proud to have you studying at either one of them. What're you thinking of majoring in?'

'Not sure yet. Maybe English Lit. Maybe Journalism.'

'Careful, kid. You don't want to end up in my racket. Too many long hours.'

'I like what you do, Dad. You're kind of like a public conscience, telling people what's going on that's wrong and encouraging them to do the right thing. I like the stories you write and the issues you cover – as long as you keep yourself from getting too involved. What're you working on now?'

I spent a few minutes telling her about the Del Norte murder investigation. She was interested, but concerned as well.

'Just take care of yourself, Dad. Don't take any stupid chances.'

'I won't.'

We chatted another few minutes, then she had an incoming call beeping and had to go. It was good to hear her voice. I wouldn't be seeing her till the end of the school year some weeks away. It was a long time to wait.

Dinner turned out great. Lorraine had heard good things about the Eel River Brewing Company, a popular pub-like bar/restaurant in Fortuna that served a broad menu. Mandy tried their special hamburger platter while Lorraine and I had avocados with shrimp cocktail to start followed by prime rib. A waiter-recommended homemade chocolate mousse and cappuccinos wrapped things up, then we made the hour-long journey back to Shelter Cove and bed. It was another school day tomorrow.

'You'll be careful down in Los Angeles, won't you?' Lorraine murmured, as we lay together in the darkness at the edge of sleep.

My passionate lady had been as good as her phone promise and for the second night running I was physically drained and feeling very relaxed, ready to drift off into soft black oblivion.

'You know I will be, sugar,' I told her, bending my head to kiss the top of her head. 'Anyway, I don't think I'll be doing anything that'll prompt the bad guys to come after me.'

'When will we see you again?'

'Don't know. Couple of weeks maybe. Why?'

'I thought I might take Mandy up to Crescent City for a weekend with Geri, if you aren't going to be around. Maybe the weekend after next. That all right with you?'

'Of course, honey. It'd be a great break for the two of you, just before Mandy has her end of year exams. I'm sure Geri would welcome the visit.'

'I thought you wouldn't mind,' she said, snuggling closer against me, her head nestled against my shoulder, one bare arm loosely draped across my stomach. ''Course, it'd be even better if you were there with us.'

'I'll do my best to make that happen.'

'I could only be away for the weekend, though,' she said, fading away. 'I've got too much work to do, setting things up for the business.'

'My busy, busy darling,' I whispered.

Two minutes later we were both fast asleep.

I didn't go back to the guest room that night. I woke up mid-morning the next day alone in Lorraine's bed with the two of them gone and a note wishing me a safe journey south signed by both on the pillow beside me adorned with several hearts and a lipsticked kiss.

I guess the transition had been made to follow Mandy's advice without any need for a discussion – which was fine with me. Waking up before dawn and moving back to a lonely cold bed had been a very painful process.

It was good to be back in my apartment after four days away. I got there just after lunch that afternoon, dropped my things, set up a clothes wash and headed on down to the paper's office to check in. There was a stack of mail on my desk, but nothing important. I had just finished scanning the last piece when Abe Rawlings, my editor, appeared at my elbow.

'Back are we?' he asked.

'Yep. For a while, at least. Why? Anything up?'

He shrugged. 'Nothing pressing. There're a few things I could put you on, but none of them are big deals. How's the Del Norte story coming along?'

'How about I grab a couple of lattes from the machine and come tell you all about it?'

'Sounds good. See you in my office in five.'

For a man with such a reputation for fierceness Abe Rawlings was really a gentle giant of a man. Tallish and thickset in his mid-sixties, with a penchant for golf, and for smart suits with waistcoats and watch chains, he had spent his life as a journalist – cutting his teeth first on local papers around Boston and Concord and then working his way up as an investigative reporter on the *Washington Post*, where, in the years after Watergate, he had helped to extend that newspaper's excellent reputation by authoring several famous exposés of the shady practices of high profile public figures and politicians. As a protégé and friend of Woodward and Bernstein, he had learned from them the thrill of uncovering and revealing to the world the unethical/criminal practices of arrogant men of power, and he had brought that crusading spirit to the little paper he had bought in the south San Francisco bay area fifteen years before (with his new San Francisco socialite wife's money), establishing for it, after only a couple years, a reputation as a veritable terrier of journalistic inquiry. As it happened, my move to the West Coast after a disastrous divorce fell just as his newspaper was beginning to make ripples and, given my experience writing for the *Des Moines Register,* Abe took a chance and hired me as part of his crew. I had been lucky with a few stories in the first year and now he considered me his number one investigative reporter, for which I was grateful. Working for Abe Rawlings in any capacity was an honor, and I was pleased and flattered that he now valued me so highly both as a reporter and as a friend.

Abe's office took up one corner of the building's second floor, with one set of windows overlooking the six-lane ribbon of Highway 101 snaking off toward San Jose and the other offering a magnificent panoramic view of south San Francisco bay, with the Diablo Range hills on the eastern side, and the tops of the Sierra Nevada mountains beyond, just visible through the haze. I carried the two large paper cups of latte into the office, shouldered his door closed, and set the cups on his desk. Then I sat in the chair opposite him.

'How's Lorraine?' he asked.

Abe and his wife had met Lorraine when they'd travelled north to Shelter Cove some months before to attend a funeral. I knew he thought I'd fallen on my feet with her, and that he worried that one day I might cut my ties with the paper altogether and move up there to stay with her permanently – which, to be honest, was something I'd considered more than once. But I wasn't quite ready for that, and neither (I believed) was Lorraine, so I assured him he had nothing to worry about in the near future at least.

'She's fine. She sends best wishes to you and Carol.'

'Good. Same back to her and Mandy. Now, tell me about this Del Norte business. What's been happening?'

I brought him up to speed on everything that Geri and the Sheriffs' Offices of both Del Norte and Humboldt Counties had discovered about the Davey Colson murder case. Abe sat back in his padded armchair, his hands clasped in his lap, frowning and occasionally nodding. When I finished he sat silently for a minute, digesting the details of the story. Then he leaned forward, resting his arms on the desk.

'Sounds like you've got plenty to keep you occupied on this for some days to come,' he said.

I nodded. 'There's stuff I'd like to do, sure. I want to contact the FBI in the city. And I'd like to spend a couple days down in L.A. looking into a few things down there. But I don't want to short-hand you if you need me here.'

Abe waved a hand, dismissively.

'It's a thin time right now news-wise and I'd rather you were out chasing leads on this story than wasting your time here with trivia. I think you're onto something big with this investigation, Arnie, and I want you to continue. Why not wrap up what you have to do here today and tomorrow, then head down to L.A. over the weekend?'

I raised my eyebrows.

'You'll cover my expenses on all this? I mean, it's all still pretty uncertain. There might not be a story at the end that warrants all this attention.'

'Let me be the judge of that,' he said. 'And don't worry about the expenses. That's what having a rich wife is all about.'

Abe's wife Carol had been previously married to a workaholic West Coast property tycoon who had amassed a fortune before he died, childless and relatively young, from prostate cancer – leaving it all to his attractive widow. Carol had met Abe three years later at a party during a visit she'd made to society friends in Washington D.C. They'd hit it off and within a year had tied the knot, Abe having agreed to restart his working life on the West Coast. He'd found the *South Bay Bulletin* wallowing in failure and bankruptcy, bought it with Carol's money, and managed to turn its fortunes around within two years. Carol loved Abe and believed in his journalistic ideals, and

– as his nominal publisher – had proved more than happy to continue pouring family money into projects that he believed would insure its ongoing success.

'Just keep me in the loop with a call from time to time, that's all I ask,' Abe went on. 'Oh. And watch your back. You're into some potentially very dangerous stuff here. I don't want the big story to be about losing you.'

I promised him I'd be careful and for the next few minutes we traded small talk. When my coffee was gone I shook his hand and made my exit.

Back at my desk I checked my diary for the year before, looking for the name of the FBI agent I'd met at the cocktail party. I keep fairly detailed records of my engagements so it wasn't difficult to find. The guy's name was Devonne Peters, and I remembered him as being African-American, very tall, very fit-looking, and very self-confident – a bit of a cross in looks between Morgan Freeman and Denzel Washington. Strong, quiet and no-nonsense. He radiated an aura of efficiency and sharp intelligence that indicated clearly why he was a Special Agent in Charge.

I found the number of the FBI field office in San Francisco and called it on my desk phone. When I finally managed to get through to a human voice I asked to be put through to Agent Peters and a minute or so later Peters' deep velvet voice came down the line.

'Agent Peters. Can I help you?'

'Hey, Devonne. It's Arnie Rednapp, of the *South Bay Bulletin*. We met last year at Fiona Bradshaw's cocktail party out at Stinson Beach, remember? We spent some time talking together about people trafficking?'

'Sure, I remember. How you doing, Arnie? What can I do for you?'

I gave him the bare bones of the Colson story, hinting at a possible connection between the murder, the Mexican cartels and corruption in the Del Norte justice system, and he immediately expressed interest. As I'd hoped, he invited me to come to his office the following morning to fill him in on the details. If he found it strange that the approach to him had been made by me and not by the Del Norte County Sheriff's Office he didn't say so. Maybe he assumed they were involved in the possible corruption I'd mentioned? I jotted down the address of the field office and the appointment time, then we said our goodbyes and hung up.

Back at the apartment an hour later, I was putting wet clothes in the dryer when my cell phone rang. It was Geri Mitchell.

'Hey, Arnie. This a good time to talk?'

'Sure, Ger. I'm at home doing my laundry. Anything that stops me doing that is welcome. What you got?'

She laughed.

'Just wanted to let you know Bridger's now working on Gregory's lily farm. He's going to call me if he discovers anything useful.'

'Good. Where's he living?'

'He found a small apartment in The Eagle in Smith River. It's an old hotel that's been converted into rentals. He left his bike with the mechanic in Gasquet and hitched in. He gets around on a used bicycle he bought in Crescent City.'

'Tell him to be careful when you next speak to him.'

'On the bicycle?'

'No, at the farm. He'd better watch his 'p's' and 'q's' around Manuel Fernandez for a start.'

'I think he knows that already, Arnie. Anyway, Manuel hasn't been there for the last couple of days. He called in sick.'

'Again? Wonder what he's up to? At least that takes the pressure off Josh for a while. Anything else?'

'Not really. What about you? Any new developments?'

'Some.'

I told her about my meeting with Sheriff Dunlap in Eureka, and floated past her the idea we'd discussed that the three men might've come from one of the local cartel marijuana plantations in the Humboldt County mountains. She thought that was interesting and said she'd pass it on to Harv Cantrell.

'You seeing the FBI soon?' she asked.

'Yep. I phoned my contact this afternoon. I see him tomorrow at 10 AM at his office in the city.'

'Good luck with that,' she said. 'Let me know what he says.'

'You know I will.'

Chapter Twenty-One

Friday, May 23

The San Francisco FBI field office is on Golden Gate Avenue, just a block or two from City Hall, in the Phillip Burton Federal Building between Polk and Larkin Streets. It's a modern white edifice about twenty stories high. At the reception counter I was told to take the elevator to the 8th floor where I would be met. I did and when the elevator doors opened Devonne Peters was waiting for me. We shook hands and I followed him down the center aisle of a long open room past dozens of agents at computer stations into a glassed-in room at one corner. Motioning me toward the chair opposite his desk, he closed the door and moved to his side, sitting in a comfortable-looking leather armchair before windows that looked out onto blue sky, the Civic Center roofs and the city skyline.

'Coffee?' he asked.

'Sure. Latte if you have it.'

Peters lifted his phone and murmured something to whoever was on the other end. Then he put it down again and sat back.

'So,' he said. 'Yesterday I contacted the Del Norte County Sheriff's Office in Crescent City and asked them to send me the file of the Colson murder investigation. I told them it was just a routine check so they wouldn't be suspicious. I received this from them this morning.' He gestured to a pile of printed papers on his desk. 'So I'm up to date on everything they currently know.' Peters put his hand on the papers. 'There's no mention in any of this of David Colson being connected in any way with anything or anyone local in Del Norte County – apart from your deputy friend's 'informant'. Or of any involvement with the cartels. So far as they're concerned the murder was almost certainly gang related – a hit squad out of L.A. that tracked him down and did him in for whatever reason. I must say the way the evidence looks so far that seems a perfectly logical assumption. Where did you get the information about his murder being connected to cartel drug dealing and local corruption?'

I took out a copy of the photograph of Colson and Gregory that Geri had given me and handed it across to Peters. He sat back, studying it. Then he looked up at me.

'Colson the kid?'

'Yep.'

He nodded. 'Who's the guy?'

'A man named Lamont Gregory. The picture was taken at the Camp Belleview facility for young offenders in northeast Los Angeles County some twenty years ago. Gregory was the founder of the camp. He was also a prosecutor for Los Angeles County and the man who put Davey Colson away for drug dealing.'

Peters' eyebrows arched. 'So?'

'A few days ago Del Norte Deputy Sheriff Geri Mitchell and I interviewed a friend of Davey's, a man named Josh Bridger.'

'That'd be the "informant"?'

I nodded. 'That's right. He'd contacted Mitchell and asked her to meet with him privately. She balked at meeting a stranger alone and asked me to tag along. That was how we found out the body's identity. Bridger had a lot to tell us. Colson had been staying with him for a few days before his disappearance. During that time he told Bridger a lot of interesting things, one of them being that during Colson's time at Belleview Counselor Gregory often visited the camp, and that during these visits – which were often over-night – Davey, along with other inmates, was sexually assaulted by him and some of the guards. This apparently went on throughout his time there.'

Peters frowned. 'Do we know where this guy is now?' he asked, his gaze fixed on the photograph.

'Yes, we do. He's the Del Norte County District Attorney. Has been for the last eight years.'

There was a quiet tap at the door. Peters looked up and beckoned and the door opened. A young male agent in shirt sleeves came into the room carrying a tray with two lattes in tall ceramic cups, a bowl of brown sugar cubes and a pair of spoons. He placed the tray on the desk and left, closing the door behind him.

'You take sugar?' Peters asked.

'No.'

He nodded and passed me one of the lattes. Then he dropped two cubes of sugar into his cup and stirred it – still frowning. Finally he swung his eyes up to meet mine.

'Go on.'

I told him the whole story, explaining my involvement in the investigation and detailing everything that we knew from Bridger and from the superficial investigations we'd made thus far in Gasquet and Smith River. While I spoke Peters leaned forward, crossing his arms on the desk. When I'd finished we sat in silence a moment. Then Peters sat back again.

'Who knows about this besides you?'

'Deputy Mitchell, obviously. And Josh Bridger. And two of Mitchell's close friends: a California Highway Patrolman named Sam Buchanan, and a former boyfriend of hers, Ryan Garrett. As well as holding down the office of District Attorney, Lamont Gregory owns a lily farm in Smith River. Garrett's the manager of that farm. He's helping us out. Oh, and my journalist friend in L.A. who's looking into things down there for me also knows. His name's Martin Taylor, a former cop. And my boss at the paper, Abe Rawlings.'

'Nobody else?'

'No.'

I didn't tell him I'd outlined the investigation to Lorraine and Mandy because I didn't think it mattered since they were positioned so far away from the case, literally and figuratively.

'Good,' Peters said.

He swung his chair around so that he could look out the window, back over the city and across the bay toward Oakland. While he was thinking he brought his hands together in front of his lips and made a little steeple of them, fingertips to fingertips.

'Okay,' he said at last, dropping his hands. 'Here's how we're going to play this.' He turned his chair again to face me. 'I'll contact your friend Deputy Mitchell on her cell and let her know what's happening. I'm going to initiate some discreet monitoring up in Del Norte County of the Sheriff's and the District Attorney's Offices. I want to know how they're treating this case, and I want to see the records of how they've handled every other drug related case over the last few years. I'm also going to get a team to dig out everything they can find about Lamont Gregory's time in Los Angeles. I'll probably also subpoena a look at his bank accounts, though he's probably too smart for those to show anything untoward. If there is a connection between him and the Varrio Pasadena Rifa or any other gang, or the Sinaloa cartel, we'll find it. I'll also see what I can find out on the quiet about Camp Belleview and what went on there.' He sat back. 'In the meantime, what're you going to do?'

I raised my eyebrows.

'Thought I'd go down to L.A. for a day or two. Maybe visit Davey Colson's mother. See if I can locate any friends of his from the Belleview period. I also want to try to find somebody that worked at Belleview during Colson's time there. Someone I can talk to that might know what was going on and who might be prepared to testify to it in a court of law.'

Peters nodded. 'Good thinking. Anything else?'

I shrugged. 'It crossed my mind that it might be useful to take a trip down to Puerto Vallarta to have a look at the houses of Gregory and his pal Baldini. While I'm there I could talk to some of their staff, see if I can discover what goes on there.'

Peters frowned again.

'You be careful, Rednapp. That country's out of control. Speak to the wrong person and you could lose your head over it. Literally.'

'I know. Believe me, I'll be careful.' I pulled out my cell phone. 'I'll give you Geri's cell number. And mine.'

Peters jotted them down on a memo pad. Then he opened a drawer in the desk and took out a business card which he handed across to me. It had his office and cell numbers on it. I slipped it into my wallet.

'You've been around that Sheriff's department, haven't you?' he asked.

'In Del Norte? A couple times. I've met the Sheriff, Harv Cantrell, and a few of the deputies.'

'What do your instincts tell you about them? D'you think they've been corrupted?'

I sat forward.

'I'd be surprised if Sheriff Cantrell is bent. He seemed a decent by-the-book guy to me. As for the others, I couldn't say. I suppose like all departments there're officers that bend the rules occasionally to get convictions, but apart from that I couldn't honestly say I've had any definite feelings one way or the other. I don't think my involvement with the investigation is welcomed by a couple of the detective deputies there, but I don't think that tells us much. Anyone in their position would resent a journalist poking his nose into their business.'

Peters nodded. 'We'll keep them out of it altogether till we know more about them. I'll do some background checks on Cantrell and his deputies and their records. If they've ever been suspected of anything shady in the past that should come to light then.' He put his hands face down on the edge of the desk. 'Anything else, Arnie? Or are we done for the moment?'

'I think we're done.'

We got to our feet.

'Can I keep the photo?' he asked, nodding down at it.

'Sure. It was made for you. As I said, Geri's got the original.'

Peters came around the desk and moved toward the door.

'I'll call if I discover anything interesting,' he said, opening it. 'I trust you'll do the same?'

'Of course.'

I stepped out and he followed me back through the ranked desks of agents to the elevator door and waited with me till it came. When the doors opened we shook hands and I stepped inside. Then the doors closed and I started down.

Back home again I called Martin Taylor on my cell and told him I was driving down on Sunday and hoped I might take him up on his offer of the spare room. He said they'd be happy to have me, that it being Sunday Connie would fix something extra nice for us for dinner. I liked that. Connie was a great cook. Martin said he'd made contact with an old friend of his in the Pasadena Police Criminal Investigation Division, a lieutenant that'd started out in law enforcement about the same time he had and who was now working on the gangs desk. Mart said he'd try to set up a meeting of the three of us for the day after my arrival. He'd also found May Colson's address in Long Beach. Already my few days to be spent down in the smog sounded like they wouldn't be wasted.

'I'm thinking I'll fly on down to Puerto Vallarta when I leave you guys,' I told him. 'I want to have a look at Gregory and Baldini's houses, see if I can find out how they spend their time when they're down there. Maybe I can meet someone who can tell me something useful.'

'I might be able to help you with that,' Marty said in response.

'How?'

'I'll tell you when you get here. Drive careful on the way down, okay?'

'I will, buddy. Thanks for everything. See you tomorrow afternoon.'

I'd hardly ended my call when the cell rang in my hand. The call window showed it was Geri. I hit the talk button.

'Hey, Ger. How's it going?'

'Going good. I'm at the office in Crescent City. How'd your meeting go this morning?'

'Very well. Agent Peters will be contacting you on your cell sometime soon.'

'He already has. And explained what he's setting up here. I told him I'd contact him if I learned anything myself.'

'Good. That it?'

'Nope. There's another piece of news. The Humboldt County Sheriff's office was called out yesterday to investigate a burned out vehicle found on a back road off Highway 299 up toward Willow Creek. Guess what it turned out to be?'

'Don't tell me. The Jeep.'

'Yep. The black Jeep Wrangler. Which is now very black indeed.'

'They're sure it was our black Wrangler?'

'They say they are. The description fits exactly, right down to the crumpled back bumper that Aikins told us about.'

'What about the license number?'

'The plates had been removed, but they should find out who it was registered to from the serial and chassis numbers. That should lead us to someone who can tell us something.'

'Let's hope so. That's great news. So that confirms the guys were based in Humboldt.'

'Very probably. But whether they're still there is another question. I would think that by now they've fled south, probably back to Mexico.'

'Quite likely. Anything yet from Bridger?'

'He called me last night. He's not noticed anything suspicious yet but he's been pretty busy settling into his new job.'

'Manuel back at work?'

'Apparently not. Bridger didn't say anything about him so I assume he's still off. What are your plans now, Arnie?'

I told Geri I was heading down to L.A. on Sunday to check into a few things, and that I'd give her regular updates on what I discovered there. She promised to do the same.

'Did you enjoy your time with Lorraine and Mandy?' she asked, coquettishly.

'You know I did. What about you? Seen that handsome CHP officer lately?'

'Had dinner with him last night as it happens.'

'Glad to hear it. I feel better knowing you've got a caring hunk of a policeman keeping an eye on you.'

'Yeah. I'm kind of glad of that, too.'

A male voice in the background said something and Geri responded, turning briefly away from her phone.

'Got to go,' she said when she came back. 'Duty calls.'

'Be careful out there.'

'I will. You, too.'

The following day, Saturday, I spent catching up with household accounts and bills. In the afternoon I watched a few innings of a Giants' baseball game on the box and drank a couple beers. Then I had a pizza delivered, ate it with an improvised salad made up from leftovers and had an early night. I went to sleep almost immediately. I must've been tired.

Driving to L.A. the next day I had two choices, the speed route on I-5 down the San Joaquin Valley via Fresno and Bakersfield, or the scenic route through Monterey, Santa Maria and Santa Barbara on wonderful Highway 1. As the weather was lovely and I was in no hurry I chose the latter, set off around 10:00 AM and spent a relaxed day driving down a relatively empty mostly two-lane highway enjoying the sea views and the salt air with my windows open and my hair blowing in the wind.

Martin and Connie's house was in a pleasant tree-lined street in Westwood not far from the Los Angeles National Cemetery. I pulled into their drive just after 5:00, and by 5:30 I was in their backyard draped over a plastic lounger beside their pool. I had a vodka and tonic in my hand and there was an assortment of nibbles arrayed on the table beside me. On the other side of the table Mart sat on his own lounger nursing a martini, his crossed legs extended before him. Connie was inside, making preparations for the promised feast.

'We're seeing Lt. Mike Brundage tomorrow morning at 10:00,' he said.

'Where? At the Pasadena department?'

'Nah. Mike thought it'd be better to meet somewhere neutral. I gather there are doubts about the integrity of some of the Pasadena detectives and she doesn't want to risk word getting back to the gangbangers that you're asking around about them. No, there's a coffee house on Sunset Boulevard that we go to sometimes. She'll meet us there.'

'She? Lt. Brundage ... 'Mike' Brundage ... is a woman?'

Martin grinned across at me.

'That's right. And a damned fine-looking one at that. Her real name's Michelle, but she earned such a reputation for being ballsy that it got changed to Mike.'

'Sounds like you know her pretty well,' I said, sipping my drink.

'We used to run around together back in the eighties. Long before Connie. Now we're just friends.'

'I look forward to meeting her.'

'Mike says she's got some news about the case. Oh, and here's something else for you.'

Martin opened a notebook lying on the table beside him and carefully ripped out a page, which he handed across to me. On it was written May Colson's Long Beach address. I nodded and slipped it into a pocket.

'Thanks for that,' I told him, picking up my drink again. 'Did you find out anything about her?'

'Only that she lives alone, and that she's almost a complete invalid because of her asthma. I gather the news of her son's death hit her pretty hard.'

'I should think it would. He was her only child and she relied on him pretty heavily.' I took another sip of my drink. 'I'll drive down and see her tomorrow afternoon. Unless you've got something else planned?'

He shook his head.

'Nope. After our meeting with Mike you're on your own. If you want more help from me, though, you know you only have to ask for it. When do you think you'll be heading south?'

'To Mexico? Probably Wednesday or Thursday. That okay with you?'

'No problem at all. You're welcome to stay as long as you like. You know that. I'm hoping before you go I'll have some news for you from my contact in Puerto Vallarta.'

My eyebrows lifted. 'You have a contact there?'

'I do. An investigative journalist like us. Guy named Paco Jimenez. Used to write for the English language newspaper in Mexico City, *The News*, as well as for various other Mexican journals. We met at a convention fifteen years ago and we've kept in touch ever since.'

'He's now in Puerto Vallarta?'

'Yeah. From the mid-nineties on the C.I.A. made a big effort in Mexico City to recruit English-speaking journalists to push their own political agendas in the Mexican press. Like others, Paco was wined and dined and offered sweeteners in an effort to pull him into their stable. But Paco wouldn't play ball, told them in no uncertain terms where to get off. As a result, the C.I.A. planted rumors about him and his Mexico City career came to an abrupt end. For the past eight years he's been living in Puerto Vallarta, working for the local rag there, the *NotiVallarta*. Like us, he hates corrupt public officials, and apart from covering the local news he spends his free time quietly researching what goes on behind the scenes in an effort to expose the bad guys as and when he can – which he's done on several occasions very successfully. He's a good man.'

'What you got him doing for me?' I asked.

'I told him you were investigating a couple of high level American lawyers who might be involved in cartel drug sales, and that you'd discovered they both have big haciendas near Puerto Vallarta. I gave him their names and Paco said he'd look into it. Said he'd be delighted to help any way he could.'

'That's great, Mart. Thanks. We'll see if he manages to learn anything interesting.'

Dinner that night was as great as I had anticipated. Prawns in garlic butter to start followed by an amazing Azerbaijani lamb dish with cous cous, green beans and broccoli, finishing off with a mouth-watering orange syllabub and fresh-made chocolate chip cookies. The meal was suitably brought to an end watching the sunset on the back deck with brandies and freshly brewed Columbian coffee. It was indeed a feast, and I went to bed an hour or two later a replete and very happy man.

Chapter Twenty-Two

Monday, May 26

Lt. Mike Brundage was everything Marty had described and more: ballsy, buxom and attractive. Though she was beginning to put on a bit of weight here and there she was still a woman who would turn heads and I took to her immediately.

She was waiting for us at a shaded table in the sparsely-peopled fenced-in side garden at the coffee shop and rose to greet us when we stepped out into the sunshine. She was wearing a light blue linen pants suit and a white shirt with two buttons undone at the neck, revealing a generous wedge of tanned cleavage. Her slightly greying blonde hair was gathered into a neat chignon, and her eyes were large and very blue. Mart introduced us and when she shook my hand her grasp was firm.

'Pleased to meet you, Arnie,' she said, smiling and resettling herself onto her chair. 'Marty's told me a lot about you.'

'Likewise,' I said, taking the seat beside her at the table. 'But all good.'

She raised an eyebrow at him. 'I hope so. He'd better not be telling you any old secrets.'

Marty laughed as he sat at her other side.

'Nothing that would embarrass you, doll,' he said. 'Anyway, all that was a very long time ago.'

A waitress appeared to take our orders. I asked for a latte, Mart an espresso. Mike already had a cappuccino. When the girl went back inside Mike turned again to me.

'Marty's told me you're covering a homicide investigation up north. I gather the thinking is that it might have ties to the gangs down here, is that right?'

'Yes, it is.'

I briefly reprised the story of the discovery of the body, explained my involvement with the case, and described Geri's and my interview with Josh Bridger and his revelations about Davey Colson. Then I brought her up to date on everything discovered thus far in the investigation, concluding by saying that there definitely seemed to be a connection with some L.A. gang. When I finished she sat looking at me, nodding her head slowly.

'That's all possible,' she said finally. 'Over the last few years we've been putting a lot of pressure on the local gangs, so it stands to reason they'd be trying to develop new operations up north, away from our intense surveillance.'

She reached down to her feet and lifted a file folder that was leaning against her purse. Opening it, she took out a sheaf of photographs which she handed to me.

'Those are the photos of the Latinos lifted from the CCTV cameras at that store in Del Norte.'

I took the pictures and glanced through them. There were five images altogether. Some were grainy and indistinct, but two or three of the faces had been caught full on and the images were clear.

'The Humboldt County Sheriff told me his department didn't recognize any of these guys.' I glanced up. 'Do you?'

She smiled. 'As a matter of fact we do. Some of them. That's the news I wanted to give you.' She took back the photos, sifted through them and pulled out three, which she handed across to me. The face in the first picture was fairly clear. It was the Latino with the scar and the tattoo. In the picture the scar showed as a dark line down the left side of his face beneath his dark glasses. The tattoo was pretty much an unclear shadow covering the front of his neck.

'Scarface is well known to us,' Mike said. 'His name is Luis *'El Gordo'* Guzman. He's a member of our most prominent Latino gang and he's been missing for several months – ever since he jumped bail from a charge of aggravated assault. One of the other men is also known to us, another local gang member, Angel *'El Duque'* Rochas, known as 'the duke' apparently because of his taste for fine clothes. He's currently on the run from a warrant for auto theft.' She glanced up at me. 'The Wrangler, incidentally, was registered in his name. He was traced via the engine block serial number. We checked the address given for him but someone else is living there now. They didn't seem to know anything about Rochas or his current whereabouts and we believed them. The third picture is of a guy we deported some months ago for illegal entry but who obviously found his way back in again. His name's Enrique 'Quique' Bardén. All three of them have known connections to the Hispanic gang I mentioned.'

While I perused the photographs Mike went on to explain that there had been gangs in Pasadena for years, but that in the late nineties and the early years of the new millennium the incidents of serious drug crime had increased alarmingly – becoming so bad by 2006 that the authorities decided to do something about it.

'Our department created a "Safe Streets Task Force",' she went on, 'to focus on reducing criminal gang activity in the San Gabriel Valley – working in tandem with the L.A. County Sheriff's Office, the L.A.P.D., the FBI and the DEA. Over the last six or eight years several operations have been initiated targeting various gangs and their thieving, drug dealing, protection racketeering, and prostitution networks. During that time our intelligence has improved markedly, with the result that every new operation we put together has had better results. Arrests and prosecutions are up, gang related murders and assaults are down, so it's obviously hitting the gangs where they live.'

'Which gangs are active in your area?' I asked.

'We have a bunch – black, Hispanic and Asian. We went after the worst ones first. Just under a year ago we mounted "Operation Thumbs Down", directed against the Rollin' 30s Harlem Crips, an African/American group that specializes in burglary, extortion and selling crack cocaine. That operation resulted in the arrest of more than two dozen gang members and the recovery of a significant cache of drugs, weapons and stolen goods. Then last December we brought to a close "Operation Rosebud", another anti-gang operation that'd been ongoing for about eighteen months and which resulted in the arrest of another couple dozen gangbangers and the recovery of over sixty pounds of methamphetamines and sizeable stocks of heroin and cocaine, with a total street value of around two and a half million dollars. That operation targeted the largest and most deadly of the local gangs – the one the guys in the photos all belong to or have close connections with – the Varrio Pasadena Rifa, which without doubt has direct connections with the Mexican Sinaloa cartel.'

'Sinaloa,' I said. 'That's the name that's been mentioned in relation to the drug dealing in Del Norte County.'

I told her about Geri's conversation with Conchita Guillén. Mike seemed to accept her story at face value.

'Which brings me to the point of this conversation,' she said, sitting forward and resting her forearms on the table. 'Marty asked me to inquire if any of our undercover informers had heard of a connection between the gangs, the Sinaloa cartel, and some major shot-caller up north. I had a few of my colleagues ask around to see what they could turn up. We all had pretty much the same results. The informers, of course, know no names or locations, except in the most general terms. It's common knowledge, however, that the Varrio Pasadena Rifa leadership has opened up in the last few years extensive growing and dealing operations in northern California, committing to these enterprises a considerable number of men – mostly illegals brought in from Mexico. They've got marijuana plantations dotted all around the Emerald Triangle that provide the bulk of their local supply. We know that from the busts that the local authorities and the DEA have made. That's quite likely where your three perps are holed up right now. In fact that's almost certainly where they're hiding, given the discovery of the burned out Wrangler in the mountains near Humboldt's eastern border. But the gangs are still running regular shipments of methamphetamines, heroin and crack cocaine from the L.A. area up the San Joaquin Valley and into Oregon and northern California to feed the distribution networks they've set up there. We know that from the vehicles that've been intercepted along the way. At least one of these networks involves an entity known as '*El Avogado,*' the lawyer, as the principal shot-caller. Your D.A. in Del Norte might well be the man in question.'

'Is there any way we can determine for sure that it's him?' I asked.

She sat back, shaking her head.

'Not unless we get lucky and arrest someone at the top end of the distribution chain who's willing to talk. That's the problem. The guys we catch who we know are heavily involved in the trafficking never say anything about their colleagues or the way they work. They know they'd be topped in prison if they did, and that if they keep shtoom their silence will be rewarded once they're out again. So they play dumb.'

I nodded. 'Well, maybe we can come across something up there that proves the link. Or someone.'

She smiled. 'That's your best bet, I'm afraid. But let me know if there's anything more I can do to help from down here.'

That pretty much exhausted the business of our meeting, so for the next few minutes the three of us just sat together enjoying our coffees and shooting the breeze. I gathered that Mike and Marty met here periodically, just as valued old friends. She apparently knew and liked Connie and was obviously considered no threat by her. This was reinforced by the presence on Mike's left hand of a sizeable wedding ring and further confirmed when she mentioned that she and her husband were vacationing in Europe in two weeks' time.

'What does he do, your husband?' I asked her.

'He's the managing director of a company called CamSec Systems that manufactures and sells commercial surveillance and security packages,' she said. 'But he started out as a cop, just like us.' She smiled at Mart.

'Alan's an old buddy of mine,' he said. 'We were all three rookies together. Alan was always jealous of my friendship with Mike, and when he realized I was too stupid to move in on her seriously he made his own advances and laid his claim.'

I smiled. 'I reckon he's a lucky man.'

'He is,' Mart says. 'And he knows it.'

'I don't suppose,' I said to Mike after a few moments of silence, 'that you know anything about the young offenders' camp that shut down in east L.A. County back in 2003, Camp Belleview?'

She turned to look at me, her face expressionless.

'Camp Belleview? Yeah, I've heard of it. Rumor had it there were some unsavory things going on there and they had to close it. Why do you ask?'

I told her about Davey Colson's time at Belleview, and the abuse he suffered there at the hands of Lamont Gregory and others. As I spoke Mike's jaw set hard.

'Dirty fuck,' she said when I was done. 'He's got to be brought down.'

'I second that,' Marty said, draining his cup and putting it on the table. 'For my part I'll keep looking for the missing information about the staff that was working at Belleview during the kid's stay there.'

Mike frowned at him. 'You couldn't find the staff records?'

'Gone,' Marty said. 'No inmate or staff records available anywhere that I could find. But as I say, I'll keep looking.'

'I'll see what I can come up with, too,' Mike added. 'There's obviously a cover-up, probably directed from somewhere high up.'

'Well,' I said, 'Lamont Gregory, the Del Norte D.A., is a good friend of Anthony Baldini. That's pretty high up.'

Mike frowned at me again. 'Baldini? The Attorney General?'

'The very same.'

'He could do it, to be sure.' Mike sat back, inhaled deeply and then let it out in a long sigh. 'Well, well. You've uncovered a nice can of worms, haven't you, Arnie?'

I smiled at her.

'That's my job, Lieutenant.'

Marty and I had come in our separate cars so after I had thanked Mike for her time and efforts and we had all said our goodbyes the lieutenant set off back toward Pasadena and Marty toward Westwood and home. I watched them go from my driver's seat, then fired up the Tom Tom GPS that normally lives in my jockey box, fed into it May Colson's Long Beach address, and aimed the battered Chevy out onto Sunset Boulevard. The pre-lunch-hour traffic was light so I made good time, turning off onto Santa Monica Boulevard, then picking up the 405 south to Highway 710, which took me straight down into Long Beach. Half an hour later I was cruising along May Colson's street, looking for her number. When I found it, the house was a pale yellow duplex that needed repainting, hers the right hand half. I pulled into the drive behind a vintage Volkswagen camper that hadn't been cleaned in a decade. The neighborhood was quiet with just a few people about, washing their cars or cutting their lawns. The day was starting to warm up.

Climbing out of the car, I stepped up to the low cement stoop and pressed the button beside the front door that was open beyond the latched screen. The buzz sounded inside above the murmur of the television that was flickering in one corner of the front room. I couldn't see the other corner, but assumed that was where Mrs. Colson was sitting. I was right. After a moment or two I heard movement and eventually she came into view, dragging an oxygen pump with her to feed the cannula that was wound round her ears, the nozzles pressed into her nostrils.

'Yes?' she said, her voice weak and breathy.

She was wearing a baggy T-shirt, wrinkled shorts and house slippers. Her arms and legs were thin and bony, her face gaunt and haggard-looking, and there were dark circles under her eyes.

'Mrs. Colson, my name is Arnold Rednapp. I'm peripherally involved with the investigation into the murder of your son and I'd like to ask you a few questions, if you can spare the time.'

She frowned, cocking her head to one side.

'Are you with the police? Because I've already spoken to them. Told them all I knew about where Davey was going and what he was doing. Which wasn't much. He never told me anything about his movements.'

'No, I'm not with the police,' I told her, 'though they know I'm following the investigation. I'm a reporter for a bay area paper.'

I produced my press card from my wallet and held it out for her to peruse through the screen.

'The *South Bay Bulletin*. A reporter, eh? Well,' she said, unlocking the screen door latch and pushing it open, 'I guess you better come in.'

She stepped back allowing me to pass by her into the room, then pulled the screen closed again and latched it.

'Damn flies. Got to keep the screen tight shut or they come in in droves.'

'Yeah,' I said. 'They're a nuisance.'

Mrs. Colson gestured to a sofa along the front wall. Then she dragged her oxygen pump back across the room and sat herself down on the large reclining armchair in the corner opposite the TV.

'Sorry to interrupt your television,' I said, sitting on the sofa.

'No trouble. It's only a stupid game show. I keep it on for company, you know. It gets pretty lonely around here now that Davey's gone.'

'I'm sure it does.'

Mrs. Colson picked up the remote from the table beside her chair and pointed it at the screen, punching a button with her thumb. The screen went dead. Without the drone of the game show voices the only sounds that I could hear now were the hum of her oxygen pump and the occasional swish of a car passing outside.

The room was small and neat and filled with well-worn pieces of furniture. Apart from the armchair, the small table beside it, and the sofa with a coffee table before it, there was only the TV on a low stand and a small chiffonier against the off-street wall beside a hallway that apparently led to the rest of the house. Ranged across the top of the chiffonier were framed pictures of what looked to be Davey at various ages, sometimes with his mother, sometimes with friends. On the wall above the chiffonier was a large framed color photograph of Davey in uniform, wearing a tan beret. Mrs. Colson caught me looking at it.

'That was when Davey got into Delta Force. He was very proud of that picture. So am I.'

'I'm so sorry for your loss, Mrs. Colson.'

'That's nice of you, Mr. Rednapp. Thank you.' She squirmed a bit in her chair. 'Now then, what did you want to ask me?'

I pulled out my notepad and pen.

'Do you mind if I take notes?'

'Not at all. That's what reporters do, isn't it?'

'That's right.' I smiled at her. 'I met a friend of your son's a couple weeks ago, Josh Bridger. Do you know Josh?'

She nodded. 'Oh, yes. Josh's been through here several times since they left the Army. He's a good boy.'

'He certainly seems to be. I should tell you he's doing what he can to help with the investigation into Davey's murder. Davey was staying with him when he was abducted.'

'Is that so?'

'Yes. I met Josh with a deputy sheriff friend of mine who's involved in the investigation,' I told her. 'During our interview Josh told us a lot about Davey's past – that he'd lost his father when he was only a toddler, that he'd spent time in a youth correctional institution for drug dealing. Josh gave us a rough account of Davey's life up to his Army years, then a pretty full one about his time as a soldier – and the bits after his discharge that Josh knew anything about. It's clear from what he told us that your son had trouble adjusting to civilian life after his release from the Army.'

'Oh, yes. Davey was always a rebel. Didn't want anyone to boss him. That's why I was surprised he was so happy as a soldier.'

'Apart from Josh, did Davey have any other good friends – people he stayed close to from his school years, say?'

'Not really, no. Most of Davey's school friends were Hispanics. Davey liked the Mexican culture, even learned a bit of the language.'

'He didn't keep any of them as friends when he got older?'

'No.' Mrs. Colson looked down at her hands, folded in her lap. 'Most of the young Chicano boys were into drugs and gangs by then. Davey didn't want that and stayed away – especially after he'd been in jail. So they finally just drifted apart.'

'What about...' I stopped. This was awkward. 'I'm sorry to ask, but did Davey make any friends while he was at Camp Belleview, the youth correctional facility where he spent his sentence?'

'You needn't be sorry. I don't mind talking about it. That camp was awful. It did something to Davey. He was never the same afterwards. He would never tell me what happened, but it was obvious they did something to him there. Something terrible. But yes, there was one boy from there he kept in touch with over the years. A fellow named Toby Hitchins.'

I wrote down the name.

'Did Toby ever visit here afterwards?'

'He did once, just for an hour or two. He was younger than Davey, and I gathered that while they were at Belleview Davey kind of looked after him – as much as he was able to, anyway. The boy never got over that. He worshipped Davey. But that made Davey nervous, so while he'd get in touch now and then to make sure Toby was all right he didn't try to encourage the friendship beyond what it was.'

'Do you have a contact number or an address for Toby, Mrs. Colson?'

'Lemme see.'

Being virtually an invalid, May Colson had arranged her little corner to contain all the important bits and pieces she might need during the day – tissues, medications, water bottles, plus address books and telephone directories, blank pads of paper and a cup full of pens and pencils. The telephone was in a stand at her elbow. Putting on a pair of reading spectacles, she sorted through the pile of address books and finally came up with a worn red one that she pulled onto her lap and began leafing through, licking her fingers to help turn the pages. After a moment she found what she was seeking.

'Here it is. "Toby Hitchins", under the "H's".' She read out his telephone number and address. 'He sends us a Christmas card every year,' she went on. 'I kept his address in here so I can send him one in return.'

I wrote the contact details down. Toby lived not far away in Torrence, which I had passed through on my way down Highway 405.

'Do you know what he's doing now?' I asked Mrs. Colson.

'Well, Toby was really broken by Belleview. That was one of the reasons Davey felt so protective of him. Again, I don't know what happened to the boys there, but it was something so bad that it twisted Toby's mind slightly. He's never been the same since. He can't hold down a job for long, and suffers from continual ill health. He's always going to the doctor about one thing or another.'

'How does he live? On welfare?'

'The house belongs to his mother's family. She's dead, but they let him live there because he's all alone now. I guess when he isn't working he lives on welfare and food stamps.'

I noted all this down. I would pay Toby a visit, but from the sound of it even if he would speak out about what happened to him at Belleview his testimony might not be allowed as evidence. That would depend on how *compos mentis* he was.

'Did your son or Toby ever mention the name Lamont Gregory?'

'Oh, yes,' she said immediately. 'Gregory was the attorney who prosecuted Davey. When he was convicted and sent to Belleview Gregory came out often to see the boys and help them settle in. For the first weeks Davey talked a lot about Gregory during my visits, saying what a help he'd been, how like a father he was toward him. Then suddenly all that changed and he never mentioned his name again. I asked him why but he wouldn't tell me.'

I nodded. 'I'll go see Toby. Maybe he can tell me what happened there. One last question, Mrs. Colson. Did Davey ever mention any other names, people who were on the staff at Belleview, guards or whatever?'

May Colson frowned, staring down at the floor, trying to remember.

'He never talked about the guards, no. At least not by name. He hated most of them, of course. As for other inmates, besides Toby the only name he ever mentioned was that of a Chicano boy that was with him there, Nacho Flores. Davey said Nacho was a hard case from the gangs who refused to follow the camp rules, and that the guards used to beat him up regularly after lights out. Sadly Nacho went back into crime after his release. I remember Davey showing me an article about him in the paper once – that he'd been convicted of a gang murder and sentenced to life in prison. Nacho was the only other inmate he ever talked about.' She paused, frowning. 'Now there was one of the staff members he got on pretty well with. One of the teachers that taught the boys during the day. What was his name? Mark? Mick?' She licked her lips. Then it came to her. 'No. Nick. Nick Parsons. That was it.'

I wrote down the name, along with that of Nacho Flores.

'Did Davey keep in touch with Mr. Parsons after he left Belleview?'

'Not that I know of, no. But he used to say that if it wasn't for Nick Parsons he would've lost his mind there. It was because of him that Davey decided to finish high school and get his diploma after he got out. Parsons told him he couldn't even get into the Army if he didn't do that.'

I nodded. 'That's true enough. So Parsons was a positive influence, obviously?'

'Oh, yes.'

'I wonder where he is now?' I asked, rhetorically.

'Heaven knows,' Mrs. Colson said. 'But wherever he is I hope he's all right.'

I left Mrs. Colson a few minutes later. She had offered to make me a cup of coffee or to fetch me a cold drink but I told her no, that I had another appointment I had to get to, and thanking her profusely I took my leave.

What I told May Colson was partly true, though the idea had only just then occurred to me.

I would stop by to see Toby Hitchins on my way back to Westwood.

Chapter Twenty-Three

Toby Hitchins lived in a small 1930's clapboard structure on a side street between Torrence and Redondo Beach. It was a single story family house set up on a high foundation, with a broad covered porch across the front that was reached via a flight of six wooden stairs. The porch had a solid railing, and on one side of it a plastic garden lounger sat beside a small wicker table – obviously a favorite hangout in the balmy summer late afternoons and evenings.

I parked the Cobalt at the curb before it, climbed out and made my way along the cracked cement pathway through a shallow band of sunburnt lawn and climbed up the stairs. The front door beyond the screen was closed but I could hear the hum of an air conditioner and so reckoned that someone was home. There was no bell so I opened the screen and knocked on the front door. On either side of the door ancient sash windows with lace curtains overlooked the porch. I waited a minute; then, when there was no response, I tried again – a bit louder this time. I was about to give up and retreat to my car when a voice came from the other side of the door.

'Who is it?'

The voice was light, treble, almost girlish.

'My name is Arnold Rednapp, Mr. Hitchins,' I told him through the door. 'I'm a reporter. I wonder if you could spare a couple minutes to answer a few questions?'

'Have you got I.D.?'

'Yes I do. I have my press card.'

I pulled it from my wallet. There was a rattling of a chain and the noise of bolts being drawn. Then the door opened a couple inches and I was gazing through the screen at a young man with tousled mousy-brown hair and dark, suspicious eyes. I held the press card up so he could read it.

'You're from San Francisco?'

'From the bay area, yes.'

He opened the door a bit wider, a puzzled expression replacing the suspicious look.

'What kind of questions do you want to ask me?'

'Mr. Hitchins, I'm covering the investigation into the murder of a friend of yours, Davey Colson.'

Hitchins looked like he'd been smacked in the stomach. His eyes bulged with shock and his mouth dropped open.

'Davey's dead?'

'I'm afraid so. His body was found in a river at the north end of the state two weeks ago.'

There was a stunned pause. Then Hitchins pushed open the screen and opened the door wide.

'You'd better come in.'

He moved back to make room for me, still looking pole-axed by the news. I stepped inside and he closed the door behind me. We were in a narrow hallway that seemed to cut the house virtually in two. Four or five doors opened off to the sides. The hallway walls were lined with dark wood up to a dado rail at stomach height. Above the dado rail stained and peeling wallpaper covered the rest of the wall to the ceiling molding. At the back of the hall a half-glazed door gave onto a fenced-in back yard. That door, too, was closed. I'd been right about the aircon. The house was almost cold, Hitchins had the temperature set so low. He stepped past me and turned back at the first door on the left.

'Come in, please.'

I followed him into the small front room and sat on the stuffed armchair he indicated to me. Hitchins sat on the threadbare sofa beside it, perching on the front edge with his hands on his knees. His mouth was still open.

'Davey's dead? I can't believe it.'

'I'm afraid it's true.'

I gave him the basic facts of the case, reducing the story to a couple minutes' exposition. By the time I was done he'd scooted back onto the sofa so that he was sitting properly, his hands clasped in his lap.

'I've just come from visiting Davey's mother,' I told him. 'She mentioned you were a friend of Davey's and suggested I might want to talk to you.'

He shook his head, confused. 'What about?'

'Mr. Hitchins... I'm sorry, but can I call you Toby?'

'Sure. Toby's fine.'

'Great. I'm Arnie.' He nodded. 'Toby,' I went on, 'I know that you and Davey were together at Camp Belleview back in the nineties. That's right, isn't it?'

He frowned, looked down at his hands, started to rub one with the other nervously.

'Yes. That's right. That was in '95 and '96.' He looked up at me, dropping his head with a look of suspicion. 'Why do you want to know?'

I reached into my shirt pocket and pulled out my notepad. 'Mind if I take notes?'

'No. Go ahead.'

I opened it to a fresh page and took out my pen.

'I met another friend of Davey's after his body was found, Toby. A man named Josh Bridger. He was with Davey in the Army. Did you ever meet him?'

He shook his head. 'No. But I've heard Davey mention his name. I know they were together in Iraq and Afghanistan, and that they had some scary times there.'

'That's right. Well, Josh Bridger told me Davey had told him that during the time he spent at Belleview some pretty terrible things were going on there. Is that true? Can you confirm that?'

Hitchins dropped his head even lower, gazing up at me from under his brows with haunted eyes.

'What kind of terrible things?'

'This isn't easy, Toby. I'm sure it's something you'd prefer not to remember, but apparently Davey was subjected to regular sessions of sexual abuse while he was an inmate at Belleview. Did that happen to you, too?'

'Why do you want to know?'

'Because we're trying ... the police are trying ... to gather enough evidence against the men who did these things so that they can finally be brought to justice for their crimes. Davey can't testify anymore against these men, but you could – if you experienced the same things. Did you?'

Hitchins looked down at his hands, worrying a thumbnail with the thumb of his other hand while he thought it over. Half a minute went by. Finally he looked up again.

'Yes. The same things happened to me as happened to Davey.'

'Can you tell me who it was that did these things? Can you give me any names?'

Hitchins shifted his position on the sofa.

'I ... I'm not sure I remember any names.'

'Please, try to remember, Toby. Any information you're able to offer that can help us nail these men will be greatly appreciated. After all, I'm sure you and Davey weren't the only boys who were abused that way at Belleview.'

He shook his head vigorously. 'Oh, no. There were several of us. It went on all the time.'

'Who did it? The guards?'

He nodded. 'Yes. Two of them.'

'Anyone else? Can you remember anyone coming from outside the camp who took part in these sessions?'

After a pause Toby nodded.

'There was one man. He was with the D.A.'s office. He came often at weekends and spent the night. When he did ... one or more of us would be taken to see him in his room.'

'Do you remember the man's name?'

'Yes. His name was Gregory. Lamont Gregory. He was an attorney who had helped to found Belleview. He liked to come out now and then to see how things were going. At least that's what he said.'

'Gregory was the only person from outside the camp that took part in these sessions?'

'No. Sometimes he would bring two or three other men with him – businessmen, it looked like. They were always well dressed, smartly turned out. Sometimes the men brought liquor, or drugs. Weed. Cocaine. They'd get drunk or stoned and then they'd make us strip and go to work on us.'

I nodded. 'Did Gregory use drugs? Did he get stoned, too?'

'No. But he'd drink sometimes.'

'What was your impression of Gregory – before the sexual abuse started, I mean?'

Toby shrugged. 'At first we thought he was just being nice, trying to help us adjust to the routine of the camp. But then the night sessions started and we knew that wasn't the reason he visited. He came because he had all of us to choose from, any boy he wanted to ... to do things to. We had no choice. If we resisted we were beaten. At the beginning I tried to stop them hurting me. That made them angry. They whipped me with their belts. Once I had to go to the infirmary because of the beating. Davey, too. They were always beating people. One Latino boy was beaten so badly he had to be taken to the hospital and he was gone a couple of weeks.'

'Was that boy Nacho Flores?'

Toby looked at me, surprised.

'How did you know?'

'May Colson mentioned he'd been badly beaten. Do you know if he was also being sexually abused?'

'I don't know. I doubt it. They might've tried but he would've fought them. He was tough – a Chicano gangboy who hated the guards and refused to do what he was told. He was beaten for that, too. But for the rest of us, we were beaten if we didn't do the sex things with them. Finally we just gave in. It was easier.'

'Was it always just one man at a time? Gregory, or one of the guards? Or did they do these things together – the guards and Gregory and the others?'

'Sometimes it was just a guard, or just Gregory. Sometimes it was a couple of them together. And the outsiders.'

'Did they bring more than one boy to abuse?'

'Yes. Usually they brought in two of us. They seemed to like it when we were both being fucked up the ass at the same time. It excited them to hear us crying with the pain. Made them feel more macho.'

'Do you remember the guards' names?'

'We weren't allowed to call them by name. We had to call them "sir".'

'Yes, but you must remember their surnames. Didn't they wear nametags?'

Hitchins looked down at his hands.

'Yes,' he said finally. 'They wore nametags during the day. One of them was a big man with a pot belly named Del Pritchard. I remember he had tattoos on his arms, an anchor and a mermaid. The other guard's name was Delgado, Robert Delgado. They were both older, somewhere in their fifties, I think. Both had been cops before they became guards at the camp.' Toby looked up, fear in his eyes. 'They told us they'd kill us if we ever spoke to anyone about what happened there. They said they'd find us, wherever we were. That's why no one ever said anything.'

I wrote down the names and the descriptions Toby had given me.

'What about the camp supervisor ... what was his name?' I flipped through my notebook pages till I found the entry I made from Marty's first telephone conversation. 'Marshall. Clifford Marshall. Did he take part in these sessions?'

Hitchins shook his head. 'No. At least I never saw him, or heard of him doing that.'

'Did you know who he was?'

'Oh, yes. We met him the day we arrived. He was scary. We were taken to his office. He was older, about sixty, and had this thick southern accent. He gave us a lecture about how we had to follow all the rules, said that whatever the guards told us to do we had to do it. He said if we didn't we'd be made to suffer for it. Then he gave us each a brand new Bible and told us to pray and mend our ways.'

I nodded. 'But he never took part in any of the sex sessions with Gregory or the guards?'

'No sir, not so far as I know he didn't. He lived with his wife in a house that was set apart from the bunkhouses where we were kept. He might not even have known what was going on after lights out.'

'And your teacher at the camp, do you remember him?'

Toby looked up. 'Mr. Parsons? Oh, sure. He was always nice to me.'

'Do you think he knew what was going on with you and the others?'

Toby frowned. 'No. I don't think so. He left the camp and went home at night. And no one would've told him about it. We were all too scared.'

I nodded. 'How old a man was he?'

'He must've been, I don't know, maybe in his late twenties or early thirties?'

'So he was pretty young?'

'Yes.'

'And you didn't keep in touch after you left? You've no idea where he is now?'

He shook his head. 'No.'

For a moment neither of us spoke, our minds still entangled in the labyrinth of horror that had played out regularly at Belleview during those years.

'Toby,' I said finally, 'I'm going to find those two guards, wherever they are. When I do, do you think you'd be able to identify them – the ones who abused you and Davey and the others? Could you pick them out of a line-up?'

'Oh, yes. I'll never forget them.'

'Fine. I'll track them down, I promise. If I do, and you can positively identify them, would you be willing to testify in a court of law against them? Would you be willing to describe what they did to you, to all of you?'

Hitchins shook his head, suddenly afraid again. 'I don't know...'

'Toby, it's not right that these men should get away with what they did. Wouldn't you like to see them imprisoned for the terrible things they did to you and the others? Isn't it time they were made to pay?'

It took a fierce inner struggle for Toby to reach a decision but eventually he did.

'Yes, Mr. Rednapp. For Davey's sake I'd be willing to testify against them.'

'Good man.'

I took down Toby's landline and cell numbers, told him I'd be in touch as soon as I had something to tell him, and left. Stepping out into the baking sunshine after spending time in the icy cool of his dark house was a shock to the system.

Before I started my drive back to Westwood I pulled out my cell, dug out Devonne Peters' card with his cell number and dialed it. It rang two or three times before it was picked up.

'Yes? Peters here.'

'Devonne, it's Arnie Rednapp. Got a minute?'

'Yeah, Arnie. Go ahead. You're in L.A. now, aren't you? What've you got?'

'I've hit the jackpot, I think.'

I told him about the morning rendezvous with Lt. Mike Brundage and the meetings with May Colson and Toby Hitchins. I finished by saying that Toby had confirmed he, too, had been abused by Lamont Gregory, as well as by some of the guards, and, further, that he was willing to testify against them all in a court of law. Then I gave him the guards' names.

'That's good, Arnie,' Peters said. 'But we'll need more than one witness to make a case stand against these men. Did your guy give you the names of any other inmates who suffered the same treatment? Or of any other people involved in perpetrating the abuse?'

'Hitchins didn't name any other victims, and he said besides the two guards there was only Lamont Gregory that regularly abused him and the others, though he did say Gregory brought occasional 'friends' from outside to the sessions. He also named another inmate who'd had a particularly rough time there, a Latino gangbanger named Nacho Flores. Mrs. Colson also mentioned him. Hitchins doesn't believe he was sexually abused, though. He said the kid was just a rebel who refused to follow orders and nearly got beaten to death for it. I gather he's doing life in some prison now. For murder.'

'Mm.' Devonne sighed. 'Okay. I'll track down the two guards and see if I can find your Latino murderer. In the meantime did your contacts name any other staff members at Belleview at that time, anyone who might be able to corroborate this information?'

'There was a teacher that Davey Colson spoke of to his mother. Apparently the guy was the only positive influence at the place. His name was Nick Parsons. Hitchins spoke well of him, too. I thought I'd try to find him. He must be still teaching somewhere. I'll try tracking him down on the internet.'

'Good idea. Let me know if you can't and I'll put somebody onto it. We have access to data bases that you don't.' Peters paused. 'You're sure this Hitchins fellow can positively identify the guards who abused him? As well as Gregory?'

'Oh, yes. Hitchins said he remembers them all very clearly, that he'd have no difficulty in identifying them again. He said he would never forget their faces.'

'I should think he wouldn't. Anything else?'

'Only that I'm thinking of heading down to Puerto Vallarta the day after tomorrow to take a look at Gregory and Baldini's properties. Maybe I can learn something useful down there.'

'As I said before, be careful, Arnie. If they are dealing with the cartels they'll have informers around keeping an eye on things. Watch your back.'

'I'll do that Devonne. And I'll call if I learn anything.'

'Thanks. I promise I'll return the favor.'

Two minutes later I was on my way back to Westwood.

I got a text while en route to the Taylors' house. It was from Geri Mitchell.

'Got news. Call me.'

I waited till I'd pulled into the Taylors' driveway and shut down before returning her call. She picked up immediately.

'What's new?' I asked her.

'Plenty, Arnie. First, one of the men in those pictures from the Hiouchi Hamlet store CCTV is definitely Manuel Fernandez, the informer at La Cantina. Ryan recognized him straight away. He also recognized the beat-up pickup as Fernandez's. He wasn't able to identify the man that was with Manuel in the pickup. The image was too fuzzy, and the man was always hunched over and was never standing clearly in shot. He also didn't recognize the three Latinos in the Wrangler.'

'He wouldn't,' I told Geri. 'Those guys are definitely from out of town.'

'How do you know that?'

I described our meeting with Mike Brundage that morning, her news that the Pasadena Police had identified the three Varrio Pasadena Rifa heavies.

'You'll probably be told that tomorrow morning,' I said. 'Better look surprised when you hear it.'

Then I told her about my meetings with May Colson and Toby Hitchins, that Hitchins had been able to name the two guards involved in the sexual abuse, and that he'd confirmed Gregory as an additional abuser. I also told her of my call to Devonne Peters. Finally I announced that I was planning to fly down to Puerto Vallarta in two days' time to take a look at things down there.

'Well,' she said. 'I wish I was going down there with you. I could use a couple days of sun and sand.'

'I won't be enjoying myself much, kiddo, I can assure you. And I won't be there any longer than I need be. This is no pleasure trip. What's been happening with Josh Bridger? Is Manuel back at work yet?'

'Josh called me this lunchtime. Manuel's still away but Josh said a strange thing happened at the morning break. Apparently he's always careful to wear gloves when he's around the other workers in the fields to cover up the tattoos on his hands. Well, Josh was sitting by himself at break time this morning and had taken off his gloves to roll a cigarette. He was just licking it closed when one of the Latino workers, a young guy named Pepe Hidalgo, turned a corner of the barn and came upon him suddenly. Josh said that when Pepe saw the tattoos he stopped cold in his tracks, his eyes big as saucers. Then he apparently turned around and beat a hasty retreat. Josh's sure the guy recognized the tats. Which means he might've had something to do with Davey's abduction and murder.'

'Unless he saw Davey's tattoos at the soccer game at La Joya and was just spooked to see them again on Josh's hands. But you're right. He could be the man in the photos that we can't identify. And if he is he'll certainly go straight to his boss and Josh'll be in the soup. What's Josh intend to do about it?'

'There's nothing he can do,' Geri said. 'He'll just have to be more vigilant.'

'Maybe he'd better quit and get back to the safety of his cabin?'

'Not a chance,' Geri said. 'He's too keen to help find Davey's murderers. He's going to call me again tonight. When will you be finished in Mexico?'

'I'm only spending one night there. I'll be back in L.A. Thursday. Why, do you need me up there?'

She sighed. 'I don't know. The way things are moving I might need you sooner rather than later. It all depends on what Gregory decides to do about Josh.'

'Let me know when something happens,' I said. 'If I'm too far away you can always call Agent Peters. You still seeing that Highway Patrolman?'

'As often as I can. I feel kind of safer when he's around.'

'I'm sure you do. You becoming an item, you two?'

'It's starting to look that way.'

I told her that made me happy on two counts – firstly for the brightening of her life, and secondly for the added security his regular presence gave. She laughed, but said she agreed with that assessment.

There wasn't anything else. We wished each other well, promising to talk again soon, and I clicked off and went inside.

Over drinks I told Marty what I'd found out from May Colson and Toby Hitchins. He smiled when I produced the names of the two guards. At last we had someone to go after. He said he'd use his contacts to see what he could learn about them.

Dinner that night was less fancy but no less delicious. It was Marty's turn this time: veal scaloppini with wild rice in a creamy mushroom sauce and fresh asparagus. Dessert was an apple sponge with English style custard, again wonderful.

After dinner I retired to my guest room and played with my laptop, surfing the net, looking for some kind of official register of educators in the State of California. I didn't have much hope I'd actually track down Davey Colson's old teacher, but I thought it was worth trying. I came across a website called 'Commission on Teacher Credentialing' which purported to have a list of all credentialed teachers working in the state. There was a search bar. I clicked on it, keyed 'Nicholas Parsons' into the slot and clicked 'Search'. After a few seconds his name popped up on the screen. No address, just his name and his teaching credentials, listed from his earliest elementary qualifications to his more recent secondary credentials and their dates of issuance. The fact that he was on the registry at all proved, I thought, that he was still in California and still teaching, though now at high school level – all this, of course, depending on whether this Nicholas Parsons was the 'Nick' Parsons I was seeking.

Then I tried another tack, searching out the California White Pages website and again keying in the name 'Nicholas Parsons'. I got a list of 34 from all over the state. The useful thing was that each person's age was given at the side of the entry, so I could immediately weed out a good number of the candidates as they were over 60. Hitchins had reckoned that when they were at Belleview together Parsons had been in his late twenties or early thirties, which would make him now somewhere in his mid to late forties. There were two Nicholas Parsons listed in their forties, one living in Chico, the other in Anaheim. I rang both. Neither was a teacher and neither had ever worked at Camp Belleview. I tried another angle.

Backtracking, I entered 'Nick Parsons' into the White Pages name slot and pressed 'Search' again. This time there were only half a dozen entries, and only two in their forties. I tried the first, who lived in Santa Cruz, south of San Francisco. This Nick Parsons was a mechanic and couldn't help me. The second 'Nick' lived in Lancaster, north of L.A. a hundred miles or so, out beyond Burbank and Palmdale and across the San Gabriel Mountains at the edge of the Mojave Desert. I called his number. It rang three or four times before it was answered.

'Hello?'

The voice was male, light and friendly sounding.

'Mr. Nick Parsons?'

'Yes. Can I help you?'

'Are you by any chance the same Nick Parsons that used to teach at the Camp Belleview correctional institute for boys in L.A. County?'

There was a very long pause, and for a moment I thought the connection had been lost.

'Mr. Parsons? You still there?'

'Who is this?' he asked at last, his voice now edgy and suspicious.

'My name's Arnold Rednapp, Mr. Parsons. I'm a reporter for a paper in the bay area, the *South Bay Bulletin*?'

'A reporter?'

'That's right. I'm currently covering the investigation into the murder of a former inmate at Belleview, a man who as a boy was taught by you there and who spoke well of you after his release. Apparently you made a big impact on his life, and were a great help to him during his time as an inmate.'

There was another pause, but not so long this time.

'What was the boy's name?'

'David Colson. Do you remember him by any chance?'

'Davey Colson's dead?'

There was shock in his voice. And a touch, I thought, of fear, which I found strange.

'I'm afraid so. He was murdered by a person or persons unknown up in Del Norte County, at the north end of the state, just over two weeks ago.'

Parsons murmured something that sounded like, 'Omigod, not another one,' but I couldn't be sure.

'What was that?' I asked.

'Nothing. Please, go on.'

'As I said I've been covering the investigation as it progresses, and I'm trying now to learn as much as I can about Davey's youth. His time at Belleview seemed to have a huge negative impact on his life, and I'd like to talk to someone who knew him there in an effort to understand what it was that affected him so.'

'I don't understand,' he said, tentatively. 'What ... do you want from me?'

I sighed. How candid could I be with this guy? Did he know anything at all about what went on with the boys at Belleview while he was away from the camp? I decided to take a chance. After all, what'd I have to lose?

'You were on the staff at Belleview, isn't that right?' I asked him. 'You were a teacher there? Of the younger boys?'

'For a couple of years, yes. A long time ago, now.'

'Then you must've had some inkling of what went on in the place ... after hours?'

'What do you mean?'

I sighed again. 'Mr. Parsons, Davey told a close friend of his from his Army years that during the time he spent at Belleview he was regularly sexually assaulted by certain of the guards there, and by another man who visited the camp from outside. I've had corroboration of this story from someone else who was there during that period, and who was able to offer specific information about the men involved in the abuse. I hesitate to ask this, but were you aware during your time there of any kind of dubious activity going on with the boys?'

Now there was a really long pause. I sat at my end of the phone and waited, hoping that he'd come back with something useful. He finally did.

'Mr. Rednapp, I'm not going to discuss this over the phone. I may be taking a huge risk, but if you'd care to come to see me in person I'll be happy to talk to you. Where are you now?'

'In west Los Angeles. I could drive to Lancaster tomorrow, be there when you finish teaching? Would that be all right?'

'I'll have to tell Audrey I'll be home late, but yes. Come to the school. Be there at 5 PM. I'll meet you at the front entrance. Oh, and bring your press I.D. There's a quiet bar nearby where we can talk. Would that work for you?'

'Mr. Parsons, that'd be great. Thank you.'

He gave me the school's address and I jotted it down in my notebook.

'So Davey was in the Army?' he asked when that was done.

'Yeah. Spent eight years in the military. Ended up in Special Ops. Delta Force. Saw lots of action in Iraq and Afghanistan and was decorated for his efforts.'

'Was he!' Parsons was obviously pleasantly surprised. 'I knew he was an intelligent boy, and courageous, but I doubted he'd ever do anything useful with his life. I didn't think he had the motivation. I'm pleased to hear that he did.'

'Davey always said if it hadn't been for you he wouldn't have survived Belleview. You were that great an influence on him. What's more, he went on to finish high school because you had urged him to. He felt he owed you a lot.'

'I'm... Well, that's... Gosh! I'm very moved. He was a good boy. Poor Davey.'

'Yeah. Poor Davey. So, Mr. Parsons. I'll be at the school's front entrance tomorrow at five in the afternoon. I'll be waiting in a blue Chevy Cobalt.'

'Right. See you then.'

We hung up.

Chapter Twenty-Four

In his home office overlooking the back deck and the Pacific Ocean beyond, Lamont Gregory paced nervously back and forth before the sliding glass doors in the late afternoon light, his second cell phone pressed tight to his ear. He was beginning to think it wasn't going to be answered when, at long last, the line was clicked open.

'Yes?'

With relief the grey-haired attorney moved to his padded armchair and settled onto it, leaning forward over his desk.

'It's me again. Sorry to bother you but the problem we spoke of earlier has gotten worse. As I expected it might.'

'Has it? In what way?'

Gregory sighed. 'I got a phone call today. One of the new casual laborers on my farm apparently has the same tattoos on his hands that the person we dealt with earlier had. Almost identical, so I'm told.'

'What's unusual about that? Lots of men wear tattoos these days.'

'These are military tattoos, Marcos. And not just your usual eagles or anchors. My informant says Colson told them his tattoos represented his unit in the Special Forces. He said every one of the men in his squad had the same tattoos on their hands. This man was hired by my manager only a couple days ago – which must mean he's one of Colson's Army buddies who's trying to find out what happened to him.'

'Special Forces, eh?' The Latino at the other end of the line chuckled dryly. 'No wonder Colson gave my men so much trouble. So, what do you want to do about it?'

There was a slight pause before Gregory spoke again.

'The fact that he came to my farm to find work means he obviously has some information already, from somewhere, and is trying to learn more. I can't have that. I'm going to try to take care of this myself, but if that doesn't work I might have to ask you to send up another team to help me. Either way there's got to be some serious housecleaning done or our whole operation's threatened. If I do need a team sent, Marcos, I want real professionals this time. No plantation amateurs. This time it's got to be done right.'

'I hear you, *amigo*. I have just the men in mind. Our friends down south have a team of former Zetas they keep on hand stateside in case a situation arises that requires their specialist talents. This sounds like just such an occasion. You know about the Zetas?'

'Yes. They were highly trained commandos in the Mexican Army who deserted and became enforcers for the Gulf Cartel. The GC used them very effectively during their war with the Juarez Cartel a few years back in Chihuahua. They were known as bloodthirsty, merciless thugs. Hundreds of people died.'

'Right. But they won their war. Six months ago our southern friends recruited a few of them from the GC and they've been temporarily passed on to us. All I have to do is give the word and they'll come to you.'

Gregory sighed again. 'I won't have them here unless there's no other choice. I don't like it, I told you that. But if my own people can't handle things I'll have to call them in. Something drastic has to be done or the whole enterprise will collapse and I'll go down with it.'

'*Claro*. Well, just let me know. If you need them they can be with you in two days.'

'Thank you for that.'

Lamont Gregory sat back, ready to close the conversation. But the man at the other end spoke again.

'Before you go...'

'Yes?'

'I'm afraid I have more bad news for you. It might mean more problems.'

'What news?'

'The Pasadena police have been making inquiries again, pressuring their snitches in the community. I hear this from my contact in the department. They're asking about connections between VPR, the cartel and a certain bigwig shot-caller in the north. They seem to know a lot about this man already and apparently are just looking for corroboration.'

There was a long silence.

'Are you saying they're onto me?'

'Who knows? They may just be fishing. I'm telling you this because if there are strong suspicions that you're involved with us in any way, you know we'll have to terminate our arrangement. You'd have to go it on your own, my friend.'

Gregory bristled.

'Wait a minute! You owe me, Marcos. I saved your ass from spending half your life in the slammer. You know that! You can't treat me that way.'

'Esteemed *señor*, with respect, I think I have repaid that favor many times over – including clearing up for you those loose ends down here that could've made your life difficult. So we are all square, I think. Now it is only business between us. And if the business becomes too risky ... well, then I'm afraid we'd have to cut you loose. I'm sorry.'

At his desk, Gregory was repeatedly running a hand through his hair, truly scared now. This was never supposed to happen. He'd planned things so carefully. But there was still a chance he could save it all.

'All right. Point taken. I'll do my best to arrange things so that neither of us suffers. If I fail I'll call again and you can send your men.

It's important that the business carries on, for both our sakes.'

'Precisely. Very well. When are you bringing another payment south?'

'The Citation is arriving Friday night. We're flying to Puerto Vallarta on Saturday for two nights. Everything's set.'

'Good. They'll have everything ready for you. Is there anything else?'

'No. I'll contact you again if I need your team sent up.'

'Very well. *Suerte, señor*! Enjoy Mexico.'

'I always do. Good luck to you, too, Marcos.'

For long minutes after he'd terminated the call Gregory sat motionless at his desk, staring out the window toward the restless sea, his face a mask of concern. Then he punched another number into the cell phone. It was a sat-phone number, for the cabin was too remote to receive a signal on an ordinary cell.

'Yes?' said Manuel, when he picked up.

The shot-caller brought his man up to date with developments, gave his instructions and hung up.

There was nothing to do now but wait.

And hope.

Chapter Twenty-Five

Tuesday, May 27

Antelope Valley High School was on the north side of Lancaster, not far from where the residential streets gave out and the great beige emptiness of the desert stretched away to the north and east. It was a modern school and probably had a large student body for the buildings paralleled the road for a couple blocks. There was a parking lot at the front of the main building and at ten to five the following afternoon I eased the Cobalt into a slot that faced the entrance and waited. The classes must've finished some time earlier for there were only a few young people still around, exiting occasionally in ones and twos from the main entrance or sitting about talking together on the thin stretches of well-kept lawn that were sandwiched between the buildings and the parking lot. Now and then a teacher carrying a briefcase or a backpack would step from the entrance squinting into the bright sunlight and head off to one of the cars parked along the front, or stride away down the sidewalk toward the nearby residential streets.

It was hot so my front windows were open. I reached into the back seat for the bottle of cold water I'd bought at a service station on the way, unscrewed its top, and took a long drink. I was just recapping the bottle when another teacher emerged from the school. This man had a backpack slung over one shoulder, was of medium height, balding, and wore glasses. He carried a light jacket folded over one arm and

213

wore a short-sleeved white shirt open at the neck and tan chinos. When he stepped into the sunlight he raised a free hand to shield his eyes as he scanned the parking lot. I stuck my arm out and waved and he waved back. Then he stepped down the steps toward me. When he approached the passenger door I reached across to open it for him.

'Mr. Rednapp?' he said, bending down to look across at me.

'That's right, Mr. Parsons.' I held out my press card with photo I.D. for him to examine. 'Please, climb in.'

He did so, reaching to drop his backpack and jacket onto the back seat. I could tell he was nervous as he kept sneaking glances in my direction, as if still not entirely convinced I wasn't in some way a potential danger.

'Where to?' I asked. 'And please call me Arnie.'

'All right. I'm Nick.'

We shook hands, then I started the car and backed out. Parsons directed me back a few blocks toward the downtown area, to a cocktail bar on the corner of the main drag. I pulled into its parking area and shut down the Cobalt and the two of us went inside. It was a long narrow room with the bar and a row of high stools on the right hand side. Opposite the bar were booths and a few tables and chairs. At the back of the room an alcove led to the toilets and on to a pair of sliding doors that opened onto an enclosed garden area. I asked Parsons what he wanted and he opted for a Dos Equis. I ordered one from the girl bartender and a Corona for myself, and the two of us walked out into the back garden. There were tables dotted around under strategically placed shade trees. We chose one and sat down. There was only one other older couple there. I liked that. Parsons might be more inclined to open up without people within earshot.

'How did you find me?' he asked, as we poured out our beers. I took a sip of mine. Cold and delicious.

'It wasn't that difficult,' I told him. I outlined my moves from the previous evening. When I finished Parsons was nodding and frowning.

'I told Audrey we should get an unlisted number,' he said. 'I don't like it that I'm that easy to find.'

'Why?' I asked, smiling. 'You got somebody after you?'

He looked across at me, then away.

'I don't know. I mean, I don't think so, but...' He broke off for a moment, looking down at the table. Then he looked up again. 'I guess you'd better hear the whole story, then you'll understand.'

For the next half hour Nick Parsons spoke of his time at Belleview, which he told me was only his second teaching job after leaving college in Oregon. He was in his mid-twenties then and was unmarried, living in a rented apartment in the nearest small town. He said that for the first weeks, though he found some of the boys a handful to deal with in terms of temper, discipline and motivation, he liked working at the camp, and managed to establish friendly relations with most of the staff and the inmates.

'I was surprised,' he said. 'Of course, these kids were completely different to the kids I'd taught up to then. I expected them to be less bright since they mostly came from deprived backgrounds in the ghettos. On the contrary, they were almost all highly intelligent, perceptive boys. The difficulty was getting them to apply themselves, but when they did it was clear they would've succeeded very well had they been born into any other environment.'

'Did you manage to get many of them to take their studies seriously?'

He shook his head.

'No. They knew that whatever I told them at the camp and however they chose to respond, once they were back in their own neighborhoods they'd be up against the same old restraints and limitations. I guess they just figured, "What's the use?" Of course I urged them to fight against all that, but it was just too great a challenge. Very soon I realized the chances of my making any real progress with their education were almost non-existent – which is why what you told me about Davey was such a surprise. Davey was one of the brightest boys, but he was also one of the most troubled.'

'Was that true from the first time you met him, or did he get worse over time?'

'He got worse over time. By the end of his sentence he'd become so introspective and suspicious that it was hard to get him to talk at all. His work became erratic. I told him if he didn't apply himself he'd never graduate, that if he didn't get a high school diploma he'd never be able to hold down any kind of reasonably paid job – even in the service.'

I took another sip of my Corona.

'Do you have any idea what made Davey change so from those first weeks to the time he left?'

Parsons sat forward, looking down at his hands clasped in his lap.

'There were rumors,' he said at last.

'What kind of rumors?'

'Davey and a few of the other boys were being shunned and taunted by the other inmates for some reason. They would call them girls' names, and make crude jokes about them being *putas* or queers or bum-boys. There were fights. Often I had to call the guards to separate them.'

I nodded. 'What did you understand from that? What did you think inspired these insults?'

'At first I thought the boys were just being cruel, as boys will be. Then I thought Davey and the others might be gay. But there was nothing really about them or their behavior to justify that theory. Then one day one of the Chicano boys in the class got angry at me for something. He started shouting and calling me names, saying I was just as guilty as the scumbags that were abusing the boys – that if I wasn't actually fucking them myself I was a gutless coward for not doing something to stop what was going on. I didn't know what he was talking about and told him so. He laughed at me. "How can you not know?" he sneered. "Are you blind? Sure, you go home at night, but every morning you see these boys after the men have had their fun with them. Can't you see they're hurting? Don't you see the cuts and the bruises? And what about all the time they spend in the infirmary? Huh? Haven't you ever asked yourself why that is?"'

Parsons shuddered, remembering the scene.

'That was your first inkling as to what was going on?'

'Yes,' he said. 'Oh, I knew some of the guards were heavy-handed, and I saw on many occasions that one or other of the boys had been beaten, and sometimes badly. But I always assumed that'd happened because of something they'd done. Up to then I'd never suspected there was anything sexual going on in the camp. Not in that way, anyway.'

I nodded. 'Do you remember a boy named Toby Hitchins?'

Parsons half-smiled.

'Toby. Yes. A good kid. Got eighteen months for breaking and entering a neighbor's house. And he didn't even take anything. Just wandered around looking in their drawers and closets. The neighbors came home and caught him red-handed. When he first came to Belleview he was pretty normal. A quiet kid but full of smiles. But after a few weeks the smiles went. Toby became silent and jumpy. He wouldn't pay attention in class, just sat at his desk staring out the window.' Parsons looked at me. 'He was one of the boys, like Davey, that the others made fun of. But he wouldn't fight back – Davey always did his fighting for him. If anybody mouthed off to Toby they had to answer to Davey. And Davey would beat them up. Finally they just left all of them alone.'

'Toby told me that two of the guards, a man named Del Pritchard and another named Robert Delgado, regularly sexually abused him and Davey Colson and one or two others. Do you remember them, the two guards?'

Parsons face darkened. 'Yes, I do. They were very violent. Very crude. I always wondered how they managed to get jobs as correctional officers in the first place.'

'Did you ever hear anything from the boys that indicated they were the scumbags the Chicano boy was referring to?'

'No. I think the boys were afraid to mention any names for fear of being beaten. Or worse.'

'Worse? What do you mean?'

Parsons sighed again. 'While I was at Belleview there were two major events that occurred involving the younger boys. The first was when one of the Chicano kids, the one who had shouted at me in the class, was beaten almost to death by the guards in a shower room. They claimed he'd gone for them with a metal bar, but neither of them were injured. Just the boy. When he was taken to the hospital he was found to have concussion, several broken ribs and two smashed front teeth. His eyes were swollen almost shut. It was a month before he was brought back again.'

'Was that Nacho Flores?'

Parson's eyes flicked toward me. 'How did you know?'

'Davey's mother, May Colson, mentioned his name. Said he'd had a particularly rough time while he was there.'

Parsons shuddered. 'You can say that again.'

'Was Flores one of the boys made fun of by the others?'

'No. Nacho was a gang boy from Pasadena. He was a loner. And he was tough.'

I nodded. 'What was the second event?'

Nick Parsons took a sip of his beer, placed the glass down on the table and sat back in his chair.

'The other event concerned a boy that disappeared.'

'Disappeared? How?'

Parsons took a deep breath and exhaled.

'One Monday morning I arrived at the camp to find the administration building crawling with police and state troopers. When I asked what'd happened I was told that overnight one of the boys had gone missing, that it was presumed he'd managed somehow to escape. I asked who the boy was and they said it was Aaron Schneider. Now Aaron was one of that handful of boys, like Davey and Toby, who were being victimized by the others. But Aaron was a year or two younger, a tow-headed stick-figure of a kid. He was from a strict family – his father was a preacher in one of those holy-roller, fundamentalist churches – and he'd been convicted of sexually assaulting a six-year old neighbor girl. The girl's parents apparently found them naked together and immediately pressed charges. Instead of giving the boy the psychological and psychiatric help he obviously needed, the authorities chose to send him to Belleview, and it broke him. He arrived during my first months there, and while he was always timid and afraid it soon became apparent that his condition was worsening, and that his general health was suffering, too. He had no energy. During outside recreation time he would always sit off by himself, clutching his knees to his chest, head down. In class he'd stare into space with his mouth open and a vague frown on his face. Toward the end he spent frequent periods in the infirmary. And then suddenly he was gone. Escaped. Or so they said.' Parsons shook his head. 'I couldn't believe it. He didn't have the self-confidence to escape. Or the strength. The cops all thought he'd run into the mountains. I suppose it's possible he could've. In any case, he was never seen again.'

'If you didn't believe he'd escaped, what do you think happened to him?'

Parsons looked at me. 'Truthfully? I think he was murdered. By those guards. That he died while being abused. Or was just considered useless to them finally – damaged goods – and was simply gotten rid of. Strangled and buried in a ditch somewhere and forgotten.'

'Didn't his parents raise a stink about it? His disappearance?'

Parsons shook his head. 'As I said they were a strict family. From what I understood at the time, they'd turned their backs on him after his conviction. Disowned him. They didn't care what happened to him after that.'

I could only shake my head in amazement.

'Did you voice your suspicions to anyone else?'

He shook his head. 'No. I was too terrified myself by that point. It shames me now to confess that I've never mentioned my suspicions of what really happened to that boy to another soul.' He took a long sip of beer. 'Not until today.'

'Why were you so afraid? Were you threatened by the guards? Or by anyone else?'

'Not threatened, no. Not in so many words. But there were hints, comments made now and then that gave me to understand I was never to question anything that went on at Belleview. That not only would I lose my job if I did, but that my career would be ruined as well. Belleview's secrets were to remain Belleview's secrets, or else. Those were the rules. And you didn't question them. These were hard, dangerous men.'

'Who made these comments? Pritchard? Delgado?'

Parsons nodded. 'Yes. But they weren't the only ones. Other guards told me the same thing – even the ones I was friendly with – that the best thing to do was to keep my eyes down and my mouth shut. That it was better for my health to take no notice of anything at the camp that appeared out of line.'

I'd been making notes on my notepad. Now I nodded and sat back.

'Did you know Lamont Gregory?'

'Yes. He came to the camp regularly while I was there, often spending the night in the guest quarters in the admin building.'

'What was your assessment of the man? What did you think of him?'

Parsons shrugged. 'Hard to say. At the beginning he seemed well-intentioned, trying to help the boys adjust. But I gradually began to have my doubts about him – especially when I saw how friendly he was with Pritchard and Delgado. He was also too much of a smooth talker. I didn't trust him. Toward the end I couldn't see any of the three of them without shuddering. They all seemed evil to me.'

'How long after Davey left did you stay on at Belleview?'

'Only six months or so. I gave my notice shortly after the Schneider boy's disappearance. I'd had enough.'

I nodded. 'Have you heard anything about what happened to Pritchard and Delgado afterward? Do you have any idea where they are now, what they're doing?'

'No.' Parsons shuddered. 'I just hope they're a long way from here.'

Chapter Twenty-Six

It took a couple of hours to return to Westwood after I'd dropped Parsons back at the school. I'd given him one of my cards, he'd given me his home and email addresses and his cell number, and I told him I'd contact him if I thought we needed him later – if and when the abusers came to trial. I thought his evidence might be useful. He said he'd be happy to be a witness, but I could tell he was still worried about the guards. Hopefully, I told him, by the time the trial came they'd both be in jail.

I was wrong, as I found out not long after I got back to the Taylors'.

Marty brought me a cold Corona at poolside and slipped into the plastic lounging chair near mine as before to enjoy his pre-dinner martini. I could tell he was troubled about something. I didn't have to wait long to discover what it was.

'Both of the guards are dead, Arnie.'

I sat up. 'What!'

He shrugged. 'That's right. Mike looked 'em up for me. Pritchard was killed in a late night hit-and-run accident when he was walking home from a bar near his house in Palmdale. There were no witnesses and he died instantly from his injuries. The car and its driver were never found.'

'And Delgado?' I asked, after swigging my beer.

'Drive-by shooting. Happened at night at a liquor store in Burbank where he was then living. He'd stopped to pick up a bottle and they nailed him as he came out the door. Again, died instantly. Again, no witnesses. And no one was ever arrested for it.'

'What about motive?'

'It was believed that in both cases the perps were former gangbangers they'd mistreated while they were inside. A squaring of accounts, as it were. So the cops pretty much gave up on the investigation.'

'When did they die?'

'Eleven years ago. 2004. Pritchard in May, Delgado in August. Just about the time...'

'...that Gregory left L.A. and moved to Del Norte County,' I finished for him. 'Interesting coincidence, isn't it? That both men should die just as he was clearing his desk to head north. Maybe that was another kind of desk clearing. Maybe he was afraid someone would get to them eventually and they'd talk?'

'Who knows? In any case they aren't around anymore to prosecute. Or to serve as witnesses for you against Gregory. Sorry.'

'Shit.'

'Yeah. So what now?'

I took another pull on my Corona.

'I'm not finished yet. I'll build a case against that bastard one way or another. I promised Toby Hitchins I would. And Mrs. Colson.'

'How you going to do that? You'll need more reliable witnesses, people that saw these things happen and who can testify to that effect.'

'I know. I'll find them.'

'Where?'

'Maybe in Mexico.' Then I frowned as a thought struck me. 'There's also that Chicano gangbanger that was at Belleview with them, Nacho Flores. Mrs. Colson said he was convicted of murder and is now doing time somewhere. Agent Peters was going to look into that for me. I'll call him later, find out what he's discovered.' I told Marty about my meeting with Nick Parsons and of his story about the inmates' ragging of Davey and the others, and of the disappearance of the tow-headed Schneider boy. By the time I'd finished Marty was leaning forward on his lounger and scowling.

'Sounds like those two bastards got what they deserved,' he muttered. 'Though I'd much rather they'd gone to trial and spent the rest of their lives in prison.'

'I'd second that. Have you heard anything from your friend in Vallarta?'

Immediately Marty brightened.

'Yeah, I did. I almost forgot. Paco called this afternoon. He's been checking around, finding out who works for Gregory and Baldini at their villas. He came up with a list of people and addresses for you. He's digging into their backgrounds now.'

'Great. Let's hope they'll talk to me.'

'He's also been nosing around the airport, using his contacts there to find out where Baldini's Citation is kept. Apparently he pays a handling firm to keep it in their hangar, so it stays inside out of the weather until he needs it again.'

'Makes sense.'

Marty took another sip of his martini, then carefully replaced the glass on the table between us.

'You know, I've been thinking. That could be how at least some of the drugs get from Mexico into the states,' he said. 'And the drug money back to the cartel.'

'What do you mean?'

Marty scratched an elbow.

'Think about it. Baldini and Gregory travel to Mexico in that plane regularly. Maybe there's a secret compartment in it somewhere where drugs can be hidden for the trip north, and cash for the trip south? That way neither Baldini nor Gregory would actually have to handle the shipment – someone else would both plant it and take it away. And they could always claim ignorance if by some fluke it was discovered. For someone of Baldini's stature and authority the security checks would be pretty superficial anyway. Besides, in Mexico you can buy off your priest with enough money.'

Now I sat forward.

'That's an interesting idea, Mart. I'll mention it to Agent Peters. And I'll try to do some gentle probing at the airport while I'm down there.'

'You watch your ass, Arnie. The place is bound to be swimming with cartel informers. One sniff of suspicion and you're likely to end up on a country road without a head.'

'I know. I'll be careful, believe me.'

Just then Connie called that dinner was ready and we retired indoors.

It'd been a long day with a lot of driving so after our meal I bid my gracious hosts an early goodnight and headed off to my room at around 9:30. The room was at the back of the house and had a small balcony that overlooked the pool and the tall poplar trees that bounded the property. I took out my cell phone, planted myself on the plastic chair on the balcony, found Devonne Peters' number in my directory and pressed 'Call'. It rang a couple times before it was picked up.

'Peters here.'

'Devonne, it's Arnie Rednapp. This too late for you?'

'Not at all. I've been watching a *Columbo* rerun with my wife and I'm happy for the interruption. What you got?'

I told him about my meeting with Nick Parsons, then what Martin Taylor had discovered about the two guards.

'Yeah,' he said. 'We found that, too. I was going to phone you in the morning. That kind of leaves you in a crack over building your sexual abuse case.'

'Maybe, but I'm not giving up yet. Did you find out the whereabouts of the Chicano gangbanger who was with Davey Colson at Belleview, Nacho Flores?'

He chuckled. 'We sure did. You'll never guess where he is.'

'Won't I?'

'I doubt it. When you were up north you passed him every day. He's in Pelican Bay.'

'Holy shit.'

Now Peters laughed. 'Yeah. I thought that'd amuse you. So, you going to see him when you go north again?'

'You can count on it. I don't suppose you happened to discover who's representing him now?'

'I did, as a matter of fact. Apparently he dropped his L.A. attorney and took up a local guy so he can contact him quickly when he needs him. Just a minute, I've got the name here in my pocket.' I could hear rustling down the phone as Devonne dug for the paper. 'His name's Thad Wilkins. He has his own practice in Crescent City. You want his number?'

'No. I can find it online or in the book. Thad Wilkins. That rings a bell.'

'Probably because he's running against Lamont Gregory in the election for District Attorney up there,' Peters said. 'He's Native American, a member of the local Yurok tribe. He's also a Democrat and a former Assistant D.A. in Sacramento with a great record. Flores made a good choice, it would appear.'

'I'll give him a call when I'm up there and make an appointment to see his client. In the meantime, has your team in Crescent City uncovered anything useful?'

'Nothing yet, but it's still early days. How's Deputy Mitchell getting on? I haven't spoken to her for a while.'

'Fine, far as I know. Oh, there was one development you might want to know about.'

I told him about Pepe Hidalgo seeing Josh Bridger's tattoos, and of our suspicions that he was the passenger in Manuel Fernandez's pickup on the Wednesday Colson died.

'If he was,' I concluded, 'he must've gone straight to Gregory with the news about the tattoos. Now we wait to see what Gregory does about it.'

'I hope your Mr. Bridger's on his toes. The response could be lethal. Want me to put a tail on him for his own good?'

'No. Bridger's former Delta Force, remember? He's keeping his eyes peeled. Thanks for the offer but let's leave things as they are for the moment. I don't think either he or Geri would want to complicate things by adding another snooper to the mixture. Geri's not going to tell her colleagues about Pepe Hidalgo yet for fear the kid might run. She can do that later, and he can be brought in when he's needed. In the meantime Bridger wants to keep an eye on him, see what he can find out about his contacts. He might lead him to Manuel Fernandez.'

'Fair enough. When you off to Mexico?'

'I booked my flight this morning. I leave early tomorrow – around 8 AM. I'll only be there one night, but I'm going to try to make the best use of the time that I can. I've got a contact down there who's offered to help me. Incidentally, my host Marty Taylor had an idea that might interest you.'

I told him Mart's theory about the use of Baldini's Citation to run money and drugs to and from Mexico. He liked the idea, said it was quite possible.

'I'm going to gently nose around when I'm down there,' I told him. 'Maybe I can find someone who can tell me something.'

'Well, I've told you before. Be damned careful.'

'I will, Devonne. I'll call when I have something to say.'

My next call was to Lorraine, who was watching television with Mandy. She took the phone into the bedroom for privacy.

'What've you been up to?' she asked.

I told her about the meetings with May Colson, Toby Hitchins and Nick Parsons. Then I told her what Martin had found out about the bent guards.

'Bummer,' she said. 'There goes your case.'

'Not really,' I said. 'Not yet. There must be other witnesses that can help nail Gregory for sexual abuse, and if there are I'll find them. How's everything in Shelter Cove?'

'We're all fine here,' she said. 'Just missing you. I called Geri tonight about coming up and she says she'd love to have us, so I'm thinking we'll leave Friday early evening. It's only a couple hours' drive, as you know. That way we'll have two nights with her before we have to come home for Monday.'

'Great. I'm sure you'll all have a fine time.'

'When are you off to Mexico?'

'Tomorrow. I'll call once I'm settled.'

'Good. I'll look forward to that. Be careful, Arnie. I want you back here in one piece.'

'Me, too,' I said. 'And the sooner the better.'

We chatted for a minute or two more, then said our goodbyes, blowing kisses down the phone. There was still no use of the 'L' word but we were getting closer, I could tell.

I spent the next hour drafting an email to send to Abe Rawlings, telling him what I'd learned over the last couple of days. I knew that would hold him. It was becoming eminently clear that I was onto something big and was sure he'd continue to let me run with it. I sent the email, then checked my inbox. Marty had sent the newspaper photos he'd found of Gregory at Belleview. The email arrived two days earlier but I had missed it hidden amongst a load of spam. They were interesting pics – one of them a large shot taken at the official opening of the camp, with Assistant District Attorneys Lamont Gregory and Anthony Baldini prominent in the midst of a group of senior police officials and dignitaries. I didn't bother to print the pictures off, just spooled through them, feeling my gut tighten as I took in Gregory's smarmy smiles and false bonhomie. One of them was a shot of him with his arm around the shoulders of Clifford Marshall, the Belleview Warden, and I squinted at it trying to make out what kind of man Marshall was, trying to imagine how he could've run an institution like Belleview and not known what was going on there. But the picture told me nothing, other than the fact that he looked bloated and smug, and I finally moved on. When I finished looking at them I shut down the computer, did my ablutions and went to bed. I was just about to drift off when my cell vibrated on the table beside me. I reached for it and pushed the talk button.

'Yeah?'

'Arnie? It's Geri. Sorry to call so late.'

'No problem. What's happening?'

'I've just been on the phone with Josh. He called ten minutes ago. He was cycling home to the Eagle tonight along a dark stretch of the road at the edge of town when a vehicle came up fast behind him. Josh said he glanced back just as it swerved toward him. He managed to throw himself off into the ditch, but the bike ended up a mangled mess. The vehicle slowed momentarily, then accelerated off down the road.'

I sat up, switching on the bedside light.

'Christ! Is Josh okay?'

'Yes, he's fine. He landed in some blackberry bushes so he got scratches and a few cuts and bruises, but nothing serious.'

'Thank God for that. Did he get a view of the vehicle?'

'Not much of one. He said it looked like a dark pickup.'

'Manuel,' I said.

'Probably. Ryan says he hasn't been to work for days. And he's not at his house. But that doesn't mean he isn't around somewhere, ready to do Gregory's bidding.'

'Looks like that's what he just did. Let's hope he doesn't try anything more for a day or two. Look, I'm off to Mexico tomorrow. I'll be there only one night and I fly back to L.A. on Thursday. I'll spend one night here, then drive up to San Francisco Friday. If all goes well I'll be with you Saturday.'

'Great, Arnie. But you don't have to come up if you don't want to. Josh says he's happy to carry on working on the farm. He'll just be more careful.'

'It isn't only that. I spoke to Lorraine tonight and she told me she and Mandy are going up to spend the weekend with you. If I can, I'd like to get there before she goes.'

'Wonderful! It'll be good having all of you here, if only for a day.'

'And there's another reason for my wanting to be there.'

'Oh? What's that?'

I told Geri about my conversation with Devonne Peters and about Nacho Flores being in Pelican Bay.

'I want to make an appointment with Thad Wilkins to talk to Flores as soon as I get back,' I said. 'I don't think Flores was sexually abused at Belleview, but he might be able to testify to things he witnessed there that will implicate Gregory in the abuse sessions. Anyway, I need to talk to him.'

'Weird that he's been here all the time and we didn't know about it,' Geri said.

'Isn't it? Anyway, I'll give you a call from Mexico with an update.'

'Do that. And now you'd better get some sleep, Arnie. You'll have a busy day tomorrow.'

'I'll do that. Give Josh my regards and tell him to be careful. And hug that woman for me when she gets there.'

Two minutes later I was making zzzs.

Chapter Twenty-Seven

Lamont Gregory was asleep when the cell on the bedside table buzzed. Clicking on the lamp, he grabbed the phone and answered the call.

'Yes?'

'*Jefe*, I did what you wanted.'

'And? What happened?'

'Unfortunately he saw me coming. He jumped into a ditch before I could clip him. I got the bike but I think he's still alive.'

'Did you stop to check?'

'No, *patrón*. The road's too busy and I didn't want to risk being seen.'

Gregory sighed. 'Very well. Go back to the cabin. I'll be in touch soon.'

Clicking off the phone, he dropped it onto the bedside table again. Then he climbed out of bed and reached for his dressing gown, pulling it on over his silk pajamas and tying the cord. Picking up the phone, he walked out of the bedroom and along the corridor to his office. The deck outside the windows was bathed in pale blue light from a half moon and he left off the overhead light and moved to his desk, where he clicked on the gooseneck lamp at its corner. Sitting, he lifted the cell phone, searched in its directory for the number he wanted, and pushed 'Call'. The man at the other end kept late nights, he knew, and it took only three rings before the phone was answered.

'*¿Bueno?*'

'It's me. Sorry it's late. I'm afraid I shall need the men we spoke of after all. My own efforts, unfortunately, have come to nothing.'

'*Lástima.* Never mind. I will phone them now. They'll be on their way to you tomorrow morning. When they arrive they'll contact you on this number for instructions. Can they stay in the usual place?'

'I have someone else there now, but why not?'

'Someone else?'

Gregory sighed again. 'He was involved in the earlier business and was identified from the CCTV films. I told him to stay there till I can figure out what to do with him.'

'If he's a liability they could always make him disappear?'

'No! Not yet, at least. Besides, he might prove useful to them. Yes, tell them to go there. You have the directions. I'll alert my man to expect them.'

'All right. This will cost you, you know? $50,000 for each man.'

'Of course it will cost me, Marcos. These things always do. But there's nothing else to be done.'

'Let me know how things go,' the Latino said. 'Hopefully your problems will soon be over.'

'We shall see. Oh, and my Sacramento friend phoned today. His share of the cargo will be loaded aboard the plane tomorrow night. Then he flies here on Friday. He's looking forward to getting away from his government duties for a few days.'

'I'm sure he is. Is he taking his family this time?'

'No. He's coming alone. He'll spend the night with me, then we'll fly down Saturday morning.'

'Excellent. I'll let our friends in the south know. Is there anything else?'

'Not for the moment.'

'Then good night to you.'

There was a click and the line went dead.

Chapter Twenty-Eight

Wednesday, May 28

Marty ran me to LAX early the following morning and I caught my Alaska Airlines flight to Puerto Vallarta without difficulty. Fortunately I always carry my passport with me.

Marty had telephoned Paco Jimenez the night before and he was waiting for me outside of Customs, holding up a card with my name on it. He was a shortish man with dark hair and eyes and a warm smile. His cream-colored linen suit was slightly crumpled, his tie loose at the collar. He took my small case and led me out to the parking lot.

I had thought the atmosphere in L.A. was pretty muggy, being used to the benign temperatures of San Francisco. But stepping from the air-conditioned coolness of the Gustavo Díaz Ordaz International Airport into the heat and humidity of tropical Mexico was like walking from a fridge into a sauna. It took a few minutes to adapt to it.

At the end of a row of flashy late-model cars and vans a battered white Honda Civic was parked under a palm tree. Paco opened the trunk to pop in my bag, then the car so that we could climb aboard. The flight down had taken almost exactly three hours, so with the added two hours of time difference between California and Puerto Vallarta it was now close to 1:30 PM. I reset my watch.

'Marty asked me to find you a reasonable hotel,' he said, starting the car and backing out of his slot. 'I got you a reservation at the Canto del Sol, at the south end of the city and not far from the beach. I know the manager and he always gives me a good rate for my friends.'

'Great, Paco. Any savings will be much appreciated by my boss.'

Paco eased out of the parking lot and onto the exit road and a couple minutes later we were weaving through moderate city traffic on a four-lane main street, heading south. The buildings on either side were modern and attractive, and the brightly-dressed people on the streets smiling and happy. To my right, the streets leading westward gave intermittent flashing views of the blue Bahia de Banderas sparkling in the sun. It felt like holiday time. I liked the place already.

'We'll go straight to the hotel,' he said, 'so you can drop your bag and freshen up. Then we'll have some lunch. I have things to tell you.'

'That sounds fine, Paco. Thanks for picking me up.'

'*De nada*,' he said. 'Anything for a friend of *Señor* Taylor.' He grinned across at me. 'Especially if that friend is another journalist.'

The Canto del Sol was big and had a sizeable pool area enclosed within its U-shaped central courtyard that was teeming with tourists – bikini-clad nubile ladies and bronzed muscular gentlemen taking the sun and enjoying their drinks and one another. It felt comfortable and friendly, and my fourth floor room overlooking the courtyard was spacious and clean. Paco remained downstairs while I dumped my bag and had a quick wash. Then I rejoined him and we walked through the air-conditioned lobby and into the restaurant at the side, where he'd reserved a table in the shade out on the terrace. We sat down, perused the menus, and ordered – a taco salad and a Corona for me, a club sandwich and a coke for him. When the *mesero* disappeared back inside Paco leaned over the table toward me and dropped his voice.

'I've been doing some research into the two men Marty mentioned. Both Lamont Gregory and Anthony Baldini have large houses near Vallarta, though Baldini's villa is much grander. It's set in a large, walled in garden with a looping drive up to the house beyond the front gate, and there's a team of security guards that patrol the property 24/7, whether he's there or not. Gregory's house has a wall enclosing the house and a smaller garden, but apart from a live-in caretaker and a CCTV camera there does not seem to be any other security.'

I nodded. 'How far away are they from here?'

'The houses? *Señor* Baldini's villa is five or six kilometers to the south in Alta Vista, up in the hills overlooking the sea. *Señor* Gregory's is about 40 kilometers to the north, in the coastal town of Sayulita. We'll drive to both of them after lunch so you can have a look.'

Our drinks came, and then our lunches, and for the next forty minutes or so we chatted lightly about our lives and work. I asked Paco why his English was so good. He told me he'd studied in the states, that his parents had been teachers of English so he and his siblings had been raised with the language. It showed. He was completely fluent.

It was while we were enjoying our coffees that Paco reached down to open his slim briefcase and produced a file, which he handed across to me. I opened it, laying it on the table before me. There were several typed pages. Two of them were lists of people and their home addresses – the staffs of the houses of Lamont Gregory and Anthony Baldini. The list of Baldini's staff was long, almost filling the page. The one for Gregory amounted to only four names, and two of them were occasional gardeners. I moved on. There followed a page of information about the company that owned the hangar at the airport where Baldini kept his Citation, Aviación Fénix. Finally, Paco had written a short fact sheet regarding the local cartels and their recent public activities, with translated quotes from various newspaper accounts of murders and kidnappings attributed to the cartel conflicts. I skimmed over it. On the whole, Puerto Vallarta itself, and its corner of the large, tequila-producing state of Jalisco, had been spared the worst of the cartel violence, with only the occasional tit for tat murder occurring here and there as the various criminal organizations vied for supremacy. In any case, whereas Guadalajara, Jalisco's capital and its largest city, had suffered increasing incidents of violence and horror in recent months, Puerto Vallarta remained safe for tourists, and the hotels and resorts were bursting with business. That didn't mean, of course, that there wasn't extensive drug activity going on locally, or that there weren't large cadres of cartel operatives in the area. It just meant that for whatever reason the levels of violence were being held down here – probably owing to a secret deal done between the local authorities, businesses and the cartel leaders. Since the advent of the campaign of President Enrique Peña Nieto to crush the Mexican cartels there has been such a tide of bloody violence and death across the country that for the sake of a modicum of stability such secret deals are often made between the locals and the cartels, with varying degrees of success. Desperate times call for desperate measures. It was sad, but entirely understandable. I turned my attention back to the lists of staff members.

'Did you talk to any of these people?' I asked Paco.

He shook his head.

'No. Most of them, I'm afraid, would not speak with you. In fact, it would be dangerous to try. Either they know what is going on and have been sworn on pain of death to secrecy, or they have their suspicions and are terrified to speak out in case word gets back and they're made to suffer for it. In either case their bosses would be immediately told about you and your safety would be compromised. This is particularly true of the staff at *Señor* Baldini's villa. They are all professionals, and would report to their superiors any approach made to them for information.' He reached across to take up the list of staff for Lamont Gregory's house. 'As for *Señor* Gregory's staff...' He ran his finger down the short list until he found a name, then pointed to it. 'There is one person who I think might speak to you. *Señora* Marielena Hidalgo. She works as a cook and housekeeper for Gregory when he is in residence.'

'Why do you think she might talk when the others won't?' I asked him.

Paco shrugged. 'It is only a guess. She lives alone at the edge of the town. Her husband was killed in one of the cartel wars four years ago – he was a drug mule, running drugs from Jalisco north toward the border. She also has a son. Rumor has it he is working somewhere in America.'

I sat back, suddenly frowning.

'Hidalgo. Is her son's name Pepe? There's a young man of that name working for Gregory right now on his farm.'

Paco made a facial shrug. 'I don't know his name. It could be him. Maybe you can find that out when you talk to her?'

'When can I do that?'

He leaned forward.

'I have been watching Gregory's house. Apparently he is expected to come to Vallarta again soon and *Señora* Hidalgo has been spending her days getting the house ready for him. But always at night she goes home to her own place. I think we could, perhaps, manage to speak to her there. Maybe this evening.'

I raised my eyebrows. 'So soon?'

'You have very little time, *Señor* Arnie. It is best that we make hay while the sun shines, as you say in America.' He lifted his cup and drank the last of his coffee. 'But now, if you are ready, we will go take a look at these palaces of the *gringo* rich.'

We climbed back into Paco's Honda and headed south, picking up the four-lane main drag again and following the curving line of the beach for a mile or two until an overhead sign for the Alta Vista turnoff prompted Paco to swing onto the exit ramp. For a few minutes we wound around through narrow neighborhood streets, climbing slowly into the foothills of the Sierra Carcoma Range. Then suddenly the buildings thinned and the houses began to look grander and richer and more luxurious. At the edge of the stunted pine forest that covered the ridge the last stretch of the roadway was flanked on its right side by a string of half a dozen palatial villas, each one set back some distance from the road on elevations that looked westward toward the Pacific, each one sequestered within massive walls with wrought iron gates, and all of them with uniformed security personnel ostentatiously keeping an eye on comings and goings. Baldini's pad was the last but one in the line, and Paco pulled to the curb fifty yards or so before it, so we were looking up at it from an angle. The high stone walls blocked off most of the lower storey of the house, but even with that the two upper stories, with their deep balconies and potted palms, flowers and ferns, clearly demonstrated the opulence of the place, and its extraordinary size. Tony Baldini was known as a socialite who loved to entertain VIP house guests, and this tropical palace was an ideal setting for just such junkets.

'Wow,' I said, impressed. 'How often does he come down here?'

'It depends,' Paco said. 'I checked with the some of the people who live down the hill. They say they always know when he's in town because of the string of vehicles that pass up and down the road. In the summer, apparently, he comes every two or three weeks – sometimes for the weekend, sometimes for longer. In winter it is not so frequent – perhaps once a month or so.'

'I wonder how often the two of them get together down here? Baldini and Gregory?'

Paco made a moue. 'Not very often, I think. From what I can discover, *Señor* Baldini is the social animal – with constant parties and visitors coming and going – whereas Gregory keeps mostly to himself.' He looked back at Baldini's villa. 'I'm sorry that we can't get any closer to have a proper look, but that would draw attention and I don't think either one of us wants to be noted by these people.'

'Certainly not.'

'Have you seen enough?' he asked.

'Yeah. I've seen enough.'

Paco put the Honda in gear and swung a wide 180 so we were heading downhill again.

'Did anyone you spoke to mention seeing any suspicious vehicles coming and going to Baldini's villa after hours during his stays here? Maybe when there were no guests in residence?'

Paco looked across at me. 'What do you mean?'

I shrugged. 'Small convoys of black Humvees, for instance, with tinted windows?'

He smiled. 'Ah. *Ahora ya entiendo.* No, they didn't say anything about that. But I wouldn't think Baldini would be so careless as to invite the cartel bosses to come to his villa. After all he is the Attorney General of the great State of California, and a friend of our President, and often invites him and other top figures of our government here as guests to his parties. He cannot afford to be so open about his association with the underworld. It would reflect badly on his high-placed friends if he did. Not to mention himself.'

'Of course. So he must contact them in some other way.'

'If he makes contact at all. Perhaps it is not even necessary? Perhaps everything is taken care of without him even being involved?'

'How do you mean?' I asked, puzzled.

Paco smiled.

'You will see. There is someone I want you to meet.'

We headed back into Puerto Vallarta again, then passed beyond to the airport and shortly afterwards took a turning along the seafront toward the north. I wondered where he was taking me. We rolled on for a few miles through a series of beach front resort complexes and parades of souvenir shops, cantinas and fast food bars until we turned suddenly inland and came to the small town of Mezcales, a few miles short of the curved northern end of the Bahia de Banderas and the thin peninsula that projected out to form the Punta de Mita. There were no tourists here, just streets of sand colored apartment buildings and – away from the main drag – poorer single storey residences where working class people have lived for decades. Paco turned off onto a side street and we went on for a bit, stopping finally at the edge of the houses before an older stucco dwelling with a tiled roof and a dusty front yard that ran straight into the road. Tall palm trees arced together behind it, framing what must have been a back yard.

'Here we are,' Paco said, smiling enigmatically. 'Come with me.'

We climbed out of the car and walked up to the house's entrance. Paco knocked on the doorframe beside the open fly-screened door and a moment later a man appeared from the darkness beyond.

'*Hola*, Paco!' the man said, pushing open the door. Then he turned to me. '*Señor* Rednapp, please. Come in. You are welcome to my house.'

I stepped past him into the shadowy interior and Paco brought up the rear, reaching out a hand as he entered.

'Antonio. *¿Qué tal, amigo?*'

The man grasped Paco's hand and shook it warmly.

'*Bien, gracias*, Paco. But we should talk English.' He closed the screen door and turned to me. '*Señor* Rednapp, my name is Antonio Sanchez. Paco has told me all about you and about why you have come to Puerto Vallarta.'

Now he held out his hand to me and I shook it. Antonio's accent was thick, but his grasp of English was good. It occurred to me that he must work somewhere where he was often dealing with English-speaking tourists.

'Please,' he said, gesturing toward the back of the house, 'come through to the *terraza*. It is cooler there.'

Antonio led the way and Paco and I followed. We hadn't far to go. The house was barely more than three rooms: the cramped front room (dominated by a new flat-screen television), a toilet and shower room, and a bedroom. The kitchen was outside, under the overhanging tiled roof that covered a third of the terrace that extended four or five yards into the dusty back yard under the palm trees. In one corner of the yard a few chickens and a rooster pecked contentedly within a rudimentary chicken run of bare poles and chicken wire, with an improvised roost at one end made up of wooden boxes cobbled together.

On the terrace, beside the cooking range situated beside the door, was a wooden table and four chairs. Antonio pulled out two of the chairs and gestured for us to sit, which we did.

'My wife Maria is at work, I'm afraid, so you will probably not meet her. You want a cool drink, *señores*? A beer, perhaps? I have some cold Modelos.'

'I'll take a Modelo,' I said, sitting. 'Thanks.'

'Paco?'

'Only water, *por favor*. And cold, if you have it.'

'*¿Como no?*' said Antonio, and busied himself withdrawing a plastic bottle from the fridge beside the kitchen work counter and a can of beer from the small case on the fridge's bottom shelf. Grabbing two glasses from the draining board next to the sink, he brought the lot to the table and distributed it between us. There was an opened bottle of Modelo at his place on the table, where he now sat, lifted the bottle to take a long drink, and then exhaled a long sigh of pleasure.

'Ahhh! There is nothing like a cool beer in the heat of the day, *no, señores*?'

'Nope,' I agreed, sipping from my own bottle. 'Nothing like it.'

Paco filled his glass from the plastic water bottle and took a long drink. Then he set the glass on the table and rested his crossed arms on the tabletop.

'Antonio is one of the surprises I've been keeping for you, *Señor* Arnie. He is a cleaner at the airport. He works, however, not in the terminal but rather in the hangar where the corporate jets are kept. Aviación Fénix.'

I nodded. 'Where Anthony Baldini parks his Citation.'

'Exactly,' Paco went on. 'I met Antonio three years ago. We both play football – soccer to you – every weekend with an amateur team in the local *liga*. When I learned that Baldini's jet was kept at Aviación Fénix I contacted Antonio and told him about you. He said he would be glad to help. So now we are here.'

'Thanks,' I said, tipping my bottle toward Antonio in a salute. 'What can you tell me about Mr. Baldini's visits?'

Antonio laughed. 'Certainly I can tell you nothing about what the great *señor* does while he is here.' He gestured to his humble house and yard. 'Clearly he and I move in very different circles.' He leant forward over the table. 'But I can tell you something about his plane. I have worked there long enough, and am trusted enough by the *patrón* and his manager, to have seen some very interesting things.'

'What kind of things?'

For a moment the twinkle in his eyes went and he looked dead serious.

'First, *Señor* Rednapp, you must swear to me that you will never tell anyone about this conversation. Or even that you have met me. *¿De aquerdo?*'

'Of course,' I said. 'What have you got to tell me?'

He sat back again, took another swig from his bottle and placed it on the table.

'I became aware of it about a year and a half ago. One winter evening I was working late at the hangar. A number of business jets had arrived that afternoon, one of them *Señor* Baldini's Citation. Just after dark there was a knock at the back door where the cars are parked and the manager unlocked it and let in two men carrying small suitcases. I was cleaning the floor at the back of the hangar and I don't believe the men even noticed me. It's a big place. Maybe the manager wasn't even aware I was still there. Anyway I kept quiet and watched while they talked with the manager for a minute or two. Then one of the men produced an envelope from his back pocket and handed it to the manager. He took it and thanked the men. Then he shook their hands and went back to his office carrying the envelope.'

'What did the men do then?'

'They went to *Señor* Baldini's Citation and entered the cabin by way of the stairs. They were inside five or ten minutes. When they finally came out they were still carrying their small suitcases. They waved to the manager through the glass windows of his office and then left. Since then I have seen this thing happen three or four other times.'

I nodded. 'Any idea what was inside the cases, Antonio?'

'No,' he said, shaking his head. 'But I would guess drugs. Or money. Or both.'

'Have you told anyone about this?' I asked.

He scoffed. 'Of course not, *señor*. I would be dead within hours if I did.'

'Were you surprised by what you saw?'

'Surprised? No. This is Mexico, *Señor* Rednapp. Everyone is corrupt here. Everyone can be bought. It is the name of the game. To survive you learn to keep your mouth shut and to trust no one.'

'Why do you trust Paco?'

'Paco is like my brother. Also, I have seen what he has written in *NotiVallarta* under the false name '*El Gallo*'.'

I glanced at Paco. He shrugged.

'It means "the rooster," or "the cockerel"', he said. 'I call myself that for safety. It is not healthy in Mexico to criticize the establishment. Also it is a fitting pen name since my articles are a wake-up call for the citizens of Jalisco to fight against the corruption in the government.'

'Paco is a brave man,' Antonio went on, 'who is trying to make things better for us here. I respect that.'

I nodded. 'Antonio, I'm going to pass on your information – without saying where I got it – to the American FBI. It's pointless asking if you would testify as to what you've seen in an American court of law. I'm not even sure you could be subpoenaed internationally and I wouldn't want to put you in any danger from the cartels. But could you do this much for me? I'll find out when Baldini's jet is coming down here next and pass that on to Paco to tell you. When it arrives could you keep watch and let me know through Paco if you see the men make another exchange? We might not be able to do anything about the corruption here in Mexico, but if we have advanced knowledge of a drugs shipment coming via Baldini to Sacramento I can have the FBI and the Federal Drug Enforcement Agency all over that plane when it arrives. Could you do that for me, Antonio?'

For a moment he stared at me, expressionless. Then he grinned.

'Of course I can, *señor*, as long as my name is never mentioned to anyone. It will please me to see the cartels lose a bit of money, and to know that in America some drug bigwigs are paying for their wickedness. I will keep good watch when the plane comes next, and you shall hear from me as soon as I see anything.'

'Thanks, amigo,' I said. 'You're a brave man.'

Chapter Twenty-Nine

It took forty minutes to drive back to the main road and then north on Highway 200 across the spine of forested hills to reach the small coastal resort town where Lamont Gregory's house was situated. We arrived there at just before five in the afternoon.

Sayulita, with a population of around 5000, was a sleepy fishing village that was discovered by tourists in the '80s and '90s. Now, in essence, it's a much smaller version of Puerto Vallarta, with the town center and the dwellings of the artisan townspeople clustered behind the gently curving modern beach frontage of flashy hotels and bars, and the richer, grander houses of the wealthy gringo snowbirds perched higher up, on the slopes overlooking the town.

Deftly skirting the tourist-thronged front, Paco took a series of back streets until at length he pulled up before the town's small Catholic church. It was modern and attractive and was flanked by two or three other buildings. One of these, a slightly larger two-storied structure, was set back from the street behind a high chain-link fence with a gate at the front. In the paved yard within the fence a couple dozen children played on climbing frames and swing sets, supervised by two nuns in summer habits. I looked back at the church.

'Nice building,' I said, then looked at Paco. 'Why are we here?'

He pointed to the building behind the chain-link fence.

'That is an orphanage, *Señor* Arnie. It is called The Orphanage of the Angel of Mercy, *El Orfanato del Ángel de la Mercéd.*'

'Right. So?'

'The orphanage was founded largely with money donated by *Señor* Lamont Gregory.'

I stared back at it, stunned.

'I'll be damned.'

'Oh, yes,' Paco said. 'In Sayulita *Señor* Gregory is very well liked. He has given a lot to the community, and he's highly respected.' He looked across at the playground, still thronging with children. 'I telephoned earlier for permission to visit. Would you like to see it?'

'Yes, I would.'

We climbed out of Paco's Honda and he locked it up. Then we walked across the street and along a few yards to the locked orphanage gate. There was a security keypad for the staff to gain entrance and a button for visitors. Paco pushed the button and we waited, watching the children running about within, some of them now curious about the two men waiting to enter.

'*Sí?*' said a feminine voice through the tiny speaker.

Paco gave his name and spoke two or three sentences in Spanish and a minute or so later another nun appeared from the main door of the building and walked toward the gate, smiling.

'*Hola, buenos días, Señor* Jimenez,' she said, opening the gate.

'*Hola, Hermana,*' Paco said. 'Do you speak English?'

'Yes,' she said. 'A little.'

'This is my friend who is visiting from California. His name is *Señor* Rednapp. Like me he is *periodista.*'

'*Mucho gusto, señor,*' she said. Then she opened the gate wide. 'Please, come in.'

We stepped inside and the nun shut the gate after us and led the way toward the building's entrance, parting the squealing children like Moses did the Red Sea.

'You are welcome here, *señores,*' she said, as we walked. 'We are always glad to have visitors. My name is Sister Josefina. I will show you around the building, then take you to meet the Mother Superior, Sister Maria Isabel.'

'Thank you, Sister,' said Paco.

'*De nada*. It is my pleasure.' She opened the dark stained wooden door. 'Now, if you will follow me?'

It was a simple structure with a white-painted central corridor and rooms opening off on the sides. Two or three of these were classrooms, but a good half of the downstairs was taken up by a small office, toilets and washrooms, a staff room, and the office and living accommodation of the Mother Superior. Apart from the latter, Sister Josefina showed us each of the rooms in turn, putting a finger to her lips before gesturing for us to peer through the small window of the closed door to the class of older children who were still hard at work. At the end of the corridor was a stairway that led to the second floor. We climbed it. Half of that floor was given over to individual bedrooms opening off the central corridor (for the nun guardians and the older boys and girls). The other half was a large open dormitory space for the younger kids, with twenty cots arranged down its length, ten on each side. All of the upstairs rooms were empty now, the children being either in class or out on the playground.

'How long do you keep the children?' I asked. 'I mean, how old are they when they leave the orphanage?'

'That depends,' said Sister Josefina. 'If we manage to find families to adopt them, then of course they can leave at any time. Some of the children, however, don't manage to find foster parents. In that case we keep them here until they are sixteen years or so. Then we try to find them positions as live-in workers, either at the local farms and *haciendas* or in the tourist hotels and resorts.'

'How many do you have here at the moment, Sister?'

'At the moment we have thirty-two souls here.'

I was impressed. The building was well-organized, clean and spacious, and the amenities for the children seemed more than adequate. I told her as much.

'Thank you, *señor*,' she said, smiling again. 'We try to do our best for them.' Now I'll take you to meet Sister Maria Isabel.'

The Mother Superior was a large woman in her sixties with a kind face and a gentle, businesslike manner. Sister Josefina introduced us and left. Then we were offered seats across from Sister Maria Isabel's desk and sat down.

'Thank you for allowing us to see your orphanage,' I opened. 'I understand that it was funded, at least partly, by an American – Mr. Lamont Gregory?'

'Yes, that is correct. Though he himself is not married, *Señor* Gregory has a soft spot for children and wanted to do something for our poor orphans.'

'That was very good of him,' I said. 'How long ago was the orphanage founded?'

'Construction on the building began in 2008, and we opened our doors to the children in 2010. It is still all very new.'

'And very nice, too,' I said. 'Does Mr. Gregory continue to take an interest in the children? Does he visit here when he is resident in Sayulita?'

'Oh, yes. He always visits. And brings gifts for them – some new piece of play equipment or a computer or books or some such. He is very kind.'

'I'm told Mr. Gregory is a rich man,' I said.

'So I understand. But rich men are not often quite so generous with their money.'

'That is true.'

'*Señor* Gregory is so generous, in fact, that while he is in Sayulita he often invites some of the children to spend the night at his wonderful house up on the hill. They always come back with little presents, too. Clothing or CD players or something he has brought from America. The children are very fond of him.'

My mind was racing. Gregory was obviously at it again, I was certain of it. Taking criminal advantage of the very unfortunate children to whom his ostentatious generosity was supposed to be offering succor. I glanced at Paco, who was looking at me with raised eyebrows and a quizzical smile. I must have shown my disgust and he was uncertain what had prompted it. Of course, he could not know of that part of Gregory's wickedness. I hadn't yet spoken of it. Only of his involvement with the gangs, the Sinaloa cartel, and drugs.

'Is there something else I can tell you?' the good woman asked, smiling. She turned to Paco. '*Señor*?'

'No, *gracias*, *Madre*.' He looked at me. 'Unless you have something...?'

I shook my head. 'No, thank you, Sister Maria Isabel. You've answered all my questions. Thank you so much for giving us your time.'

Once back in the car, I told Paco about Camp Belleview. He was shocked to hear it, of course, and vowed to keep an eye on the orphanage in future. I told him that if all went as we hoped Gregory would soon be behind bars anyway, and no longer a threat to the children. But if, as I suspected, there were other local abusers, friends of Gregory, then something else would have to be done about them.

'*Claro.*' He sighed. 'So. Do you want to see Gregory's house now?'

'Of course. Unless it's time for us to visit the housekeeper?'

He looked at his watch.

'She will be at home now, certainly. But let's give her some time to get settled before we invade her privacy, shall we? We'll look at the house first.'

Paco started up the Honda and pulled away from the church, heading east toward the rising hills and the nicer houses. Three or four minutes later he turned onto a road that led away from the main concentration of smart snowbird dwellings and climbed a hillside where there were no houses and walls to interrupt the scrub pine forest blanketing the upper slopes. A hundred yards further on we rounded a curve and slowed almost immediately as we approached an entirely isolated modern white-painted house of two stories perched behind a ten-foot high wall with an attractively designed black wrought iron gate separating its front drive and entry portico from the roadway. Beyond the building and its walled garden the tree and brush-covered hill rose another hundred feet or so. Across the house's second floor a broad terrace six or eight feet in depth looked out over the front entrance. Opposite the house, a steep bank dropped away from the road, offering anyone on that terrace an uninterrupted view of the town, the white sand beach and the sea beyond.

Paco was not so afraid this time of being seen by anyone and pulled to a stop immediately in front of the gates so that I could have the best view of the house and garden beyond it. It was an attractive place, of a proportion in keeping with the needs of a single resident family, and I liked it a lot. Gregory may have been an evil bastard but he certainly had good taste.

'Can I get out and have a look?' I asked.

'Sure. Why not?'

I opened the passenger door and climbed out, walking the few feet to the closed gate and peering through the railings. There wasn't much more to see, other than the shadowed entry portico under the terrace and the dark, heavy-paneled wooden front door. On either side of the house, within the surrounding wall, formal garden beds flanked tiled walkways, bordered by low box hedges and filled with geraniums, cacti and palms interspersed with clusters of desert rose bushes and dragon trees. As I was taking all this in a man in a long-sleeved work shirt and jeans suddenly appeared from around the corner of the house and strode toward me, scowling. He asked me something in Spanish that I couldn't understand. I smiled.

'Sorry, sir. I don't speak Spanish, I'm afraid.'

He reached the gate and glared at me through the railings.

'What do you want here?' he asked in heavily accented English.

'Nothing. I just wanted to see the house. I come from Crescent City, in California,' I lied. 'I heard that our District Attorney, Lamont Gregory, had a house here and I thought since I was vacationing in

Sayulita I'd find out where it is and take a look at it. Very impressive, I must say.'

The man's scowl relaxed somewhat and he nodded. Then he glanced beyond me to the car, bending and squinting to check out Paco in the driver's seat.

'*Señor* Gregory is not here. I am the caretaker.'

'I see. I don't suppose I could take a look at the place, could I? I'd love to see what the inside of the house looks like.'

He shook his head sharply. 'No. It is private.'

'Ah,' I said, still smiling. 'Pity. Well, thanks anyway.'

I gave the man a little wave, turned and climbed back into the Honda. Paco slipped the car in gear and we drove off down the hill again.

I was sure the man was watching us all the way out of sight.

'Where to now?' I asked as we reached the town again. 'Do we go to see the woman, or should we have something to eat first?'

Paco smiled across at me.

'*¡Hombre!* You only had lunch a few hours ago. Are you hungry already?'

'Actually, no. But it's habit. It's about this time in the evening that we *gringos* sit down to our evening meal.'

'In Mexico, *Señor* Arnie, we eat much later, in order to miss the heat of the day. In any case I would rather we didn't eat anything until we get back to Vallarta. I wish you to come home with me tonight to have dinner with us. My wife Rosa is preparing a feast of welcome for you and I know you will not be disappointed. Rosa is an excellent cook.'

I looked at my watch. It was now 6 PM.

'That's very kind of you, Paco. Of course, I'd love to come. But can you drop me at the hotel for an hour or so beforehand? I want to make some phone calls, and I need a shower.'

'Of course. But first we will go to see Gregory's housekeeper.'

Chapter Thirty

Señora Marielena Hidalgo lived on a packed dirt road in the midst of a line of small, single-storey cement structures standing in a row like decaying, badly discolored teeth. Hers was basically the same as the others, with the exception that the small front yard before her house was carefully tended and sported an assortment of low palm trees and lush tropical plants and flowers arranged around a tiny patio with a bench and a trickling brick fountain. *Señora* Hidalgo was obviously proud of her garden and took pains to keep it neat and flourishing. The rest of the houses in the row took no such pains, and the general impression was of dust and weeds and dog do. However the street was quiet, and aside from a scraggy-looking hound sleeping in a patch of shade and a man watering his geranium-filled window boxes a few houses down there was no sign of life. Paco passed by the house slowly, turned at the next corner and pulled the Honda to a stop. Then we both climbed out and stepped back around the corner toward *Señora* Hidalgo's front door.

There was a beaded fly-screen suspended in the open doorway, so Paco reached out to knock lightly on the door frame.

'*Señora* Hidalgo?'

A moment later a hand parted the fly-screen and the stern face of a woman in her fifties stared out at us, her dark hair tied back in a bun. She wore a simple dress with an apron over it, and her hands were covered with what looked to be corn flour.

'*Sí, señores. ¿En qué les puedo servir?*'

'*Perdón, señora, pero...*' Paco looked at me, then back to her. '*Señora* Hidalgo, do you speak English? My friend is American and does not speak Spanish.'

'Yes. I speak some English. What do you want?'

I spoke now.

'*Señora* Hidalgo, my name is Arnold Rednapp. I'm a reporter from a paper up near San Francisco in California. I'm here to do some research on your employer, Mr. Lamont Gregory, and I wonder if you might be willing to answer some questions? I know that you are his housekeeper and cook, whenever he is here.'

'*Sí.* Yes, that is correct.' She frowned. 'What kind of research are you doing on Señor Gregory?'

I looked at Paco. This might require some delicate maneuvering.

'It's for an article I want to write. I understand that Mr. Gregory is highly regarded here, and that he's done a lot for the local community – including founding an orphanage at the church. I'm interested in learning more about his philanthropic works here in Sayulita.'

Señora Hidalgo looked at Paco.

'Philanthropic?'

'*Su generosidad con el pueblo,*' he said, translating for her.

'Ah. *Ya entiendo.*' She looked back at me for a moment. Then finally nodded, pulling the fly-curtain beads aside with one hand. '*Adelante señores.* Please, come in.'

I stepped past her into her house with Paco close behind.

Beyond the beaded screen the front room was darkly shadowed and cool, with a gentle afternoon sea breeze blowing through from the front toward the back yard. Like that of Antonio Sanchez, *Señora* Hidalgo's house was small and compact, with only two or three rooms. From what I could see, it was furnished simply and comfortably and was kept neat as a pin. As Antonio had done, she led us through onto the *terraza* at the back of the house, where there was a small table and four chairs arranged under a splaying palm.

'Please,' she said, gesturing toward the table. 'Sit down. I will get us some cool water.'

Paco and I pulled out two of the chairs and sat while *Señora* Hidalgo disappeared inside. She returned a moment later with clean hands and a plastic bottle and three tumblers which she set down. Uncapping the bottle she filled the glasses, then took a seat across from us. Lifting her glass, she raised it toward us in a toast.

'*¡Salud caballeros!*'

'*¡Salud!*' Paco and I responded together, returning her gesture.

The cold water tasted good. The afternoon was still warm and sultry, even though the shadows now were growing long.

'So,' she said, setting down her glass. 'What would you like to know about *Señor* Gregory?'

I pulled out my notepad and pen.

'I have visited the orphanage at the church,' I told her. 'It's very impressive.'

She nodded. '*Señor* Gregory paid for the materials to build it.'

'Yes, I know. I'm told he is very fond of children.'

She looked at me for a moment, then looked away.

'That is so.'

'The Mother Superior at the orphanage told me he even has some of them to stay at his house sometimes while he is in residence here in Sayulita. Is that right?'

Señora Hidalgo seemed suddenly ill at ease, scratching her elbow nervously.

'Yes, that is true. He often has two or three of the children spend a night at the house. It is a great treat for them. I make them nice food and they spend the day playing in the garden and swimming in the pool.'

'How old are the children usually? Does he invite the younger ones or the older?'

'They are usually around twelve or fourteen years old, *señor*. But sometimes they are younger.'

'Boys and girls?'

'Boys, yes. But sometimes a girl will come as well.'

I decided to jump in with both feet.

'*Señora* Hidalgo, I've not been entirely truthful with you. It is true that I am doing research on Lamont Gregory – but not into the good deeds he has done. Up in California your employer is suspected of being involved in a number of criminal activities, including drug dealing and possibly even murder. He also has a history of sexually abusing young boys, and I have reason to suspect that he might well be taking advantage of those orphanage children during their visits to his house.'

Señora Hidalgo was looking at me, her face creased in a frown.

'Wait, please, *señor*,' she said, shaking her head. 'My English is not so good. I did not understand what you said just now. He has a history of what?'

Paco leant forward, speaking to her for several seconds in Spanish. As he spoke, *Señora* Hidalgo's face lost all expression and she sat back in her chair. When he was finished the woman looked back at me.

'You see, *señora*,' I said, 'Gregory has been known to engage in that kind of activity before, in California. Can I ask you, do you believe anything like that is happening during the visits of the orphanage children to his house here?'

The woman was as silent as the sphinx, staring implacably first at me, then at Paco, then at the table before her.

'*Señora* Hidalgo, I promise you no one will ever know of this conversation. You have nothing to fear. I am only trying to find out if these things are happening so that I can warn the Mother Superior at the orphanage of the dangers the children are facing. Believe me I have no wish to put you in any danger. I only want to know if you ... if you've ever had suspicions yourself that such things might be taking place there.'

There was another long silence. Then she sighed, looking straight into my eyes.

'*Señor* Rednapp,' she said, finally. 'I have never spoken of these things to anyone. I have been too afraid to speak. When I explain why you will understand. I have worked for *Señor* Gregory for ten years, now. He has always been a good employer and has paid well. When my husband died...' She looked down, momentarily reliving that grief, then looked up again. 'When my husband died *Señor* Gregory was very kind to me. He gave me a small gift of money to pay for the funeral and the burial. I have a son, who had then only seventeen years. I didn't know how I would be able to raise him without a father. *Señor* Gregory offered to take him to California with him, to give him work on his farm. I cannot tell you how happy that made me. My Pepe is a good boy, but he has not a strong character. He is easily influenced by his friends. And if his friends are bad, then...' She looked down at her hands clasped in her lap. 'I let him go to America because I thought it was the best thing for him.'

'And has it been?' I asked.

She shrugged. 'I do not know. Pepe writes to me once a month. His letters are always full of praise for *Señor* Gregory, and he tells me what he is doing on *Señor* Gregory's farm. But he has been there now almost four years and he is still just a laborer. He hasn't learned any new skills. Only his English is better, I think, which is good.'

I nodded. 'So Mr. Gregory has been good to you, and you've worked for him a long time. When did you start to notice things that didn't seem right?'

Señora Hidalgo sighed.

'As you know, I do not live in that house even when *Señor* Gregory is in Sayulita. When my work is done I come back here to my home. So I am not there at night when ... when these things happen. But I have noticed on many occasions that the morning after the children arrive they are different from the way they were the day before.'

'How different?' I asked. 'In what way?'

She frowned, concentrating. 'They are no longer happy. They are quieter, almost sad. And they seem afraid. Whenever there is a noise they jump and turn around to see what it is. Sometimes they don't come down for breakfast but stay in their rooms instead. I have to take their food up to them. Often I find them crying.'

I nodded. 'I see. Anything else?'

'Sometimes later on, when I make up their beds after they've gone, I have found blood on the sheets. Not a lot of blood, but some. So I knew something was happening to them while I was away but I didn't know what it was.'

'Does Mr. Gregory come down in the morning to be with them?'

'Yes, but he does not spend much time with them. And then a car comes after breakfast to take then away again to the orphanage. When they are leaving *Señor* Gregory always gives them each a nice gift of some kind – a toy or some candy or something from America.'

I nodded. 'Did you ever find out what was happening to the children?'

She looked down at her hands for a long moment.

'One night I had to go back to the house. I had forgotten my purse and had no money to buy food, so I had to go back up the hill to get it.' She looked at me. 'When I got to *Señor* Gregory's road there was only the light from the moon to see by. I got to the gate and let myself in with my key. It was about ten o'clock. *Señor* Gregory had visitors. There were two cars parked before the front door.'

'Did you recognize the cars?' I asked her. 'Could you tell who it was that was visiting?'

Señora Hidalgo nodded. 'Yes. One of them was a police car. The other was that of the priest at the church, Father Anselmo. I recognized it because he sometimes comes to visit Señor Gregory in the daytime.'

'Does someone in the police also visit Gregory during the day sometimes?'

'Yes. The Chief of Police of Sayulita, *Señor* Gregorio Gutierrez, has paid him visits. I didn't know if it was him that night because all the police drive the same kind of cars. At least, I didn't know it then.'

Señora Hidalgo reached into a pocket of her apron and produced a handkerchief, which she clutched in her hands.

'That night when I was inside the gate I tried to be very quiet,' she continued. 'I entered the house through the back door and went into the kitchen, found my purse, and was about to leave again when I heard one of the children cry out upstairs. A boy. He was clearly in pain. Then I heard the sound of a slap and the child stopped his screaming and started sobbing and whimpering instead.'

My face tightened.

'Was that all you heard, *señora*? Did you hear any of the men's voices?'

She dipped her head. 'Yes. I first heard the voice of the policeman, *Señor* Gutierrez, telling the boy to shut up. Then I heard a girl whimpering, and after that the priest's voice, trying to soothe the child. But he didn't sound like he usually does. He sounded ... evil, *como un boracho*. Like a drunk.' She shuddered. 'Then I left, as quietly as I could. No one knew I had been there. At least I hope that is so.'

I nodded. 'There's a caretaker living at the house, isn't there? How do you get on with him?'

'Fernando?' She made a face. 'He is a brute, but I try to stay on his good side. He can be very difficult.'

'Do you think he takes part in these sessions with the children?'

She looked at me. 'I do not know. I did not hear his voice. But he lives in the house so he must know what is going on.' She shook her head slowly. 'He is a bad man. It would not surprise me if he too did things to the children.'

I looked at Paco. He was sitting with his head down, staring hard at the ground. Then I turned my attention back to *Señora* Hidalgo.

'*Señora*, tomorrow I shall speak with the Mother Superior at the orphanage. I will find a way to persuade her to end the overnight visits of the children at Mr. Gregory's house – and even day visits, unless they're accompanied by a chaperone. That should stop the activity taking place there. I'm afraid I can't prevent it happening elsewhere, or do anything about the police chief and the priest.' I looked at Paco. 'Perhaps that is something you could do, *amigo*?'

'Perhaps I could,' he said nodding, his face grim.

I turned back to *Señora* Hidalgo.

'I also have to tell you, *señora*, that your employer will probably be arrested soon for his many crimes and brought to trial for them in America. When that happens you will lose your job. For that I am truly sorry.'

She smiled ruefully. 'I have been waiting for such a thing to happen. *No importa*. I would rather work for someone who is not evil. I shall start asking around. Sooner or later there will be something. But it is not for me that I worry.' Her eyes were starting to tear up, and she dabbed at them with the handkerchief. 'Please forgive me, *señores*. I am ashamed that I have not spoken of this before to anyone, but I was afraid. *Señor* Gregory has my son with him. He is also the friend of many important people. I did not believe anyone would believe me, and I didn't want him to do anything to my Pepe.'

Paco sat forward on his chair.

'*Señora*, no one can blame you for keeping silent.' He reached out a hand to touch hers on the tabletop. 'And you will not suffer from speaking of it now, I promise you. I am a reporter at *NoviVallarta*. I will ask around myself to see if there is anyone who knows of a position you could fill. I will do my best. If I hear of anything I will contact you.'

Now her smile was genuine.

'*Gracias, señor. Es usted muy amable. Un caballero. Gracias.*'

All this time I had been debating within myself whether or not to tell her about her son and his possible involvement with Davey Colson's murder. I decided finally to share with her at least part of the truth.

'*Señora* Hidalgo, I have one more thing to tell you. This is going to be even more painful, I'm afraid.'

Now she frowned again, alarmed. 'What is it, *señor*?'

'Your son, Pepe. I know of him. And I have to tell you that there are suspicions he's become involved with Mr. Gregory's drug business, and that he may have taken part in some violent crimes that are currently being investigated by the authorities there.'

Her eyes widened and the color drained from her face.

'*¡Ay Dios!*' she said, putting a hand to her mouth. 'Not my Pepe!'

'I'm afraid so. But I believe the boy has not done anything bad yet himself, just been witness to terrible things. Perhaps if he is willing to help the police they will go easy with him. Let us hope that is what happens. Believe me, if I can find him and speak with him I will urge him to take that road.'

'Please, *señor*. If you find him tell him his mother wants him to give himself up. He must tell the truth. If he does, surely the police will understand?'

Señora Hidalgo was weeping openly now, quietly, into her handkerchief. For a minute or two none of us spoke, waiting till she could compose herself again. Finally she dried her eyes and sat back.

'You have not met my Pepe?' she asked me finally.

'No, *señora*. Not yet.'

'Then I will show you his picture. He sent it to me two months ago.'

She got to her feet and disappeared into the house. While she was gone I looked again at Paco. This time he was staring at me, his face sad and troubled. Catching my eye he shook his head. I nodded.

'Here he is,' *Señora* Hidalgo said, reappearing at my elbow with a photo in her hand.

It was a color picture, taken at the lily farm against some sort of wooden-sided outbuilding. Pepe was standing with his arm around the shoulder of another young Latino about his own age. Both were smiling and both had open bottles of beer in their hands. The second guy was wearing a baseball hat, back to front.

'He's a good looking boy,' I told her. 'The other man, isn't that Alejandro Moreno?'

She looked at me, shocked.

'¡*Sí!* Yes. That is the name Pepe told me. He said they are best friends.'

'I know of him, too,' I told her. 'Alex's not involved with the drug people, as I understand it. He would be a good man for Pepe to have as a friend.'

'¡*Gracias a Dios!*' she said again, crossing herself. Then she took back the photo and gazed at it, lovingly.

There was really nothing more to say, so we thanked the good woman for her time and took our leave.

Chapter Thirty-One

Far to the north, in his luxurious house overlooking the Pacific, the Del Norte County District Attorney was not happy.

Firstly, the court recorder had telephoned him in his office that morning to tell him that some clerical official from Sacramento was going over the county trial records for the last several years, and he had no idea why such a review would be necessary. That worried Gregory. Why should such a thing happen now? Not that there was anything overtly wrong with any of those trials – so far as the casual observer could discern. But it was not good that such old ground was being dug over again.

Then after he'd arrived home that afternoon from his office he'd had a phone call from the caretaker of his Mexican property telling him that a gringo stranger had been to the house that afternoon asking to be shown around it. Someone who claimed he was a neighbor of his up here. Of course he'd been refused. When asked to describe the man the caretaker had been vague, but had promised to look through the house's CCTV security footage to try to send him a picture of the visitor. An hour later the picture had arrived via email. It was hard to see the man clearly through the bars of the front gate, but once his face had been enlarged by zooming in his identity was immediately revealed. Someone Gregory had met only a few days before. The reporter from the *South Bay Bulletin*. He was supposed to be following the investigation into the mysterious body in the river. Why should he suddenly turn up in Sayulita? Coincidence? Or did he actually know something?

If that was the case then Gregory was in danger. And that woman Sheriff's Deputy – what was her name, Mitchell? She must also be in the know, and therefore also dangerous. She was there when he had met the man and must be his friend. They were clearly working together. Something would have to be done about them. And soon.

Then another call came in on his second cell, this time from Los Angeles. More bad news. A mountain marijuana plantation in Trinity County, managed jointly by the VPR gang and the Sinaloa Cartel, had been over-run earlier that day by Sheriff's deputies and DEA agents. The men guarding the plants were none other than the three who'd been involved with the earlier botched mission in Gasquet. Two of them had fought back and been shot dead in the firefight. The third had escaped and was still at large somewhere in the forest.

'I thought you were going to have those men moved south!' Gregory had barked down the phone. 'Now there's someone running around out there who knows things that could get both of us into deep trouble!'

'Calm yourself, *amigo*,' said the smooth Latin voice at the other end of the line. 'I am in touch with the man via his satellite phone. He is making his way to another plantation of ours. The men there will get him south somehow.'

'Well, that's something,' the grey-haired attorney had grunted. 'Let me know when he's out of the area.'

'I will do that. With regard to the other business, the Zetas will be with you tomorrow. They've been given directions to the cabin. You will be contacted the minute they're in place and ready.'

'Good. I'm afraid, much as I hate these things, that I have a number of tasks here that require their special expertise. I've also decided to take up your suggestion and have them dispose of the person I've got currently hiding out up there. He's proved less than useful to me and now he's a millstone around my neck. I'll instruct them to take care of that business first.'

'Very wise. Loose ends are dangerous. The Zetas will do it and you will not need to worry about him again. You are flying this weekend?'

'Yes. My friend arrives tomorrow. He'll spend one night with me here, then we fly down to Vallarta together on Saturday.'

'Excellent. The friends to the south will be pleased to hear it.'

'Speaking of whom ... I learned this afternoon of the presence in Sayulita of a man from up here, a reporter, who seems to be nosing into my affairs. He may already know more than is good for either of us. If I email you his details and a photo of him taken from my CCTV do you think they might be able to do something about him down there?'

'That depends. Do you know where he's staying? And how long?'

'He told my caretaker he was vacationing in Sayulita, but who knows if that's the truth?'

'Then it is doubtful, unless he is going to be there for some time. But send the picture and his details anyway and I will forward them. We'll see if they can do anything for you. If he's in Sayulita they'll find him. If not ... you'll probably have to take care of him at your end.'

'Thanks. I appreciate it.'

When the two men had severed their connection Lamont Gregory went to his liquor cabinet and poured himself a double Glenfiddich malt. Then he sat again at his desk and swiveled it around so that he could watch the golden sun set on the rim of the sea.

As he sat ruminating on the day's troubling events, he began slowly to feel less stressed about them, more positive.

There were problems, yes, but their solution was on its way. And when that solution was effected life would return to its usual routine. It would cost him, but no matter. Resolving problems always resulted in expenditure of some kind. Some form of sacrifice.

In the meantime there was some good news. He'd spoken to the caretaker at the lily farm. The money was being collected from the network of local dealers. Come Friday night it would be ready to be loaded into the plane, placed beside the drug proceeds brought up from the valley by his friend. The caretaker would see to that; it was his responsibility. And while that operation went on in the small airport's dark hangar Gregory and his friend the Attorney General would be entertaining here – a dinner party for a few locally important invited guests. No one would know anything of what was happening a mile or two away. Only the one man involved. No one could suspect. And then, on Saturday, the two friends – together with their secret cargo – would travel to their idyll in the sun. The exchange would be made as usual and all would be well.

Things would continue on as before.

So long as the hard men from the south did their jobs well.

Chapter Thirty-Two

It had gone eight o'clock by the time Paco dropped me at my hotel in Vallarta. I asked for an hour to make some phone calls and to take a shower and he said he'd return to pick me up at around nine-fifteen.

I watched him drive off in his Honda, then went up to my room.

I found a cold Corona in the room's mini-bar fridge and settled with it and my cell phone on the chair on my balcony overlooking the pool. Below me scores of bronzed people were still cavorting in the water, or lying stretched out on loungers between the potted palm trees, enjoying drinks and the soft evening light. This time of year there were hardly any children around. I was glad of that for the quiet.

The first person I called was Devonne Peters. I caught him at his office and spent several minutes telling him about Paco Jimenez and our visits to the houses of Baldini and Gregory, the orphanage, and the interviews with Antonio Sanchez and *Señora* Marielena Hidalgo. As I'd promised, I did not mention Antonio's name. Devonne was excited by Sanchez's story about the exchange in the hangar, and promised that when the next shipment from Puerto Vallarta was expected in Sacramento he would have his men ready to swoop on the plane after it landed.

He was also interested, of course, in *Señora* Hidalgo's story of the pedophile ring of VIPs using Gregory's house as its base during the time he was in residence. I told him I intended to advise the orphanage's Mother Superior against allowing such overnight visits in future, perhaps suggesting that there were disturbing rumors being circulated, and Devonne liked that. I also told him Paco had shown an interest in exposing the local members of that circle of perverts, and Devonne liked that even more.

'Long live the free press,' he said, chuckling. 'You heard about the drug bust in Trinity?'

'No,' I said. 'What drug bust?'

'I thought your deputy friend might have told you. The Trinity County Sheriff's Department, along with a bunch of DEA agents, over-ran a hilltop marijuana plantation this afternoon. A hiker had come across it, seen armed men patrolling its perimeter, and informed the authorities when he got back home. The guys guarding the plantation were none other than the three Latinos in your CCTV footage from the store north of Crescent City. Two of them fought back, and in the fire fight both the big guy with the tat and the scar and the Wrangler owner were killed. The third guy unfortunately got away. The tattooed guy, incidentally, was carrying a Springfield Armory 9mm XD pistol – just the right caliber for putting that hole in Colson's head.'

'I'll be damned,' I said. 'If the third guy can be found and brought in he might now be tempted to spill the beans on the whole operation.'

'Maybe. We've got people out there looking for him. The chances are he's making for some other plantation nearby where there're other gang people he can hide up with. When're you back?'

'I fly to L.A. tomorrow after lunch. Then I'm driving home on Friday. How're your investigations into the Del Norte trial records going?'

'Slowly. There do seem to be some anomalies, but it's going to take careful scrutiny to identify any real criminality or negligence. They're still working on it.'

There was nothing else. I told Devonne I'd be in touch again soon and clicked off. Then I called my long-suffering editor, Abe Rawlings, at his home in the Palo Alto hills and brought him up to date.

'This story sounds more sensational every time you check in,' he said when I'd finished.

'Abe, I think there's enough here to be riveting reading for the entire state, let alone the bay area.'

'When do you think you'll be able to wrap it up?'

'Not until arrests are made. As to when that'll happen there's no way of knowing. I reckon the way things are moving it won't be too much longer. I'm heading up to Del Norte this weekend to poke my nose into a couple more wasps' nests. Hopefully that will provoke some kind of response. Anyway, we shall see.'

'When are you back here?'

'I fly to L.A. tomorrow and I'll drive up Friday. I'll stop by the office when I get there.'

'Good. Have you encountered any cartel heavies down there?'

'Not that I've seen. I've been pretty discreet.'

'Well, like I always say, Arnie, watch your ass.'

'I'll do that, boss.'

I was about to phone Lorraine next when my cell buzzed with an incoming. It was Geri Mitchell.

'Hey, Ger. What's happening?'

'Hi, Arnie. I got news.'

'If it's about the drug bust and the demise of Scarface and his partner, I've already had it from Devonne Peters.'

'Amazing break, isn't it?' she said. 'If they can find that third guy and bring him in, he might sing like a canary.'

'Let's keep our fingers crossed. How's Josh doing?'

'He's been fine. The only thing he's noticed over the last couple of days is that Félix, the Latino caretaker of Gregory's family house at the farm, has been making lots of trips out and about in his car, God knows for what reason. But he's away most of the time.'

'Is that unusual?'

'I asked Ryan. He says it's not when Gregory's about to make one of his trips to Mexico.'

I sat upright. 'Is he? Soon?'

'Ryan says Lamont told him they wouldn't be meeting this weekend because he was leaving on Baldini's jet Saturday morning. Apparently Baldini's coming up Friday afternoon to spend the night.'

'Any idea when he plans to come back?'

'Ryan says he should be back Monday or Tuesday.'

I made a mental note to let Paco know the details so he could pass them on to Antonio.

'Josh say anything else?'

'No. Except that the kid that saw his tattoos and freaked hasn't been seen since. Ryan doesn't know what's going on. He went to his place but he's not there.'

'Hmm. Sorry to hear that. I was hoping to speak to him when I get back there. I met his mother down here.'

'You what?' she asked, amazed.

I told her about my day, all of it. When I had finished she was silent for several seconds.

'Boy, it sure was useful for you to go down there. If everything falls right we could have this whole thing wrapped up in a matter of days.'

'Let's hope so,' I said. 'How are Nelson and Ross taking the news about the deaths of the two gangbangers?'

'As you'd expect. They reckon now that they're dead the Davey Colson case should be closed. They're making a big deal of it with Harv, but I don't think he's going to agree. Anyway, it'll be the D.A.'s decision to make, not his.'

'Yeah,' I said. 'But the D.A. is Lamont Gregory. He'll want it closed, without doubt.'

'Of course. So we've got to wrap this up as soon as possible, before he can make that happen. When are you coming back?'

'I'm flying up to L.A. tomorrow and will drive to San Francisco on Friday. I'll be hot-footing it up to you Saturday morning. Partly to see Lorraine and Mandy, of course, but also because I want to see some people – including the gangbanger who's in Pelican Bay, Nacho Flores.'

'That'll be interesting. What you going to ask him?'

'Don't know yet. Want to have a chat with his counsel, Thad Wilkins, first. That might tell me where to go.'

'I know Thad. He's a nice guy. You'll get on well with him.'

'Good.' I checked my watch. 'Anything else to report?'

'One other thing,' she said. 'Remember Alex Moreno? The boy who got beat up and wouldn't tell us what happened or who did it to him?'

'Sure do. What about him?'

'When I talked to Ryan today I asked after him. Ryan says he came back to work a few days later, then quit. Apparently he's now working at Ray's Market as a shelf stocker. His girlfriend Hayley's mom, my friend Verity, got him a job there.'

'Good for him. At least we know where he is if we need him.'

And that was it. Geri said the house key would be under the flowerpot on Saturday if I managed to arrive when no one was around, and we hung up. Then I called my angel.

'Arnie!' Lorraine squealed when I announced myself. 'I've been hoping you'd telephone tonight. How's it going down there?'

I told her the bare bones of the day's history, then asked after the two of them. All was fine in Shelter Cove.

'Ardelle and I have been buying furniture and equipment for the tea shop and we're both very excited. We managed to get some great deals from close-out sales in San Francisco, and the delivery charges aren't that steep.'

'Good news,' I said. 'How's work?'

'Oh, that. Boring as ever. I'm counting the days, Arnie. I tell you, I haven't felt this excited about anything in years! I can hardly wait for it all to come together! When we get back from Crescent City we're going to start redecorating the place.'

'That'll keep you in shape. If I'm around I can help.'

'That'd be awesome, but it's not necessary. Ardelle and I are both practical gals.'

'How's Mandy?'

'A bit stressed over her end-of-year exams, but otherwise fine. She's looking forward to our weekend break. And she's looking forward to seeing you.'

'Well, I'll be there Saturday afternoon so maybe we can do some things together. I've got people to see, but I should have some free time after that.'

'Oh, Arnie. I'm looking forward very much to being with you again.'

'Me, too, honey. Me, too.'

Paco was right on time, his white Honda sweeping to a stop outside the hotel entrance exactly at nine-fifteen.

I'd been waiting for him just inside the lobby doors, enjoying the cool of the air-conditioning, and walked out to meet him as he pulled up.

'Did you make all your calls?' he asked as I slid onto the passenger seat.

'I did. And had a shower. And I stopped by the shop in the lobby and got this for you guys as a thank you present.'

I handed him a box of chocolates and a large bunch of flowers, which he ooed and aahed over for a bit before depositing both on the back seat, thanking me profusely.

'You really didn't need to buy presents for us,' he said. 'It is my pleasure to be helpful to you. For your sake and for Marty's.'

'You've been more than a help, Paco,' I told him. 'Without you I'd never have been able to find out the things we discovered today. With that information we'll have no trouble bringing down Gregory and his minions. Oh, and there's a message for you to deliver to Antonio.'

'What's that?' he asked, swinging the car south onto the main drag again.

I told him about Gregory's plan to fly to Vallarta on Saturday with Baldini, and to remain until Monday or Tuesday. So there'd be at least two nights the Citation would need watching.

'No matter,' Paco said. 'Antonio will do it. And if he needs help, I'll be available, too.'

'Well, be careful, both of you. All we need to know is that the exchange has been made and the time the plane will leave the airport with them onboard. Baldini will probably fly first to Crescent City to drop Gregory, then fly back to Sacramento. By the time he arrives the place will be swarming with agents.'

The evening spent with Paco and his lovely wife, Rosa, was very pleasant indeed, with an extended meal of spicy Mexican dishes and a generous assortment of fine wines, red and white. They both insisted that as soon as I was able I was to bring my daughter and Lorraine and Mandy down for a holiday, and I told them I would talk to the boss and see what could be arranged – probably for later in the summer.

Paco dropped me back at the hotel entrance just short of midnight and we agreed to meet the following morning to make one final trip to see the Mother Superior in Sayulita.

Then I waved him away and went up to my room.

Chapter Thirty-Three

Thursday, May 29

Paco met me at the hotel at nine the following morning. I had already checked out and had my bag with me when I saw his white Honda ease to a stop outside the glass front doors. I threw the bag into the back seat and climbed in front and he pulled out into the traffic.

We drove straight across the hills to Sayulita where Paco parked outside the orphanage on the other side of the quiet street. This time the playground was empty. The children were obviously in class. The nuns weren't expecting us, but when we had identified ourselves and told the voice at the other end that we wanted another short interview with the Mother Superior the same nun from before, Sister Josefina, let us in.

Sister Maria Isabel was surprised to see us again.

'What brings you back to us so soon, *señores*?' she asked when we had seated ourselves. 'Was there some question you forgot to ask me yesterday?'

'No, *Madre*,' I told her. 'I'm afraid that since our visit yesterday we've heard some rumors that might cause trouble for the orphanage if they're not dealt with. We decided to talk to you about it.'

The good sister leaned forward over her desk. 'What have you heard, *señor*?'

'It has to do with the children's visits to Mr. Gregory's house.'

The woman looked puzzled, cocking her head to one side. 'What about the visits?'

I sighed. This was not going to be easy.

'Sister Maria Isabel, as you know my friend Paco here and I are both journalists. Last night we were told about certain stories that are circulating locally that have to do with Mr. Gregory and a few other local dignitaries and officials. The rumors hint that when the children from your orphanage spend the night at Mr. Gregory's house, they are...'

I hesitated. What I had to say was awkward enough to tell anyone let alone a nun with vulnerable young lives under her care. I tried again. 'I'm sorry, Sister. This is most unpleasant, but I'm afraid there's no other way to put it. The gist of the rumors is that while the children are visiting Mr. Gregory they are being sexually abused by these men.'

Sister Maria Isabel stared at me without moving an eyelash.

'Sexually abused?'

'Yes.'

She shook her head. 'That cannot be true. I do not know about the other men you mentioned for I do not know who they are, but as for *Señor* Gregory, he surely is incapable of such a thing. He is a good man, *Señor* Rednapp. Look at what he has done for these children!'

I nodded. 'I know, Sister. It is possible that the rumors are groundless and that the men are totally innocent. But for the sake of the reputation of the orphanage – and that, of course, of Mr. Gregory – can you not see that it would be better for everyone if these visits to his house were suspended? At least for a time?'

The good woman stared at me, running the implications of my suggestion around her mind. Then she sighed and nodded.

'The Mother Church has suffered much over the last years with reports of such evil things,' she said at last. 'So perhaps yes, it would be good to stop the visits for a time. *Señor* Gregory can always see the children here, can he not?'

'Exactly,' I said, smiling.

'It saddens me,' she said, shaking her head, 'that people have so little to do in their lives that they can entertain such disgusting thoughts.'

'It is a pity,' I agreed. I stood up. So did Paco. 'That is all we came to say, *Madre*. We thought you should know of these rumors as soon as possible.'

She stood as well, clasping her hands.

'Thank you for coming, *señores*.'

By the time we got back to Vallarta it was approaching noon so Paco took me straight to the airport and the two of us walked into the terminal together. There was plenty of time before my flight's departure so we found a table at the back corner of the little snack bar and ordered coffees. When they came, Paco stirred a sachet of sugar into his.

'Well, Arnie. I think it has been a useful twenty-four hours, *no*?'

'Very useful, Paco. None of it would've been possible without your help.'

He shrugged. 'It was nothing.' He took a sip of his coffee. 'Your visit has given me a new project. If I can find the evidence to bring down these men that molest the children, believe me I shall do so. You have given "*El Gallo*" another good reason to crow.'

I raised my cup to him. 'I wish you luck with that, *amigo*.'

Ten minutes later I had checked in and Paco and I stood before the barrier leading into the departure lounge.

'Give my regards to Marty, please,' Paco said, shaking my hand again. 'He's another good brave man. And take care of yourself, Arnie. I think there are some dangerous times ahead for you.'

'I'll be careful,' I told him. 'Tell Rosa I look forward to seeing her again.'

And with a wave of my hand I took up my bag and walked through to the security check.

Marty Taylor was waiting for me on the other side of customs when I got to LAX and led me outside to the short term parking lot. Five minutes later we were winding our way through lunch hour traffic back toward Westwood in his Crown Vic.

On the way I filled him in on the developments of the previous twenty-four hours and passed on Paco's best wishes.

'He's a great guy,' I told him. 'Without Paco the trip would've been a wasted effort. Because of the work he did before I arrived we learned things that will have a huge impact on bringing down Gregory, Baldini and their entire operation. Thanks for putting me onto him.'

Marty smiled across at me. 'I thought he'd be useful.'

'He was more than useful. Without him I'd have been nowhere.' I glanced out at the neighborhoods whizzing by outside my window. It was good to be back. 'Any new developments while I've been away?'

'Matter of fact there is one. Mike Brundage called last night. She managed to track down the whereabouts of the former Supervisor of Camp Belleview, Clifford Marshall.'

I turned to him. 'Oh, yeah? Where is he?'

'In Bakersfield, believe it or not. He's retired now, lost his wife to cancer a couple years ago. He's in an assisted-living complex at the edge of the city. I've got the address.' He patted his shirt pocket.

'Great, Mart. Tell Mike thanks for me, will you? I'm driving home tomorrow morning and can stop and see him on the way – though I'm not sure what he'll be able to tell me, or if he'll be any help to us at all.'

'Well, here's the address anyway.'

He pulled a piece of paper from his shirt pocket and handed it across to me. The assisted-living place was called Sunset Apartments. It meant nothing to me. I stuck the paper in my notebook.

'I had a thought on the plane, Mart,' I told him. 'Paco says he's going to work on bringing down Gregory's little pedo ring in Sayulita and exposing all its local VIP members. As for me, I've almost got enough evidence now to bring Lamont Gregory down both for his drug dealing and for his sexual abuse of minors.' I glanced across at him. 'How would you feel about tackling the Attorney General, Anthony Baldini? Exposing his drug connections and his manipulation of the state's legal system at the highest level? Think you could work that angle?'

He smiled. 'Arnie boy, I've been thinking of nothing else for the last three days. And I've already made a start. After you go tomorrow I'm heading up to Sacramento to spend a few days digging around. I still have connections there and they might be able to open a few doors for me.'

'Go for it, Mart. I'll let you know if I come across anything that might help.'

Connie was waiting for us with a lunch of cold cuts and salads when we got in. After we'd eaten I spent a couple hours in my room getting my notes in order, answering emails and packing. I had just decided to lay down for a few minutes' rest when my cell buzzed. It was Devonne Peters.

'Hey, Arnie. You in-country yet?'

'Got back just before one. Got something for me?'

'I have indeed. We've picked up the third member of the Latino group that did in Davey Colson. Remember, the one on the run?'

'I remember. Where'd you find him? On another marijuana plantation?'

'Nope. He was in a southbound van full of illegals that was stopped by chance by the CHP just below Fresno on I-5. His name's Enrique Bardén, by the way. He tried to run off, but the Smokey put a bullet through his calf and dropped him. No broken bones, however, and he's due to be released from the hospital within the next twenty-four hours. When that happens I've got agents ready to interrogate him. We're hoping he's gone through so much by now that he might be willing to talk.'

'That's great news, Devonne. I'll keep my fingers crossed. Anything else?'

'Only that I've got agents watching out for the Attorney General's Citation flight plans. They'll be on hand in numbers when he touches down in Sacramento on Monday.'

'You going to arrest him then?'

'No. They'll keep him and the plane under close surveillance for a couple of days first, see who collects the goods and where they're taken.'

'Good idea. Better to get as many of the bastards as you can at one go.'

'That's the thinking. You going north tomorrow?'

'That's my plan.'

'Well, I'll call you if I have any news. Otherwise, take care of yourself.'

'I'll do that, Devonne. And thanks for keeping me in the loop.'

Just before the close of business hours I looked up the Crescent City attorney Thad Wilkins' office number and gave him a call. I was lucky. He was in. I explained that I was a San Francisco journalist following the David Colson murder, and told him that I was a friend of Deputy Geri Mitchell.

'Great lady. How can I help you, Mr. Rednapp?' he said.

'You have a client I'd like to speak to, counselor. A prisoner at Pelican Bay named Nacho Flores.'

'Ignacio, yes. Why would you like to see him? What can he have to do with the Colson murder?'

'Nothing. But there are issues raised by the investigation that have to do with L.A. gangs – the VPR in particular – and I'd like to ask him a few questions. When I get to Crescent City I can meet with you to explain in greater detail.'

'When do you expect to be here?'

'I'm driving up to Del Norte County Saturday afternoon. Any chance we might meet then?'

'Saturday? Is it that urgent?'

'Given how close we are to resolving this investigation I'd say yes to that. As long as you don't mind the intrusion into your home time?'

He laughed. 'I'm a bachelor, Mr. Rednapp. My Saturday home time is watching a Giants game on the television with a couple of beers and a pizza. I think I can spare a few minutes to hear what you have to say. I'll give you my cell number so you can call me direct.'

'Great, counselor. I'll call soon as I hit town. Thanks.'

He gave me his number and I wrote it down.

'How's the electioneering going?' I asked.

He sighed. 'I don't know. Gregory's so entrenched in this county I wonder sometimes if it was even worth my challenging him. We'll see, I guess.'

'Your campaign might be given a big boost shortly, Mr. Wilkins. Something in fact that could make your election a virtual walkover.'

He laughed. 'Short of a miracle I can't imagine that happening. What kind of boost are you talking about?'

'You'll know after our meeting on Saturday. But I think it'll certainly lift your morale.'

'Intriguing. I look forward to hearing from you, Mr. Rednapp. In the meantime I'll contact Flores and suggest that he agrees to see you.'

'Thanks, Mr. Wilkins. See you Saturday.'

My last day with the Taylors was very pleasant, with another relaxed late afternoon swim in their pool and another splendid evening meal – this time a Thai feast created by Connie. I went to bed again a thoroughly contented man, with a full stomach, a quiet mind, and a sense that in spite of all the evil in the world there were still marvelous things that people could share together and wonderful times to be had.

Chapter Thirty-Four

Friday, May 30, AM

Former Delta Force Sergeant Joshua Grant Bridger stood bent over the stained enamel sink in his tiny apartment bathroom at the Eagle, splashing cold water over his cheeks in the grey early-morning light. Then he straightened and reached for the towel, scrubbing dry his weathered skin and tawny beard. He had to bend down slightly to see all of his face in the square of mirror above the sink and the face he saw was deeply tanned. He finished his drying and hung the towel back on its nail, hovering a moment longer before the mirror, stroking the trimmed beard down over his cheeks and chin, grooming it. He smiled. It was a neater Josh Bridger now than the one that had greeted the little deputy and her journalist friend at the highway rest stop eleven days earlier. Even his hair had been cut back from ragged shoulder length to curl in smoothly below his ears. He was more modern-looking now and less wild – a far cry from the mountain man image his former look had suggested.

He wondered how Deputy Mitchell was doing. He hadn't spoken to her for a couple days and was curious as to how the investigation into Davey's death was progressing. And where was the reporter? The last thing Geri had told him was that Arnie was off to Mexico to take a look at Gregory's house and to learn what he could about how the man spent his time there. He should be back by now. Hopefully he'd learned something useful. Josh would call Geri later to find out. For now, though, he had to finish dressing. Pablo would be by to collect him in ten minutes.

For the first couple of days at the lily farm Josh had kept to himself, remaining cordial but virtually monosyllabic in his communications with his workmates. But after a few days of working closely with them he began to open up slightly, finding in Pablo Ortega in particular a man of quiet wisdom with whom he could relax and in whom he could – to a certain extent – trust. Then, after Pepe Hidalgo had seen Josh's tattoos and had reacted with evident shock, the word had soon spread that Josh was more than simply a new field hand. It was clear now that he was in fact a close friend of the blond gringo that had gone drinking with the Gregory employees and then been found dead in the Smith a few days later, and that he was working on the farm to try to discover how and why his buddy had died. Josh knew that his cover was blown. Even Pablo had reacted differently with him after that day, reserved and taciturn, and Josh found it necessary, finally – when by chance one afternoon they were working together apart from the others – to explain his purpose in taking on the job. He did this without mentioning Geri Mitchell or any connection with the investigation – hinting that his decision to look into things had been entirely his own. Pablo had listened soberly and then had clapped him on the back, wishing him luck in his efforts. He also told him to watch his step, for the powers that had brought about Davey's demise were still out there and anything they considered a threat to them or their operation would be dealt with strongly. Josh acknowledged that warning, but told Pablo that that was what he was hoping for – some overt move that might reveal who the shot-caller and his lieutenants were and how they operated. When Josh had been knocked off his bicycle Pablo had been even more concerned. But Josh had diffused his worries by reminding him he'd been a Delta Force soldier and could handle whatever they threw at him. Pablo shook his head, grinned at him, and appealed to the Blessed Virgin to protect his crazy *gringo* friend.

Josh reached for his shirt, pausing long enough to inspect his right arm to check the healing of the cuts and scrapes he'd sustained when the pickup had swerved out of the darkness to pitch him into the briary ditch. All was progressing well. In a few days the scabs would be gone. Satisfied, he finished pulling on his shirt.

Five minutes later he was waiting outside the Eagle's front door when Pablo Ortega's white Nissan Navara pulled to a stop next to him. Josh climbed inside.

'*Buenos días, Señor* Josh,' said Pablo, putting the pickup in gear and pulling away. 'How are you this morning? No one has tried to kill you again in the night, I hope?'

Josh smiled wryly. 'Nope. No excitement last night. Except for discovering Perlita's taco shack up the road. I stopped there on my way home, had three of her tamales, chicken and beef. They were awesome. She does good stuff.'

Perlita's was run out of a parked van in the lot across from Ray's Market at the top of the town, near the entrance to Highway 101. In the few months of its existence it'd earned a widespread reputation for excellence.

'*Sí*,' Pablo agreed. 'Perlita and her husband Juan come from a village in Chihuahua not far from where I was born. Their food is pretty good. Conchita's at La Cantina is better. You should try it.'

'So I hear. I'll stop there one day and give it a go.'

'You should. But the best Mexican food of all here is that of Juanita, my wife.'

'You're a lucky man.'

'I am that, yes. A very lucky man. But you are lucky, too. Because tonight I am inviting you to come back with me to my house to meet Juanita and to try her enchiladas. What do you think of that?'

Josh smiled broadly.

'That's awesome. Thank you. I look forward to it. We can stop at the store after work and I'll get some beer.'

Paco turned right onto Highway 101 at the top end of Smith River and headed south. There was no fog that morning, and the broad lily fields flanking the roadside basked under a sky that was a clear cornflower blue.

Josh had kept clear of Ryan Garrett after his initial interview with him for the job. Ryan had intimated then that he knew why Josh was there and was completely *au fait* with what was going on. But he also told him that he mustn't expect any special favors – he would be treated just like every other worker. If Josh had something to tell him he was to do so discreetly. Josh had agreed to that.

Deputy Mitchell was another matter. Josh had contacted her on her cell soon after he'd been given the job on Gregory's farm. Since then he'd spoken to her on two other occasions – once to tell her about the boy seeing his tattooed hands and fleeing, then again after the hit and run. He knew it was best to keep their communications to a minimum and he had refrained from checking in with her just to solicit news on the investigation. But things were moving more quickly now. He'd have to contact her again soon to find out if there'd been any developments.

He smiled, thinking of her. She was an attractive woman, in all ways. Had it not been for the buxom waitress in Grants Pass that'd become a regular feature in his life over the last eighteen months Josh might have been seriously interested in her. At the beginning, while he'd been looking for a suitable law enforcement officer with whom to share Davey's photograph and story, he had followed her Sheriff's Office SUV at a distance one afternoon on his Indian, had watched her pass by Smith River, then turn off onto Ocean View Drive, the old Highway 101, and eventually turn up the sloping driveway of a smallish farmhouse perched on the hillside opposite the distant ocean. He had stopped a quarter mile beyond beside a low stand of brush and watched her climb out of her ride and enter the house with a key. So he knew where she lived if he needed to get to her. For the moment, however, the cell phone contact was enough.

Pablo slowed his pickup at the centerline of Highway 101 and turned left onto the paved track that led up to Lamont Gregory's house and farm. Beyond the large white family home, outside the barn, a dozen men loitered in clumps awaiting the arrival of Ryan Garrett, who would assign them their duties for the day. Josh Bridger scanned the men's faces. Manuel Fernandez had not yet turned up for work again, though he was expected every day. Josh wanted to be prepared when he faced him for the first time. But there were no new faces. All of these men he had seen and worked with before.

Pablo parked the pickup at the side of the barn and the two men climbed down. As they joined the rest of the men Ryan Garrett's Chevy Captiva pulled up and the big man descended, slamming the door shut behind him. The men moved toward him and soon he was giving them their instructions. The work day had begun.

It was just after lunch when Josh, working with a group of three other men clearing a culvert of brush and dead leaves, noticed a dark van slow and pull to a stop on the shoulder of 101 near to them. The van was a hundred yards away but Josh could see the passenger side window slide down and the silhouettes of two men looking his way from the front seat. He thought he could make out a third in the van's back seat, but he wasn't certain. Then the driver produced a set of binoculars and trained them toward Josh and the others. Josh felt his eyes lock momentarily with those of the watcher. Then the binocs were dropped, the window raised again and the van pulled off the shoulder and moved on down the highway.

Josh watched it go, his old Delta Force instincts kicking in automatically, flashing warning signals in his brain.

So. The professionals had arrived.

From now on he'd have to be extra careful.

Chapter Thirty-Five

Friday, May 30, PM

Traffic was moderate when I left Mart and Connie's at ten Friday morning and it took just two hours to reach Bakersfield and to find the address Marty had given me for Sunset Apartments, where Clifford Marshall, the former Camp Belleview Supervisor, was now living. My faithful Tom Tom led me right through the sprawling city directly to it. The place was laid out in a broad U-shape with the main entrance at its center. There was a long parking lot across the front of the building. I pulled the Cobalt into the first slot I could find, shut it down and climbed out. The morning air was heavy and still, without even a breath of breeze moving the trees.

Fortunately the Sunset Apartments building was air-conditioned. Just inside the glass front doors was a reception desk with an African-American woman manning the phone. She looked up at me with a bright smile. The nametag pinned over her heart read 'Yvonne'.

'Good morning, sir. Welcome to Sunset Apartments. How may I help you?'

I smiled back.

''Morning, Yvonne. I'm here to see Mr. Clifford Marshall. I believe he's living in one of your apartments?'

'That's right. Mr. Marshall is in No. 18, just down the hall to the right and around the corner.'

'Do you know if he's in now, or might he be out?'

The girl sobered slightly.

'Oh, he'll be in his room. Since his stroke six months ago Clifford doesn't get around too well. We take him out in the late afternoons, but during the mornings he stays in his room after breakfast. Does he know you're coming?'

She lifted the phone and was about to dial.

'Ah, no. I'd like it to be a surprise if you don't mind.'

She raised her eyebrows and put the phone down again.

'Are you a member of Mr. Marshall's family?'

'A distant cousin,' I lied. 'Clifford's my second cousin on my mother's side. I was just passing through and thought I'd pay him a quick visit.'

She nodded, smiling again.

'Would you like a member of staff to accompany you, Mr...?'

'Rednapp. Arnold Rednapp. And no, I'll be fine on my own, thank you.'

The phone started ringing and she reached out to grasp it.

'Very well,' she said, distracted now. 'Let us know if we can be of any help, Mr. Rednapp.'

She picked up the phone and I set off toward Marshall's room.

Just beyond the corner the hallway became all glass on the left hand side, with the apartment doors opening off to the right. The view through the windows was of a lush well-watered lawn crisscrossed by cement pathways leading to a central gurgling fountain. There was an abundance of benches and here and there residents sat on them in the sun, or lounged in wheel chairs with an attendant or a relative at their sides, their aged faces turned upwards, taking the rays.

No. 18 was only a few steps beyond the corner. On the door was a brass number plate and, below it, a white card with Marshall's name hand-printed on it. There was a Christian fish symbol at its bottom. I stopped at the door and listened. Inside I could hear the murmur of morning television. I rapped on the dark wood. It took a couple of minutes, but finally the door was opened and I was staring into the pallid face of a heavyset man in his late seventies, his thin, wispy hair tousled as if he'd just woken up. This bewhiskered face little resembled the one I'd seen in the newspaper photos Martin Taylor had sent me. The left side of Marshall's mouth dragged downwards slightly – a legacy of his stroke, I reckoned. He stared out at me through rheumy eyes.

'Yes?'

'Mr. Clifford Marshall?'

'That's right.'

His slightly slurred voice was cracked and old, the voice of a man now unused to speaking, and his accent was definitely southern.

'My name is Arnold Rednapp. I'm a reporter for a San Francisco paper. I'm writing an article about youth correction facilities in California. I believe you were in charge of one of those for some years at the edge of Los Angeles County – Camp Belleview. Is that right?'

His frown deepened.

'Yes, that's right. What about it?'

'Would you mind if I asked you a few questions about your time there, sir? It won't take long.'

His mouth worked as he considered my request. Then he opened the door wide and stepped back to let me enter.

'Come on in,' he said. 'I guess I can give you a few minutes.'

The apartment was small – only a short hallway leading from the door to a studio front room with a tiny kitchen area built into one wall and a bed in the opposite corner. A door in the hallway led into the bathroom/toilet. A flat-screen TV was mounted on the wall of the front room next to the double window. There was an overstuffed armchair across the room from it, a small cluttered table at its side. Prominent on the wall above the television was a carved image of Christ on the Cross wrought from some dark hardwood. It dominated the room. There was one more chair, a straight-backed wooden number resting against one wall.

Marshall hobbled forward toward the armchair, his left arm swinging limply at his side. When he reached the chair he lifted a large black-bound Bible off the seat, and then dropped heavily onto it. Then he picked up the television remote from the table beside him and punched the screen to black. He was wearing patterned yellow pajama trousers and a white t-shirt under a loosely tied pale blue dressing gown. His bare feet were in slippers. I pulled the straight-backed chair closer and sat down.

'Mind if I make some notes?' I asked, reaching for my notepad and pen.

'I guess not,' he said. 'What do you want to know?'

'As I said, I'm researching youth correctional facilities in California for an article I've been commissioned to write. In my reading I came across the name of Camp Belleview, and noticed that it was closed in 2003 after only ten or twelve years of service. I thought that was curious, and I wanted to ask you about it – since you were in charge of the place throughout its existence. Your name was listed as the camp supervisor. Can you tell me why it was shut down so soon?'

Marshall's eyes bored into me, his face still locked in a half-frown, as if he had registered a bad smell and couldn't yet determine its provenance. He was still clutching the Bible in his lap.

'Are you a Believer, Mr. Rednapp?' he asked finally.

'Ah ... no, sir. I'm not.'

'Shame,' he said, nodding. 'You'll go to hell, son. You know that, don't you?'

'Maybe so. But I've always tried to lead a good life, so if there is a God maybe he'll be merciful and spare me from the hot place.'

'That's not good enough, Mr. Rednapp. No matter how hard you try to be good we're all sinners at heart. Born that way. Without actively seeking His forgiveness...' he glanced up at the dark wood crucifixion, '...you haven't a chance.'

'About the camp, Mr. Marshall. Can you tell me what happened there that made the authorities close it down?'

He swung his eyes back to mine.

'That camp was an evil place, Mr. Rednapp,' he said. 'An evil place. The hand of the Devil was at play there.'

'In what way, sir?'

'I didn't know what was going on. Not for a long time. Then my wife told me about it. Edna. She died two years ago. That's her picture on the bedside table there. She found out bad things were going on and she begged me to do something about it.'

'What kind of bad things, Mr. Marshall?'

He shook his head, his whole body shuddering.

'Perversion. Profane things. Wicked things.'

'Sexual, you mean? Was some kind of sexual abuse taking place there? Is that what you're saying?'

He stared at me for a long moment, motionless. Then he nodded.

'My wife found out about it. One of the boys told her. Then she told me, tried to make me do something to stop it.'

'And did you?'

'I couldn't.' He lifted the Bible, clutched it to his chest, staring before him and shaking his head. 'He told me he'd ruin me if I ever said a thing to anyone. He said he'd make sure everyone knew what'd happened in Arizona, that I'd never be able to work again.'

I sat forward. 'Who was "he", Mr. Marshall? And what happened in Arizona that was so terrible?'

'Gregory!' Marshall spat out the name like a curse. 'Lamont Gregory. He was with the D.A.'s office. A bigwig. Important. Powerful. He'd founded the camp. He threatened to ruin me when I challenged him about his visits, about what he was doing to the boys, he and the others. He said he'd make the whole thing come back again. So I backed down, kept mum. Had to. My wife never forgave me for it.'

'What had happened in Arizona, Mr. Marshall?'

He looked up at me again. A pathetic, wheedling look.

'You won't tell anybody, will you? You won't give away my secret?'

'I promise, no.'

Nodding, he sat back, still cradling the holy book.

'I had a man killed there. In Arizona. A young black man. While I was warden at another institution.' He looked up at me. 'He was a bad one, violent and mean. He was always causing havoc, giving us trouble. One night he started a riot, got all the boys on the rampage. I had to call in all the guards to put it down. When we finally got control again I'd had enough. I thought it'd quiet things down if he was got rid of, make our lives easier. So I asked a couple of the boys to take care of him, hardened COs who'd had enough of his shenanigans themselves and were mad and bad enough to do it. I told them to make it look like it'd happened during the riot. So they ... they beat him to death.'

'And word got out?'

He nodded. 'The Arizona Department of Corrections thought the death was suspicious. They sent a team down to investigate. Somebody must've said something. Anyway, I was called to Phoenix and told to resign. Either that or they'd bring charges. I resigned. I didn't work for five years.'

'And then Gregory found you and offered you the job at Belleview?'

'That's right.'

'Because he knew he had a handle on you, knew he could count on you to keep silent about what was going on at Belleview for fear of having your past brought up again, knowing what your wife would've suffered had she known the truth. The shame of it. Not to mention the possibility of you finally having to face charges.'

He nodded, staring down into his lap.

'I had to go along with it,' he said, quietly. 'Had to. I kept quiet. But when the inmates started to die ... first the Schneider boy, then the two others that hung themselves ... I'd had enough. I was going to ask for early retirement, but before I could do that the State closed the place down, gave us all our walking papers.' He looked up at me, suddenly frightened. 'I don't know why I've told you all this. You won't tell anybody, will you? You won't write all that in your article? Please don't, I beg you. I've been in hell ever since Gregory threatened me, made me keep quiet. I keep seeing those boys' faces, hearing my wife's pleadings. I was a bad man, Mr. Rednapp. A weak man. I was damned for what I'd done, condemned to hell. But now I'm saved.' He smiled, lifting the Bible in his hand and holding it out toward me. 'The Lord Jesus Christ has forgiven me my transgressions and I'm reborn. None of that can touch me anymore.'

I nodded. 'I'm glad for you, Mr. Marshall. And no, I won't be writing about your secret, I promise you.'

He smiled then, dropping the Bible back into his lap and sitting back.

'Thank you, sir. Thank you. You're a good man.'

I stood, replaced the chair against the wall and stepped toward the door. Then I turned back.

'One last question, Mr. Marshall.'

'Yes?'

'The Schneider boy. You said he died. I've heard that he escaped and was never found. What was the truth?'

The old man shook his head. 'I never knew for sure. Pritchard and Delgado – two of the guards – said he'd escaped and run off. They'd found an open window, they said. There was no way to disprove them. But it wouldn't surprise me if they'd just snuffed him and dumped his body somewhere. I've known a lot of bent correctional officers in my time, Mr. Rednapp, but those two were about as bad as they come.'

I nodded, looking down at the broken figure in his chair desperately clutching his Bible. And for a moment I saw a monster, a vile demon every bit as guilty as Gregory himself, and a part of me felt like decrying that guilt to the world, in spite of my promise to him. But then I reconsidered. Clearly he'd suffered enough. His silence had cost him the happiness of his marriage and the serenity of his old age. Who was I, after all, to cast judgment? Looking down at him now I saw only a sad, scared pathetic old man awaiting his end. I reached out to touch his shoulder.

'Thanks for talking to me, Mr. Marshall.'
And I left.

I got home at six that evening – leaving me time to run a bunch of dirty clothes through the washer and dryer, to go through the stack of mail that awaited me in my mailbox, to pay a few bills and make a few phone calls.

Abe Rawlings was very interested to hear about all my discoveries since we'd spoken last.

'Sounds like this thing should end soon the way things are shaping,' he said. 'You going up to Del Norte again?'

'Tomorrow morning,' I told him. 'I reckon I'll only have to be up there three or four more days. By then we should have the whole story. And hopefully an arrest.'

'Good deal, Arnie. Let me know how it's going.'

I told him I would and we hung up.

Five minutes later my cell buzzed. It was Paco Jimenez in Puerto Vallarta. I pushed the talk button.

'Paco, *amigo*. How're you doing?'

'All is fine, *Señor* Arnie,' he said. 'I wanted you to know that I have found for *Señora* Hidalgo a new position with a family in Vallarta. A colleague of mine needed a housekeeper and cook. She'll have a little apartment of her own on their property. There is even a room for her son if he comes back to visit.'

'That's good news. When is she taking up the job?'

'She thought it would be best to make her move after Gregory returns to California. Then her son would not be at risk.'

'He might not be anyway. The boy's gone into hiding, and I think not just from the authorities. I think he's also scared of Gregory now.'

'Why?'

'It's almost certain he was witness to a murder up in Del Norte that was set up by Gregory. I think he's afraid Gregory will have him popped so he won't be around to tell any tales.'

'In that case, if the son is safe, *Señora* Hidalgo could make her move earlier. Maybe even tomorrow. I will contact her and arrange it.'

I smiled. 'That'll make Gregory's day, to turn up Saturday and not have a cook or a housekeeper. I love it. He'll have to make his own breakfasts, poor man.'

'Ha!' Paco laughed. 'Perhaps he can persuade the caretaker to do the cooking?'

'Let's hope he poisons him,' I returned. 'But no. I'd rather see the bastard rot in jail for all he's done.'

'So would I, *Señor* Arnie. So would I.'

I told Paco to pass on my regards to Antonio and to Rosa and hung up.

Fifteen minutes later I was fast asleep.

Chapter Thirty-Six

It had gone 11 PM by the time Pablo dropped Josh Bridger outside the front door of the old Eagle Hotel. Before he climbed down Josh shook the man's hand again and thanked him for the evening. He'd had a good time, and Juanita's food had been as good as her husband had boasted.

As Pablo swung the pickup in a tight U-turn to head off back to his trailer home Josh's eyes strayed to the small parking lot across the street behind the old Bank tavern on the corner. The Bank was the second of Smith River's bars, and its regulars were mostly local trades people and workers – long-standing white residents. Nestled amongst the four other vehicles stationed side by side in its small parking lot, its nose pointed out toward the street, was the same black van Josh had seen pull onto the highway shoulder that afternoon. He couldn't see if there were men in the van because there was too much shadow. But he suspected there were, and that they were watching him.

Josh watched Pablo's pickup disappear down the road. Then, turning away, he unlocked the building's front door and went inside.

His apartment was at the back of the building, up a flight of rickety stairs that had clearly needed attention for some time. The hallway was deeply shadowed, the only light coming from a shaded low wattage bulb dangling from the ceiling near the foot of the stairs. Josh climbed the stairs, moving quickly. When he reached the upstairs landing he turned toward the front of the building. The upstairs hallway was unlit and ended at a window overlooking the street. Moving past the doors of the two front apartments, Josh edged along the wall toward the side of the window. Cautiously he peered around the window's edge through the full-length lace curtain. As he did so there was a sudden explosion of sound as two men reeled laughing from the back door of the old Bank tavern. Josh watched as they approached the car at the left of the van. One of the men pointed his key fob at it and punched the unlock button, causing the car's interior lights to flash momentarily. In that flash Josh could clearly see three forms inside the black van, facing his building. Oblivious, the two men climbed into their car, started it up and drove away, leaving the street empty again under the pale light of the lone streetlight beside the tavern.

For a long while nothing happened. Everything was quiet, save for the distant thrum of crickets.

Then the van's doors opened and the three men stepped down, all wearing balaclavas and dark jumpsuits, all three carrying pistols with long silencers held down at their sides.

Josh didn't wait any longer. Turning, he retraced his steps along the hallway to his own door and unlocked it. Stepping across the threshold, he pulled the door to and locked it again from the inside, closing the sliding bolts at top and bottom.

Ever since the hit-and-run incident Josh had expected such a move from Gregory's hirelings and he was prepared for it. Without switching on any lights he quickly gathered his few belongings into a backpack and moved to the window at the back of the room. This he unlatched and quietly slid open.

The old hotel was T-shaped, with a two-storey projection pointing out from the center back of the building. The projection had originally housed the former hotel's restaurant and kitchen on the lower floor. Now it was converted into apartments. Josh's window overlooked the scruffy yard at its right side.

Poking his head out, he glanced down at the ground. There was nothing but a few clumps of grass, which would help to break his fall. Slinging the backpack over his shoulder, Josh eased himself out onto the window ledge, then turned and lowered himself down to hang by his fingertips from the sill. Then he dropped to the ground, landing in a crouch and stifling his involuntary gasp.

Josh knew exactly what to expect. He'd done the drill himself dozens of times, going with his Delta Force unit after insurgents holed up in ramshackle hideouts in Faluga or Mosel.

Like him his pursuers were professionals. They'd play by the rules. That gave him an advantage. He knew the rulebook, too.

The men would divide up in the street – two to breach the hotel's entrance lock and approach the apartment from its front door, one to skirt around behind the building in case their target tried to escape that way. Josh had only seconds to prepare himself.

Dropping his backpack to the ground, he flattened himself against the wall at the building's corner, listening and watching. The light from the streetlamp beside the tavern angled down the alleyway at the hotel's side, washing the ground beside him in a pale glow. Almost immediately he heard soft footsteps on gravel, saw a man's shadow moving down the alleyway toward him.

When the man turned the corner he was looking upwards, searching for Josh's window, his gun raised toward it. He didn't see Josh lunge at him from the darkness until it was too late. With one arm Josh struck the gun upwards while at the same time swinging a rabbit punch into the man's throat. Before he had time to react Josh delivered a second sharp blow with his clenched left fist to his diaphragm, driving the breath out of him. Then as the man started to buckle Josh swung his right, crashing it into the side of his head. Instantly the man dropped, unconscious, to the ground. The whole thing was over in a nanosecond.

Josh hovered over him a moment, listening. His victim was still breathing, but he didn't move. His pistol, a Glock 22 .40 caliber, was still in his hand. Josh prized it from the senseless fingers, slipped on the safety and jammed it into the back of his pants waist. Then, slipping on his backpack, he dashed down the alleyway toward the street, pausing at the hotel's corner long enough to peer around toward the front door. The street was empty. The two men had obviously gained entrance and gone inside.

Hoping they were on their way upstairs, Josh pelted on tiptoe across the street to the tavern parking lot, reaching the cover of the black van and crouching down behind it. Leaning out slightly, he peered back at the hotel. There was no movement. No sound.

So far so good.

Pulling from its scabbard at his back the hunting knife he'd taken to carrying since the attempt on his life, Josh eased around the side of the van far enough to swing his right arm in a wide arc out and down, plunging the sharp point into the tire's side. There was a sudden whoosh of air as it deflated, the van slowly settling over it, popping and creaking.

Sheathing the knife again, Josh vaulted the fence at the back of the lot and launched himself into the darkness beyond.

It took half an hour to work his way through the town, moving from back yard to back yard, keeping to cover whenever possible and well away from street lights. Fortunately the quarter moon had not yet risen and he managed to avoid rousing all but a couple of the dogs along his way, finally reaching the last fringe of houses at the north end of town. Here he slipped over a fence into the adjacent field and worked his way east along it till he reached the barbed wire barrier at the edge of Highway 101.

At his left, on the far side of the field, a line of scrub trees marked a narrow stream that continued through a culvert to the other side of the highway. Keeping low, Josh sprinted along the fence toward those trees. When he reached them, he hovered behind a low bush, awaiting a gap in the highway traffic. When one came, he picked his way between the barbed wire strands and sprinted across the two lanes in the darkness. Climbing another fence, he kept to the trees and brush flanking the stream, following it as it angled upwards toward Ocean View Drive.

Geri Mitchell was seated in her reclining armchair in her pajamas and dressing gown, working at her laptop, when she heard the low tap at the French doors across the room. Turning her head toward them, she slowly slid open the drawer in the table beside her and extracted the snub-nosed Colt .38 she always kept there when it was not in her purse.

'Who is it?' she called out, holding the gun ready in her lap.

'Bridger,' came the voice from beyond the glass.

She frowned. 'Josh?'

Carrying the Colt she rose and crossed the room, pulled back the curtain and peered through the glass. It was Bridger all right, standing on the back deck with his backpack. In his right hand was a gun, pointing downwards. Geri unlocked the door and pulled it open.

'There's a strange car in your driveway,' he said quietly.

'That's right. I have guests staying.' Geri cocked her head to one side. 'What're you doing here? How did you know where I...?'

'I've known where you live since before we met,' he interrupted, grinning sheepishly. 'Part of my checking you out process.'

'I see. Well, you'd better come in.'

Geri stepped back and Josh moved into the room, pulling his backpack from his shoulder and glancing around.

'Where're the guests?'

'One's asleep. The other's having a shower.'

Josh nodded. 'Sorry to come so late but I had no choice.'

Kneeling, Josh opened the top of the backpack and jammed the Glock inside. Watching this, Geri frowned.

'What's happened, Josh? Where did the gun come from?'

Josh stood again, clutching the backpack.

'Could I have some water first? Then I'll tell you. I've been stumbling through fields for the last forty-five minutes and I'm thirsty.'

'Of course. You can have a beer if you want? Or something stronger?'

'No. Water's fine, thanks.'

Geri replaced the Colt in its drawer, closed down her laptop and went out to the kitchen. When she returned with the water Josh had dropped his backpack on the floor and was sprawled on the sofa.

'Hope I didn't get dirt on your carpet,' he said, taking the glass from her.

'It wouldn't matter if you did. That's what vacuums are for.'

She watched as he drank half the water down, then wiped his mouth with the back of his hand. Then she returned to her armchair in the corner.

Clutching the glass in his lap, Josh sat back.

'Okay,' he began. 'Here's the story...'

Josh outlined the events of the previous ten hours. When he had finished Geri was on the edge of her chair, her brows drawn in a tight line.

'Oh, my God,' she said, blinking. 'So they're back.'

'Not the originals, Geri. Those guys were amateurs. Remember how they butchered Davey's body, how they panicked and dropped it in the river? They were just scared greenhorns. These guys today are the real deal. I could tell from the way they handled things from the first.' He took another drink of water. 'And now I've pissed them off. Given one of 'em some severe aches and pains, stolen his gun and embarrassed them with the flat tire. They'll really want my ass now.'

Geri looked around apprehensively.

'They couldn't have followed you, could they?'

Josh grinned. 'No way. No, they didn't follow me, and they don't know where I've gone.'

Geri visibly relaxed. 'Thank God for that.'

'But we can't rely on that for long. Sooner or later the man at the top is going to put two and two together and figure out we're working together. Then he'll tell his goons, they'll find out where you live and come to check us out.'

She tightened. 'Tonight?'

Josh shook his head. 'No. It should take twenty-four hours at least. Hopefully longer.'

Lorraine walked into the room from the hallway leading to the bedrooms. She was wearing a fluffy white dressing gown and toweling dry her long honey-colored hair. When she saw Josh she halted.

'I thought I heard voices out here.'

Geri stood up.

'Lorraine, this is Josh Bridger. Josh, my friend Lorraine.'

Josh rose and Lorraine stepped toward him extending her hand, which he shook.

'Lorraine and I were roommates at Sac State years ago,' Geri went on.

Josh smiled. 'Very pleased to meet you, Lorraine.'

'Same here,' Lorraine said, returning the smile. She glanced down at his hands. 'Nice tats.' Then she retreated to sit on the sofa beside Geri. 'Given the hour I take it this is a business call, not just a casual drop-in?'

'That's right, Lo,' Geri returned. 'Josh is helping with the investigation into the mysterious body in the river.'

Lorraine nodded. 'Ah.'

Geri explained Josh's part in the investigation, briefly describing what he'd been doing and why he'd turned up so late on a Friday night. When she'd finished Lorraine's mood had morphed from light to serious and she was staring at the floor, deep in thought.

'Sounds like it's not really a good time to be here,' she said at last. She turned to Geri. 'If these guys really are after Josh, then based on what you've told me they're bound to figure out you two are connected and turn up here sooner or later. I think maybe I'd better get Mandy out of here and back to safety in Shelter Cove.' She put her hand out to touch Geri's arm. 'You'd better find somewhere else to stay, too. This place is pretty remote. I don't want anything to happen to you.'

Josh sat forward. 'Nothing will. I'll hang around for the next day or two till we're sure the danger's passed. Things are heading up fast now. The end should come soon. Either the baddies will be found and arrested, or we'll at least know where they are. Who's Mandy?'

'My thirteen-year-old daughter,' Lorraine told him. 'We've came up to spend two nights, but I'm thinking maybe we'd better go back tomorrow instead.'

Josh nodded. 'Probably a good idea.'

Geri made a sad face. 'Sorry, Lo.'

Lorraine sighed. 'No matter. We'll do it again when this thing is over. I'll stay long enough tomorrow to see Arnie, then we'll go.'

Josh looked at Geri. 'Arnie? Is he due back tomorrow?'

Geri nodded again. 'Yes. Sometime in the afternoon.'

'Wow,' Josh said. 'The gathering of the clan. Looks like he chose his moment well.' Then he stood up. 'Well, ladies. Tomorrow's going to be a busy day so we'd better get some sleep. If you've got a blanket and a spare pillow, Geri, I'll curl up here by your French windows and keep an eye on things.'

'I've got better than that,' she told him. 'A folding camp cot and a flannel sleeping bag. You should sleep well in that.'

Ten minutes later the ladies had retired and Josh was settled into his cocoon beside the double-locked and curtained French doors.

Just for safety, the Glock – without its silencer now – lay ready on the floor beside him.

Chapter Thirty-Seven

It was midnight when Lamont Gregory's last dinner guests had departed and he was left alone with his overnight visitor. Leaving him nursing a whiskey nightcap in the living room he passed into his study, retrieved his second cell phone from the desk drawer and checked it. There were two missed calls, both from the same number. Pushing the button to return the last call, he settled himself in his desk chair. After four rings the phone was answered.

'Yes?'

'You called me tonight. Twice. I'm sorry I didn't pick up. I was away from my phone.'

'Yes.'

'So have those matters been taken care of as I wished?'

'The first was handled successfully. You won't need to worry about that one anymore.'

The District Attorney shuddered. 'Good. And the other? The ex-soldier?'

There was a long pause.

'Well?'

'Sorry, *señor*. He got away.'

'He *what*?'

'He must have seen us waiting for him. He climbed out a window at the back of his building and ran off. We didn't see which way he went.'

'I'll be goddamned,' Gregory breathed, hunching forward. 'Do you have anything else to tell me? Any other good news?'

'Do not worry, *señor*. We will get him,' the Latino returned. 'I want him, too. He hurt one of my men and took his gun. It is now more than just a job. It is a mission. I promise you, we will find him and he will pay.'

Gregory sighed. This business was growing ever more exasperating. And dangerous. It had to be wound up properly, and soon.

'All right. Go back to the cabin. Wait there. I'll try to find out where he could be and call you in the morning before I leave. I'm leaving at ten so it'll be before then. I won't be reachable after that till mid-afternoon, but don't bother calling me unless you have good news. I should be back in Crescent City Monday.'

'Understood, *señor. Bueno*. We'll go to the cabin and sleep. I'll await your call in the morning.'

And the connection was cut.

Lamont Gregory sat in the shadowy study staring into space, distracted now, and worried. Where could the man be? Where could he have run to?

Then he remembered. The woman deputy, Mitchell. And the journalist. They must all be working together. The journalist was not from here. There'd be no local address for him where the ex-soldier could find refuge. But the woman...? She was also a Smith River resident, he knew. And wherever she lived, it couldn't be far from the old Eagle Hotel.

Gregory smiled.

Now he knew his instructions for the morning. Two birds with one stone. Very neat. He nodded to himself, pleased with the idea. And if by chance the reporter was visiting at the same time ... then all three could be eliminated. That would leave only the missing boy to be silenced, once they'd tracked him down.

To strengthen their resolve he would offer the Zeta assassins another $50,000 each, to be delivered when all four of the troublemakers were dead. But it must be done cleanly, in such a way that the deaths seemed accidental. There must be no potentially dangerous investigations.

Above all, there must not be any more unnecessary killing – no collateral damage, as they said in the military. Just those four.

Then it would be finished and he would be safe once again.

Rising, he snapped off the desk lamp and left the room to return to his friend.

Chapter Thirty-Eight

Saturday, May 31

I awoke in my own bed bright and early Saturday morning after a long and very sound sleep. It was good to be back in my own apartment, if only for a few hours.

I showered, breakfasted on cereal and fruit, and was just getting my things together to head north when my cell buzzed. It was Geri.

'Arnie! Glad I caught you before you left. Things have been happening up here.'

I took the phone to my favorite chair and lowered myself into it.

'What kind of things?'

'There's been another attempt to kill Josh.'

'What! When?'

'Three Latinos in a van were waiting for him late last night. Josh reckons they're pros. He saw them in the parking lot across from his apartment building when he got back from visiting Pablo Ortega. He went inside and watched from an upstairs window, saw them climb out of their van and move toward the building's front door. All three had guns with silencers. Josh escaped by climbing out a back window, knocking one of the men out on his way. He also took the man's pistol.'

'That'll piss them off. Where is he now?'

'Here with us. He came last night, just after midnight. Scared me half to death.'

'Is Lorraine with you?'

'Yes. She and Mandy arrived last night around nine. They're both fine, but after hearing Josh's story Lorraine's decided they'll drive back home later this afternoon. They'll wait for you to get here first. Things are getting too scary for them to stay here just now.'

'I think that's a good plan. It's bad enough you might be in danger. I certainly don't want them running any risks.'

'Nor do I. But Josh is still here and he's keeping an eye on things. He doesn't think the men will try anything else until tonight at the earliest. It'll take them that long to make the connection. Or to be told of the connection.'

'Let's hope so.' I looked at my watch. 'It's half past seven now. If I get away in the next half hour I'll be up there by 2:30 or 3:00. I'll come as quickly as I can.'

'We'll be waiting for you. Oh, and there's other news, too, Arnie.'

'What's that?'

'I had a call from Harv Cantrell. The CHP were called to a blazing wreck up on the South Fork of the Smith last night. An old pickup went off the road and crashed down into the gorge. The gas tank must've exploded on impact. The driver was trapped behind the wheel. He was burnt to a crisp.'

'You don't have to tell me. The driver was Manuel Fernandez, right?'

'They think so. It was his pickup, all right. But the body was burned so badly they'll have to identify it in some other way. The autopsy's this morning.'

'So,' I said. 'If they've gone after Manuel it looks like Gregory's decided to eliminate all the loose ends that might connect him to Davey Colson's murder. I think maybe you'd better warn that boy that saw Josh's tats and ran off. What's his name? Pepe. Pepe Hidalgo. Remember, he saw it all happen. Or so we think.'

'I remember. But Ryan said he hasn't been around since that day. Not even at his house.'

'In that case it's not so pressing. He's probably hiding.'

'Where?'

'When I was in Mexico Pepe's mother showed me a picture of him with Alex Moreno. Remember, the kid that got beaten? The two of them are pals. I think Alex will know where he is. Or Alex's girl, your friend's daughter. If you have time, you might try asking Alex first, then the daughter.'

'I'll do that. Arnie, shouldn't we tell Harv Cantrell the truth about all this now? I think it's time we brought in the department, don't you?'

'We should tell Harv, yes, but I don't know about anybody else. Maybe we can talk to him after I get there this afternoon. Can you arrange a meeting with him somewhere neutral, say at his house? Make it for around four o'clock if you can – I've got to see Thad Wilkins first about arranging an interview with the Latino prisoner in Pelican Bay. I'll also call Devonne Peters and suggest it's time he came to Crescent City and saw things up close. He could start by joining us at that meeting. But we only want to meet with the Sheriff. He can decide afterwards if he wants to trust the rest of his deputies.'

'Okay,' Geri said. 'I'll call and arrange it. That's it, I guess.'

'All right. One more call and I'm out of here. Let me know Cantrell's address. You can text it to me. And I'm sorry about Lorraine and Mandy. Maybe we can all have an early dinner together before they head south.'

'We'll try for that. Anyway, we're here waiting. Want a quick word with Lorraine?'

'No time. Just give her my love, and say that I'll see her soon.'

Devonne picked up after only one ring. I knew he'd be on the job, even this early on a Saturday. Too many things were happening for him to afford the luxury of a lie in.

'Yeah, Arnie. What you got?'

I told him the news Geri had just given me, also that we'd decided to meet with Sheriff Harv Cantrell to tell him all we knew about the murder, Lamont Gregory and the men in the black van. I then suggested that Devonne might well want to be at that meeting.

He sighed, thinking. 'Yeah, I'll come. It might be a risk to tell him, but if you think Cantrell can be trusted then I agree, it's the thing to do. You need backup, you two. I'll brief my number two here, then I'll head north after you. I'll bring a couple of other agents with me, just in case. When are you going to be there?'

'I should get to Crescent City around three. Then there's someone I want to see. I've asked Geri to arrange the meeting with the Sheriff at his home for four o'clock. Can you make that?'

'As soon as I can square things away here I'll be on my way. With luck, we'll be there by four. If the meeting's set for then we'll go straight there. Let me know the address when you can.'

'I'll do that. Incidentally, have your agents been able to question the Latino the CHP picked up in the van near Fresno?'

'They're working on him but so far he's hanging tough. Won't give out anything but his name, Enrique Bardén. Still, it's early days. We'll see what happens after he's been grilled steadily for thirty hours or so.'

'Fingers crossed. We could sure use his testimony if he can be broken. Maybe you could offer him witness protection?'

'He'll have that put to him. Oh,' he added. 'You might be interested to know, Gregory and Baldini have just taken off from Crescent City in the Citation. They'll be in Puerto Vallarta by the time we meet up.'

'Fingers crossed the usual exchange is made in the hangar.'

'If it is we'll have 'em,' Devonne said. 'Drive careful, Arnie. See you in the redwoods.'

And he hung up.

The traffic was moderate through the city, but I wasn't able to make any real time till I got north of Santa Rosa. From then on things went pretty smoothly. An hour into the trip I heard the little musical phrase from my cell that tells me I've got a text. I pulled it from my pocket and took a look. Confirmation from Geri of the meeting with Sheriff Cantrell at his house at 4 PM, with his address and a brief description of how to get there. She also told me Lorraine had decided to stay in Crescent City for one more night. She and Geri had taken rooms at the Bayview Inn on the harbor front, and she'd also booked a room for me. That was good news. That meant we'd have one night together at least, and that she and Mandy would be out of danger. At the first rest stop I came to I pulled off the highway long enough to text the meeting time and the Sheriff's address to Devonne Peters. Then I set out again into the traffic. I was feeling good. Everything was set. And the game stakes were rising.

I got to Crescent City just before three and swung off the road into a service station at the edge of town. While the tank was filling I produced my cell and dialed the number I had for Thad Wilkins.

'Hello?'

'Mr. Wilkins, it's Arnie Rednapp. I've just got to Crescent City. Okay if I swing by your place now?'

'Sure. Come ahead.'

He gave me his address and told me how to get there and within ten minutes I was parked outside his modest house and walking up the cement pathway to the front door. He had it open before I got to the porch. He was a little shorter than me, and stocky, but his full dark-hued face projected genuine friendliness and self-confidence. His black hair was styled slightly long and he was wearing a white shirt with the sleeves rolled up and a pair of chinos with wide red suspenders. He was a good-looking man.

'Good to meet you, Mr. Rednapp,' he said, shaking my hand.

'Please, call me Arnie.'

'Then you must call me Thad. Come on in.'

I stepped inside and he closed the door, then preceded me along a hallway to a kitchen with a breakfast counter on one side dividing the food preparation area from the broad living room beyond. The house was simply but tastefully furnished and bore the hallmarks of being a man's space with no female touches apparent anywhere. There was a television on in one corner, a Giants baseball game by the sound of it.

'Can I get you anything? Coffee? Cold drink?'

'Coffee would be great, if it's made.'

'It is. I'm a bit of a caffeine addict, I'm afraid. Goes with the job.'

'Fine. Then I'll have a cup, thanks. White, no sugar.'

Wilkins filled two mugs from a glass coffee pot, added a dash of milk to mine and handed it to me, then led us through into the living room.

'Take a seat. And tell me about this news you've got that's going to make my election a walk-over. I'm dying to hear it. Right now I can use all the help I can get.'

He sat in the armchair that was obviously his command post, reached for a remote and killed the TV. I sat on the sofa, took a sip of my coffee and rested the mug on the coffee table before me.

'How well do you know Lamont Gregory?' I asked him for starters.

He shrugged. 'I've been up against him in court a fair number of times, and I respect him as a counselor. Wily and shrewd. As a man ... I'm not so sure.'

'Why do you say that?'

'Well, my feelings about the way he's run the D.A.'s office over the last eight years are well documented. I think he plays favorites, and I think he's too soft – especially with the cartel-affiliated perps. With those he tends to lay down open and shut plea bargain charges that move them on into prison temporarily but are not in my view harsh enough penalties for the severity of their crimes. Ironically, the ones he goes after hard are the locals, the guys who grow their limited pot crops in the mountains nearby. He throws the book at them, gets them all sent away for long sentences. That's never seemed right to me.'

'Doesn't the public notice what he's doing? Going after the locals but giving the cartel thugs a relatively easy ride?'

'As long as the dealers are seen to go to prison the public doesn't care that much. Sad but true.' He sipped his coffee. 'Anyway, it's always hard to prove negligence or malpractice in a D.A.'s office. Bad or unfair decisions can often be blamed simply on too heavy a workload.'

'That may be so,' I said, 'but what does Lamont Gregory's apparent double standard suggest to you, Thad?'

Wilkins smiled. 'Gregory's no fool. He knows what he's doing. If I'm honest, it suggests to me he's got an in with the cartels, that he's treating their boys lightly in return for kickbacks of some sort.'

'What if I told you it's worse than that? What if I told you that Gregory, in fact, is the godfather of all of the drug dealers in Northern California, that he's running the whole shebang?'

Wilkins sat back, his mouth open. 'What?'

'Yep. He's had close connections with the L.A. gangs ever since he practiced law down there in the 80's. He's even formed a partnership with his old buddy Anthony Baldini, the State Attorney General, so that they split the profits from a state-wide drug dealing syndicate. Their organization's being protected by a network of corrupted officials and law enforcement officers all across the state.'

This was a lot more than what I actually knew, and far beyond what had been mooted thus far in the investigation into Gregory's illicit activities. But even as I said it, it seemed more than likely the truth. If Gregory controlled the cartel drugs in Del Norte County why shouldn't he also control the supply for the whole northern half of the state? And wouldn't that broader involvement be more in line with the notoriety of the senior shot-caller from the north that Lt. Mike Brundage had spoken of – 'El Avogado', 'the lawyer'? That would also explain, at least partly, the need for Baldini's regular trips in his Citation to Crescent City – to supply the northern demand for cartel drugs. I'd said it to get Wilkins' attention, to draw him onside so that he'd be willing to help. But the more I thought about it the more I believed I was probably right.

Thad Wilkins put his cup down on the small table beside his chair.

'I think you'd better tell me what you know, Arnie.'

So I did. By the time I'd finished Wilkins knew almost everything.

'What part does my client, Nacho Flores, play in all this?' he asked finally.

'None,' I told him. 'Nacho's only connection is that he spent time in Camp Belleview during the period Davey Colson was there. He almost certainly knew about the sexual abuse. His testimony could tie Gregory in with that and with certain other criminal events at Belleview. Anyway, I'd like to question him about his time there. He was also a member of the Varrio Pasadena Rifa gang, and might know something about Gregory's association with the gang leaders.'

Wilkins nodded. 'Okay. I'll get on to the prison right away, see if we can arrange a meeting with Nacho for tomorrow morning. If you give me your cell number I'll let you know the time.' He stood up. 'I'll need to be there, too, of course.'

'I wouldn't have it any other way.' I emptied my mug and stood up. 'Great, Thad. I'll expect your call later regarding the meeting time.'

Wilkins walked me to the front door. I gave him my card and he tucked it into his shirt pocket.

'Good meeting you, Arnie. Thanks for briefing me on all this. You were right. My election prospects do suddenly look a hell of a lot brighter.'

I smiled.

'Like I said, a walkover. See you tomorrow at Pelican Bay.'

Chapter Thirty-Nine

Sheriff Harvey Cantrell lived in a big ranch-style place on one of Crescent City's residential streets a few blocks north of the Sheriff's Office. By the time I got there Geri's sporty red Toyota was already parked in the drive in front of the closed doors of the double garage, beside the Sheriff's new departmental white Ford Explorer Interceptor SUV. The house was surrounded by a large well-trimmed lawn, with tidy flower beds and blossoming rhododendron and azalea bushes dotted here and there.

I pulled up outside the house at five minutes to four. Gathering up my notebooks I climbed out, locked the car and headed up the drive. I had just reached the porch steps when a dark blue Crown Vic pulled to a stop behind my car. I waited while Devonne Peters climbed out of the front passenger seat and two other agents from the driver's side and back seat. The driver was a woman. I waited as they locked their car, then walked up the drive toward me, Devonne in the lead, carrying a briefcase. When he reached me he pushed out a hand, which I grasped.

'Arnie,' he said.

'Good to see you, Devonne. You made good time.'

'Not bad for a Saturday.' He turned to the other agents. The man was medium height, in his thirties, with a slim, fit body, a square jaw and a tense smile. The woman was older, mid forties, also of medium height with short chestnut hair and a trim figure. Devonne pointed to them in turn. 'Arnold Rednapp, Agents Tom Walker and Elaine Fischer. Two of my finest. I've briefed them on the way up and they've had a look through the Del Norte investigation reports to date.' He glanced at the red Toyota. 'That Deputy Mitchell's car?'

'Yep.'

'Then it looks like we're all gathered.' He looked at me. 'There's no one else coming to this meeting, right?'

'Not so far as I know.'

He nodded. 'Good. Well, then. Let's get started.'

Harv Cantrell's face as he opened the door went from a welcoming smile to a puzzled frown.

'Hello there, Arnie,' he said. 'Who're your friends?'

'Sheriff Cantrell, this is Special Agent in Charge Devonne Peters from the FBI's San Francisco field office. And these are his assistants, Agents Walker and Fischer.'

'Feds, huh?' he said, shaking each of their hands. 'Well, I guess you'd better come inside and tell me what this is all about.'

He stepped back and we filed through into the house. When he had closed the door Harv led the way through a wide arch into a spacious front room that took up virtually a quarter of the house. Geri was standing in front of a sofa on one side of the room. She nodded at me and smiled at the other newcomers.

'Have a seat, please,' Harv said. The agents moved toward a second sofa and matching armchair beside it, Peters taking the armchair. I moved to sit beside Geri on her sofa. 'Geri and I were having coffee and there's a full pot on in the kitchen if you'd like a cup. Or I can get you water. Or a beer if you'd prefer.'

'I'll have coffee,' Devonne said, smiling. 'White with two sugars.' He turned to the others. 'You guys?'

'Coffee sounds good,' said Agent Fischer. 'But black, please, and no sugar.'

'Same for me,' her colleague added.

'I'm okay,' I said.

'Fine,' Harv said. 'The wife and kids have gone out so we have the house to ourselves. Oh, and if any of you need the convenience it's down the hall on the right.'

He smiled and disappeared toward the kitchen.

During his absence I took the opportunity to introduce Geri to the others. Then Harv reappeared with a tray upon which four mugs were placed, filled with steaming coffee. There was a sugar bowl and spoons alongside them. Harv moved first to the two agents on the sofa, who each took a mug. Then he placed the tray on a coffee table before Devonne and stood back.

'Hope that's enough milk, Agent Peters. Help yourself to the sugar.'

'It's fine. Thanks.'

Devonne spooned sugar and stirred as Harv moved to sit in his large recliner in one corner of the room.

'Now then, gentlemen and ladies,' he said. 'To what do I owe this visit? Geri and I were just small talking, waiting for Arnie to get here – and of course I thought it was to be only Arnie joining us. I assumed we'd be discussing the Colson murder case. Am I still right? Is that why you're here?'

He was looking directly at Devonne Peters.

'That's right, Sheriff Cantrell,' he said, smiling.

Harv held up a hand. 'Please, everyone. Let's cut the formality. I'm Harv, okay?'

'All right, Harv,' Devonne went on. 'I think maybe it'd be best if Deputy Mitchell answered your question, since she's the one who made the discovery that got us involved in the case.' He looked toward her. 'Geri?'

'Sure,' she said, and cleared her throat. 'Harv,' she said, turning toward him, 'I know you warned me about keeping anything important in this case from you, but once you hear the whole story I think you'll understand why I did.'

Sitting forward, she began. Forty-five minutes later all the facts had been presented and everyone in the room was finally singing from the same hymnal. From the look on his face, however, Harv Cantrell didn't like the tune.

'You're asking me to believe,' he said when Geri had finished, 'that my effective boss, the Del Norte County D.A. Lamont Gregory – who also happens to be a friend of mine – is a criminal drug baron and a *pedophile*? And that he's also responsible for Colson's murder?'

'That's right,' Peters said, nodding.

'He's been corrupt for years, Harv,' I said. 'From long before he left L.A. to come back here. Based on information I've gleaned about his law practice down there, and his years as a Los Angeles County Assistant D.A., he's clearly been working with the gangs almost from the beginning.'

Cantrell was shaking his head with amazement – a man stripped of his belief in Santa Claus and the tooth fairy all at one fell swoop.

'I'll be goddamned,' he said at last. Then he looked at Geri. 'But why couldn't you have told me about this before, Geri? Didn't you trust me?'

'Harv,' she said, squirming slightly in her seat, 'I didn't know what was best to do. I didn't think you would knowingly put up with such corruption, but I couldn't be absolutely sure.' She looked at me for support. 'Based on Bridger's information Arnie and I thought it would be best to keep the department out of it altogether for the time being. And to bring in the FBI. Arnie had met Agent Peters so he went to talk to him about it. I always intended to tell you as soon as ... as soon as we felt we could.'

Devonne Peters raised a hand. 'Sheriff Cantrell, you mustn't be too hard on Geri for holding back. After all, if what we suspect is true Gregory is controlling illicit operations all across the north of the state, probably maintaining them with bribery and covert manipulation. How was she to know you or your department wasn't complicit?'

Cantrell was still shaking his head. 'My department? Do you really think we've got bad apples in my force, Agent Peters?'

Peters raised his eyebrows. 'Who knows? Hopefully not, but we can't be sure. In the meantime I suggest you keep all this to yourself, Sheriff. Either Deputy Mitchell or myself will bring you up to date with any new developments.'

'All right,' Cantrell agreed. 'I'll keep silent. But how much longer is this going on?'

'Not long,' Peters replied. 'As you probably know, Gregory is in Mexico with his friend the Attorney General and won't be back till Monday. We hope by then to have put a case together against him and to make an arrest by Wednesday at the latest.'

Harv nodded. 'I knew he was in Mexico. The wife and I were at a dinner party at his place with him and Anthony Baldini the night before he left.' He shook his head again. 'I still can't believe it. Lamont Gregory a drug baron and a murderer?'

'Maybe he didn't intend it to be murder,' I said. 'Maybe things just got out of control. We've got to find someone who was there that can tell us what really happened.'

Harv looked up. 'Do you know of such a witness?'

'I know of two,' I said. 'One of them is in custody down south, currently being interrogated by some of Devonne's agents. Hopefully he'll crack and spill the beans.'

'There's another?' Devonne said, glowering across at me.

'Yes,' I said. 'Manuel Fernandez's mysterious passenger in the black pickup, the one seen in the CCTV pictures.' I looked at Geri. 'We believe it was a young man named Pepe Hidalgo, one of Gregory's lily farm workers – the son of someone he knows down in Sayulita.'

'Where is this guy now?' Sheriff Cantrell asked.

I looked at Geri, who shook her head, chagrined.

'Sorry, Arnie. I didn't have time to check into that, what with moving and booking motel rooms and everything.'

I smiled. 'Never mind, kiddo.' Then I looked at Cantrell. 'He's in hiding. But Geri and I think we know how to find him. When we do, we'll try to persuade him to give himself up and tell what he knows.'

Harv Cantrell nodded, frowning. He was unused to having a serious investigation in his patch removed from his control and he wasn't liking it.

'What about the three Latinos that are after Colson's friend?' he said at last. 'Shouldn't we put a tail on him for his own safety?'

'Bridger's at the Bayview Inn as we speak,' Geri said. 'He's got a room there. So do I and my house guests. After what happened at the Eagle Hotel last night we won't be staying at my place for a while – not until this is all wrapped up. Josh's not going out, and he should be safe there.' She looked at me. 'I reserved a room for you there, too.'

I nodded. 'Thanks.'

'So what now?' Harv asked.

'We've got rooms at the Best Western Plus,' Devonne said. 'Across the highway from the Bayview Inn and facing the road. We'll keep watch on the Bayview through the night. Then tomorrow morning we can all meet and decide how to usefully spend the day.'

'There's a restaurant close by that does great breakfasts,' Geri said. 'The "Good Harvest". It's a couple blocks south of the motels. We could meet there, say, at eight tomorrow morning?'

Devonne nodded. 'Sounds good to me.'

The rest of us mumbled our compliance and that seemed about it for the meeting. The next few minutes were spent making sure we all had one another's contact numbers. Then Geri and I and the FBI agents left the house and headed toward our cars, Geri and I bringing up the rear. When we reached her red Toyota, Geri turned to me.

'I sent Lorraine and Mandy off to Brookings to do some shopping,' she said. 'To keep them entertained while I was here. They should be back anytime now. I suggest you drive on over to the Bayview and sign in, Arnie. I'll be right behind you. When the girls get in I'll call you and we can have dinner together.'

'Great,' I said. 'See you in a while.'

Geri pulled her cell phone out of her pocket and I turned away toward my car. When I looked up from my driver's side door she was behind the steering wheel of her Toyota apparently listening to a voice message. I unlocked the Cobalt's door and climbed inside. The three agents had already boarded their Crown Vic and as I started up they moved out past me on the way to their motel. I slid the Chevy's shift into drive and was about to pull out when Geri backed out of Cantrell's driveway and stopped alongside me, lowering her passenger window. I lowered my window too.

'Something's just come up,' she called across. 'You go on ahead and I'll see you at the motel in an hour or so.'

'Fine,' I said back. 'Take it easy.'

'I'll do that.'

And with a muffled roar of her Toyota's hot engine Geri drove off up the street, disappearing around the next corner.

My room at the Bayview was pleasant and comfortable, with – as expected from the name – a view out over the enclosed bay at the back. I had a quick shower, changed clothes and spent forty-five minutes bringing my notes up to date and checking and answering emails on the room's free Wifi, none of it important. Picking up my cell I was pleased to see that Thad Wilkins had texted me the time for the Pelican Bay interview: 10 AM the following morning. I sent him a 'thank you' in reply.

When an hour and a quarter had passed and I still hadn't heard from anyone I called reception and asked which rooms Lorraine and Geri were in. I also asked for the room number for Josh Bridger. Then I pressed the cut-off button and dialed first Geri's and then Lorraine's rooms in succession. There was no answer from either. Finally I called Bridger.

'Yes?' he said, when he picked up.

'Josh, it's Arnie Rednapp.'

'Hey, man!' he said. 'How the hell are you? How'd the meeting go?'

'I'm good. And the meeting went well. Josh, have you heard anything at all from Geri or Lorraine?'

'No. Why?'

'As we were leaving the Sheriff's house Geri told me she had something to attend to, that she'd see me back here in an hour. Then she drove off. It's been an hour and a half now and she's still not back. None of them are. I'm beginning to wonder if I should be worried.'

There was a long pause at the other end.

'What do you think, Josh?' I prompted. 'Any idea where they might be?'

'They could be anyplace,' he said at last. 'One place I'm hoping they're not is back at Geri's house.'

'Surely they wouldn't go back there?' I said, the hackles on my neck rising.

'Maybe one of the girls left something behind they needed to pick up?' he suggested. 'Maybe Geri went to let them in?'

'I hope not,' I said. 'She should know better. From what I've heard, Geri'd be no match on her own for the guys that came after you.'

'Too right. She wouldn't be.'

There was another pause before Josh spoke again.

'Arnie, I think we'd better go out there and have a look.'

We went in my Cobalt, me fighting to keep within the 55 mile per hour speed limit all the way up the straight two-lane road to Smith River. Twenty minutes later we passed the town and swung right onto Ocean View Drive.

When we reached Geri's driveway and turned into it a surge of nervous apprehension mixed with relief swept through me. Lorraine's and Geri's cars were both parked beside the house's front porch. I guided the Chevy to a stop behind Geri's Toyota, killed the engine, and Josh and I climbed out, Josh holding down along his right thigh a pistol that he'd withdrawn from inside his jacket.

'Lorraine!' I called. 'Geri!' I moved toward the porch steps.

'Hold it, Arnie,' Josh whispered behind me.

I turned. Lifting a finger to his lips, he set off around the side of the house toward the back deck, raising the pistol before him and motioning for me to remain where I was. But I was too worried to do as I was told. Cautiously I climbed the porch steps and tried the front door. It was locked. I bent down and moved the flower pot where Geri always left the spare key. It wasn't there. Then I tried peering through the front windows, hoping to see one or other of the women coming to unlock the front door for me. But there was no movement. I stepped back, suddenly very afraid. A minute later there was the rattle of a key in the lock, the front door swung open and Josh stood in the gap, his face grave.

'They're gone,' he said, grimly. 'It looks like they've been abducted.'

It would take forty minutes for Sheriff Cantrell, Devonne and the other agents to get to Geri's house. During that time Josh carefully searched all the rooms, pointing out a smudge of blood on the carpet a few feet inside the front door – which brought a chill to my soul. Then he went out the back to check the outbuildings, ordering me to keep to the deck so as not to contaminate the house's interior for forensics. I did so, though it was hard for me not to turn the house over myself, looking for clues as to where the girls might've been taken.

'The men were waiting in the house when they arrived,' Josh said, returning. 'There're fresh tire marks and crushed grass beyond the barn where they parked the van out of sight. One of the bad guys probably snuck in first, found the place empty, then contacted the other two and they brought the van in and parked it up back there. Then they picked the French door lock and waited inside. They must've jumped the girls the minute they came in.'

'But the front door was locked when we got here. Was the French door at the back unlocked?'

'Yes.'

I threw myself down on one of the benches beside the redwood deck railing.

'Why in God's name would they have come back?' I muttered.

Josh stepped into the house and returned a minute later carrying a thin laptop by one edge, a handkerchief separating it from his gripping fingers.

'This was in the bedroom where Mandy was sleeping. Recognize it?'

I nodded. 'Yeah. That's hers. It would've had all her exam review material on it. Obviously Mandy forgot it and she needed it.'

Josh nodded. 'That's what it looks like to me.'

I buried my face in my hands, shaking uncontrollably.

Geri, Lorraine and Mandy were in the hands of cartel killers.

And we had no clue where they'd been taken.

Chapter Forty

Geri shifted on the van's hard floor, trying to find a less painful position. The violent bouncing and swerving had been going on for some time now and she knew they were following some kind of mountain track well off the main roads. Beside her she could sense the near presence of Lorraine and Mandy, both occasionally whimpering when the going became particularly rough. All three were lying on their sides close together, bound tightly with duct tape, their hands behind their backs and their feet bent up behind them, their mouths taped shut. What's more, the men had also blindfolded them so they couldn't see. All that was left was their hearing and their sense of movement and smell. The latter was of no help. Quite the contrary. Their captors had obviously not showered in days and the air in the van was rank with man sweat.

Geri Mitchell knew her county well after having patrolled it for years. From the moment the van had left her house she had concentrated on determining the route it was taking and for a long time she followed its course without difficulty. The driver had turned left into Ocean View Drive, then left again onto Highway 101. She tried to calculate how long it was before the van turned next, and when it did, after only five minutes or so, and to the left, she knew they'd taken the North Bank Road flanking the Smith River, and were making for the T junction with Highway 199 – the road leading north to Gasquet and the Oregon border. This was confirmed when at length the driver came to a stop, then turned left onto the highway. Counting the minutes again Geri was able to trace their progress past Jed Smith State Park, then past Hiouchi Hamlet. Shortly after, the highway swung sharply to the left and followed the narrow, twisting Smith River gorge – all still very familiar. Twenty minutes or so later the van slowed suddenly and turned right, following another winding paved road. It seemed they'd left the highway now and were climbing into the mountains – possibly toward French Hill. This was country she knew less well, for the number of houses trickled to zero a quarter mile off the main highway and she'd never driven beyond them. From that point on the roads pushed into Forest Service land, empty of dwellings. Or so she had thought.

The van wound around a series of sharp bends for several minutes, climbing, then dropping down, then climbing again. Then the pavement ended and the rutted gravel road and the bouncing began. It had been at least fifteen minutes since that had occurred, and now Geri hadn't a clue where they were. Somewhere east of Gasquet she reckoned, but she wasn't sure.

She wondered what time it was. Probably around 7:30 or 8:00 PM. By now Arnie and the others would know they'd been taken and would be desperately worried. Geri shuddered with shame at the thought of her stupid mistake. She should've known better.

When she had discovered Lorraine's voice mail upon leaving the meeting at Sheriff Cantrell's she'd been more irritated than concerned. Mandy had forgotten her laptop at the house and would need it to prepare for her exams next week. It was essential that they get it, and Lorraine had said she was going to drive straight to the house and collect it, using the spare key. Josh Bridger had told them, after all, that it would take the Latino assassins at least twenty-four hours to make the connection between him and Geri, so there'd be no danger in approaching the house in the late afternoon. That, at least, had been Lorraine's thinking. Geri had tried phoning her back, but her cell went straight to message. Geri had cursed, but had decided the best thing to do was just to get there as soon as possible, retrieve the blessed laptop, and get everyone back to the safety of Crescent City and the Bayview Inn as soon as possible.

It occurred to her to see if there was any backup available that could join her at the house, and she had called Dispatch on her cell – only to be told that the two deputies on patrol were currently at opposite ends of the county, miles away from Smith River. Then she'd tried Sam Buchanan on his cell, and he had pulled over his CHP rig to take her call. Unfortunately, however, he, too, was out of reach – way to the north on Highway 199, patrolling just south of the Oregon border. It would take him at least forty minutes to get to Smith River, but he said he'd get there as soon as he could. Geri told him not to bother, that she would probably have come and gone by then – and, blowing him a kiss down the phone, had said goodbye. Sam said he would join her at the Bayview Inn later that evening, after his shift had finished. She had smiled. That was something good to look forward to.

So Geri had driven out to her house beyond Smith River and turned into her drive, her eyes scanning the area for anything suspicious. There was nothing. Lorraine's car was parked beside the porch and Geri pulled her Toyota to a stop behind it.

Pulling her Colt from her handbag as a precaution, Geri opened the car door and climbed out.

'Lorraine?' she called, as she took the steps up to the porch. 'Mandy? Are you two in there?'

The front door, she could now see, was slightly ajar, and for the first time Geri sensed that things were not quite as they should be.

'Guys?' she called out, clutching her pistol now with both hands and training it toward the door.

She thought she heard a stifled murmur from within. Lorraine? Mandy? Geri's concern for her friends overrode the guidance of her professional training. Moving to the door, she pushed it open.

In the corner across the room Lorraine sat on the edge of Geri's armchair, her hands behind her back. She stared at Geri, a look of tense apprehension on her face.

Geri had then stepped into the room, her gun still raised.

There was movement to her left, down the hallway toward the bedrooms. She turned her head. A man in dark clothes and a balaclava stood holding Mandy before him like a shield, the blade of a large knife pressed against her throat. Mandy's terrified eyes were as big as saucers.

Geri swung her pistol round to train it at the head of the man with the knife.

'Drop the knife, scumbag, and step back,' she barked. 'Or you're dead meat.'

'If you fire the girl dies,' said a voice behind her. A male voice with a smooth Latino accent. 'Do not turn around. Do not move.'

Geri could sense the man moving into the living room from the kitchen behind her, imagined the pistol trained on her back. Glancing toward Lorraine on the chair, she could follow the man's movement with her friend's eyes. Then she felt a sudden pressure at the back of her head as the muzzle of the silencer was pushed against it.

'Now,' the voice said, 'I want you to bend down and place your gun on the floor at the side where I can reach it. Do you understand?'

'Yes.'

Geri had slowly done as she'd been instructed, laying the Colt on the floor at her right side. When she straightened again she felt the gun's muzzle move down from her head to her back. A gloved hand reached out to take up her weapon. Then the man stood again.

'Now you can turn around,' he said.

As she did so Geri noticed a third masked man standing by the side of the French doors at the back of the room, his silenced pistol trained on Lorraine. Geri glanced to her right, to the man who had taken her gun. He, too, was masked, and the Glock he aimed at her head was exactly the same as the one his colleague held on Lorraine – the same that Josh had brought with him to the house the night before.

'Where is the man with the tattoos?' the man beside her growled, obviously the leader of the three. 'And the journalist, Rednapp. Where is he?'

'I don't know,' she had lied. 'I don't know where they are.'

The blow came from nowhere, a sudden swipe with the pistol's butt that crashed into the side of her head and brought her swiftly to her hands and knees. Geri nearly passed out, but after a few seconds she was able to fight through the throbbing pain and nausea and pull herself back to full awareness. She put a hand to her head and felt blood oozing. The man beside her had not moved.

'You are lying, little deputy,' he said. 'I think you know very well where they are and are just trying to be brave. *Una puta con huevos*, eh, Rafa?'

He laughed, and the man beside the French doors laughed with him.

The leader stepped closer, jamming the silencer into her side.

'But your bravery is stupid, *gringa*. Either you tell me where these men are or we will kill you. All of you. Is that clear?'

Across the room Lorraine smothered another gasp and Geri could hear soft sobbing coming from the hallway to her left.

'You'll probably kill us in any case,' she thought to herself. Then she faced her masked captor, holding her chin up in spite of the pain.

'As it happens, I don't know where either of them is. You're wrong to think that I would. But it'd be stupid of you to kill us, all the same.' She nodded across the room toward Lorraine. 'That woman is the journalist's girlfriend. He will be crazy with worry for her. Maybe you could use us as bait, to arrange a meeting with the two men?'

Geri knew she was suggesting a plan for their murder but she stifled her scruples. If all went well Harv, Josh and the FBI agents would free them before the worst could happen. If it didn't then it didn't really matter what she said. But offering such an option to their captors at least rendered the three of them potentially useful, and therefore less expendable.

The man had considered her words, then smiled and nodded. Giving terse instructions he supervised the taping of all three women's hands behind their backs. Then he stepped into the kitchen and returned with a drying up cloth, which he ripped into three long strips. Doubling one of them into a narrow band, he moved to Mandy, making to cover her eyes, but she had pulled her head to one side.

'No!' she'd moaned. 'I want to see. Don't cover my eyes. Please!'

'You must have your eyes covered, *niña*,' the leader said to her gently, moving closer. 'You mustn't see where we are taking you. And if you were to see our faces then we would have to kill you, don't you see? You'd be able to identify us, describe us to the police. So if you want to live, and I'm sure you do, you'd better put up with the blindfolding. Perhaps later, when we get to where we're going, we can remove them.'

The blindfolding was done without any further objection.

Five minutes later Geri heard the sound of a vehicle pulling up and stopping at the back of the house. Then the three women were bundled out the back door, across the deck, and down the stairs to level ground. Geri heard the back doors of a van being opened and then, one by one, the women were forced inside it. Their feet were taped together, then bent up behind them and tied in a loose sling to their bound hands so that they could not even sit up. Then the doors were closed and locked, the men climbed aboard and the van drove off down the drive.

All that had occurred well over an hour before, and now Geri thought of Sam. By now he, too, would know of their abduction. At the thought of his worry for her Geri's eyes teared up. If only she had waited for him!

Suddenly the van slowed, the driver shifted into the lowest gear, and the vehicle turned to the right and lurched up an incline over even rougher ground. The buffeting of before was nothing to what the girls experienced now, being thrown from side to side and over one another as the vehicle fought for purchase on the rutted track. This went on for five minutes or so, crawling upward only feet at a time, until at length the van reached a flat area and pulled to a stop. Then the key was switched off and there was only silence.

The men climbed out from the front, slamming the doors. A moment later the back doors were unlocked and swung open.

'*Bienvenidas* ladies,' said the leader. 'Welcome to the Buena Vista Hotel.'

Chapter Forty-One

Devonne Peters and the other two FBI agents had only just arrived in their dark Crown Vic when Sheriff Harv Cantrell pulled up behind them in the department's white Ford SUV. Geri's drive was beginning to look like it was party time. To add to the jam Sam Buchanan pulled in five minutes later in his CHP rig, and by the time Josh and I had reported to everyone the details of what we'd discovered it was nearly 7:30 and the light was beginning to fade. Despondent, almost in a state of shock, the seven of us sat on the back deck, gravely considering the implications of the situation.

Sam Buchanan seemed to be taking the news particularly badly, and now he sat on one of the chairs beside the table, leaning forward, elbows on knees, wringing his hands and shaking his head.

'It's all my fault. Geri called me a little after five asking if I could drop by to give her a hand with something. I was up above Collier Tunnel then so I told her I'd get here soon as I could. I didn't know how dangerous the situation was. Well, I started back down the road at five-thirty, but then I came across an accident involving two tourist rigs and had to stop. What with waiting for the tow truck to arrive to pull one of the RVs out of a ditch, I wasn't able to get away until almost an hour ago.' He sat back, running his hands through his sandy hair. 'If I'd gotten here sooner I could've prevented it happening.'

'Don't be too sure of that, Officer Buchanan,' Devonne Peters said. 'You might well have walked straight into a trap that could've left both you and Geri dead, not to mention the other two. I wouldn't be too hard on yourself.'

Sam nodded. 'Maybe so.'

'Well, I guess I'd better call in the forensics team,' Harv said, getting to his feet. 'Geri's abduction's going to upset a lot of folks around here.'

Devonne Peters rose from his position on one of the benches and strode over to the open French door, staring back into the living room.

'I think it'd be best, Harv, if we kept this to ourselves for a time.' He turned back toward the Sheriff. 'And I wouldn't worry about forensics just yet, either. There's nothing here that won't keep. As long as the kidnappers think their work has gone publically unnoticed they might feel less pressured to terminate their victims and run. What's more, they might think they can use the ladies as bargaining chips to get what they want.' He turned to Josh and me, seated together on one of the rail benches. 'Which, I think, basically, is you two. I reckon their instructions were to take out the pair of you so that the case building against Gregory could be buried – literally.' He looked at Josh. 'When you searched Geri's car you found her purse, right? And there was no cell in it, and no handgun?'

'That's correct, sir. No gun and no phone.'

Devonne nodded. 'They must've taken them. I gather there's been no attempt made to contact either of you yet?'

Josh and I looked at one another.

'You mean from Geri's phone?' I asked.

'Yes.'

'No,' I answered for both of us. 'We've had no such calls.'

'Well,' said Peters, 'keep your phones turned on, just in case. If they do call try to keep them talking as long as you can. Give Agent Fischer your cell numbers and she can set up a watch on them so that any incoming calls can be traced. If they use Geri's cell to call, with any luck we can determine their location. Once we have that we can go after them.'

Josh and I gave the woman agent our cell numbers and she retreated to the far end of the deck with her own phone to set up the surveillance. Meanwhile Devonne pulled a chair around so that it faced both Josh and me and sat down.

'I believe you saw the kidnappers and their vehicle last night,' he said to Josh. 'Is that correct?'

'Yessir. There were three of them. They were in balaclavas so I can't give you any descriptions, except to say they were all of medium height and slim build. When I saw the van yesterday afternoon the faces inside looked Latino, but I'm not absolutely certain even of that. Last night all three of them were carrying Glock 22s with suppressors when they came for me. Like this one.'

Josh pulled the weapon from behind his back to show him. The suppressor had been removed. When Devonne nodded Josh pushed it back into his pants waist.

'Their vehicle was a black Ford Cargo Van,' he went on. 'An E-150 I think it said on the side. It had California plates.'

Devonne had pulled out a notepad and was scribbling notes.

'Did you get the number?'

'No, sir. I was a bit busy at the time.'

'Hm.' Devonne looked at me. 'Arnie, we're going to have to get moving on finding that second witness to Colson's murder.' He glanced at his watch. 'There's still some time left tonight. Do you think you can track down his whereabouts? He might well know where the girls have been taken.'

I nodded. 'Yes, I can do that.'

'Good. You mentioned that Gregory's manager on the lily farm is helping with the investigation, is that right?'

'That's correct. A man named Ryan Garrett.'

'And there's a Latino caretaker that looks after the family house on the farm?'

'Yes. Félix something. There's some indication he's also involved in Gregory's drug business. Josh told us he seemed to be very busy just before Gregory left for Mexico.'

'He was,' Josh confirmed. 'His pickup was gone most of Thursday and Friday.'

Devonne nodded, then turned to Sheriff Cantrell. 'Harv, I'm sorry to muscle in on your investigation, but now that kidnapping's involved the case has definitely become federal.'

Cantrell shrugged. 'Let's just find these guys and get Geri and the others back to safety. Is there anything I can do?'

'Yes, there is. You can go to the lily farm and arrest the Latino caretaker. Better bring his wife in, too, in case she's involved. If you can get them to your office my agents and I will work on them, see if we can get him in particular to open up about his boss and the whole operation. Now that murder and kidnapping is involved the guy might agree to work for us in exchange for witness protection.'

'I'll go get him now.'

As Cantrell rose to his feet Sam Buchanan stood with him.

'I'll come along as backup, Sheriff. My shift is up but I'm damned if I'm going to quit working so long as Geri's still in danger out there.'

'Thanks, Sam. That'll be a help. I'll talk to your dispatcher.' He looked at Devonne. 'I'll give you guys a call when I've got them at the station.'

The two men stepped down the deck stairs and disappeared around the corner of the house. The rest of us got to our feet.

'Well,' Devonne said, 'I guess we'll head back to the motel.' He looked into the living room. 'You say the key was in the front door, Bridger?'

'Yes, sir. On the inside. That's how I was able to open it.'

'Then I suggest you lock the French doors from inside. Then you can relock the front door.'

'I'll do that,' Josh said. 'And put the key under the flower pot on the front porch where Geri usually leaves it.'

'Good idea,' Devonne said. Then he turned toward Walker and Fischer. 'Let's hit the road, guys.'

Ten minutes later we had locked up the house and gone our separate ways – Devonne and his FBI colleagues back to Crescent City in the Crown Vic, Josh and I toward Smith River in the Cobalt. Turning off 101 at the top of the town, I swung the car into the parking lot of Ray's Market and pulled into a slot near the front doors. The place wasn't too busy and there were only a few cars in the lot. Josh hadn't said a word. I cut the engine and we both climbed out and walked inside.

There were three people working the tills, two women and a man. All three were young and white and I reckoned neither of the women was Geri's friend Verity. At one side a counter stood under a sign that said 'Customer Service'. There was an older man in an apron behind the counter looking through some invoices. I went up to him.

'Excuse me, sir. Is Verity around?'

The man looked up.

'No. She finishes at five. Can I help you?'

'What about Alex Moreno? He still working by any chance?'

The man glanced toward the back of the store.

'Yeah, he is. You're lucky. He works late Saturdays.' He turned back to me, reaching for a PA microphone. 'Want me to call him?'

'No, thanks. I'll go back and see him, if that's all right?'

'Sure, go ahead. He's unloading boxes. We had a shipment this afternoon and he's puttin' stuff away.'

'Right. Thanks.'

Josh and I made our way to the back of the store, found the rubber swinging doors that led to the storeroom and pushed our way through. As the man had said Alex was unloading boxes from pallets and stacking them in storage bays. When he heard the doors slap closed he turned in our direction. The bruises had almost gone and he looked now just like any other good-looking Chicano kid.

'Sorry,' he said, turning toward us. 'Only staff back here.'

'It's all right, Alex. We got the okay from the guy at the Customer Service counter. We wanted to see you.'

His face clouded. 'I know you,' he said, looking at me warily. 'You came to my house one night with *Señor* Garrett.'

'That's right. We wanted to know how you got banged up so bad.'

He nodded. 'What do you want now?' he said, eyeing Josh with trepidation.

I put up a hand.

'Don't worry, Alex. We're not here to hurt you. We just want some information.'

'What information?'

'We need to know where we can find Pepe Hidalgo.'

The boy's face went to stone. But there was tension behind the dark eyes.

'I don't know where he is.'

'I think you do. Like I said, you don't have to worry. We're not here to harm him either. We're not working for Gregory.'

'Then what do you want with him?'

This was difficult. How much could I tell him? I sighed.

'Alex, we know that Pepe was involved in Gregory's drug dealing business.'

'Wait a minute,' he interrupted, bristling. 'I don' know nothin' about any drugs.'

'Yes, you do,' I insisted, 'and you were beaten up for talking to Davy Colson about it. You were worked over by the same men that killed him. Then you quit working at Gregory's farm and found work here at Ray's through your girlfriend's mother.' The boy looked at the ground, sheepishly. 'I know you know about the drug dealing, Alex, and about Pepe's involvement with it. We also know that Pepe was with Manuel Fernandez and the three gangbanger heavies when Davey Colson was abducted and murdered.'

Alex looked up, shaking his head forcefully. 'No! That's crazy.

You are wrong!'

I stepped closer to him. 'Alex, I know you and Pepe are buddies. I was in Mexico two days ago. Pepe's mother showed me a picture of the two of you together taken at the farm. If you care about him you've got to tell me where he is. I need to talk to him, to persuade him to give himself up. Otherwise he's in danger.'

He stared at me. 'What kind of danger?'

I shrugged. 'You know what happened to Manuel. The same thing could happen to Pepe. I know he didn't have anything to do with Colson's murder. But he did witness it. He could tell the truth about what happened that day, and about the other criminal activities Gregory's involved in. If he comes clean I guarantee he'll be treated well and given a reduced sentence. That's what I want to tell him. That's what his mother begged me to tell him.'

It took the boy a while to come to a decision. As he debated the pros and cons his eyes flicked from me to Josh to the floor and back again. Finally he nodded.

'All right. Pepe's staying in a friend's trailer just outside of town to the north. He's on his own. We – my girlfriend and I – bring him what he needs. I will call her. She can take you to him. If you go without her he might run away.'

Alex walked away a few steps, digging out his cell phone from a back pocket. Speed dialing a number he spoke a few hushed sentences when it was answered, then clicked the phone off and slipped it back into his pocket, turning again to us.

'She's coming. She'll be here in five minutes.'

Chapter Forty-Two

Hayley Thomas's eyes widened with recognition when she saw me and for a moment Alex was confused and somewhat alarmed by her reaction – until she explained that we had met when Geri and I paid a visit to Alex's house while he was sleeping one afternoon after his beating. Hayley asked after Geri and I told her she was fine, that we were actually following up on a few things for her while she was otherwise tied up – an unfortunate choice of words under the circumstances. Once Alex had repeated to her what I'd told him Hayley was happy to take us to Pepe's hideout.

She had walked the few blocks to the store from her parents' house so she rode with us in the Cobalt and gave directions from the front seat, pointing me down and around several narrow roads until we came to a long barn surrounded by a cluster of outbuildings. Off to one side, almost totally concealed behind a wide open-fronted garage housing tractors and equipment, was a thirty-foot trailer home. Laying a hand on my arm Hayley made me stop well before we reached it.

'You'd better wait here. He won't know your car. I'll talk to him first. Then I'll call you. Okay?'

'Fine. We'll wait.'

She turned to look at Josh. 'I'm sorry. I noticed the tattoos on your hands. Pepe told us about the tattoos. He saw them first on your friend Davey's hands. When he saw them on your hands at the farm he panicked. Pablo told us you were okay, but all the same you'd better stay in the car, all right? Otherwise he might freak out.'

Josh nodded. 'Okay. I'll sit tight here.'

'Thanks.'

Hayley climbed out and walked to the trailer, where she knocked on the front door. After a moment the door was opened and she stepped inside.

There followed a hiatus of several minutes until finally the door opened again and Hayley stood in the frame, beckoning. I climbed out and crunched across the gravel toward her. It was nearly dark now, and the trailer's lights threw Hayley's shadow down onto the ground outside. When I reached the trailer she stepped back and I climbed the two steps up and into the small space.

Pepe Hidalgo was standing in the hallway toward the back of the trailer. He was my height and thin as a rail, wearing a black 'Iron Maiden' T-shirt, jeans and running shoes. His hands were in his pockets, and he was eyeing me with great misgiving.

'Hey, Pepe,' I said. 'Thanks for seeing me.'

I moved into the front room and sat at one end of the ragged sofa that faced the hallway and the back bedroom. There was an armchair to the left of it by the door and a small kitchen table with two chairs on the right. Hayley pulled out one of the chairs and sat down. Pepe moved forward enough to stand leaning on the doorjamb, ready to run if need be.

'Hayley says you saw my mother in Mexico.'

I smiled. 'That's right. Three days ago, at her house in Sayulita. I told her I would try to help you. That's partly why I'm here.' I nodded toward the armchair. 'Why don't you sit down? You don't have to be afraid of me, Pepe. I'm here to help you.'

He stared at me for a time.

'I didn' have nothing to do with that man's death,' he said at last. 'I was still in the pickup. When they tried to move in on him Davey went crazy. He was knocking them around like they were children, giving them a real bad time. It was the fat one with the scar, Luis, who finally shot him. He was the only one with a gun.'

I nodded. 'I was sure you had nothing to do with it, Pepe. But you were there all the same. Technically that makes you an "accessory to murder", which means you're legally just as responsible for Colson's death as the man who actually pulled the trigger.'

The boy moved to sit in the armchair, bending forward and wringing his hands.

'That is not fair, *señor*. I was there only because Félix made me go. He said *Señor* Gregory wanted me and Manuel to go with the others, to help them out. Davey knew Manu and me so they wanted us to persuade him to come with us to someplace away from people. Then the others would come and beat him up. That was the plan. There was nothing about any killing, *señor*. Otherwise I would not have gone along.'

'I believe you,' I said. 'But you still need my help, Pepe. And I need yours.' I sat forward. 'Look, my name is Arnie Rednapp. I'm a newspaperman from San Francisco. I got involved in the investigation into Davey's death because I happen to know the Sheriff's deputy, Geri Mitchell, who responded to the call when his body was found. Quite by chance I was riding with her that morning and I went along. I'm following the investigation now because I'm going to write an article about it when the case is closed. But tonight I'm on a different mission altogether.' I stopped, sorting carefully in my mind what I wanted to say and how I wanted to say it. 'You know what happened to Manuel Fernandez, don't you, Pepe?' I said at last.

The boy sat back, suddenly afraid.

'Yes. Alex told me. He said it was an accident.'

I shook my head. 'It was no accident, and you know it. What's more, you know who was responsible. Ever since Davey Colson's arrival in Del Norte County things have been going wrong for Lamont Gregory. First Davey was murdered rather than just being worked over. Then Josh Bridger appeared at the farm. Now Gregory knows there are people after him, trying to tie him to Colson's death, to expose his corruption and to close down his drug-dealing operation. He found out about Josh Bridger because of you. You saw Josh's tattoos and knew he was Davey's friend. You passed the word to Félix and Félix passed it on to Gregory. Three nights ago Manuel tried to run Josh Bridger down in his pickup but Josh jumped clear. Clearly, Gregory's now a frightened man. He almost certainly called on his L.A. gang contacts to send him a team of professionals to clear up his problems. One of those problems was Manuel.'

Pepe was shaking his head in consternation.

'But Manuel worked for *Señor* Gregory. He was one of his right hand men, the most important after Félix. Why have him killed?'

I shrugged. 'He'd failed to kill Josh Bridger. What's more, like you he was a witness that could tie Gregory to the Colson murder if he was ever caught. Manuel was the assassins' first assignment. Then the night before last they went after Josh Bridger again, tried to kill him at his apartment. But Josh got away. Today these men did something else – they kidnapped three women, one of them Deputy Geri Mitchell. The other two are friends of hers who happened to be visiting when they came for her. These men are professional killers, Pepe. If we don't find them they will kill those women. And if they do their next target will be you.'

He blanched. 'Me?'

I nodded. 'You were with Manuel. You saw Davey shot. You're a witness that can tie Gregory into his murder. You'll have to die, too. Don't you see?'

He shook his head. 'It cannot be. My mother is *Señor* Gregory's friend. He would not have me killed.'

'Oh yes he would,' I told him. 'He's fighting for his life, Pepe.' I bent toward him. 'Which is why it's vital that you give yourself up so that you'll be out of their reach. If you tell the authorities everything you know they'll go easy on you. There may be jail time but it won't be long. In the meantime I need your help. We have to find out where the women have been taken. Anything you can tell us that will lead us to them is vitally important. Do you understand?'

'I am sorry for those women, *señor*,' he said, 'but there is nothing I can do to help you.'

'Yes there is, Pepe.' I took a deep breath. 'I know – we know – that the gangbangers that came to beat Davey up, Luis and the other two, came from a marijuana plantation in Humboldt County. They were loaned to Gregory by his VPR friends down south. While they were here they had to have someplace to stay.' I looked at him, intently. 'It stands to reason that these new men, these cartel assassins, are probably staying in the same place the others stayed before. When you were with Manuel did you ever go to that place?'

He shook his head. 'No. I was never there.'

'Please, Pepe. If you know anything at all that can help us find it we might be able to save those women.'

'We didn't go to their place. We met them at the store in Hiouchi.'

'That's the only time you saw them, that one day?'

'Manuel may have met them on other days, but I was only with him then.'

I felt the strength drain from my neck and shoulders. Only Manuel knew where they had stayed. And Manuel was dead.

'All right. I believe you.' I paused for a moment to collect myself. 'Maybe if you think about it you'll remember something later. In the meantime I suggest you get your things together and come with me. The sooner we get you into custody the sooner you'll be safe.'

Pepe hesitated a moment, thinking it over. Then he stood up.

'All right. I'll come with you.' Then he frowned. 'But what about my mother? If I talk Gregory will do something to her. She's his cook, after all.'

I shook my head. 'Not anymore.' I told him what Paco had told me – that he had found new employment for her elsewhere, in Puerto Vallarta. 'So you see, Gregory has no idea where she is now. She's perfectly safe.'

The boy smiled at me, relieved. And nodded. Then he went to the back of the trailer to gather his possessions. Three minutes later he reappeared with a small hold-all and a black plastic bag filled with clothing.

I stood up. 'Ready?'

Hayley led the way out, then stopped halfway to the car.

'You'd better explain about Mr. Bridger,' she said to me.

At the mention of Josh's name Pepe froze.

'Josh is in the car, Pepe,' I told him. 'He is not angry with you for what happened to his friend. He knows you didn't do it, that you wouldn't even have been there if you'd known killing him was on the cards.'

The boy looked toward the car nervously. As he did so the back door swung open and Josh climbed out. He closed the door, then stepped toward us.

'Hello, Pepe,' he said, smiling. 'Long time no see.'

He held out his hand. After a moment's hesitation the boy reached his own forward and they shook. Then Josh looked at me.

'We going to stand here all night yacking, or are we going to get this young man to a safe place?'

Minutes later we dropped Hayley at Ray's Market. Before climbing out, she gave Pepe a hug and told him she'd see him soon.

Then we set off for Crescent City.

Halfway there my cell buzzed. It was Devonne Peters. I punched the talk button.

'Hey, Devonne. What's happening?'

'Not a lot, unfortunately. When Sheriff Cantrell went to get Félix and his wife at the lily farm they'd gone. The door was unlocked so Cantrell and Officer Buchanan went inside and had a look around. There were signs of a hasty packing job – drawers in the bedroom open, clothes strewn around – and some dirty dishes on the table, remnants of their last meal, apparently only hours old. The Sheriff's put out a call for their arrest with a description of Félix's car – which we got from the California DMV along with the license number. He also organized a search for the kidnappers' black van. I doubt they'll be moving around much, but I should think Félix and his wife will be. They're surely on the run. Hopefully they haven't gotten too far away yet.'

'That's bad news,' I muttered, suddenly realizing. 'Félix would certainly know where the girls were taken. I imagine one of his jobs was to keep the place stocked with food and basics for any gangbanger colleagues that were passing through.'

'That's why we're hoping they'll be picked up sooner rather than later,' Devonne said. 'What about you? Did you find your witness?'

'We did. He's with us now. We're bringing him in. Shall we go direct to the Sheriff's Office?'

There was a slight pause.

'No. I'm still not convinced Harv's department's clean. I'd rather not expose the witness to any of his deputies until we know a bit more about things. Why not bring him here to the Best Western? Agent Walker's in a double room. The boy can stay with him till tomorrow anyway. Could he tell you anything about where the girls were taken?'

'No. He only met the gangbangers with Manuel that one time at the Hiouchi store, the day of the murder. He says he was never taken to where they were staying.'

'Crap. I was hoping he'd have the info we need.'

'So was I. And neither Josh nor I have had any messages on our cells.'

Peters sighed. 'Well, that's not necessarily a bad sign. It might mean they're still trying to decide what to do with them. Or awaiting Gregory's instructions. Let's hope they hold off making any decisions for a while yet.'

'I've got all my fingers and toes crossed, Devonne.'

'I'm sure you have. Okay. See you here in a few.'

And he clicked off.

Chapter Forty-Three

In his luxurious holiday home in Sayulita Lamont Gregory was not a happy man. Firstly his cook/housekeeper had been absent on his arrival, and when the caretaker was sent to her house to investigate he'd found it empty, the woman having apparently moved out. None of the neighbors knew where she'd gone.

Then when he'd called the orphanage to arrange for some children to spend Saturday night entertaining him and his cronies at the house he was told by the Mother Superior that such a visit was not convenient at this time. The children were having end-of-year examinations, she explained. She was sorry, for she was sure the children would have loved to come, but they needed to concentrate on their studies. Gregory tried to pressure her into relenting, but she had grown strangely adamant and finally he'd given up. Then he'd had to suffer the embarrassment of phoning his friends to tell them Saturday's licentious revels were off. Naturally everyone was disappointed. He'd looked and felt a feckless fool, and none of it was his doing.

Then in the evening after he'd returned from suffering a mediocre dinner at one of the tourist restaurants on the beachfront, his second cell phone had rung and the ensuing conversation had given him even more cause for concern.

'*Patrón*,' said the former Mexican Army officer, 'we have a problem.'

'What kind of problem?' he had asked.

'We went to the address you gave us – the house of the lady deputy. We gained entrance when it was empty and waited inside. But neither the tattooed man nor the newspaperman ever came.'

'Disappointing. So?'

'While we were waiting two women friends of the deputy turned up and entered the house with a spare key – a woman and her teenage daughter. Then the deputy herself came. So now we have all three of these women. We brought them here, to the cabin.'

'To the cabin!' Gregory rasped, aghast. 'Why in God's name did you do that?'

'We had no choice. You said you wanted no unnecessary killing. Besides, they might be useful to draw the men we want to a meeting where we can deal with them. If not they should be terminated and their bodies buried where no one will find them. We can do that. The decision is yours, *señor*. What do you want us to do?'

The grey-haired attorney dropped his head, screwing his eyes tightly shut. He wanted to scream with exasperation. Could things get any worse? How was he to cope with this new setback, this new horrendous complication? If it was only the two strange women it would be easy enough to arrange another fatal car crash. But with the deputy as well...? No. It was far too risky.

He was beginning to sense that in spite of all his careful planning the whole beautiful operation was about to collapse in ruins around him. And if he was not careful it would take him down with it. How could he save himself?

Certainly he had money enough stashed away to simply disappear somewhere – to Patagonia or Malaysia or the South Seas. He could buy a new identity and retire to some quiet corner where with a few backhanders the locals would accept his presence without questioning. It'd been done before. He could open that escape route at any time, but was this the right moment? Or could he bluff his way through a few more days, liquidate even more of his assets before fleeing?

'*¿Patrón?*' the voice prompted. 'Did you hear me? Did you understand what I've told you?'

'I understood you perfectly well,' Gregory growled. 'This is a tricky situation and I will have to think about it. In the meantime keep the women secure. Have they seen your faces?'

'No. We wear balaclavas when we are with them. If we let them go they probably could not identify us later.'

'Well. That's something to bear in mind.'

'But if we let them go, esteemed *señor*, surely that would cause you even more problems?'

'I'm aware of that! As I said, I need time to think this through. Leave it with me until tomorrow. I'll give you a call when I've made a decision. All right?'

'Of course, *patrón*. Do you still want us to go after the others? The tattooed man, the journalist and the boy?'

'Yes. No! I don't know. I'll tell you tomorrow.'

'Very well. We'll be waiting. Have a good night.'

And thus the conversation had ended.

Now Lamont Gregory stood on his bedroom balcony overlooking the town and the sparkling Pacific under the slice of moon. Even his malt whiskey didn't taste as it usually did, didn't give him the familiar blurring of tension. He sat the glass on the railing and stared out at the black line of the horizon.

Should he tell Baldini about this new problem? Would he be able to help? No, he decided. There was nothing Tony could do that Gregory couldn't do himself. In fact it would probably just alarm him, cause him to explode in one of those terrible Italian rages of his, the way he used to do during their shared law practice in L.A. No. Better to keep this to himself and work it out his way. One way or the other.

With a great sigh Gregory lifted the glass again and drained it in one swallow.

Then he went to bed to try to sleep.

Chapter Forty-Four

Sunday, June 1

Breakfast at the Good Harvest restaurant the following morning was a somber affair for all concerned. Everyone had slept badly and the long faces around the table showed it. The chirpy waitress did her best to raise our spirits with regular trips to freshen our coffee, and the food was as good as Geri had avowed, but Geri's absence at the table – not to mention my nagging fears for Lorraine and Mandy – was a heavy damper on all our spirits.

Devonne had turned up with only his female colleague, explaining Agent Walker's absence by saying he'd left him to do some telephoning. That satisfied Harv Cantrell and Sam Buchanan, neither of whom appeared to give it a second thought. Clearly it would've been silly for the FBI to have turned up escorting Pepe Hidalgo as their mysterious guest. For the moment Pepe was to be kept under wraps.

I did have one piece of good news to share, however. During the night I'd received a text from Paco in Puerto Vallarta. The exchange in the *Aviación Fénix* hangar had been made. There were now drugs on board Anthony Baldini's Citation waiting to be delivered to Sacramento. When they arrived Devonne's agents would be watching, awaiting their collection.

But there was still no word of Félix Calderón and his wife, though both Harv and Sam were optimistic something would happen later in the day.

'Wherever they're going,' Harv said, 'they almost certainly had to stop in the night to sleep. When they hit the road again this morning Highway Patrol units up and down the coast will be looking for them. Don't you worry. If they're on a public road anywhere in the western states, sooner or later they're going to get caught.'

I sighed. 'Let's hope it's sooner for the girls' sake.'

The next few minutes were taken up discussing who was doing what. I, of course, had my meeting with Thad Wilkins and Nacho Flores at Pelican Bay at 10 AM. After that the day was open for me – unless new information gave us a lead to chase. Sam Buchanan was due to start his patrol in an hour, but he'd be keeping in touch with developments and had been given permission to offer backup if necessary. I knew the FBI agents were going to start debriefing Pepe at their motel, which would take some time. The boy had worked for Gregory for years and probably knew a lot more than even he realized about his boss's criminal operation. Harv Cantrell said he was going to his office to tackle some paperwork and to hang by the phone and radio in case any news came in. Josh Bridger would stay in his room at the motel and await further developments.

Everyone at the table was antsy with frustrated energy. The sooner something happened that triggered using that energy the better for us all.

Thad Wilkins was standing beside his car at the entrance to Pelican Bay State Prison when I arrived at five minutes to the hour. He accompanied the guard who walked over from his security hut to check my ID, and confirmed that I was there for a pre-arranged visit with one of his clients. The guard nodded, conferred with his colleagues inside by radio, and a moment later Thad had climbed back into his car and was leading me past the hut and along to the right outside the grim prison wall with its strategically placed watchtowers to a large parking lot adjacent to a public entrance. We pulled in side by side, I climbed out to join him, and together we made our way to the door. Once inside our IDs were checked again and we were frisked for concealed weapons or drugs. Then we were told to wait while a Correctional Officer was summoned to escort us to the visiting area. Finally we were led across the outer yard to a single storey building which housed the visiting facilities, then along a corridor and into a private room.

The room was divided into halves with a wall-to-wall counter at its center dissected by a thick Plexiglas sheet fixed between the ceiling and the countertop. There were two chairs on our side of the glass, and two telephones. On the prisoner's side a single chair and a telephone was all there was in the tiny barred cell. Wilkins and I sat down and waited. Five minutes later the door at the back of the cell opened and Nacho Flores shuffled into the room wearing a white jumpsuit with 'PBSB Prisoner' printed in bold letters on the back. His wrists were handcuffed behind his back and clipped to a belly chain that also stretched down to his closely shackled ankles. The cell door was closed behind him and Flores, knowing the routine, backed up to the door's narrow hatchway and offered his hands through the opening. While we watched, one of his two escorts undid the handcuffs and removed them. Then as Flores stepped forward to sit on the single chair the two guards withdrew – one out of sight down the corridor, the second to lean against a wall, watching through the bars from a distance.

Once he was settled Flores picked up the phone on the counter before him and Thad and I picked up ours and held them to our ears. As previously agreed, Thad began the conversation.

''Morning, Nacho,' he said, smiling. 'I hope you're well?'

Nacho Flores grimaced. 'As well as I can be in here.'

Thad nodded. 'Thank you for agreeing to this interview. This is Mr. Arnold Rednapp. He's a journalist from San Francisco who's following a murder investigation here in Del Norte County. His research has unearthed some connections with Los Angeles and certain events in which you were involved. He'd like to ask you some questions about that. While you're under no obligation to answer them I would recommend as your counsel that you do so – unless you have good reasons for holding back. Any help you can offer Mr. Rednapp might be favorably considered by the parole board when your case comes up for review before them in a couple years. All right?'

Flores nodded, smiling tightly. Thad turned to me.

'Go ahead.'

I leaned forward. 'Mr. Flores, the man who was murdered here two weeks ago is someone you knew in your youth. His name was David Colson. Davey Colson. Does that name ring a bell?'

Flores didn't move, nor did his eyes flicker. He continued to stare at me.

'You would've known him at Camp Belleview, the Los Angeles County juvenile offenders' institution where you spent two years in your teens. Does that help place him?'

Flores nodded. 'I remember Davey Colson.'

'There was another boy there at the same time, a friend of Colson's named Toby Hitchins. Do you remember him?'

Flores nodded again. 'Yes.'

'Good. I spoke with Hitchins a few days ago in Los Angeles. He confirmed what I'd already heard from another reliable source – that while he was at Belleview he, Davey Colson and several other inmates were regularly sexually abused by certain of the guards and others. Did you know about that?'

'Yes, I did.'

'Were you yourself abused?'

Flores' smile broadened.

'They tried, but I wouldn't let the motherfuckers touch me. I fought back. Hard. They beat me for it, but they never tried to butt-fuck me again.'

'Do you remember the names of the guards who beat you?'

'Yes, but it doesn't matter now.'

'Why?'

'Because they're both dead.'

I sat back.

'All right. While this sexual abuse was going on did you know of anyone else involved in it besides the guards? Any other members of staff or anyone from the outside?'

'I only know of one person, though I heard there were others who came with him sometimes.'

'Who was this person, Mr. Flores?'

'A *maricón* named Gregory. Lamont Gregory. He'd founded the camp. He was an Assistant D.A. then.'

'Do you know where he is now?'

'Yes. He's the District Attorney for Del Norte County.'

'Was Gregory present when the attempt was made to sexually abuse you, Nacho?'

'Yes. When I refused to do what he wanted he told the officers to beat me. Gregory left and they worked me over with their batons. When they'd finished I was unconscious. Later, when they checked me and I still hadn't moved, they took me to the hospital. They told their colleagues I'd attacked them, that they'd only been defending themselves.'

'If we're able to bring Gregory to trial would you be willing to testify to that in court?'

Flores sneered. 'Why would anyone believe me? A Chicano murderer?'

'Nacho, do you remember the teacher that taught the younger inmates at Belleview? Mr. Parsons?'

'Yes. He was *un payaso*, a fool.'

'That may be, but he's never forgotten the time he spent at Belleview. Nor has he forgotten you and what happened to you. He remembers how badly you were beaten. And he remembers what you told him that day in class, when you shouted at him for doing nothing to stop the sexual abuse of the others. I have spoken with him and he, too, is willing to testify. If he is there to corroborate your story your testimony should be believed. In any case there's also Toby Hitchins. He's also agreed to speak out in court against Gregory.'

For the first time Flores seemed to relax and his smile became more natural, less guarded.

'It would make me very happy to see that bastard crucified.'

I shifted tack slightly. There was another angle to be explored with this guy.

'Mr. Wilkins told me that it was Gregory that prosecuted you for the murder rap. Is that so?'

He nodded. 'Yes.'

'From what I've learned, Nacho, at the time you were arrested for killing the rival gang leader you were pretty high up in the Varrio Pasadena Rifa hierarchy, is that not so?'

'You could say that.'

'Did you know Marcos Galvéz?'

'*Hijo de puta*,' he said, and spat to one side. 'Of course I knew him. He and I were the gang's bosses. But then Marcos and Gregory set me up.'

I shifted position on my chair.

'They set you up? How?'

'Because of what'd happened to me at Belleview I never trusted the *pendejo* Gregory. But Marcos and he were close. So was Marcos and the other Assistant D.A., Tony Baldini. For months Marcos had been paying them both off to work things in our favor whenever one of our soldiers was taken in. They got several of them off altogether and managed to plea bargain short sentences for the others. At the same time they were both ruthless in prosecuting our enemies.'

'And you say Gregory was being paid for this?'

Now Flores grinned. '*Claro que sí. Por supuesto*. They both were. Handsomely.'

'But you didn't trust him?'

'Gregory? No. I hated him. And I hated the fact that Marcos continued to work with him.'

'Did Marcos know that?'

'Of course. I'd told him so many times.'

'So they set you up?'

'Yes. Marcos told me to take out the MS-13 motherfucker who was trying to recruit our dealers in the valley. It seemed routine business. So I trailed the guy one night and cut his throat. Immediately the cops were all over me. They'd been on my tail. Catching me that way the case was open and shut. I would spend the rest of my life in prison, and Marcos could run the VPR on his own with the help of his friends without any hassle from me.'

'Nacho,' I asked, changing direction slightly, 'at the time of your involvement with the Varrio Pasadena Rifa was there a connection between the gang and any of the Mexican cartels?'

'Yes. With the Sinaloa Cartel.'

'Would Gregory and Baldini have been aware of this?'

'Of course. It was even rumored they met the cartel bosses in Mexico themselves and set up their own connection with them.'

Thad Wilkins sat forward. 'The bosses? You mean Joaquín Guzmán Loera and Hector Palma?'

'Exactly. *"El Chapo"* himself, and his right hand man.'

I pulled the conversation back on track. 'Nacho, did you ever actually see gang or cartel money change hands between Marcos, Baldini and Gregory?'

Flores showed his teeth. 'Oh, yes. Many times.'

'Would you testify to that as well?'

'I would. But it'd probably mean the end for me. The gang would take me down for ratting.'

'In here?' I scoffed.

'*Señor* Rednapp, the cartels and the gangs are all over this prison. They do what they want here. It might take time, but sooner or later someone would get to me.' He shrugged. 'And then it would be all over.'

352

I shook my head. 'You would still testify? Knowing that?'

He shrugged again. 'Why not? What kind of life do I have here anyway? I've been a walking dead man for years. To see Gregory brought down would at least let me die a happy one.'

I'd had more than enough useful information from Nacho Flores. I thanked him, and Wilkins and I watched him being restrained again and led away. Then we made our own exit from the prison and back to our cars. There I shook Thad's hand and thanked him for his help.

'It's nothing,' he said, smiling. 'In fact, I owe you, Arnie. When this breaks my election victory's almost a certainty. You were right, you've given me a gift. Maybe one day I'll find a way to return the favor.'

I had pulled away from the prison and was on the road back to Crescent City when my cell phone buzzed. There was a store parking lot ahead so I pulled into it and stopped, bringing the phone from my pocket and punching the talk button. It was Devonne Peters.

'How'd it go?' he asked.

'Very well. I'll tell you all about it when I get back. We've got Gregory nailed now, no question. Any news about Félix Calderón?'

'Not yet. But there's something else.'

'Yeah? What's that?'

'Pepe Hidalgo remembered something this morning while he was telling us about meeting the gangbangers at the Hiouchi store. He said the men were staying in an old cabin somewhere, that they were complaining because it was so primitive, with no electricity or hot water.'

'A cabin, huh? Did they say where it was?'

'No. Only that it was up in the mountains.'

Something nagged at the back of my mind, the memory of a mountain cabin being mentioned recently, but I couldn't remember when, where or by whom.

'Thanks for that, Devonne,' I said. 'I'll think about it and see if it suggests anything.'

'Right. Where you headed now?'

'Nowhere in particular. Thought I'd see how Josh Bridger's doing.'

'Okay. I'll call if I hear anything. Catch you later.'

We hung up and I pocketed the phone and pulled back onto the road.

I'd driven another quarter mile when it suddenly hit me where I'd heard that recent mention of a mountain cabin.

Ryan Garrett had spoken of one when he was describing the close relationship between his family and the Gregorys in the old days, the fact that his father and Lamont's had hunted together, had stayed for days in the mountains – at a cabin Lamont Gregory's father had built there for his hunting trips. Ryan hadn't been a hunter himself, I remembered, but he'd been to the cabin once.

I slowed the Cobalt at the next wide place and executed a smooth 180 back toward Smith River and the Gregory lily farm.

If Ryan still remembered the way to the cabin we could go there.

We might even get there in time to save the girls.

I pressed down hard on the accelerator.

Chapter Forty-Five

Geri Mitchell woke from a doze and jerked upright, shaking her head to clear the cobwebs and shifting her position against the rough boarding of the wall behind her. To her right Mandy and Lorraine were seated like her on the plank floor of the cabin storeroom, their legs stretched out in front of them, their feet bound, their hands pinned behind them with plastic ties. Geri felt Mandy's shoulder warm against her own and turned to look at her. The youngster's head was flopped forward, apparently asleep. Beyond her Lorraine, however, was awake, her head turned toward the small barred window beside her that offered a view of distant trees and somber grey skies.

'You okay?' Geri whispered.

Lorraine sighed. 'Yeah, I'm fine. Just scared.'

'Me, too, darling. Me, too. How's Mandy coping?'

'She's all right but she's obviously terrified. She hardly slept last night.'

'Sorry, Lo. I can't tell you how gutted I am that you two've been caught up in this.'

Lorraine smiled across at her, weakly.

'It wasn't your fault, Ger. If I hadn't stupidly gone back to the house none of this would've happened. But Mandy needed her laptop. I had to do it. It was just our bad luck, I guess.' She swiveled her head around, working and stretching the neck muscles. 'Wonder what time it is?'

'Sometime around noon I should think.'

'Have you heard anything from inside? Any conversations?'

'Nothing clear enough to understand. There was a phone call earlier. I heard ringing. They must have a sat phone in there because there probably wouldn't be signal up here for an ordinary cell.'

'Could you hear what was said?'

'No.'

There was silence for a few seconds. Then Lorraine turned to her again.

'Are we going to get out of this alive, Geri?'

'I don't know, babe. By now Harv and the others will know we're missing, and if I know him and Sam as well as I think I do they'll be busting their butts to find out where we are so they can rescue us. Not to mention your Arnie. And the FBI.'

Lorraine shook her head. 'But will they find us in time? Seriously?'

'We have to hope that they do. In the meantime let's just keep quiet and avoid causing our hosts any aggravation. And keep your ears open, Lo. If you hear anything – a helicopter or a plane or any movement outside – tell me immediately.'

Lorraine nodded. 'I will.' She looked back toward the window.

Geri rolled her own shoulders, trying to flex her muscles, keeping the circulation moving down to her tightly pinioned hands.

It'd been almost twenty hours since they'd been taken by the Zeta murderers. When they'd arrived late the previous afternoon the men – again wearing balaclavas – had pulled them out of the van one by one, cutting first the ties that held their feet and hands together behind their backs, then removing the blindfolds and the tape from their mouths – with a warning that they'd be shot if they made a sound. Finally they'd cut the tape binding their feet and marched them up the steep track another hundred yards or so around the edge of the hill to an old hunting cabin nestled amidst tall fir trees and set against a dense forest of madrones, tan oaks and firs. The minute she saw it Geri knew what it was, a remnant from the old Gregory dynasty – Lamont's father's hunting chalet, where he and Ryan Garrett's father had stayed back in the '40s and '50s. Geri remembered Ryan speaking of the cabin to her and Arnie only days before. And wondered if Arnie, too, would remember and put two and two together? If he did there was still a chance they could get out of here alive. But it would not be easy for them to find this place, unless they discovered someone who knew exactly where it was. She herself had pored over Google Earth on her computer screen for several evenings, tracing rutted Forest Service roads from Gasquet up, over and around the foreshortened mountainsides, searching for a place where the first Latinos might have stayed, an old trailer home or a shack of some kind. But she'd found nothing. Using a helicopter to find the place would be equally ineffectual – the thugs' black van, she had seen, was well hidden in thick brush and low trees, and the cabin itself effectively shrouded from the air by the forest canopy. Still, someone in the county must know of the cabin and remember how to get there. Geri could only hope Harv and the others would find that someone and use their directions to get here as soon as possible. Otherwise there was no hope for them.

The previous evening had been terrifying for all three women. From the van they'd been taken to the cabin and led up the steps onto its slant-roofed front porch. At the right side of the cabin a covered breezeway extended from the porch through to the back of the house, separating the cabin from an adjacent storeroom. A few yards beyond the back of the house, along a well-worn track, was a primitive one-holed outhouse – a facility with which they would soon become familiar. Led initially down the planked passageway to the storeroom door, the three women were pushed inside and forced to sit on the floor against the wall. There they'd had their feet re-bound with gaffer tape. Then the men had retreated and closed the door behind them, the sound of a padlock being clicked into place following shortly thereafter. The last thing they heard was the cabin's side door opposite opening and shutting.

It had taken some seconds for the women's eyes to adjust to the relative darkness of the storeroom. On the opposite wall floor-to-ceiling shelving was crammed with cans of food, bottles of drinking water and boxes of stores and equipment. Geri had carefully scanned the shelves, searching for anything that could help them effect their release. But there was nothing. In any case it'd be difficult if not impossible to break out of the storeroom without making considerable noise. Smashing their way out only to be immediately shot by their captors was clearly not an option worth considering, so Geri had reluctantly abandoned any idea of escape. If they were to get away it would have to be through the efforts of some external agency.

An hour or so after their arrival the storeroom door was reopened and two of the balaclavaed men stepped inside, pulled Lorraine to her feet, and dragged her out, shutting the door behind them as before. Geri felt her absence like an open wound, counting the minutes until the door was thrust open again and her friend reappeared, tearful now, between her guards, to be lowered roughly back to her place on the storeroom floor. Then Geri herself was jerked upright and dragged across and into the cabin, leaving Lorraine and Mandy locked away once more behind her.

Inside the cabin Geri was dropped unceremoniously onto one of the four chairs surrounding a wooden table at the large room's center. Shifting her position she had glanced around her. The inside of the cabin was rustic but comfortable, with a stone fireplace on the west wall and doubled bunk beds in the back right corner. Lined with old growth redwood boarding the place looked snug and cozy, capable of comfortably sleeping four people at least, and must have seen that many visitors often back in the day. In the rear left corner a galvanized sink with a cold-water tap, almost certainly fed from a spring somewhere on the hillside above, stood at one end of a hardwood counter with cupboards beneath. Above the sink, a narrow horizontal window looked out onto the wooded slope at that side. A small wood-fired cooking stove and oven stood beside the sink on the back wall. At the front of the cabin, flanking the heavy wooden door, two gingham-curtained windows overlooked the approach trail, the ravine below and the distant mountains. The cabin was positioned, it seemed, on the side of a cleft in the mountain, with a spring-fed creek cutting its way down below it to eventually join the distant South Fork of the Smith. In spite of its remoteness the cabin clearly had everything needed to provide shelter and sustenance to a handful of people for some time and Geri was impressed in spite of herself. Clearly in this, as in so many other things, Lamont Gregory had proved a master at preparing for the unexpected.

The man Geri assumed was the Zeta leader – also wearing a balaclava – had pulled out the chair opposite her and sat down. One of the other men had retreated to the kitchen area where he was rinsing plates and pots. The second was looking out one of the front windows.

'Why have you brought us here?' asked Geri, deciding to go on the offensive. 'What do you want from us?'

The man opposite, dressed in a green camouflage jumpsuit, leaned forward over the table, resting on his arms.

'You know very well what I want, little deputy,' he replied. 'At the house you told me you could be useful. So be useful.'

'How?'

He sat back. 'You know the men we are looking for – the ex-soldier and the journalist. Your friend might be the reporter's *puta* as you said, but she clearly knows nothing of his whereabouts at this moment. However, you do, I am sure. You know where both of the men are. And if you don't tell me where they are I shall have to kill you. All of you.'

Geri half-smiled. 'Even if I did know it wouldn't do you any good now. Your work here is done.'

'What makes you think that?'

'By kidnapping us you've blown your cover and your time is running out. My colleagues know I'm missing. They also know Manuel Fernandez's death was no accident. They know you and your thugs killed him and that you then attempted to kill Josh Bridger. They know all about you, and they know who controls you. And sooner or later they'll find their way here to free us. It's only a matter of time.'

The man laughed. '*¡Chingada! ¡Muy lista!* You have it all figured out, don't you, brave little *gringa*?' He sat forward again, clasping his hands before him on the tabletop. 'If that is so, perhaps we should just kill all of you now? Would not that be sensible? To cut our losses and to run?'

Geri's smile tightened. 'That would be stupid. I'm an officer of the law. If you kill me you'll have every law enforcement agency in the country after you. You wouldn't get twenty miles without being stopped. As it is you might still make it. You're only responsible for one death in this county. Wouldn't it be wiser to leave us here and just go? Remember, it's not just the local law officers after you now. In kidnapping us you've committed a federal offence. Now the FBI are involved, too, and the FBI only play hardball.'

The man stared at her for a moment, motionless. Then he rose to his feet. Trailing the fingers of one hand across the tabletop he moved slowly around it until he was standing at her side, staring down at her. Then he raised the hand to her cheek, tracing with the backs of his fingers the line of her jaw from ear to chin.

'You're a pretty little *gringa*, aren't you? *Guapa de verdad.* Perhaps we could play some games together to pass the time, huh? What do you say, *guapa*? How 'bout a rough Latino gangbang?'

Drawn by his tone the other men eased closer, watching. Geri could sense them leering behind their balaclavas, licking their lips. Abruptly she jerked her head away from the man's caress.

'No?' he said, feigning hurt. 'You don't want to play with us, *chica*? *Qué lástima.* What a pity. It would've been a good way to pass the time, *no*?'

'Go fuck yourself.'

The man drew his arm back sharply, ready to strike her. Then he restrained himself, brought the hand down again to grasp her chin, pulling her head sharply upwards.

'You'd best watch what you say, *pendeja*. Or who knows? You might lose your tongue.'

Geri said nothing. After a moment the man released her and stepped back around the table.

'I'm going to give you a little time to think things over,' he'd said finally. 'When I bring you in here again you will tell me where the men are. Or you will die. All of you. It's that simple. *¿Comprendes?*'

Geri remained silent, her jaw tight.

Crossing his arms the leader barked an order. The other two had jerked her upright and dragged her back to the night-darkened storeroom.

That had been sixteen hours before, and now the physical discomfort all three women felt from maintaining their positions against the storeroom's wall and floor was reaching a critical level. Twice since their arrival they'd called out asking to be allowed to relieve themselves. Eventually the three men had arrived in their balaclavas, the women's feet were freed and they were led, one at a time at gunpoint, out and up the track to the privy on the hillside. Once there their hands were freed and they were allowed to enter the small structure to do their business in private. When finished, their hands were re-bound behind their backs and they were returned to their prison room.

They had also been fed twice. Once the night before, when two of the masked men suddenly reappeared – one to stand guard with an automatic pistol aimed toward them, the other to free their hands and then to pass to them bowls of warm stew and chunks of bread. Then the same routine had occurred mid-morning, when they were freed and given bowls of cereal and canned milk with bread and butter. For drink each time a bottle of water was opened and placed where they could share it. They had fed themselves, then the remains were taken away, their hands re-bound behind their backs, and the men had retired again to the cabin, locking the storeroom door behind them. These were the only breaks for the women in all their long hours of waiting. And worrying.

It must be nearly 2 PM, Geri thought now, staring through the window at the grey clouded sky. How much longer would it be before help arrived? Would it arrive? And if it did would it arrive in time? These men would not hesitate to kill them all, she knew, if that was the decision of their employer. Even if it meant their own eventual certain death.

Bowing her head, Geri prayed silently for succor to a God she wasn't even sure she believed in anymore.

Chapter Forty-Six

Far to the south at his Mexican home away from home in Sayulita Lamont Gregory paced his bedroom balcony in the late afternoon sunlight and prayed for the day to pass quickly. In the morning he would meet his friend the Attorney General at the airport and they would return to California. He needed to get home, to contain the rapidly unfolding events that were threatening to destroy him. It was a lost cause, however. He knew that now. Even if he managed to stave off the inevitable another day or two the truth would eventually come out. His cozy illegal organization would be exposed and he would be forced to flee or be arrested. But he had not spent the day panicking and wasting time. On the contrary he'd been busy and was pleased with his achievements. Everything was slowly coming together for his escape.

Ordering his caretaker to drive him into town he had withdrawn most of the funds from his Mexican bank accounts and converted them to dollars in high denominations. Then he'd returned to the house, emptied the wall safe of the jewels and cash stashed there, stuffing the combined lot into the money belt he carried under his shirt.

Using his second cell he'd then contacted a former client in Los Angeles who was a master forger. Years ago Gregory had secured the man's release from a counterfeiting charge on a procedural technicality that had spared him a decade of jail time. Now he was calling in the debt: he needed a new identity and a new passport, one that would pass inspection at any national border he might wish to cross. The man told him he could certainly provide such a document – but for a fee. The so-called debt was from years before, he pointed out, and besides in his desperation Gregory was in no position to enforce the return of favors. Grumbling, Gregory had agreed to pay the exorbitant fee and had arranged a transfer of funds into the forger's off-shore account. Then another problem arose. The work would take two days to complete and the new passport wouldn't be delivered to his home in Crescent City until Tuesday at the earliest. Never mind. If that was the way it was then he'd have to accept it.

Once that business was concluded he'd then made several calls on the cell to other criminal contacts. Could they help him? Many couldn't. But one finally could – again for a fee. There was a safe haven for him in Uruguay, the house of a bankrupt planter who was moving back to Spain. He could have the house for a song – after meeting the sizeable fee demanded by his contact to facilitate the business. Bribing the local officials into silence wouldn't cost him that much more. The situation would serve for the short term at least. So now there was an escape route planned, and a plane being held ready to collect him at short notice if a hasty retreat was required. All he needed was time to liquidate as many of his assets as he could.

The call to the Zeta team had been more difficult. If he instructed them to kill the three women and run there was always the possibility the bodies might be discovered before he'd made his escape – or of the Zetas being captured – and the risk of becoming embroiled in the aftermath was too great. On the other hand, if he instructed the team to continue with their mission to kill off Colson's ex-soldier friend and the meddling journalist they might fail again, creating an even more chaotic situation. No. Better to forget the men. It was too late, anyway. The best thing now was for the Zeta assassins to sit tight with their prisoners in the mountains until his return to Crescent City. Then he could assess the situation and decide on a plan. Perhaps they at least could be gotten rid of? He would see. For the moment, however, the men had to wait. And do nothing.

The smooth-voiced leader had been unhappy with that news. He'd insisted on immediate payment of the promised extra money to compensate for the increased risk of their ongoing situation. If the money wasn't delivered within two hours, he threatened, they would leave the women at the cabin and go – which would've been like abandoning a ticking time-bomb. Gregory was forced to accept their terms, arranging the transfer of funds immediately so that the cartel hirelings could confirm the transaction via their sat phone. He'd made sure the money was transferred into their account on time.

There was only one problem he hadn't been able to solve. When he'd telephoned the caretaker at his lily farm in California there had been no answer. Each time he tried the number rang and rang and was never picked up. And when he tried the man's cell it was never turned on. Where could Félix be? And Teresa? They never went away without his permission. The whole thing was suspicious. And dangerous. Félix had been with him for years. He knew too much about the entire operation to be running loose.

He glanced at his watch again. 5 PM. Time for him to shower and change. Thanks to the desertion of his cook/housekeeper he would have to be driven down to the town again to search for a restaurant that could give him a meal that didn't leave him with burning indigestion in the night.

Never mind. In less than twenty-four hours he'd be back in Crescent City where he could see for himself what was going on, could contain the damage long enough to free as many of his assets as possible. Then he would disappear.

He smiled. He would not fall even if his beautiful organization was collapsing around him. He'd made millions from it over the years, money waiting now in numbered accounts spread across the world. He wasn't afraid. He wasn't even very concerned.

After all, he thought smugly, money buys everything.

Even impunity.

Chapter Forty-Seven

It was almost 1 PM by the time I tracked down Ryan Garrett to his house. Trying to control my excitement, I described to him what'd happened over the preceding two days and why we desperately needed to find the cabin his and Lamont Gregory's fathers had used during their old hunting expeditions. Ryan, of course, was deeply shocked by the abduction of Geri and the girls and wanted to do everything he could to help. But he was unsure whether he could remember how to get to the cabin. It'd been too many years since he was there and the country must have changed in the interval. But he knew someone who would know how to find it.

One of his father's old hunting buddies was a former U.S. Forest Service employee named Floyd Anders who, in his day, had known the mountains of Del Norte County like the backs of his hands. He was retired now, but was still clear-headed, and was certain to be able to provide the information we needed. So we set off, Ryan and I, in his Chevrolet Captiva to find this man.

Anders lived with his wife off old Highway 101 on Lake Earl Drive, between Smith River and Crescent City, on the edge of the lake itself. He spent his time these days fishing, and Ryan had apparently passed many a pleasant afternoon with the old man in recent years angling from Anders' boat on the lake, or fly-fishing at various spots on the Smith River. It being Sunday, however, and close to mid-day, it was unlikely that Anders was off somewhere pursuing his hobby.

When we reached Anders' modest house Ryan slowed and turned into the drive. There were two vehicles parked in front of the double garage: an old rust-colored Jeep 4 by 4, and a newish grey Nissan Maxima, the latter obviously the family car. As we climbed down from Ryan's SUV I glanced around at the well-groomed, fenced-in yard – a closely-mowed lawn with flower borders and decorative bushes and trees planted here and there at the edges – obviously a source of pride for the house's inhabitants. I followed Ryan up the cement pathway to the door and waited while he pushed the bell button. After a few seconds the door opened and a short, round man with a white beard and a shock of white hair stood in the door frame. He had on a red Pendleton shirt and denim bib overalls, and was wearing glasses with heavy black rims.

'Hey, Ry,' he said, boisterously. 'You come to do some fishin'?'

'Not today, Floyd. Got a few minutes? Got something I need to ask you.'

'Sure, come on in.' He stepped back, opening the screen door for us and calling over his shoulder, 'Honey, it's Ryan.'

I followed Ryan inside and the old man closed the door.

'This is Arnold Rednapp, Floyd,' Ryan said, introducing me. 'He's a newspaperman from San Francisco.'

'Pleased to meet you, sir.' He grasped my hand with surprising force. 'Come on through to the kitchen. We've just finished our lunch. You boys eaten?'

'Yeah,' Ryan said. 'We're fine, thanks, Floyd. But we'd take some of Ferne's coffee if there's any brewing.'

'There sure is.'

Floyd Anders led us through to the large kitchen at the back of the house where a Formica-topped table stood to one side, half of it covered still with empty serving dishes and used plates. Ferne Anders was standing at the counter, pouring coffee from a pot into four mugs. Ryan stepped over to her, gave her a quick hug and kissed her on the cheek. She beamed.

'Hello, Ry,' she said. 'Good to see you. Been awhile.'

'Yes, it has. Too long. Lots going on at the farm just now. Hard to get away. This is a friend of mine, Ferne. Arnold Rednapp.'

'Glad to meet you, Arnold. Any friend of Ryan's is most welcome here.'

Floyd was clearing away the dishes.

'You boys go ahead and sit down,' he said. 'Coffee's coming right up.'

Ryan and I sat at the table's other end and a moment later Floyd joined us. Ferne brought the mugs over two by two, then sat down beside her husband.

'So,' Floyd said, after taking a sip. 'What can I do for you?'

Ryan leaned forward.

'Floyd, this is a serious business and we need your help with it. Arnie can explain things better than me so I'll let him do the talking.'

He turned to me and for the next few minutes I briefly described the course of the investigation into Davey Colson's murder and the events of the last two days. As I spoke, both their faces – Floyd's and his wife's – lost their smiles and took on somber casts.

'I went to Ryan,' I concluded, 'hoping he'd remember where the cabin was. He doesn't, but he said you'd be sure to know and that's why we're here.'

'You do know, don't you Floyd?' Ryan asked.

'Yep,' the old man confirmed. 'Ought to. Spent many a weekend there over the years before your daddy died.'

'Can you take us there?'

'I could. But I can also show you on a Forest Service map how to get there, so you won't need me. I'm a little too old to bounce around on mountain roads anymore. Hang on a minute.'

Floyd got up and returned moments later with a folded map. While he was away Ferne had wiped down the table with a cloth, and now Floyd opened the map and laid it out on the clean surface.

'This map,' he said, 'covers the area around Gasquet and French Hill. It runs south to just beyond Craig's Creek Mountain, and the scale is pretty large so there's a lot of detail. Now here,' he bent closer to the map, adjusting his glasses on his nose. 'Here's where the French Hill Road takes off from Highway 199, just below Adams Station.' He traced the road with his finger. 'It winds around the mountains as you can see and eventually peters out clear over here in the east, close to the Siskiyou County line. Off of that road a bunch of smaller access roads branch out to cover the higher areas, a lot of 'em not marked on the map and most of 'em impassable except for four-wheelers. The road to the cabin is just about here,' he said, pointing again. 'It ain't that rough so your bad guys could definitely get their van up there, though some of the ruts'll probably knock hell out whoever's inside. Now the cabin itself...' he bent closer to the map, squinting behind his glasses, '...is situated here. See this draw coming down from the top of the mountain? Well the access road comes up off of French Hill Road right here, and winds up that draw to a parking place below the cabin, just about ... where the end of my finger is. The cabin's hard to see from the air because the forest around there is pretty thick. But it sits just here, below the mountain top on the west side.' He turned his head to check the sides of the map. 'Yep. There's lat and long lines on the map as well, so you can figure out exactly where it is that way, too.'

'Can we borrow that map, Floyd?' Ryan asked.

''Course.'

'Could you put an X exactly where the cabin sits, sir?' I added. 'So we can show it to the Sheriff and the FBI?'

Floyd looked at his wife. ''Honey, can you get me a pen?'

Ferne stepped away to the counter and returned with a ballpoint which she handed to her husband. Bending forward, Floyd carefully traced the roadway up the mountain with his finger to a certain point, then put a cross on the map a short way above it.

'That's it. You'll find the Gregorys' cabin right there.'

'Thanks, Floyd.' Ryan put his arm around the man's shoulder and squeezed. 'This could save those girls' lives.'

We finished our coffees, reiterated our thanks and said our goodbyes. Once back in the Captiva, Ryan backed out and we roared off down the road toward Crescent City.

On the way in I used my cell to tell Sheriff Harv Cantrell of our breakthrough.

'That's great news, Arnie,' he said, excited. 'I'll contact the others and let 'em know. Where are you now?'

'With Ryan Garrett. We should reach town in about ten minutes.'

'Say "hi" to Ry for me, will you?' Harv said. 'I've known him a lot of years.'

'I'll do that, Harv. He wanted to come along and I told him he'd be welcome. Where should we all meet up?'

Cantrell thought a minute. 'Shirley and the kids are away again this afternoon,' he said eventually. 'Why don't we meet at the house like before? You all know where it is, it's private and we won't be disturbed. I'll tell Agent Peters to go there, too, and I'll swing by to pick up Josh Bridger from the motel on my way.'

'Good, Harv. See you there.'

'Oh, hey,' he said. 'I almost forgot. Got another piece of good news.'

'What's that?'

'Had a call this morning from the U.S. Border Patrol down at the Calexico/Mexicali crossing into Baja. By a stroke of luck one of their officers noticed a license plate on one of the cars waiting to cross that rang a bell. He did a quick check and found my warrant, so Félix Calderón and his wife have been arrested.'

'Fantastic!' I said. 'It's amazing they got that far without being picked up.'

'Sure is. Must've travelled at night and on back roads all the way down. Anyway, I've made arrangements to have them transported back to Del Norte as soon as possible.'

'Great news, Harv! Now let's get those girls back. Once that's done all we'll have to do is pick up Gregory on his return and the case is closed.'

It had gone three o'clock by the time everyone was gathered in Harv Cantrell's living room. Ryan had come in with me and I introduced him to the FBI people when they arrived. Peters had brought both Agents Fischer and Walker with him, and also Pepe Hidalgo, whose presence caused Sheriff Cantrell's eyes to grow saucer-sized when they were introduced. Peters had decided he'd need all his agents to rescue the girls, so they'd had no option but to bring him along. But what to do with the boy while they were away? Cantrell offered a solution: his wife was expected back in a while. The boy could stay with her and the rest of the family until everyone got back, spending the night in the guest room. He'd be safe here, and there was no fear of his trying to escape. Until she returned, however, he was sent off to the family room at the back of the house to watch television.

I unfolded Floyd Anders' map and laid it out on a coffee table and the seven of us crowded around it.

'According to Ryan's friend here's the position of the cabin,' I told them, pointing. 'You get there by following the French Hill Road for about ten or twelve miles into the mountains. There's a turning here,' and I pointed to it, 'where a road branches off up along a small stream. That's the road that leads to the cabin. There's a flat area here. That's probably where the van will be parked. The cabin's just above it where the "X" is, nestled in a stand of trees.' I looked at Ryan. 'You've actually been there, Ryan. Can you describe what you remember of the cabin and the approach to it?'

Garrett did his best, though he hadn't been there for almost half a century and it was pretty certain the hillside would've changed a lot over the years. His most useful memories were those relating to the layout of the cabin itself, and with the aid of paper and pencil he was able to draw a fairly clear picture of the cabin's interior.

'That's about it,' he said. 'I can't remember anything else.'

'You've done fine, Ryan,' Devonne Peters said. He looked at his watch. 'What time's sunrise this time of year?'

'Around 4 AM,' Harv Cantrell said. 'Why?'

'It's a long way out there and by the time we'd got ourselves ready it'd be too late for us to head out there tonight. We'd never get set up before dark. I hate to make the girls spend another night with those killers, but it'll be better if we get up there early tomorrow morning, an hour or so before sunrise. Most of them will probably be still asleep and we can get ourselves settled in before the sun comes up.'

'It's going to be a pretty short night then,' Ryan said.

'True,' Devonne agreed. 'So let's use the rest of the afternoon to prepare ourselves, then get some supper and have an early night.'

'Who all we going to take?' Sheriff Cantrell asked. 'Want me to order out the SWAT team?'

'No,' Peters said. 'We still don't know if any of your deputies have been turned by Gregory. I don't want to run the risk of the kidnappers being warned and running. We'll do fine on our own. We know there're at least three of them up there. Hopefully there'll be no more.' He looked around at Fischer and Walker. 'On our side there's us three, plus the Sheriff and Mr. Bridger – if you wouldn't mind swearing him in as a temporary deputy, Harv. I took the liberty of checking his service record yesterday – very impressive. I'd kind of like having Sgt. Bridger's Delta Force experience working with us.'

Cantrell nodded. 'Sure I can deputize him. What about Arnie?'

Devonne looked at me. 'Do you want to come?'

''Course I do,' I told him. 'But I don't know how useful I'd be. I'm a reporter, not a cop or a soldier. And I hate guns. I might get in your way rather than be a help.'

'I think he should stay down here,' Josh said, nodding. 'Arnie knows too much about Gregory to risk him being shot. But you're forgetting the other man we could use. Why not call in Sam Buchanan? When we were out at Geri's yesterday he and I had a talk. He's a former Navy Seal. He's also part of the local CHP SWAT team. We'd work well together. We speak the same language.'

Harv Cantrell nodded. 'Good idea. I'll get on the phone to his dispatcher and arrange to have him released to us.'

The rest of the hour was spent discussing logistics, strategy and armaments. Sheriff Cantrell said he would drop by the office and pick up some stun grenades, Kevlar vests, radio gear and five assault rifles and ammunition. If there were any suspicions aroused he would simply say he wanted to take the stuff home to check out how well it'd been maintained. Sam would turn up already armed and kitted out, so the entire team was covered for fire power and equipment. That was about it for materiel. There wouldn't be time to use any sophisticated surveillance or eavesdropping gear so there was no point in bringing it. Finally it was decided that everyone involved in the operation should rendezvous at the junction of French Hill Road and Highway 199 at 2 AM, where they would shift themselves and their gear into the two vehicles best suited to handle the mountain roads – the two SUVs belonging to Harv Cantrell and Ryan Garrett. Ryan would go along as a driver only, and would remain with the vehicles at the bottom of the road leading up to the cabin, away from danger.

The meeting broke up just before 4 PM and we all headed outside. Devonne's cell phone pinged with an incoming text and he hung back to open it. When he joined the rest of us his face was wreathed in a big smile.

'What's tickled you, boss?' Fischer asked.

'Baldini's pilot just filed his flight plan for the return trip tomorrow,' Devonne said. 'They're leaving Puerto Vallarta at 7:30 AM our time, and the expected ETA in Crescent City is around four hours later, just after noon.'

'Great,' said Josh. 'Just in time for you to arrest him, after we've got the girls back.'

'Let's take things one at a time, shall we?' Harv Cantrell said, frowning. 'No sense in tempting fate.'

There being nothing further to be said we all went our separate ways – me going with Ryan in his Captiva back to his house to pick up my car.

When we got to his place we both climbed out and stood silently together for a few seconds. It was an awkward moment. So much depended on what happened over the next eighteen hours.

Then we shook hands and I watched him walk to the house.

In nine hours' time, in the dark early morning, Ryan would be off to meet with the others to free the girls. I could see he was already charged with adrenaline for the mission.

As for me?

All I could do was find somewhere to make myself comfortable, turn on my cell phone, and wait.

It wasn't until late that night that I realized I'd left my cell in Ryan's SUV.

Chapter Forty-Eight

Monday, June 2

By the time the two SUVs reached the turning to Gregory's hunting cabin it was just before 3:30 AM and the eastern sky was already pink with the coming dawn. The last miles had been made without lights, the two vehicles crawling along the graveled road at barely 20 miles per hour. Pulling past the rutted track, Harv Cantrell eased his Ford Explorer onto the shoulder and shut it down. Ryan Garrett, following in his Captiva, swung in to park behind him and the drivers and passengers of both vehicles stepped out into the twilight, Sheriff Cantrell clutching Floyd Anders' map.

They were still a quarter mile from the cabin and it was unlikely the sound of their slow-moving vehicles would've carried that far through the trees. It was possible, of course, that the cabin had a view down over a section of the road, and if that was the case the kidnappers might well have seen the Sheriff's white rig and be waiting to ambush them. But that was unlikely given the early hour, the density of the forest and the steepness of the sloping hillside.

The three FBI agents had ridden with Ryan Garrett, and now Devonne Peters stepped out onto the graveled road, holding his smart phone with its GPS app open and nodding his approval.

'Damn thing works,' he said, smiling. 'I put in the lat and long coordinates for the cabin and it's telling me it's only a little way up there.' He nodded toward the mountain. 'Useful gizmo.'

'Leastways it confirms I didn't stop at the wrong turning,' said Harv, with a grin. 'Well, boys and girls? Shall we get ready?'

The next ten minutes were spent strapping on Kevlar vests, checking and loading weapons, and making sure spare ammunition clips and water bottles were carried. The five mobile radio transmitter/receivers were allocated to Devonne Peters – as the overall mission commander – to Bridger and Buchanan, who'd be making the initial approach to the cabin, and to Fischer and Walker as their backup. Once they were fitted and tested and seen to be working correctly Devonne called the group into a close huddle.

'Okay,' he said, shifting into business mode. 'We've already talked about how we're going to do this thing, so just to review. Ryan stays here with the cars. The rest of us will move carefully up the hill to take up a base position at the point where the black van is parked – assuming it is parked there. After me, Sgt. Bridger's next in command, then Sheriff Cantrell. Bridger and Buchanan will be on point, clearing the way for the rest of us. Once we've set up, they'll then continue up the track to check out the cabin and surroundings. When ready Bridger will summon Tom and Elaine. Tom will then circle around and up to the ridge to approach the back of the cabin and settle in at the tree line above it. Elaine will move to take up a position at whatever angle still needs covering – that'll be Josh's call. Communications are to be minimal. Once everyone's in place we'll decide what our next step will be. That'll depend on what we find up there. Are we clear?'

There was a chorus of muttered 'yes's from the group.

'All right. Let's get those ladies out of there.'

Leaving Ryan with the vehicles the five men and one woman, all now wearing camouflage caps and clothing and carrying various pieces of equipment and weaponry, walked back to the turning and started up it – Josh in the lead, his AR-15 assault rifle pointing ahead. Twenty yards behind him, Sam Buchanan, similarly armed, followed. Then, after another twenty yards, the rest of the party. Progressing feet at a time from cover point to cover point, Josh slowly advanced up the road and around the curve of the hillside. Each time he cleared a section he beckoned Sam forward and, signaling to those behind him to move up, Sam complied. Thus for the next fifteen minutes the little group shuffled in increments up the rutted roadway.

Moving up the track in a crouch, his face beneath the dark navy cap blackened with swipes of camouflage paint, Josh marveled at how easily he'd slipped back into the familiar Delta routines. It was as though the preceding six years of civilian life hadn't existed. While certainly aware of the seriousness of the mission – three women's lives were at stake here, after all – there was another part of him that thrilled at being back in harm's way. It gave him a sense of purpose and self-respect he hadn't felt for years.

It was a relief to all when the black van was discovered at the point indicated by Floyd Anders, parked nose outward under a canopy of fir trees and tan oaks. That meant the kidnappers were still there. Hopefully the women would be, too.

When the rest of the group had joined Josh and Sam at the van Devonne Peters nodded to the two men and they set off together again toward the cabin, moving in stages as before, leaving the others behind.

The sky's overcast had cleared during the night and the day dawned quickly now. By the time the two former commandos had worked their way upwards sufficiently to get their first glimpse of the cabin front a bright band of sunlight bathed the ridge above them. The cleft of ground where they and the cabin were situated, however, was still in deep shadow. Lying side by side in thick brush, Josh and Sam held position for a time, watching the cabin's windows and door for any movement. There was none.

'Base, Eagle One,' Josh whispered into his mic. 'We're below the cabin and there's no movement inside. Eagles Three and Four can move up.'

'This is Base. Copy, Eagle One.'

Five minutes later Josh heard a faint rustle behind him and Agents Walker and Fischer, both in camouflage gear and face paint, slipped into position alongside them, the muzzles of their AR-15s thrust forward through the brush.

With a glance at Sam, who nodded his approval, Josh signaled for Agent Walker to make his move up the hill. Giving them a thumbs-up Walker quietly eased himself backwards, then cut sideways and uphill, disappearing into the trees.

Josh turned his attention back to the cabin. As Ryan had described there were windows on either side of the front door and another narrow horizontal window high in the wall at the back west corner. As he watched, a dark shape moved across one of the front windows. Then it returned, framed in the opening. A face looking out. A Latino face. Even from forty yards away Josh could see the man's eyes scanning the area. Then the face retreated and a moment later the front door opened.

'Eagle Three, hold position,' Josh whispered, urgently. 'We've got a man outside.'

Walker's voice came back. 'Eagle Three. 10-4.'

He would delay his forward progress, keeping still until Josh gave him the all clear.

The man who stepped out of the front door was dark-skinned and slim and was carrying an M-16 rifle in the crook of his left arm. Stepping forward to the corner of the porch, he stood smoking for a few moments, scanning the slope around him. Josh and the others, well-concealed amidst elderberry brush and bracken, watched him, unmoving. Stepping forward, the man parked his cigarette in the corner of his mouth, fumbled with both hands at his fly, then urinated onto the ground at the side of the porch steps in a high arcing stream. Josh could hear the spatter of piss on the dry earth. When he'd finished, the man zipped himself up and stepped back. Taking a last puff on his cigarette, he dropped the stub onto the porch floor and shredded it with his boot. Then, with a final look-round, he turned and re-entered the cabin, closing the door behind him.

Man One had been clocked and noted. How many more were there?

'Man back inside,' Josh whispered into his mic. 'You're clear to go, Eagle Three.'

'Eagle Three, copy.'

Walker would now continue his scrambled progress through the trees to the ridge, to work his way down to the cabin from above.

Josh stared at the redwood structure. Were the girls inside? Or had they arrived too late? Maybe they'd never even got here? Without seeing through one of those windows he couldn't be sure. From their current position he couldn't even properly see the far side of the cabin, and it looked from where he lay as if there might be some kind of structure stuck onto that side that Ryan hadn't mentioned – possibly a later addition. He would have to work his way down into the ravine below the cabin, then up again on the far side, to see what that was all about.

'Eagle One to Base. I'm moving position to the east of the cabin. Eagles Two and Four are holding here on the west side.'

Devonne's voice: 'Base. Copy that, Eagle One.'

Nodding to his comrades, Josh eased himself backwards and set off, carefully selecting his route.

Fifteen minutes later he'd reached his new position in the trees on the east side of the cabin. Now he could clearly see the small privy sitting on the hillside above it, and the room that had been added at its right side. A storeroom? Probably. During his transit he had clocked the covered passageway that led from the front porch to the back of the building, separating it from the added room. He'd also noticed the small barred window in the storeroom's southern wall. Given the slope of the ground it was too high for him to see into, even if he were able to get close enough to stand beside it. But the unexpected room raised questions.

'Base, Eagle One. In position now east of the cabin. There's some kind of a storeroom on this side with a barred window on its south side. That could be where the girls are being held. There's an open passageway between it and the cabin that runs from the front porch to the back yard. There must be a side entrance to the cabin from that passageway. Suggest Eagle Four moves down and across the stream to take a position on the opposite slope that offers a view of that passageway and the front windows. We need to see what's going on in there.'

'Eagle One, Base. Copy that,' Devonne returned.

Then came Fischer's soft, feminine whisper: 'Eagle Four deploying.'

'Careful, Eagle Four,' Josh warned. 'The spics check out the front regularly. Keep yourself hidden.'

'Will do. Thanks.'

Two minutes later Tom Walker's voice whispered down the radio link.

'Base, Eagle Three. In position above the cabin.'

Devonne Peters' voice came back online. 'Copied, Eagle Three. This is Base. What can you see?'

'Not much. I'm about twenty yards uphill in the trees. As already reported, there's a single high window at the back west corner of the cabin. There're no windows in the rear wall. There's an outhouse at the back a few yards to the east of the storeroom. If they let the girls loose occasionally to do their business that might be the time to make our move.'

'I'll bear that in mind,' Peters replied. 'But let's confirm the girls are in there, first. Nobody else has made an appearance?'

'Negative.'

'That true for you, too, Eagles One and Two?'

'Affirm,' Sam and Josh responded.

'Okay,' Devonne whispered. 'We'll wait now till Eagle Four's in position.'

It took three-quarters of an hour for Agent Fischer to traverse the narrow stream and cautiously work her way up the opposite slope to a point across from the cabin, concealing herself in a stand of scrub oak brush.

'Eagle Four in position,' she told the team when she was settled. 'Got a clear view of the passageway. Can't see anything through the cabin or storeroom windows. Too much glare. But I'll keep watching.'

'This is Base. Copy, Eagle Four. Report any movement.'

'Eagle Four, 10-4.'

Listening to the exchange Josh knew that this operation could take some hours to bring off. Devonne Peters would not sanction any action until it was known where the girls were and how many men were guarding them, and without a clear view into the windows there was no way of determining that with certainty. They had to hope the cabin's inhabitants would sooner or later show themselves of their own volition. Then they could assess the risks and plan an attack.

For the moment, however, for all of them, there was nothing to do but wait.

Geri awoke from a nightmare in which she'd been crushed under a pile of dead bodies, their inert mass forcing her into the hard ground. Struggling back to consciousness, she realized the dream had been prompted by the aches and pains she felt in her hips, back and shoulders from sitting for so many hours on the hard storehouse floor with her arms pinioned behind her. Straightening her back she looked around. Lorraine and Mandy were still asleep, slumped against one another beside her, their breathing relaxed and regular. Geri glanced up at the window and saw a clear blue sky. She reckoned it must be somewhere around 6 AM.

The second full day of their captivity had begun.

The previous evening had been much like the first, with another escorted visit for the ladies, one by one, to the outhouse, followed by a crude meal of lukewarm stew and bottled water. Then just before dark the masked men had reappeared, dragged Geri again into the cabin and dropped her onto the chair by the table.

'So, *gringuita*,' the smooth-voiced leader had said, sitting opposite her once more in his balaclava, 'are you going to tell us where we can find the reporter and the ex-soldier? If you do we might let you live.'

'I've already said,' Geri had reiterated, wearily. 'I've no idea where they are. How could I have? I've been your prisoner for two days now.'

'And as I've already said I know you're lying. Perhaps with a little persuasion you could be made to talk, eh?'

Reaching behind him the man produced a large knife with a shiny blade. For a moment he toyed with it, wiping the wide steel across his palm, testing its edge with his thumb. Then in a sudden movement he brought the knife down with a crash onto the table, burying its point deep in the wooden surface. And sat back.

'We have plenty of time, little deputy. And we're very good at getting information out of people when we need it. Would you like for us to prove that, huh? We could start perhaps by chopping off a finger or two, *no*? Or an ear?' He chuckled. 'You don't like the thought of that, do you, *güera*? Soon you'd be singing like a bird.'

Geri shuddered. 'Whatever you do to me won't make any difference. I've told you I don't know where they are and that's the truth. I'm not even sure they're in the county. So what would be the point of torturing me?'

'Oh, for the pleasure it would give us, of course,' the man said, his voice caressing, seductive. 'It's so exciting to hear a woman screaming for mercy, begging for us to stop. *¿A poco no, compañeros?*'

The two other balaclavaed Latinos looking on from either end of the room murmured their agreement.

'Of course we could also try our methods on your friends, couldn't we?' the leader continued, leaning toward her over the table. 'What about the girl, eh? Shall we bring her in, see what she could tell us? You could watch. After a little of her virgin blood has been spilled there's no knowing what she might tell us, *no*?'

'It'd be a waste of time,' Geri said. 'They've only just arrived in Del Norte County. They know nothing about any of this.'

'Hm.' He nodded. 'That is probably true. Certainly the mother seems to know nothing. But we could still amuse ourselves for a time with the girl, couldn't we, *amigos*?'

'*Claro que sí, Capitán*,' one of the others purred. '*¡Y con mucho gusto!*'

'You sick bastards,' Geri said. 'Anyway, what use is it knowing where the men are? You can't go after them. Not anymore. You know that. You've been made. Your van is known now. I've told you, your business here is finished, and the sooner you free us and go the better your chances are of getting away.'

Ignoring her, the leader rose to his feet and moved around the table to stand at her back. Reaching out a hand he stroked her short hair, then rested both hands on her shoulders.

'Even if you won't tell us about the men,' he murmured, 'you could still please us in other ways, *gringa*. You're a sexy woman. It has been hard for us stuck away up here in the mountains. Very boring. Very ... lonely.' The man moved his fingers, caressing her tense shoulders. 'If you are good to us I might even decide to let you live. It is not much of a sacrifice, *no*? Your body ... for your life?'

When Geri said nothing the man gripped her shoulders harder, pressing his finger ends into her flesh, hurting her.

'Is that not so, *puta*?'

'Perhaps,' Geri grunted through the pain. 'But frankly I'd rather you killed me. At least then I'd die knowing I'd not been contaminated by a bunch of shitface beaner assassins.'

The blow sent Geri sprawling onto the wooden floor. For a few seconds she thought the slap might have burst an eardrum, but as she slowly recovered from the shock of it she realized the ear was still functioning, in spite of the ringing within it that strove to drown out all other sound. Then she became aware that the man was beside her again, hunkered down close. With a wrench, her face was jerked upwards toward his.

'I am disappointed in you, *bonita*. I had hoped you might want to save yourself. But clearly you do not. You are nothing but a stupid *hija de puta*. And it will give me pleasure to kill you when the time comes.'

Forcing herself to smile Geri glared up at him.

'*¡Chinga tu madre, cabrón!*' she croaked, and spat into his face with all the venom she could muster.

The man had dropped her head onto the floor with a thump. Then he had stood, wiping the spittle from his face and staring darkly down at her.

'*¡Sácala de aquí!*' he'd barked, angrily.

And the men had taken her back to the storeroom.

Now, twelve hours later, Geri rolled her shoulders and her neck, waking up the muscles and stretching them. How much longer, she wondered, before something would happen? Their fate, she knew, depended upon what Lamont Gregory would decide, and from what she could recall he was due back in Del Norte County that afternoon.

Sometime after that he would contact their captors and tell them what to do with the women prisoners. What would that be?

Whatever his orders the Latino leader had said he intended to kill her. And if he really meant to do that there wasn't anything she – or even Lamont Gregory – could do to stop it.

Only rescue could prevent that happening. And rescue, for the moment, seemed as far away as Christmas.

The morning dragged on. When the four observers were secure in their positions, Devonne Peters and the Sheriff had moved up the hill to a point near Sam Buchanan where they, too, could watch the cabin from cover. Now the entire team was in place and ready, but until they knew more about what was going on inside they could not move or formulate any plans.

By 10 AM the sun's rays had reached the cabin level and Josh Bridger and the other members of the stakeout team were suffering aches and pains caused from lying motionless on the hard ground for so long a time.

Over the hours there'd been several episodes of observed movement both within and outside of the cabin, and it was clear now that the women were being kept together in the storeroom.

At around eight o'clock Agents Fischer and Walker had seen two of the Latinos wearing balaclavas – from the description of their clothing, the one Josh had seen on the front porch and one other – move across the passageway from the cabin's side door to the storeroom, unlock the padlock, and then, carrying automatic pistols, escort the women one by one to the outhouse, returning them to their prison room when they had finished. All three of the women, Sam was pleased to hear, were in fair condition, though Geri seemed to have a bruise on the right side of her face. At least they were moving freely and seemed otherwise unharmed.

'Thank God for that!' Devonne Peters breathed down the radio link.

Then, at nine, the two balaclavaed men had appeared again with a plastic water bottle and bowls of some kind of breakfast, which they took into the storeroom. They remained there for some time. While the two men were thus occupied a third man, without balaclava, had appeared on the front porch. He looked to be in his forties, with a hard face and short black hair. As the man before had done, he too stood for a few minutes smoking and surveying the surroundings. Then, flicking his cigarette end onto the gravel path, he'd gone back inside. That brought the count to three men – the number Josh had seen at the Eagle Hotel. But was that all of them?

Minutes later the two masked men reappeared from the storeroom with the bowls, relocked the door and re-entered the cabin. Since then there'd been nothing.

What to do now? Josh wondered. No doubt Devonne Peters was debating that at that very moment with Harv Cantrell. It was possible, of course, that there were other men in the cabin that they had not seen, and the uncertainty about that made it difficult to plan any kind of extraction. And even if there were no more men an attempt to storm the cabin from three sides was problematical. There was too much sloping open ground to cover to get to the building without detection, and no definite means of effecting a surprise entry once they got there.

Watching the cabin from his cocoon in the trees Josh knew what was going through Devonne Peters' mind. There was only one sure way to do it. They had to make their move when all of the men were in the open and away from the girls. Unless and until that happened there was nothing that could be done.

Hours passed and the sun continued to climb into the early summer sky. The day was warming – uncomfortably so for the watchers in their camouflage jumpsuits. Given their few hours of sleep the night before, there was also the temptation to drowse during the long period of inactivity, to let the eyelids droop – just for a moment. The distant calls of hawks floating over the valley below them, and the hum of the cicadas in the nearby brush, provided a lulling background soundtrack, dulling their senses, inviting them to succumb to the urge to drift off. But they were all professionals and had done this kind of thing often in the past. They knew the dangers such temptations posed and they wouldn't give in to them. They couldn't. It might cost them their lives.

Just before noon, when Josh was wondering if there would ever again be any movement from the cabin, Elaine Fischer's voice came down the radio link.

'Eagle Four here. Two men in balaclavas have just appeared in the passageway. They're unlocking the storeroom. Now they've gone inside. Stand by.' There was a brief pause, then: 'They're back. They've got Deputy Mitchell. She's tied up, hands and feet, her hands behind her back. They've relocked the storeroom and hauled her into the cabin. I repeat, Deputy Mitchell is now inside the cabin.'

Josh frowned at the report.

What the hell was that all about?

He checked his assault rifle, resetting it on the fallen log before him, training it on the porch and the front door, clicking off the safety, ready for whatever was to happen next.

Geri was dozing again when the door was suddenly jerked open and the two masked men once again pulled her to her feet and hauled her off into the cabin. This time, however, they did not drop her onto the chair by the table. She was dragged instead to the center of the room and dropped to the floor on her knees facing the closed front door. Then the two men stepped away. She looked around her. Piled beside the front door were several backpacks, rifles and automatic weapons. Obviously a move was being prepared. But who was going? Were they taking the women? Or did they have other intentions for them?

Geri had not heard any telephone ringing, but then she had been asleep. From what she understood Lamont Gregory was not due back in Crescent City until early afternoon. Was it afternoon now? Had she been asleep that long?

'You're getting ready to leave,' she said, without turning. 'Are you going to let us go?'

'Yes and no,' said the smooth-voiced leader behind her.

Swiveling on her knees, she turned herself around.

And gasped.

The man was no longer wearing a balaclava. None of the three men were, the two that brought her in having stripped theirs off. While the two underlings moved about the room collecting gear and stowing it into bags, the man who was their chief stood beside the table, loading bullets into the clip of his Glock 22. Geri swallowed, dryly, an awful thought forming in her mind.

'What do you mean, yes and no?' she asked.

The man looked up from his work to smile at her.

'The others we are going to leave as they are in the storeroom. They mean nothing to us. Either they will find a way out of their prison and survive or they will perish. That will be up to them.'

'That's good news,' Geri told the man. 'But what about me? Am I going with you?'

The leader smiled again, showing his even teeth.

'No, *gringa*. You are staying here, too.' He slipped the now loaded clip into the Glock, cocked the weapon and lowered it to his side. 'Only you will be dead. You had a chance to save yourself but you refused it. Now, I'm afraid, you must die. Executing you will also relieve my conscience a little. At least I will be carrying out one of the assassinations I was paid for. What a pity I'm unable to kill the journalist and that *cabrón* with the tattoos. But at least I shall leave having achieved part of my mission.'

Geri felt an icy chill ripple down her spine and her stomach tightened.

'You can't do that,' she stammered. 'You said you had to wait for your employer to tell you what to do. You said there was no hurry.'

'Yes. But that was before you pointed out it would now be impossible for me to carry out the rest of my mission, before you urged me to leave it unfinished and escape. You were right, *guapa*. If we are to get away we shall have to leave now. Thank you for your good advice.' He walked toward her, putting one hand flat on the top of her head in a gentle caress. 'What a pity you had to be such a *pendeja, no*? You might have been able to stay with your friends.'

Geri stared at the pistol in his hand, only inches away. She shuddered uncontrollably.

'I'm so sorry, little deputy,' the man said, withdrawing his hand. 'One last question: do you want to leave this world with your eyes covered? Or would you rather die looking out onto the mountains? It is a spectacular view, as you know. Tell me, which is it to be?'

'I don't want my eyes covered,' she said at last, in a whisper.

'Very brave.' He turned back to the others. 'Rafa! Juanito! *¡Vamonos! Llévala afuera.*'

'*Sí, Capitán.*'

Geri felt tears well in her eyes as the two men stepped forward and lifted her to her feet. The leader moved to open the door and stood watching as his men dragged her limp form through the opening onto the porch and down the stairs, dropping her onto her knees on the hard ground a few feet below the cabin, facing away from it. Then the two men returned to the porch, one of them re-entering the cabin as the leader stepped past them toward the stairs, pistol in hand.

It was a spectacular view, as the man had told her. But Geri had no urge to look at it. Instead she stared at the ground before her, numb with fear.

Geri could hear the man's footsteps on the wooden steps, then the faint whisper of his boots moving over the earth. Until he stood right behind her.

'*Adios, hija de puta.* Kiss the Blessed Virgin for me.'

Geri imagined him looking down at her kneeling form, raising the pistol, aiming it at the back of her head. Tensing, she closed her eyes, awaiting the end.

The shout came from the right, a little distance away. But it was loud. And authoritative. It was a voice she recognized, though strained and charged with adrenaline.

'FBI! Drop your weapon!'

And then all hell broke loose.

Chapter Forty-Nine

Monday morning's breakfast at the Good Harvest restaurant tasted no better to me than it had the day before, though that had nothing to do with the food. It also didn't help being alone.

I'd woken up late, at around 9:30 – with a throbbing head and a mouth that tasted like sick. The fact is I'd been so upset with myself and depressed about having stupidly left my cell in Ryan's Captiva that I had bought a bottle of Jack Daniels Tennessee sour mash whiskey and spent the late evening in my motel room, drowning my sorrows in Old No. 7 and trying not to think about Lorraine and Mandy in the hands of evil cartel assassins. If that was not enough, there was also the thought that I wasn't even going to be a part of the team that was hoping to rescue them in a few hours' time. It didn't help, of course – the booze. A man my age should've known better.

It took me half an hour to pull myself from the bedclothes and into the shower, and another half hour before I was shaved and respectable enough to set off to find some kind of breakfast. Which was mostly coffee.

I had no idea when Devonne's group would reach Gregory's cabin, or how long once there it would take for them to do whatever they had to do to get the girls out. Of course I'd no way of knowing the girls were even there, and that in itself was enough to make me want to drink myself to oblivion. What if the whole operation was too late? What if the girls were already dead?

That was a horror too great to contemplate.

They had to be alive. And Devonne's team had to rescue them. That was the only scenario my quaking soul was willing to accept.

In desperation I looked up Sheriff Cantrell's home number and telephoned from the restaurant – getting his wife. No, she hadn't had any word from him yet. And yes, it was not unusual for such an operation to take a long time. The best thing for me to do, she advised, was to immerse myself in doing something useful so that I wouldn't be torturing myself thinking about it. It was a technique, she told me, that she had worked at developing herself over the years – with only moderate success, she admitted – to enable her to cope on the not infrequent occasions when her husband was away from his family, putting his life on the line. I thanked her for her advice and told her that if she didn't mind I might call again later on.

Sitting now at a corner table in the restaurant with my fifth cup of black coffee slowly cooling in front of me, I wondered what it could be – that useful thing I might occupy myself with to take my mind off my worries. Until I remembered that Lamont Gregory would be flying in to Crescent City Airport sometime just after noon that day on Anthony Baldini's Citation. And reflected on the fact that the grim circumstances currently causing such angst in my life – and in so many others' lives – were entirely of his making. Remembering that left me with only one option as a worthy pass-time: I would be there to watch the bastard's plane come in.

Accordingly I finished my lukewarm coffee, paid the bill (tipping the waitress handsomely as a reward for her unstinting attempts to cheer me up) and made my way outside to the car.

It was 11:50 by the time I pulled into a slot in the back row of the airport parking lot, backing the car in so I'd have a clear view of any aircraft taxiing in to the little terminal. I didn't have long to wait. At ten past noon the sleek silver bird banked in the distance and descended, settling onto a runway just out of my vision. Reappearing moments later, it taxied majestically to a parking area near the terminal and shut down. Immediately the door at its front opened, the stairs mechanically unfolded to the ground, and the Del Norte County District Attorney himself stepped down carrying a small suitcase – followed shortly thereafter by Anthony Baldini, who I recognized from having researched him online only a few days before. While Gregory was looking somewhat preoccupied, the Attorney General was full of smiles as he followed his friend. Gregory was wearing a beige summer suit with a pale blue shirt and wine-red tie. Baldini was in chinos and a yellow polo shirt, with deck shoes.

As they talked a tanker truck appeared from beyond the terminal building and with the help of one of the flight officers the driver commenced to load jet fuel into the plane's wing tanks. While this was going on a stewardess appeared at the airplane's door and descended the stairs carrying a small case. This she deposited at Gregory's feet, smiling, after which she re-entered the plane. It took about ten minutes to do the refueling, then the flight officer climbed back aboard the plane and the tanker drove off. Throughout this time the conversation between the two old friends was seemingly inconsequential, Baldini even managing at one point to raise a smile on Gregory's somber face. There certainly didn't seem to be any serious concerns being discussed. Then Baldini turned and retraced his steps up and into the plane and, collecting his two cases, Gregory stepped away toward the terminal. As he entered the building the Citation's door was closed, its engines re-started, and the plane taxied back toward the runway, disappearing again behind the stunted pine trees lining the taxiway. Two minutes later it took off, the engines roaring as it climbed through the clouds and disappeared, banking toward the south.

So I'd seen Lamont Gregory. I'd confirmed that he was back in Crescent City, available for arrest as soon as the girls had been freed. I should've just left it at that. But somehow I couldn't. And instead of starting up the Cobalt and heading back to the motel to wait by the phone like a good boy, I sat waiting for the man to reappear.

Ten minutes later a city taxi pulled into the lot and drove up close to the terminal entrance. Gregory pushed his way through the doors carrying the cases and the taxi driver jumped out to place his VIP passenger's luggage in the trunk. Then the two men climbed into the vehicle and the taxi drove off.

I waited until it was almost out of sight. Then I followed them.

Lamont Gregory's town house was not far from the airport – a large ranch-style home at the end of a string of new houses lining the bluff overlooking Pebble Beach. Set back from the road on a rise, it sat sideways to it, an extensive redwood deck evident at its back. It was an attractive house, and large – too large for a man living on his own. It was also fairly isolated, with fir trees rising above it at the back and a tall board fence at the side marking the boundary between his property and that of his neighbor, some dozen yards away.

Pulling onto a conveniently placed parking area above the beach and opposite the house – for tourists wanting to view the impressive beachfront – I watched as the taxi made its way up the drive and stopped before the house. The driver and his passenger stepped down, the luggage was retrieved from the trunk, money was paid, and the two men separated – Gregory carrying his cases up to his front door, unlocking it and stepping inside, the taxi driver climbing into his rig and then driving away.

For several minutes I sat in the Cobalt, wondering what to do next. In spite of my better judgment I had a very strong urge to head up that driveway myself to confront the man. 'Why should I want to do that? What could I possibly achieve?' I asked myself. There was no justification for it, nothing to be gained by doing it. It was a stupid idea. I should just leave it to the authorities to arrest the man when the time was right. But did I do that?

No I did not.

Shifting the car into drive I turned across the empty roadway and drove up to park outside Lamont Gregory's front door.

I had turned away after pushing the button of his doorbell and when I swung back around at the sound of the door opening the shock of recognition that registered on Gregory's face was almost comic. But he recovered himself quickly.

'Mr. Rednapp, I believe?'

'You're right, sir. I just got into town yesterday and thought I'd take you up on your offer of a chat.'

'But that was to be at my office,' he purred, reminding me of Vincent Price in one of his more oily characterizations. 'I've only just returned from out of town myself.'

'I know, Mr. Gregory. I called Annabelle and she told me you were due back this afternoon but weren't expected to come to the office today. I had nothing to do so I thought I'd drop by to see you here. How about it? Can you spare me a few minutes?'

He looked at me like I was a plate of rotting fish. Then the unctuous smile returned.

'Of course. Come in, please.'

Gregory had undone his jacket and had been sorting through his mail, it appeared, as he still held a bunch of letters in his hand. Stepping back he allowed me to pass him, then pulled the door closed behind me.

As expected Gregory's house was very comfortably and tastefully furnished, with a large living room on the ocean end of the house filled with expensive-looking stuffed furniture, a baby grand piano, a bar in one corner and an assortment of elegant hardwood end and coffee tables. Above the flagstone fireplace a large portrait of himself in an ornate gold leaf frame dominated the room. A pair of picture windows at the room's end offered the sea view, and it was magnificent. But he didn't invite to me sit on one of the plush looking chairs or sofas. Instead he led me down a hallway toward the back of the house, into a room that must've been his study. The walls were lined with bookcases filled with legal and other books, and a large mahogany desk sat near the sliding glass doors overlooking the back deck. There was a low leather-covered armchair opposite the desk and he motioned me toward it. Then he moved behind the desk, settling himself onto a swiveling armchair and dropping the unopened letters onto the desk before him.

'Can I get you anything, Mr. Rednapp? A drink of any kind?'

'Thank you, sir, but no. I'm fine.' Reaching into my jacket's inside pocket I withdrew the small battery recorder I sometimes use for interviews and switched it on. 'You don't mind if I record our conversation, do you, sir?' I asked innocently, showing him the device. 'It's easier than taking notes sometimes, you know?'

He clearly was not happy with the idea, but realized it would seem churlish to refuse.

'No, I don't mind. Use the recorder if you like.'

'Thanks.' Checking that the machine was working I laid it on the desk between us. 'I've thought a lot about your offer to speak about your record as Del Norte County District Attorney, sir, and there are several questions I'd like to ask you, if you don't mind?'

He sat back, steepling his fingers before him over his stomach.

'Be my guest.'

'I believe you returned to Del Norte after serving some years as an Assistant D.A. in Los Angeles County, is that correct?'

'Yes, that's right.'

'During that time you prosecuted a good number of cases relating to gang crime, isn't that so?'

'Yes. What of it?'

'Was one of the gangs whose members you prosecuted the Varrio Pasadena Rifa gang?'

Gregory's mouth set in a hard line and he stared at me for several seconds before answering.

'Yes, but so what? The VPR was only one of a number of gangs whose members came before the court.'

'Yes, but I've looked into it, sir. I had a glance through the prosecution records during your years as Assistant D.A. down there and I found an interesting thing.'

'Oh? What's that?'

'It seems that members of the VPR gang, when brought before the court, always ended up being prosecuted by you for charges far less serious than the ones the police originally booked them for. Whereas members of other L.A. gangs were usually hammered with the heaviest charges possible, and prosecuted ruthlessly, seeking – and in most cases getting – the maximum sentences available.' I gave him my cod puzzled expression. 'How can you explain that, sir? Why were the VPR soldiers treated with kid gloves while other gang members weren't?'

Gregory frowned, angry now.

'I thought you wanted to discuss my work here in Del Norte County, Mr. Rednapp? What does the VPR have to do with that?'

'Hm,' I said, nodding. 'A fair question. Well, let me answer it by asking you something else. How well do you know Marcos Galvéz?'

His eyes hardened.

'Marcos who?'

'Galvéz, Mr. Gregory. Marcos Galvéz. The present boss of the VPR. I believe you once defended him on a murder charge, and got the case dismissed on the grounds of police negligence. Isn't that right?'

He sat forward on his chair, resting an arm on the desk in front of him.

'I once defended someone named Galvéz, yes,' he said. '*Is* he head of the VPR? That's news to me.'

I nodded. 'I see. And what about the Sinaloa Cartel? Have you ever prosecuted anyone involved with the Sinaloa Cartel, Mr. Gregory?'

He began to tap his fingers on the desktop, nervously.

'There may have been cases where the defendant had connections with the cartel. I cannot remember.'

'Uh-huh. What about here in Del Norte County? Have you ever had a case involving anyone here at all associated with the Sinaloa Cartel?'

'As I said, I cannot remember.'

'Then let me jog your memory.'

I was on thin ice here, I knew. For though I had discussed this matter with Thad Wilkins, and it was his contention that Gregory had always shown leniency toward Sinaloa connected dealers, there had been no actual cases mentioned nor any statistics. I was going to have to make it up, and it had better be believable.

'Mr. Gregory,' I continued, winging it, 'I have researched the cases relating to drug dealing that have come before the Del Norte County Court over the last seven years, and I have discovered no less than ten occasions when dealers with known connections both to the VPR gang in Pasadena and to the Sinaloa Cartel were prosecuted by your office. In every one of those cases the defendants were charged with the lowest level felony charges available under the law – much lower charges than were sought by the enforcement agencies. On top of that the defendants were often offered plea bargains that gave them their freedom after only a year or two of incarceration. In some cases the full evidence discovered by the police was not even brought into the prosecution case. That smacks to me of favoritism, Mr. Gregory. And it suggests there was a reason for it, an agenda that prescribed who was to be hit hardest and who to be let off with a slap on the wrist. Would you care to comment?'

Gregory was truly angry now. I could see the veins in his forehead pulsing, and his eyes glared hatred at me in waves.

'I think this interview is at an end, Mr. Rednapp,' he said at last, and stood up. 'I would like you to leave my house. At once.'

I stayed in my seat.

'The same thing happened,' I went on, 'when you were law partners down in L.A. with your old friend Tony Baldini, now the state Attorney General. His record, too, both as defender and later as prosecutor for Los Angeles County, shows evidence of manipulation of charges and plea bargaining done for the benefit of the members of only that particular gang – the Varrio Pasadena Rifa.'

'That's nonsense, Rednapp, and you know it.'

'Is it, sir? You're a friend of Marcos Galvéz, Mr. Gregory. So is Anthony Baldini. You've been his friend ever since you arranged his release on the murder charge all those years ago. You and Baldini. Ever since then Galvéz has fed both of you regular bribes to look after his VPR people, to reduce or have struck off the charges raised against them, or to plea bargain their sentences down to virtually nothing – while at the same time being ruthless in prosecuting and convicting rival gang members for the severest felonies resulting in the longest sentences. You're a mercenary bastard, Gregory. A true scumbag. And so's your friend. You did it down there. You're doing it here in Del Norte County, letting *your* busted drug dealers get off lightly while you hammer the locals and anyone else who tries to elbow into the market.'

He blanched. '*My* drug dealers? What're you talking about? This is outrageous!'

Now I stood.

'Is it?'

Reaching into my jacket I pulled out the second copy of the Camp Belleview photograph Geri Mitchell had given me of Gregory with the boy Davey Colson and I tossed it on the desk. Just like in the movies it landed so that he saw the two figures right side up. The Gods must've been smiling at me.

'Recognize that picture?' I asked him. 'Do you know who that is with you? Where it was taken?'

For a long moment Gregory didn't move, just stood staring down at the photograph, expressionless, his breath tight in his chest. Then he sat down again.

'Yes, I recognize the picture. A copy of it was sent to me just two weeks ago.'

'By Davey Colson himself.'

'Yes.'

Gregory seemed to have made some kind of decision, for his

manner suddenly changed and he seemed far more self-assured, no longer intimidated by the evidence I was laying before him of his guilt. He sat back, half-smiling again.

'He sent it to me at my office,' he went on, calmly. 'Wanted to blackmail me, the little shit.'

'Not a little shit anymore though, was he? But you weren't to know that, of course. You never saw him as a grown man. Only the men you sent to work him over did.'

Gregory nodded. 'Yes. I sent him a check, to the General Delivery address in Gasquet that he mentioned in his letter. The check was bogus, of course. Just a ruse to get him to the Post Office where my men could collect him.'

'But they got more than they bargained for, didn't they? Davey Colson had been a soldier, a Delta Force commando. He almost wiped out your little bunch of persuaders, didn't he? Until one of them put a bullet in his head. And all because you and your guard colleagues at Camp Belleview had repeatedly fucked him as a young boy and he'd never forgotten his vow of revenge. Camp Belleview – an institution you founded solely to provide yourself and your sick friends with a steady supply of boys to sexually abuse. You did the same thing in Sayulita, founding an orphanage so that you and your VIP cohorts could have easy access to young vulnerable ass. You're not just a corrupt attorney and a murderous drug dealer in bed with gangs and a cartel, Gregory. You're also a pedophile, a sexual exploiter of children. In short, sir, you're the scum of the earth. I'm going to rejoice seeing you brought to trial for all of it, you sick bastard. And that's just about to happen.'

Now I was ready to go, but before I could even turn away Gregory had opened a drawer in the desk and withdrawn a small automatic pistol from it, only slightly bigger than the fist he held it in. Pointing it at me, he sat back again.

'Sit down, Mr. Rednapp. You're going nowhere.'

I sat down.

He sighed. 'It's a shame you're so good at your job, Rednapp. It's going to be the death of you, I'm afraid. But before I shoot you I shall enjoy making you suffer a bit. Remember the three missing ladies? I know you're friends with that troublesome deputy, Mitchell. But I believe you also know the women that were taken with her. If I'm not mistaken the older one is your current flame. Am I right? And the younger is her daughter. Is that not correct, Mr. Rednapp?'

'What of it?'

Reaching into the inside pocket of his jacket, Gregory pulled out a cell phone.

'Being the smart reporter you are you'll also know that the men holding the three women are in my employ. I have used them to ... clear away certain problems that have arisen since the man Colson was killed.' He lifted the phone to show it to me. 'This is the cell I use to communicate with them. Now you can sit and watch me as I telephone their leader and instruct him to take the three bitches out of their prison room and to execute them. Immediately. I will even put on the speakerphone so that you can hear their screams and the sound of the shots that will end their lives. And when it is all over, and you know that they have all died because of you and your blasted meddling, then I will kill you.'

'You're even sicker than I thought,' I breathed. 'How do you expect to get away with it, huh? Not only the girls' murders, but mine, too? How are you going to dispose of my body? Had you thought of that?' I shook my head. 'It's no use, Gregory. The authorities are on to you. Your game is up.'

Gregory used one hand to bring up a number in the phone's directory and then pressed the call button. Sitting back in his chair with a tight half-smile, he raised the cell to his ear, keeping the gun levelled at my chest.

'Your body can lie here until someone finds it, Rednapp. It is of no matter to me. By tonight I'll be miles away from here, on my way to a new life. So you see,' he chuckled again, 'crime *does* pay, Mr.

Rednapp. Pity about the girls, though,' he said, feigning a sad face. 'They're going to die. And all because of you.'

He was listening obviously to the ringing in his ear. Hearing it repeating again and again, waiting for it to be picked up.

And then even I could hear the ringing. But it wasn't the buzz of the ringing down the line that I was hearing. It was the jangling ring of the phone itself.

Approaching.

Puzzled, Gregory held the cell out to look at it, then returned it to his ear. Then dropped it to his lap, as Devonne Peters stepped into the room holding a gun in one hand and a sat phone in his other that rang, and rang, and rang.

Until Gregory, the realization finally hitting him, punched the end call button. Then silence filled the room. And resignation.

'Lamont Gregory,' Devonne said, pocketing the sat phone. 'I'm FBI Special Agent in Charge Devonne Peters. I'm here to arrest you for the murders of David Colson and Manuel Fernandez, and the attempted murder of Josh Bridger. Further, you're to be charged with the kidnapping of Sheriff's Deputy Geri Mitchell and Lorraine and Amanda Adams, all of whom are now free and safe.'

'Thank God!' I said, exhaling a gasp of relief.

'You will also be booked for perverting the course of justice while in public office, and for regularly sexually abusing inmates at the Camp Belleview youth correctional institute in Los Angeles County,' Devonne went on. 'We've got strong evidence for every charge I mentioned, and there are more if we choose to bring them. Your little reign of evil is finished, counselor. So put the gun down. The house is surrounded and you haven't a chance of escape. Be sensible, Gregory. It's all over.'

Seconds passed. Long seconds, with Gregory still holding the pistol pointed vaguely somewhere between me and Devonne, and with Devonne standing rigid by the door, his pistol lifted high and aimed at Gregory. A true Mexican standoff. Then Gregory sighed and

I thought it was all over, thought he was about to comply and lay the pistol down on the desktop. But he did something else instead. Something totally unexpected. Sitting back, he suddenly brought the gun up to his mouth, shoved the muzzle inside and squeezed the trigger.

'Nooo!' I shouted, leaping from my chair and grabbing at the gun.

It was a reflex action and perhaps a foolish one. But in those seconds I did manage to pull his gun hand back and away from his head, by which time Devonne Peters had lunged across the room and snagged his wrist, bending it back sharply so that the lawyer cried out and the pistol dropped from his hand to the floor. Then he pushed Gregory back onto his chair and stood over him, his own gun trained at his head.

In the stunned silence that followed, Devonne knelt briefly to recover Gregory's gun. He looked at it. And grinned.

'Not used to guns are you, counselor? For future reference you have to take the safety off before you can fire it.'

Gregory glowered up at him.

On the desk top my little device was still recording, its lights flashing, still laying down the sounds of that bizarre interview and its aftermath. I switched it off and dropped it into my coat pocket.

Now Harv Cantrell appeared at the study door with two of his deputies, neither of them Nelson or Ross.

'You okay, Arnie?' he called out, brandishing his own pistol.

'I'm fine, Sheriff,' I told him.

'Then you'd better get your ass over to the motel,' he said. 'You're one lucky dude. There're three good-looking women over there who all want to see you pretty badly.'

'I'm on my way,' I said, tears welling up in my eyes.

And I left them to it.

Epilogue

Labor Day Weekend, September
Playa de Oro, Puerto Vallarta

'Going to sleep?' murmured the velvety voice beside me.

I opened an eye and rolled my head to the right. Two feet away the tanned face of my lovely Lorraine smiled across at me under her sunglasses from her deckchair, the two piece swim suit she wore revealing just enough of her body to set my blood aflame once more.

'I had thought of it. Would you mind?'

She reached out to grasp my hand, holding it tightly.

'Of course not. You probably need it.' She raised herself to glance beyond me to the deck chair on my left where Geri Mitchell – also very tanned – lay snoozing in her bikini, her face covered by a large sombrero. 'After last night you should be tired,' she whispered. 'You stallion!'

Giggling she lay down again, still holding my hand, pressing it.

I lifted my head and looked down past my feet toward the long swathe of white beach and the lapping waves beyond. There was Mandy, splashing and laughing in the rolling surf with her boogie board. A few yards away my daughter Lisa – now graduated from high school and about to start her Freshman year at Santa Cruz University – paddled her own boogie board into the waves and laughed back.

Beyond them Sam Buchanan lay on his back on the calm blue water, face upwards, eyes closed, a man at peace.

We'd come down for a final ten days of sun and conviviality before the routine of winter, work and school reclaimed us altogether. Sam and Geri, Lorraine and Mandy, Lisa and I. Paco and Rosa Jimenez had found us a seaside villa to rent in the south of the city, just the right size for the six of us and not too far from them. Tonight we would meet them again for dinner at their house, our final evening together before the six of us would return to California and the real world in the morning.

It'd been ten wonderful days and we'd enjoyed them – a vacation all of us had craved ever since those chaotic days of early June when our collective world had been almost broken asunder. There had been no time for getting away before this – too many days taken up putting together the bits and pieces of evidence from all sources for the upcoming trials of Lamont Gregory and his drug-dealing lieutenants, days for me spent finalizing the article covering Davey Colson's murder and its aftermath. The article had appeared in a late summer special edition of the *South Bay Bulletin*, an edition devoted to the corruption scandal involving officials at both ends of the state and in its capital city. In any case the idea of being in Mexico in the middle of boiling summer was daunting, so it had been easy enough to wait. It was still hot now, in early September, but at least the evenings were cooler, and one could sleep at night without the feeling of being roasted slowly in a cotton-lined oven.

I turned my head to look at Geri, snoring gently under her huge hat, and smiled. Closing my eyes I let my mind drift, revisiting the events of the last three months, the frenetic period of activity that had started on the day of Gregory's arrest.

Geri had come so close to death that day, a whisker's width away from being blasted to oblivion by the Zeta leader. Josh told me later how it all went down, how when the man had raised his pistol Devonne Peters had challenged him and the man had instead swung his Glock toward him, ready to fire. But before he could do so bullets from the rifles of both Sam Buchanan and Josh Bridger had smashed into his head from two sides, sending a momentary puff of blood and brain matter flying into the air, and the man had collapsed backwards onto the ground. His colleague on the porch had ducked inside long enough to grab an M-16 and was able to fire two quick bursts in the vague direction of Sam and the others, but fortunately had missed. Then, before he could pinpoint their position and direct his fire with effect, a single shot from Josh Bridger had dropped him, stone dead, onto the porch floor. The third and last man had tried to escape through the side door and along the passageway to the back of the cabin, but had run smack into Agent Tom Walker, who'd been drawn down from the trees by the shooting and who challenged him with his rifle aimed at his head. The man had dropped his weapon immediately and raised his hands, the only member of the Zeta team to survive.

Fearing that Lamont Gregory would flee before he could be apprehended, Devonne Peters had left the scene with his fellow agents and the handcuffed Zeta survivor shortly afterwards, arriving at Gregory's town house just in time to make his spectacular entrance and to save my bacon.

Lamont Gregory would face justice in a month's time, and in all likelihood would spend the rest of his twisted life behind bars for corruption, sexual assault, drug dealing and murder. To add to the evidence already gathered – which included the fresh drug haul from the small case brought from the Citation – the desktop computers at both of Gregory's houses were found to contain copious files of explicit child pornography, and in a locked desk drawer grueling DVDs were discovered of films taken during his sex sessions with the children in Sayulita. The man's culpability as a drug godfather and rampant sexual predator was without doubt – even without the testimony of Toby Hitchins and the teacher, Nick Parsons.

Further afield, Martin Taylor in Los Angeles had been able to dig up a fair amount of hard evidence documenting both Gregory's and Anthony Baldini's corrupt practices during their shared tenure as criminal defense lawyers and as Assistant D.A.s for L.A. County. On top of that his weeks spent in Sacramento investigating the Attorney General had unearthed undeniable evidence of Baldini's continued high-level manipulation of justice in the capital city on behalf of his gang and cartel friends. Together with the evidence collected by the FBI team that'd followed the Citation's drug delivery to its distribution point, Taylor's reportage had brought down not only Baldini but also a large sector of the extensive sales network for his imported drugs. The former Attorney General, too, was certain to spend much of the rest of his life in prison. Martin's story of the man's corruption, when it reached the pages of the *Los Angeles Times* in late July, created a state-wide sensation, and his prestige as an ace investigative journalist was enhanced even further.

For his part, Paco Jimenez had also been busy, surveilling – with the help of his friend Antonio – the Sayulita Police Chief, *Señor* Gregorio Gutierrez, and the priest, Father Anselmo. Though they had lost their friend and sometime host Lamont Gregory, these dedicated pedophiles had wasted no time in setting up a new venue to which the orphanage children could be sent and abused. With care Paco and Antonio had photographed the men and the children arriving and departing the sessions – pictures that left no doubt what the youngsters had suffered during the hours spent with the men. Using *Señora* Marielena Hidalgo's anonymous testimony together with the photos they had taken, Paco had, as '*El Gallo*', written a stinging exposé of their perverse activity in *NoviVallarta* and public opinion had swung immediately against them. The men went into virtual hiding, but their iniquity was too great not to provoke a serious response – and from a quarter quite unlooked for.

One evening Chief Gutierrez was visited at his home by four men wearing dark clothing and balaclavas. As he opened the door of his palatial house the men raised their machine pistols and emptied them into the startled policeman, leaving him a bleeding, lifeless bundle on the threshold. That same evening, across town at the priest's house, another group of dark-shrouded villains forced their way past the housekeeper at his front door and chased the holy man into a bedroom closet, where they emptied their pistols into him as the others had done. Thus retribution was exacted, by cartel command. Even murdering drug barons, it appears, have scruples.

As for the others? Pepe Hidalgo, by agreeing to testify about both Gregory's drug enterprise and the murder of Davey Colson, would almost certainly receive a short prison sentence. Visited in the county jail often by Alex Moreno and his girlfriend Hayley, and once for an entire week by his devoted mother flown up from Mexico by Ryan Garrett, Pepe remained up-beat about the time he'd have to endure behind bars, knowing that Garrett had promised him another job on the lily farm – with more responsibility – as soon as he was released.

Enrique 'Quique' Bardén, the sole surviving VPR gangbanger who had been a part of Gregory's first 'persuaders' group – the group responsible for Colson's death – and who had been arrested trying to flee south in a van full of fellow gang members and illegals, was eventually persuaded to testify about the events leading to Colson's murder and the firing of the shot by his scarred colleague. That testimony, with Pepe Hidalgo's corroboration, would surely be enough to secure him a slightly lesser charge – from Murder One to Accessory to 2nd Degree Homicide – meaning he would probably spend only a dozen years or so in prison before being again deported.

As had been hoped, Gregory's caretaker Félix Calderón and his wife, after their forced return to Crescent City from Calexico, had been persuaded, by Sheriff Harv Cantrell and Agent Devonne Peters working in tandem, to tell everything they knew about Gregory and his operation, in return for enrolment in the witness protection program and a new life and identity for both somewhere far away from Del Norte County.

Investigation into the records of detectives Craig Nelson and

Nick Ross over the previous several years resulted in discoveries of egregious evidence tampering and collusion with the District Attorney's office that, if not exactly proving guilt, at least gave solid grounds to warrant their expulsion from the department. Given they would have no recommendations to take with them, almost certainly the best employment the two could hope for in future would be lowly jobs as security officers in some dusty industrial complex.

Having retrieved her laptop Mandy had done well in her exams and was looking forward to being a Fortuna sophomore. Lorraine, together with her friend Ardelle, had completed the work on the Shelter Cove tea shop and had opened it at the end of June with a special celebration attended by a few dozen locals, her former boss, and myself – having made a special trip up to be there. Since then the place had done well and the girls were delighted with their prospects.

Josh Bridger – off currently spending a few weeks in southern Oregon picking grapes and canoodling with his waitress girlfriend, and having decided to abandon his mountain eyrie to pursue instead a career in law enforcement – was due to commence training at College of the Redwoods near Eureka in the next few weeks.

As for me life was looking up. My published account of the events that followed Davey Colson's visit to Del Norte County went down splendidly with both the public and my colleagues. Abe Rawlings had been delighted, and as a result had not quibbled about me taking ten days off for a vacation in early September.

Regarding my love life, Lorraine and I now often used the 'L' word – even in front of Mandy and Lisa – and it's now very likely that one day soon our two worlds will become one. Still, making that decision's a way off, for both of us. Better now just to enjoy what we have with no strings.

Squeezing Lorraine's warm hand once more I sighed, listening to the girls' cries and the wash of the waves on the sand.

Moments later, just as the warmth of the Mexican sun was about to lull me into open-mouthed, snoring oblivion, another piece of recent news flitted across my dimming consciousness, making me smile as I savored it.

With Lamont Gregory out of the picture the promised walkover had been secured. Thad Wilkins had easily won his election as the new Del Norte District Attorney, ushering in a new era of fair and honest judicial practice in the county.

So you see?

In spite of everything the good guys do sometimes win.

About the Author

(Photo by Bob Bailey)

William Roberts is an American actor, writer and voice artist resident in the UK for over forty years. Born and raised in the Pacific Northwest, he was educated in California and at Manchester University, England, and still proudly carries only a US passport. He currently lives and works in London, enjoying his writing, flying his small airplane around Europe and watching his grandsons grow. *An Ill Wind* is his second published work, and he hopes others will follow.

Also by WERoberts

The Humanist

When a young man's body is found near a remote northern California town sprawled over jagged rocks at the base of a seaside cliff, the authorities dismiss the death as an accident or suicide. But there are suspicious circumstances surrounding the tragic event. Sent to investigate, crack San Francisco reporter Arnold Rednapp soon discovers that the boy's unorthodox beliefs had turned a large section of the small town against him, leading the journalist to suspect a community-wide conspiracy to hide the truth of what happened. Rednapp's suspicions are hardened when he himself receives anonymous threats...

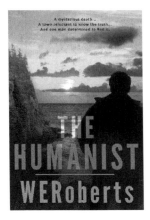

A gripping, intriguing tale of detection with a strong cast of memorable characters that offers just a bit more than the usual.

Available on Amazon as a quality paperback, in Kindle format and as an audiobook read by the author.